HOCKEYVERSE

LOVING LADYBUG

PART ONE

JANE HANDLER

Loving Ladybug Part One

A WHY CHOOSE OMEGAVERSE FRIENDS TO LOVERS HOCKEY ROMANCE

JANE HANDLER

To everyone who's watched a hockey game and wanted to take a
couple of them home.
This one's for you.

About This Story

Welcome to the HockeyVerse! *Loving Ladybug* is a full-length why-choose, friends-to-lovers, non-shifting, omegaverse, hockey romance *duet*. Part One ends on a cliffhanger, but there is a happy ending in *Part Two!*

You don't need to have read the *Finding the Forward* duet to enjoy this book. But if you have, you'll recognize a lot of familiar faces. It starts not long after the end of *Finding the Forward, Part Two.*

This is a 'why-choose' romance, so the female main character gets her happy ending with more than one person and it's ultimately m/m/f. It might look a little different from the omegaverse endings you're used to but it's still happy.

The HockeyVerse is part of what I like to call 'the parallel omegaverse.' It's a *parallel universe* that's similar to ours. However, this world has evolved a bit differently, which affects everything from physical places to technology to laws. For example, the drinking age and driving age are both eighteen. The biggest difference is that alphas, betas, omegas, and many other designations exist. Each designation has specific characteristics.

In this world, all love's legal and accepted, with same-sex and polyamorous relationships being common. Many people live in packs. Registered packs have all the legal rights of families, no matter what designation comprises them. There are also plenty of couples and throuples. Gender and racial equality are widespread. Birth control is freely available for all genders and designations.

While this story and world aren't particularly dark, **there's on-page domestic violence between Gwen and her boyfriend (who quickly becomes an ex) in chapter two**. There's on-page bullying toward one of the main characters, but not within their love group, as well as a motor vehicle accident, and a pregnant side character who has complications (but everyone's okay.)

All characters have past trauma with relationships. There are also mentions of past traumatic incidents including family bullying, neglect, death, stalking, kidnapping, and gun violence.

This book is spicy and meant for adult readers. It contains knotting, oral, group scenes, and other spicy acts.

There's a lot of characters, so there's character guides and a glossary in the back. I hope you love Gwen and her guys.

About the Sports in the Story

The HockeyVerse is *not our world*. While many things are the same, there are plenty of differences. Even familiar sports may have different rules, terminology, leagues, and teams–both because it is a parallel world and how having a/b/o designations and gender equality can change things. If you're looking for a hyper-realistic sports romance, this might not be for you.

For example, in this world, WAGs (wives and girlfriends) are MASOs (mates and significant others).

Ice Hockey is a co-ed, mixed-designation sport. It's alpha and male heavy, with very few omegas, especially at the professional level. The Professional Hockey League (PHL) has thirty-two teams in four countries. They have a minor-league and draft system. The hockey season runs October-March, with pre-season in late September and playoffs in April and May. The PHL falls under the International Association of Team Sports (IATS).

It is common for a drafted player to not be signed until they finish university. Teams can also "sweep up" their drafted players at any time–not just during the free agent window. Some teams participate in the goalie development program, where collegiate-age goalies have an opportunity to train with a pro-team and act as their EBUGs (Emergency Backup Goalies.)

Skate Smash is like roller derby on ice held at a rave. It's a high-energy contact sport with lots of dance breaks. It's co-ed, mixed-designation, but tends to be alpha and female heavy. The Professional Skate Smash League (PSSL) falls under the International Coalition of Ice Sports (ICIS). They have a draft system, a minor league, and a team-sponsored junior system (Discovery League). Skate smash players also have more control over the team roster than in many other sports.

Soccer (Football) is extremely popular, especially among betas, and is known as ***fútbol*** worldwide. **Rugby** and **Lacrosse** are also very common team sports.

Many collegiate sport programs fall under the National Association of Collegiate Athletics (NACA). The NACA has very strict rules for athletes, which includes regulations on where they can be employed and what they can participate in.

Chapter One

GWEN

"**G**wen, we're going to Marabou Mike's later for wings and beers. Come with us?" Bonnie, my teammate and co-worker, pleaded as we cleaned up after our hockey campers had left the rink for the day.

"I'd love to, but I'm spending tonight with Austin." Not that I had the money for extra things. Since classes ended for summer, I'd been all work, no play.

But, priorities, since my hobbies included eating regularly and doors that locked.

"Right, today's the day," she breathed, gathering her things. "I hope it goes well. See you tomorrow."

Bonnie and I played hockey together at the New York Institute of Technology, so she understood the gravity of my boyfriend's situation.

"See you tomorrow." I grabbed my bag and stick, then entered the area of the main rink, went past the snack bar and skate rental desk, and through a door marked *Employees Only.* Tony was in the back, sharpening skates.

"Tony, I'm done with camp. I'm going to get a quick workout in. Do you need any help?" One of the perks of working here was that Tony let me have ice time. Something especially helpful in summer, since I couldn't afford fancy off-season training.

"Do you have a shift at Tito's tonight?" The weathered older alpha had once been an Olympic speed skater and now managed the New York Ice Training Center.

"I took tonight off, but I can help you restock for a bit. I could use the hours." Also the distraction. My phone had no missed calls or texts from my boyfriend. I'd been hoping for news, for his sake. I eyed the boxes of skates piled up near Tony. "Did they come?"

Tony's eyebrows arched as his black coffee scent flared with annoyance. "They're too big for you."

"They're for Austin. I'm so glad they came, because well, today's the day. He might need cheering up if they don't call." While I direly needed new skates, so did he.

"I got you the wholesale price because I thought they were for *you,*" he grumped.

"I'll get new skates, eventually." A reminder on my phone popped up that I had another tuition payment due.

Tony put down the pair he'd been sharpening. "You should have dumped him and taken the offer from PacTech."

"Tony." It was an old argument. I was happy here in New York with Austin. "I... I found a ring when I was putting his clothes away. I think he's going to propose once he gets signed." I'd been expecting it for a while.

Austin was my world. We'd been together since high school. He was my best friend, my ride or die. We were going to make it in hockey together.

I waved and left for the small rink.

The training center was home to both the professional ice hockey team, the New York Knights, and the professional skate smash team, the Manhattan Maimers. The New York Knights had gone all the way and won the championship, making them the top team in the Professional Hockey League.

During the off-season, we reserved the smallest of our three rinks for players who stayed and any other pros who might be here. The small rink was my favorite. It smelled like the barn I grew up skating at.

Putting on my skates, I hoped they held out for a while longer. My goalie skates had fallen apart shortly after finals. My hockey skates would have to suffice for now. I was picky about my goalie skates and saving up for exactly what I wanted.

Sweat dripped down my face as I went through my usual on-ice workout. While I'd spent my day doing drills, workouts, and conditioning on and off the ice with my hockey campers, I liked to get in my own time.

As I worked, a giant guy came onto the ice. He was probably six-foot-eight. While not *huge* like Grif Graf, one of the Knights' wingers, he was taller, and still a large and well-proportioned guy.

Huh. Hadn't seen him around.

I braced for him to tell me to leave, but he didn't. He simply moved to the other side of the rink and got to work. Better for me. I could only stay if they let me.

Out of the corner of my eye, I watched him critically. He was several years older than me and was good—and graceful for his size. He took off his helmet for a moment, wiping off his face and taking a drink of water. The Asian guy was *nice* looking, with golden skin, dark hair, brown eyes, a strong jaw, and chiseled features.

He looked over at me, gave me a nod, and went back to work—as did I. The big guy still worked away as I finished. Leaving the ice,

I showered and changed in the employee locker room, so I could help Tony restock.

My phone beeped as I worked.

Austin

Pick up Chello's on your way home? I already placed the order.

Aww. How sweet. I'd been planning on splurging and grabbing something from his favorite restaurant. Chello's was mine.

Me

Of course. Love you.

I finished up the inventory and went to Tony's office to grab the skates. They'd cost me more than I'd ever spend on skates for myself, but Austin had *really* wanted these. Maybe one day they'd be his sponsor.

"Those skates are too good for him. The Philadelphia Aces had years to sign him. They're not going to magically call him today," Tony grunted, looking up from his computer.

"One can hope. Good night, Tony." I picked up the box. Tony might be right. But that didn't mean there weren't other teams waiting for the deadline to either sign Austin or give him a chance if the Philadelphia Aces passed.

Sure, him getting signed wouldn't solve all our problems. After all, getting drafted hadn't. Still, him becoming part of a hockey team, any professional team, would alleviate a lot of stress.

And I didn't mean financial stress. I was fine with being poor, but happy. It was the mood swings since Austin graduated a month ago that gave me whiplash.

"Hey, Ladybug, going already?" Clark called as I walked down the hall to grab my backpack out of my locker.

Clark Edwards bounded over to me like a brown-haired golden retriever that hadn't been walked all day. He was this drop dead gorgeous, dark-haired, alpha forward for the Knights. The kind that should, and did, sell underwear, with muscles honed from years of hockey, tossing hay bales, and fixing tractors.

He also wore these nerdy black glasses, had a penchant for ugly sweaters, and knew everything there was to know about the Defender League movies and comics.

"Yeah, heading off. We could work out tomorrow, either after I'm done with camp or first thing?" I offered. I enjoyed working out with the Knights and learned so much from them.

Clark was last year's wonder-rookie, the kind that was signed from a community college team in farm country and made the Knights' lineup straight away. Something that didn't happen often. A lot of people called him *Wonder Boy*.

"After you get off would be perfect. Oh, the few of us that are still in town are having a little get-together tomorrow night at Dimitri's," he told me. "After that, I'm heading home."

"Austin's bartending at Tito's tomorrow night, and I'll probably be called to sub." Disappointment leaked into my voice. Dimitri's parties, even the 'little get-togethers,' were always a good time. Austin liked it when I brought him.

"You *can* come without him. We all know how much you love Austin. We're not going to steal you." He laughed. Clark looked at the box. "Oh, did you get your new goalie skates?"

"Not yet. These are a surprise for Austin." I opened the box and showed him. They were maroon with gray stitching, which I'd had to order custom.

Clark whistled. "I hope he knows how lucky he is. If you work at Tito's tomorrow, let us know and we'll stop by."

"Sure. See you tomorrow." I waved. They always tipped big.

"Bye, Ladybug!" He smiled and hustled off.

I left the building and headed for the subway, hoping that when I got home Austin had some good news.

Chello's in hand, I walked to our apartment from the subway. It was a worn-down area, but it worked for us. We needed a place convenient to the University of New York City that we could still afford. UNYC had offered Austin a tuition scholarship and a meal plan, but not much toward living. We didn't want to take loans, so we lived off-campus and worked. A lot.

Sure, I had little time to enjoy university life. I often went to class, hockey practice, and work, exhausted—especially since transferring to NYIT from community college. With him graduated, I could now focus more on myself.

One year to go.

My phone rang—my boss from Tito's, possibly calling me in for tomorrow. "Hey."

"Hey, I need you to work tonight," Ernie told me.

"I have tonight off."

I entered our ramshackle building, which didn't even have a working lock on the main door.

He huffed, "I know, which is why I'm asking you to work."

"I can't. I specifically took tonight off." With a sigh, I started up the five flights of stairs, since we didn't have an elevator.

Ernie huffed again. "This isn't a request. Show up or you're fired."

"I... I can't. It's a big night for Austin." My heart twisted. I needed all the hours I could get. Austin hadn't gotten any extra summer jobs this year so he could be free in case a team was interested.

"You're both fired. I'm so sick of your bullshit. Especially his. You at least make sure your shifts are covered, while he's been out every day this week and hadn't even called in," he snapped.

"What? Don't punish me for whatever he did." As far as I knew, he'd been on lunch shift all week–including today.

"I'm done with both of you," he retorted. The line went dead.

Fired? Tears pricked my eyes. I wiped them away. I'd deal with it tomorrow. Maybe Tony would give me more hours.

There was surely a good explanation for Austin not going to work. His agent must have him doing phone meetings or extra practices. Maybe one of his rich friends included him in their summer training group and he forgot to tell me.

Mrs. Jenkins' door flew open as I passed. She probably saw me on her door camera.

The older beta woman had her red hair in curlers. Her marabou feather robe was pink, a cigarette dangled from her lips. "Keep the fighting down."

The door slammed in my face before I could reply.

Well, then. What was she talking about? We hadn't had any loud fights lately.

I unlocked our door and called, "Hey, are you home?"

We'd gotten this one-bedroom furnished, but tried to make it a home. Right now, boxes of his stuff were everywhere, in case he needed to move quickly when a team called.

"In the kitchen making you brownies," he called.

I came into our tiny kitchen as he took a pan of chocolaty goodness out of the oven and set them on the counter. The scent made my mouth water. Mmmm. While I did most of the cooking, because I liked it, he was the baker.

Austin dyed his blond hair blue, wearing it long and shaggy. A blue eye winked at me, and he gave me a dimpled grin, chin clean shaven.

"Hi." I fell into his arms. I was almost five-eight and had an average athletic build. He was six-foot-one. Not a giant alpha, but still tall and solid, with classical broad shoulders, a narrow waist, and lots of muscles. His large hand stroked my wavy hair, which was currently shoulder-length and pale pink with an undercut.

Austin planted a kiss on my forehead. His scent whirled around me, stronger than mine, since he was an alpha, and I was just a beta. It always reminded me of fabric softener. Of comfort. Safety.

Nothing else mattered because with Austin, I was *home.*

We'd met in junior hockey back when we were teenagers. Both of us had moved to play on that team, so we lived with host families that were down the block from each other and fell in love. After we'd graduated high school, we'd moved to New York together.

Neither of us had any family we really spoke to. But we had each other—and that's all that mattered. Sure, we argued, especially when money was tight and stress was high. All couples fought.

"Chellos, brownies, movies?" Austin asked, getting mismatched dishes down from the cupboard, his large body filling the small space.

"Perfect. I got you a present." Placing the box on the cracked counter, my belly fluttered. *Please like them.*

"Gwen." He opened the box and took out the custom, top-of-the-line hockey skates, sucking in a sharp breath. "This is too much. I thought you were saving to get *you* skates."

"You've got to look good out there when those teams call at 12:01. They'll call." I wrapped my arms around him.

Plenty of players were drafted, but not signed right away. The teams could sign them at *any* time until thirty days after university graduation. After that, the player became a free agent and could play for whoever they wanted as soon as the signing window opened.

We were on day thirty. Lucky for him, the signing window recently opened, so he didn't have long to wait if the Aces passed.

"I've been doing informal interviews all week. Though the most promising teams are abroad," he told me slowly.

"Oh, is that why you missed your shift? Not prying, Ernie called me." I'd mention us being fired later.

He nodded. "Yep. That's weird that he called. I traded shifts."

Did he? But I wouldn't push it.

He continued, "I think the Aces will sign me and they're just being coy."

"I hope that's the case. Though plenty of players do a season or two abroad first. I'll support you either way and we'll make it work," I replied. It would be hard being away from him, but we'd manage.

Austin pouted as he wiggled out of my grasp and made himself a plate, his scent sour with hurt. "Don't you believe in me, Babe?"

"Of course I do. I've done nothing but support you for the past five years," I soothed, hating when he got like this. It had been happening far too much lately. I wanted my big sweetheart back.

"Oh yeah? So why aren't we going to the two Knights' goalie weddings this summer, huh? Do you know what a networking opportunity that could be for me? Considering how much time you spend with the goalies, and how much lasagna you make them, you'd think you'd get an invitation." His big form crowded me and the spicy scent of angry alpha made me flinch. Austin smirked.

I'd been invited to both weddings. One wasn't an actual goalie wedding, it was a goalie's packmate. It had already happened *in Greece*. While my friends had offered to cover me, I didn't want to deal with the fight with Austin it would have caused. The other I hadn't mentioned because it was in Canada, and I was afraid of traveling there.

"Well, I guess we know what they think of you. I mean, you do all that unpaid work for the Knights. They *won* a championship. But I don't even have an offer to go to their training camp?" He sneered.

I flinched again. *I* didn't have an offer to go to their training camp either. It wasn't how the program worked. I was a part of the

Knight's goalie development program. We acted as EBUGs–emergency backup goalies–and sometimes practiced with them. We weren't paid to avoid breaking both collegiate eligibility rules and the PHL's rules for EBUGs.

"Your agent would probably have better luck. If you want, I can try talking to Coach next time I see her," I promised, not wanting to be yelled at by Austin. I was tired, hungry, and needed snuggles.

Not that me talking to Coach Kirov would do anything. She was the goalie coach and Austin was a forward, but I knew her best out of the Knights' coaches.

His scent changed from angry to happy, and his expression brightened. "You'd do that for me, Babe?"

"Of course. We're a team." I added a piece of bread to my plate, holding my breath. The plan had always been for Austin to go pro first, then he'd help me.

Austin kissed the top of my head. "I'm sorry. I didn't mean to snap at you. I'm just stressed. You choose the first movie?"

"I know. Sure." We took our food and snuggled up on the battered couch.

He handed me the remote, and I chose a silly feel-good hockey movie. As the movie started, I took a bite, letting the sauce explode over my tongue. It was almost as good as my nonna's.

Almost.

She and her neighbors had encouraged my love of hockey. Something my dads never liked–especially after my mom passed away.

"Oh, I made your tuition payment," he added, taking a bite of pasta. "Only a few payments left."

"Thank you." My university had a weird rule that if you played a sport that crossed semesters, tuition and fees for the entire year had to be paid by mid-August.

Austin had pushed me to transfer to NYIT, instead of a cheaper public university. He'd promised that if I figured out that year, he'd cover the next—my last—to make up for all the years I'd worked multiple jobs and gone to community college to support him at UNYC. So, he'd been making payments for month.

NYIT had a great hockey program that produced several PHL players. An amazing school academically, it had a top accounting program. But it was pricey, even with all my scholarships and aid.

So here we were.

Austin kissed me again, sweet and full of hope. "Always. After tonight, we'll be golden."

Chapter Two

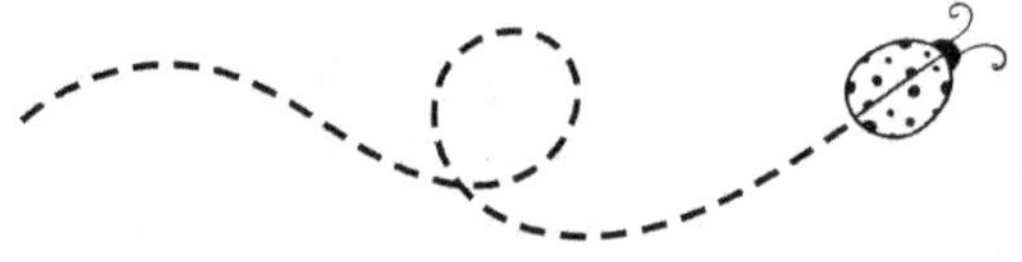

GWEN

NOTE: This chapter contains content that might be upsetting to some readers.

I held my breath as the clock on my phone changed to midnight. His phone rang, and we jumped from our spots on the couch as we watched TV. My heart squeezed. *Please be good news.*

"Tell me they sent a contract?" Austin hopped up from the couch and paced our small living room.

The look on his face said it all. Austin knocked the lamp over.

I flinched as his spicy anger filled the small space. He'd had too much to drink as we'd waited for midnight. I hated it when he got like this.

One thing that had attracted me to Austin when we were teenagers, was that while he was a beast on the ice, and an ass with his friends, he was gentle with me. He *saw* me. Remembered little silly things about me. Was kind and undemanding.

Until recently...

"Did anyone else send a contract? What about Hungary? I have to have a contract *now* or I'm screwed. How many times do I need to tell you that? Not an invitation to a camp. A contract." His anger flooded the space, and I made myself small on the couch.

He needed a *contract* by tonight? That was news to me–and not part of our plan. We should have done things differently if that was the case.

Why did he need a contract by tonight, when no one but the Aces could offer him a contract until right now?

"Get me a fucking contract by morning," he yelled, then ended the call.

"I'm sorry you didn't get a contract. Don't you think you were a little hard on her though? I'm sure she's trying her best." I wrapped a blanket around myself for comfort.

"She works for me," he snapped.

The entitlement made me frown. Like me, he valued hard work.

"What did you mean about needing a contract tonight?" I prodded, puzzled. We'd talked about our plan in great detail–and he'd never mentioned that.

His shoulders hunched and he plopped back down on the couch, but didn't cuddle me. "When I moved to Rockland to play junior hockey, I made a deal with my dad and grandfather. I had until one month after university graduation to sign with a team. I had to do it on my own with no help–no connections, no financial assistance, no family name, nothing."

"Didn't your parents pass away?" Back in high school, he'd told me that he lived with his grandpa after his parents died and that it was so bad he basically ran away to junior hockey and went no-contact.

The similarities of our stories drew us to each other.

Austin grimaced. "I wish he died instead of my mom. He's an asshole–so is my grandpa. I want nothing to do with them."

"Is Austin Blake not your name?" I chewed on my lower lip.

"I lied. It's not like you don't have secrets," he snapped.

"Hey, I'm not mad about that. I can only imagine what you must have gone through to feel like you needed to tell everyone your dad was dead," I soothed.

I could forgive lying about his family, his past, and his name. After all, I understood that completely. My dads were assholes too, and I hadn't talked to them in years.

Though I didn't wish they were dead.

I surveyed him. "What now?"

"I have to go home and take my place in the family business. I hate them. They're so toxic. Even my brothers." He grimaced as he raked a hand through his blue hair. "They're shitty, small-minded, conceited people, who want you to do everything their way."

"Why didn't you tell me about the deal? We should have structured the plan differently." Sure, he didn't talk much about his family, but this was an important detail.

"I... I almost told you so many times, but I was so sure the Aces would sign me," he confessed.

"Me, too." I squeezed his shoulder. "It's awful that your family put you in this position."

"I feel like I failed you. We were supposed to be a team. Play together, take the PHL by storm, form a pack, have a cute little house and kids," he told me, remorse crossing his face.

"We can still do all that. You have until morning, right? We can come up with a plan by then." I nodded.

His phone rang. There was no name on the screen, and it wasn't an area code I recognized. Hope built within me. Maybe a team was contacting him directly? The international teams did things differently.

Austin looked at it, scowled, and hit the silence button. Oh.

"Maybe we should go to bed?" I offered, trying to make the best of things. "In the morning, hopefully, your agent will have a contract for you. If not, I'll get out the spreadsheet, and we can go over all your options. We'll make a presentation and convince your dad to give us more time."

Surely, his father would listen to reason if we made a good case. There'd be plenty of time for Austin to take his place in whatever they did after he retired. Hockey players didn't have long careers.

"Now I have to go work for them and do what they say." He stood, the spicy scent of alpha anger raining over me. His phone rang again.

I took a deep breath. "I understand that you're hurt and frustrated. But hey, I'm here. We can do this."

"There's no *we.* It's over. That plan, that dream, is gone," he roared, flipping the coffee table over

Confusion coated me and I took a step back at the violence. "I don't understand. Just because you have to move home and work for your family doesn't mean we have to break up. We've been together for so long, been through so much, we aren't going to throw it all away for one setback, are we?"

My hands balled into fists as hurt and fear shot through me. I'd never seen him direct his anger at me like that. It was one reason he played hockey– a way to deal with his rage.

Was he truly going to end things because he didn't get a hockey contract? Given how long and hard we'd practiced, the nights we spent dreaming, the sacrifices we made, it seemed ludicrous.

"I'll fight for us, including convincing them to give you more time. We can still make it in the PHL together," I assured. All this anger confused me. Did we mean nothing?

Was he using me?

"Oh, come on, if the PHL wanted you, you'd be on a team by now." His face contorted with so much loathing that I didn't recognize him.

My heart dropped. Was this the frustration and stress talking, or had he somehow hid this part of himself from me for all these years?

Was the man who brought me flowers and told me he loved me, the one who twirled me around on the ice, the one who'd lay in the dark and talk about the future with me, a lie?

"*You* didn't want me to put in for the draft, remember?" Now I was too old. "I haven't signed with an agent or networked, or declared free agency since *your* plan called for us putting you first. Which is fine, but it also means that you can't put me down for not being signed yet." I didn't raise my voice, but I put an edge to it.

The plan made sense given I was a goalie and we took a little longer to develop. Not to mention starting over at sixteen had slowed me down prospect-wise.

He sneered. "You're not that good. I mean, you were when we were younger. I also thought you'd be an omega–and that would be our ticket. But no, here you are, just a dumb cunt beta who hasn't even finished university yet. You're too stupid to even take advantage of your job with the Knights."

"You don't get to talk to me like that," I snapped, my face growing warm with anger. How dare he?

He thought I'd be an omega? Yeah, no.

"You know what, tensions are high tonight. I'll stay with a friend so you can cool off, and we can talk this out in the morning." Yeah, I needed to leave before I said something I regretted. This conversation was leaving me hurt, angry, and confused.

I grabbed my phone and backpack. In the bedroom I threw some things inside, not that I had much. This was his frustration talking, right? Doubt crept through me.

He blocked the bedroom doorway with his shirtless frame. "Where the fuck do you think you're going?"

"I told you, I'm going to stay with a friend, and give us time to cool off. Do you want me to come by before or after work so we can talk this out?" I did a few deep yoga breaths as I threw more things into my bag. Something about this mood differed from usual.

"Friends? You have no friends." A cruel grin toyed on his lips. Lips that had kissed me so many times.

"I do so." My voice shook. His words hit me in the chest. While I knew a lot of people, I was always so busy with work, school, and hockey that I didn't have many friends who I could call at midnight and ask to crash on their couch. Austin was my bestie.

"Fine, call someone right now." He smirked.

"Okay." Most people were away for summer. The few here barely had a place to live, let alone a place for me to stay. Bonnie was working late and her phone was off.

Oh, Clark had texted me? I'd try him. No answer. Shit. My stomach dropped. Carlos? He'd absolutely help me. But his phone was set to *do not disturb.*

"Wow. Sucks to be you. I guess you're not fucking one of them. Always wondered with all the extra shit you did this year," he spat.

"I'm not fucking anyone but you. The Knights made it to the playoffs, then won the championship, which makes the season *longer.* Please, let me pass." I made my voice hard as I tried to find a space to squeeze through.

He thought what? Austin sometimes got jealous of me hanging out with the Knights without him, but I'd thought it was because they were pros. Not shit like that.

My shoes were by the door, my keys were already in my bag. If I had to, I'd go to the rink and work off my frustrations on the ice until my head cleared.

His phone lit up with texts.

Ris

Sorry you didn't get the contract. If you want to stay with me instead of your dad, let me know. Love you.

It was like plunging into an ice bath.

"Who's that?" My heart sank. Had he been *cheating* on me? I wasn't sure how else to take that text.

"That's your fault, you know. If I'd gotten the contract, we could stay together. Now we can't and I have to mate with an omega they chose. I wasted *so* many years on you. I thought you were special, but you're just some useless beta bitch."

His words made me recoil.

"You don't get to call me names. Do you honestly think our relationship was a *waste?* You didn't think that when I was paying your tuition, making your food, and washing your underwear. When I put my goals, my dreams, on hold for *you.*" The words turned bitter in my mouth.

How could he have kept all this from me? How did I not see it? No, I knew how I didn't see it. Sometimes I was too tired to even finish my homework, let alone look to see if the man I trusted more than anyone was someone else.

"Sure, we had good times. But it doesn't matter anymore. We can't be together because *I didn't get a contract.* You didn't even end up being a fucking omega," he spat.

There he went with the omega thing again. While sure, omegas were made for alphas, plenty of alphas married betas. Omegas were less than ten percent of the population to alphas, who were over a quarter, while betas were more than half.

"I never said I'd be an omega. People just thought that when we were in high school because I like fairy lights. I don't *want* to be an omega. I... I thought you loved me." All the life drained out of me as my voice broke. "I loved you. You were my everything."

Tears pricked my eyes. I thought he was my forever alpha. My love. My one and only. I'd *trusted* him. Believed in him.

"I did love you. I wanted to be with you. Now I can't. I told you, it's over. There's no *we,* because *I didn't get a contract.* Also, my family would eat you alive. With your pink hair, your clothes, your tattoos and nose piercing, and your manners. They didn't even fix your nose right the last time you took a puck to the face," he sneered.

"It's only hair. I can be fancy when I want to be." I flinched. Most of it was intentional, including taking several pucks to the face.

I ducked under his muscular arm. He grabbed me by the back of the shirt and threw me into the living room. Not only did he work out a lot, but alphas were stronger and faster, with better reflexes, by nature. They were leaders and protectors. Betas were the average everyday people who got shit done.

All the air whooshed out of me as I hit the couch.

"You bitch," he roared.

Red swam before my eyes as I tried not to let the force of his anger overpower me. While we'd fought, he'd never, *ever* laid a hand on me.

"That's it. We're over. You *don't* get to touch me like that." I peeled myself up off the floor, grabbing my phone and backpack.

That was my uncrossable line.

"Get back here," he yelled, tripping over the table he'd thrown.

"We're done." Voice and body shaking, I shoved my feet into my shoes and unlocked the door. When I turned to get my hoodie off the hook, something hit me in the forehead, knocking me backwards.

Pain seared through my head as an object clattered to the ground.

An ice skate. He'd thrown a fucking skate at me. It felt like the blade nicked me. Shit.

Without waiting another moment, I slipped out the front door and ran down the apartment hallway, shoving my phone in the pocket of my ratty sweats, so I didn't drop it. Sure, he was bigger than me, stronger.

But I was *fast.*

"Where are you going?" he shouted down the hallway.

"You hit me, I'm out," I yelled back, blood running into my eyes, which I wiped away. I had to get out of here. As much as leaving hurt, this wasn't the man I loved.

This was someone else entirely. One that could kill me.

A body slammed into me, knocking me face first into the hallway wall, further aggravating the cut on my head. He spun me around, alpha body crushing me, as his hand smacked my face, then wrapped around my throat.

A tear trickled down my face as pain shot through me. How could I have ever loved him? Wanted to spend forever with him?

I kneed him the balls, and he let go.

"Fuck," he yelped.

Free, I ran, fueled by fear.

"You're nothing. You're a fucking nothing who will never fucking make it," he yelled as I careened down the stairwell, taking them as fast as I could.

I didn't hear or see him follow, but I kept running until I reached the subway station, stopping occasionally to wipe the blood out of my eyes. I pulled my hoodie on to cover the blood on my face and continued to try to stem the flow. First, I'd go to the rink, use the first aid kit, and get myself together.

That sounded good.

Getting on my phone, I changed *all* my passwords. I blocked my location from him and took a picture of my face.

And ignored Austin's mean texts.

"Are you okay?" a man who'd gotten on at my station asked. "Are you bleeding?"

"I... I'm on my way to get fixed. It'll be fine." I ducked my head more, not liking the attention.

Clark had texted.

Clark

Sorry I missed your call. Is everything okay?

Me

Broke up with Austin. Going to the rink to work shit out.

Someone should know where I was for safety.

By the time I reached the rink, Austin had stopped rage-texting me, so I replied.

Me

It's over. I'll be by after work tomorrow to get my things.

That was my only response. Maybe Clark and Carlos would come with me. I didn't want to go by myself.

Where I'd put my stuff–or go–I didn't know. It wasn't like I had much. My hockey and class stuff, and some clothes.

The rink was nearly always open, but nighttime was quiet. I should find the first aid kit and get cleaned up. Instead, I found myself at the small rink, my tennies slipping slightly as I walked to the center and laid down in the darkness on the ice, exhaustion coating me.

It was comforting to lie on the ice, reminding me of better times when I'd do this on the pond at my nonna's.

What had happened? I'd come home to a guy who made me brownies and left to someone throwing a skate at my head.

He'd never even raised his voice to me until this past year, let alone pinned me to a wall and tried to choke me.

I swallowed a sob. There was so much I didn't understand. His deal. The complete mood shift. Why couldn't we still be together even if he had to work for his dad?

Not that I'd give him a second chance. He hit me. That was it. No amount of apologies in the world would fix that.

My phone rang, but I was too tired to answer it as I sobbed.

What was I going to do? I couldn't afford to live in New York on my own–or finish my degree. He was right. I'd lost my best paying job. I was homeless. Friendless. I didn't even have a place to crash.

I'd trusted him. Invested everything in him. Never did I think I needed more than him and I'd made him my world. I hadn't seen us as simply dating. To me, we were a young couple, starting our life together, figuring things out... together.

He'd betrayed me, leaving me with *nothing*.

The tears flowed fast and hard as I cried and cried until the world slipped away. Someone called my name as everything grew dim.

Hopefully, it wasn't Austin coming after me.

But I was too tired to care.

Chapter Three

GWEN

"Do you want to know what I think?" Tony perched on the end of the exam bed at the hospital. There were shadows of stubble on his weathered face. He wore shorts and a T-shirt, not the nice pants with a rink polo I usually saw him in.

"I'm not taking him back. But I have no idea how I'm going to live or get through my last year," I sobbed. "I still don't understand how he could hurt me, say such cruel things."

Apparently, I'd been found passed out on the ice and brought here. The doctor had stitched up the cut, the police had taken pictures and a statement, and we were now waiting on the results of my scans.

"You got a shit deal, and I'm so sorry. You've spent years supporting that knothead, and *his* education, and *his* dream. It's time to focus on you. *Your* goals, *your* education, *your* dreams. Contact your university coach and the financial aid office and see how they can help you. Go live in the dorms. Have a year to be a student and not work so many jobs, so you can focus on what's important." He took a sip of coffee as the hospital bustled around us on the other side of the curtain.

"How can I live without all my jobs?" I gave him a skeptical look. All this made my head ache more than it already did.

"Take out a loan. I know you don't want to, but a little debt so you can breathe might be exactly what you need. All your jobs take away from hockey and class—you're too tired to always do your best," he told me. "That could cost you *everything* if you still plan on going pro after graduation."

"Ouch." It was true. I'd found out the hard way when I started at NYIT that I couldn't work as much as I had before. During collegiate playoffs, Tony forced me to not work at the rink, and I'd taken off from Tito's due to scheduling. I'd felt so much better on the ice with only having class and practice. But you needed money to live.

"If you honestly and truly want to play professional hockey next year, you have to get *noticed.* I know you're used to keeping your head down, but you need to stop that. Sometimes in this business, being good isn't enough. As you know, teams will choose the giant alpha with a lower save rate because they don't know better. So you have to *make them look,*" he told me. "Make them reconsider, make them *regret.*"

"True." I knew this. Well. I'd spent the past year proving to NYIT that I deserved my spot. Something that would be easier to do if I wasn't so tired all of the time.

Plenty of betas played goalie. There were even omega goalies. The Knights had both. But their omega goalie was also well over six feet, and even most beta goalies were on the tall side for their designation.

However, I was afraid that making them look would get me noticed in all the wrong ways.

"Do you think I have what it takes? After all, Austin didn't." My voice trembled. Being a PHL goalie had been my dream since my nonna and her neighbors had taken me to my very first game when I was tiny.

"Austin's an ass who can't take feedback." Tony rolled his eyes. "Honestly, I'm not sure he could make it in the PHL. You, however, if you're not tired and prioritize, focus, and sparkle on the ice, could be the next Maria Barilla." He grinned, knowing I admired her.

"That's the dream." I grinned back. She'd been a legendary goalie for the Knights, still holding the record for shutout games all these years later. Maria was also the first beta goalie in the PHL.

"Also, practicing isn't enough. You have to network and build relationships," he told me.

"True. It might be nice to live in the dorms, or my own little place." This whole thing hinged on me qualifying for a loan or somehow getting major financial aid. Because I couldn't afford rent for my own place, let alone a security deposit and the tuition payments I still had left.

Tony nodded. "That might be good for you. Figure out who *you* are without Austin. It's been you and him for so long that he's become part of your identity. There's so much more to you, out there for you. Take some time to figure that out."

The words rubbed my soul raw. Who was I without Austin? I mean, I was someone without him. But I had zero experience being that woman.

Tears pricked my eyes as I pulled my knees to my chest, careful of the bruises on my ribs, neck, and face. "I thought he loved me."

"You're allowed to feel hurt, to be angry. It's shitty what he did. I'm not going to let you wallow though, because then that fucker wins," he told me.

"We don't let the assholes win. Double D says that." I bit back a smile.

"He's a smart man, and a good goalie. Not as good as Maria Barilla, though." He chuckled. "The best revenge is to *thrive*. Show Austin you don't need him. Just wait until you get signed by a PHL team."

"Okay. I could hop on a group chat, check some housing boards, maybe ask around the rink." I nodded. We didn't have to give much notice for our place, thank goodness. I couldn't afford rent on two places, anyways, and I wouldn't want Austin to be stuck.

"Yes, ask around. If you need someplace for a couple of days while you get things sorted, my daughter is at camp. You can always put your things in a storeroom at the rink. You should get your things sooner rather than later, so he doesn't do anything to it," he offered.

"True—and thank you." I rubbed my head.

"It might take a little time, but you'll get this figured out. After all, you were the fixer in your relationship. You know how to make things work. Unlike him." He snorted. "Here's your phone and stuff. Oh, call Clark. He was upset to find you passed out and bleeding on the ice." Tony handed me my bag.

"*Clark* found me?" I blinked. "I thought you did."

"He found you, got the rink night manager, who then called me. He rode with you in the ambulance, which someone had already called. I made him go home as soon as I got here. I said you'd call," he told me.

"Oh." I sat up and looked at all the messages and missed calls on my phone. Clark had come to the rink. He'd *found* me.

"Why did you *lie down on the ice?*" Tony made a face.

"I enjoy lying down on the ice." It was comforting.

"Hey, you can't go back there," a nurse said to someone.

"Don't worry. Mariquita is my sister," a familiar voice said. Mariquita was Spanish for Ladybug, which was the nickname the

Knights had given me, since I was an EBUG–an emergency backup goalie–and a woman.

Hockey players were so silly sometimes.

Carlos Rodriguez, winger for the Knights, came in, wearing a Knights shirt, workout shorts, and flip-flops, his hair tousled like he'd just rolled out of bed... with someone. Which might explain the *do not disturb* on his phone.

He'd grown up here and had gone to the same community college I had. We'd played together my first year there. Then he'd gotten signed and spent a year with the Bantams, the Knights' farm team, before becoming a Knight.

With him was Dimitri Belikov, a defender, who, like Carlos, was going into his third year with the Knights. He'd played for Russia first. The Russian alpha was about the same height as Clark, but broader. His dark hair was slicked back, and he looked put together–and a little threatening–even in jeans, a T-shirt, and loafers.

Clark followed, wearing a green shirt advertising his parent's tractor repair company, some workout shorts, and Defender League slip-ons, he also had a sweatshirt tied around his waist. He clutched a paper sack.

He rushed over to me, concern brimming in his big brown eyes as his black-rimmed glasses slipped down his nose. "Hey, how are you? Your clothes are covered in blood."

"I told you she'd *call*." Tony gave them a hard look.

Clark held up the sack, unbothered. "Breakfast delivery. Also, I needed to make sure she was all right." His hand brushed my pink hair out of my face, so he could see the gash. "That looks nasty. Not as bad as when I found you, but still."

He'd brought me food? Clark was always thoughtful, which Austin saw as a threat.

"Why did you go to the rink if you were hurt, Bozh'ya Korovka?" Dimitri rumbled, using the Russian word for ladybug. He'd semi-adopted me since he was raising his teen siblings.

"I was going to use the first aid kit and get my head together while I found someplace to crash. Maybe hit some pucks and pretend they were Austin's face," I replied. "But... I'm glad you came, Clark."

I'd texted Clark for safety, not because I'd expected him to find me.

Tony stood. "I'm going to find the doctor and see when you can leave."

"Of course." Clark's brows furrowed. "I came straight to the rink when you didn't answer my calls."

Oh. A phone had been ringing. I looked away. "I was afraid it would be him. Thank you."

"That's what friends are for," Clark told me, taking the hoodie from around his waist and throwing it at me. "Oh, here's a clean sweatshirt. I have a washer at my place and we can wash yours."

"I'm going to kick his sorry ass." Carlos eyed my other injuries. The tan, dark-haired kappa wasn't as tall as the other two, and more compact. However, he was taller than me. Also, *fast* and a daredevil on the ice.

Kappas were crazy fuckers. Literally, they were a designation of fun-loving adrenaline junkies with questionable judgment. There weren't too many of them.

"I kneed Austin in the balls," I admitted. He'd deserved it.

"That-a-girl." Clark grinned, revealing dimples.

He sat down on the foot of the bed, his brows knitting together as worry filled his scent, which was reminiscent of hay on a hot summer's day.

"Tell me what happened? All I know is you texted me that you two broke up and when I found you, you were *bleeding*." Clark's brow furrowed, and his scent soured.

I took a bite of the breakfast sandwich, letting the tastes and textures explode over my tongue. *So good.*

As I ate, I told them what had happened. Normally I wouldn't get this personal with them, but I was still struggling to process everything. Not to mention questioning myself. Was this my fault? Could I have done something different, better?

How could I have trusted Austin for so many years?

"I did the right thing, didn't I?" I scrunched up the wrapper, wishing it was Austin's face.

Clark's arm wrapped around me, Carlos by my side. Dimitri looked like he wanted to punch someone.

"Yes. He doesn't get to hurt you. You were right to leave him. He turned out to be a fucking asshole," Clark assured.

"Real alphas don't hurt people. None of this is your fault," Dimitri added.

"It was shitty of him to take advantage of you and to lie to you," Carlos told me.

"I understand his lies and I understand wanting to make it on your own. But I can't wrap my head around how quickly it escalated." I sniffed. It was too much. Though their words made me feel better. *None of this is your fault.*

"Where are you going to stay for now? I have a spare room if you need it. I'm going to be gone most of the off-season, anyway. Because I have to go back and forth for stuff, I kept my place," Clark offered.

"Thanks. I think I'll stay at Tony's for a few days, then check with my teammates, see who might need a summer roommate." Like I could afford rent wherever Clark lived. It was kind of him to offer though. "Will you come with me to get my stuff?"

"Of course. That's why I brought them." Clark grinned. "I can't promise I won't punch him."

"I've been wanting to take a swing at him since he got mad at you at the holiday party for giving Clark a present," Carlos replied, punching one hand with the other.

"You heard that?" I winced. It wasn't like I'd gotten Clark some extravagant or inappropriate gift. I'd drawn Clark's name in the team holiday *gift exchange*.

"I heard him at Dimitri's party accusing you of flirting with Dimitri. Last time I checked, *thanks for inviting us, is your sister here?* isn't flirting," Clark told me.

My belly twisted. "The stress of the last year made him a little insecure. He's usually not like that."

Carlos gave me a look like he didn't believe me. He'd known me the longest, and by extension, Austin, since I'd bring him to things.

"When he snapped at you at Mercy's birthday party for not spending enough time with him, he was stressed about finals even though graduation had already happened?" Dimitri's eyebrows rose.

My head bowed as self-loathing consumed me. "How did I miss all this?"

Clark tipped up my chin, his touch gentle. "Don't beat yourself up. It'll be okay."

I hoped so. Right now, I felt like someone had ripped my heart out of my chest.

"This is where you live?" Dimitri's voice went rumbly as we approached my building.

It was still early. I might even make it to work on time. Tony had told me to take the day off, and he'd let the camp know.

But if I didn't work, I didn't get paid.

"We can't all live in adorable townhouses," I shrugged. His place was *cute,* mostly decorated by his sister. She was nice and attended one of the omega academies here in the city. Sometimes we got together for pedicures.

"It's kinda far from your campus." Carlos frowned.

"It's not that far from UNYC." I shrugged. We walked down the hallway and I shuddered.

Clark put an arm around me. "It'll be okay, Gweny."

Mrs. Jenkins' door flew open. She scowled at my stitched-up forehead. "Please tell me you're not going back to him."

"We're here to get her stuff." Clark pushed his black glasses up the bridge of his nose.

"Good. Do you want the video for the police report? You filed one, right? I called them, too," she told me. Today's marabou feather robe was blue.

Video?

"Your door cam caught part of it," I breathed. "Yes, please."

I'd filed a report. While the police had clucked sympathetically, at this point there wasn't much they could do other than the standard things. The more information I had, the more they might be able to do. Especially if he didn't leave me alone and I needed more than the basic restraining order that was automatic with these sorts of alpha-on-beta domestic violence cases. Every bit would help.

"Good." She held out her phone.

I held out mine, and she sent it to me, then slammed the door.

"Austin, I'm coming in to get my stuff. I'm not alone." I unlocked the door and opened it, looking around.

All the boxes in the living room were gone. The table he'd knocked over had been righted. The posters were off the walls.

"I think his stuff is gone," I breathed, noting what was missing from the kitchen. "We got the place furnished."

"Makes things easier. Can you afford rent here on your own? I mean, I know you may not want to stay, but it might give you time," Clark said.

"I could do it for a few weeks, but that's it." It would give me a moment to develop a plan. I'd be asking the landlord if Austin's share could come out of his half of the deposit. It would be hard to live here, but better than imposing.

"Good idea," Carlos told me.

I opened the bedroom door and sucked in a breath. Shredded clothes were strewn everywhere. Makeup smeared the walls. My laptop, which I'd gotten at Christmas, sat smashed into tiny pieces. My books were torn up–including my favorite series from when I was a teenager and one of the few things I'd brought from home when I'd fled. Posters had been ripped off my wall.

Every memento was ruined, each stuffie decapitated. All my good hockey stuff, versus what was in my locker at the rink, was destroyed. *Beta whore* marked up my custom goalie mask that he'd bought me when I'd gotten into NYIT. He'd even broken my stick into pieces. Someone destroyed the custom goalie pads he'd bought me for my birthday.

My jewelry box had been upturned, everything stepped on. All my spices that I'd gotten little by little, mostly from the campus needs pantry, were dumped on the carpet.

"Shit," Clark muttered, looking around at the devastation.

A small box on the dresser caught my eye, in a pile of confetti that was the few hockey cards I hadn't sold because they weren't worth anything. It was the ring box I'd found with his clothes. Inside was a piece of paper with the words *it wasn't for you* scrawled in his messy handwriting.

I'd never take him back. But the words were still daggers in my heart.

The *only* picture I had of my mom was cut into pieces inside it. Tears pricked my eyes. How could he be that cruel?

Clutching the box, I fell to my knees on the spice-filled carpet and began to cry.

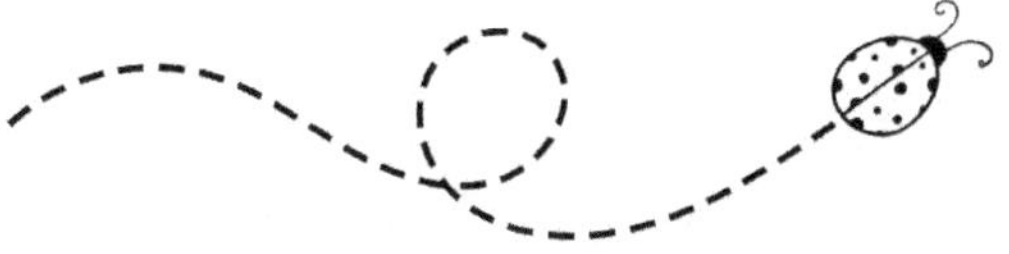

Chapter Four

TENZIN

My phone rang, and I silenced it as I exited the subway, weaving through the throng of people bustling on this Friday morning in New York City. A few people gave me looks as I made my way down the busy sidewalk.

It could be because I was six-foot-eight, tall even for an alpha. It could also be because I was a professional hockey player.

A small child stopped and stared at me, tugging on his mom's pant leg. I waved, but didn't stop.

My phone rang again. No. I didn't want to talk to any of them. It buzzed with a text.

Morgan

You're selling our house?

It was my house and I could sell it if I wanted. Maybe I should have told her before I put it on the market, but she'd moved in with them some time ago.

Did I even answer her? I should block her. After all, we'd broken up. She'd moved on. Yet there was something so *final* about doing so.

I entered the New York Ice Training Center. Yesterday, I'd come by on my own out of curiosity. Today I was here to sign some papers, shake some hands, and make a *big* change.

The Portland Sasquatches had been good to me. I loved my coaches, my teammates, and the city of Portland. We were the second-ranked team in the PHL. I'd been ready to re-sign with a big contract. I'd been happy.

Then my life blew up.

My agent had been beyond supportive of helping me find a way to quickly and quietly leave the Sasquatches without making enemies. She'd done phenomenal work, considering she was literally in labor right now.

I didn't want to leave the Sasquatches. But, it was better this way. Not only was New York City across the country, my ex hated it with a passion.

A group of kids carrying hockey sticks waved at me as they filed past. I waved back, my heart breaking a little. I followed the signs for the Knights' offices.

"You're the Yeti," the security guard at the elevator said, as he confirmed my appointment with Bunty Longfellow, the Knights general manager.

"I am." That had been my hockey nickname in high school. The Sasquatches had found it *hilarious* when they'd discovered it while I was a rookie and it stuck.

His eyes got wide. "Are you..."

I put a finger to my lips. I didn't want this to get out yet.

He pretended to zip his lips. "Understood."

I took the elevator up, and it opened into a reception area. A man in a suit waited for me. He was an older alpha, gray in his hair and lines on his face. While Bunty Longfellow had been a good GM for a long time, many had called for his retirement–and for the owner of the Knights to step down–after a debacle last season, involving them trying to illegally fire one of their most popular players.

Bunty extended a hand. "Mr. Brooks, I hope you had a pleasant flight from Portland. I'm honored that you came all the way out here, instead of handling it over the phone and through your agent."

"I wanted to show you that I'm serious. Which is also why I wanted to sign with you sooner rather than later." I didn't plan on going back to Portland other than to handle some business.

"Come into my office." He ushered me into his large office, and we went through the usual coffee and niceties.

Bunty leaned forward over his big wooden desk. "We're beyond excited that you want to join the Knights. We could use a defender like you since Elias Royce retired."

That's why we'd approached the Knights. They'd be looking for a solid defender to fill the void left by their captain.

"I could use a team just like you. After all, the championship win is where Grif Graf is, right?" I joked, trying to get comfortable in the too-small chair, even though it was clearly meant for large alphas.

He laughed. "Absolutely."

The Sasquatches had lost the PHL championships two years in a row. First to the Biscayne Bay Hurricanes, the second to the New

York Knights. Both times, forward Griffin McGraff had been part of the winning team.

"He'll be sad that he's no longer the biggest guy on the Knights," Bunty chuckled.

Grif Graf was a big guy, but not as tall as me.

We got down to business, going over the contract, which was *incredibly* generous. I'd expected them to counteroffer and had been prepared to accept. But they hadn't. They'd even added things, as if I needed enticement.

All I'd asked for was the caveat that while other players could know, I didn't want me joining the team announced to the press until closer to the start of the season.

I signed the contract and shook Bunty's hand again.

He handed me a black and silver Knights hat. "Are you sure you don't want it announced today? Usually a player like you would have all the fanfare, like a press conference, and photo ops with your new jersey."

"I'm not really a fanfare sort of guy and I appreciate your willingness to keep this quiet. Closer to the start of the season, I'll be happy to participate in whatever promo you want," I replied, putting the hat on my head.

"I can respect that." He clapped me on the shoulder. "Let me give you a tour and introduce you around, and we'll get everything set."

"When you're ready to move, I can help you with arrangements. We have an agreement with an apartment building if you're looking to lease. I know real estate agents if you're looking to buy. Car leases, moving companies, we can get it all handled. I even have a cheat sheet with utilities, grocery delivery, and everything you need to get started," someone in operations, a man named Devon, told me.

"Perfect. For now, I'd like to get an apartment," I replied. I'd already gotten a tour, had lunch, met with HR and had given them all my documents, as well as had a chat with their PR person. The new assistant GM hadn't started yet. Theirs had left after Bunty hadn't been fired.

"Great, were you thinking of moving here in late August? Give you a chance to get settled before training camp?" Devon typed on his laptop. He was a very efficient beta in his early thirties.

"How quickly could I move in? I'm staying at the Stonefeld Manhattan Hotel right now," I replied. While my hotel was nice, it would feel more real once I'd gotten settled.

I needed something to feel real right now.

"Oh. So soon. Okay. Do you have friends or family here?" He started typing.

"Not really. I'm looking forward to exploring all the museums. I had a graphic arts minor back at university," I replied. My ex hated art museums and always rushed me through them. I had one friend here, but he was out of town.

"There are some nice museums here. Let me see what I can do. How many bedrooms? Sorry, I don't remember if you have a pack or mate, or anything."

"It's just me. Whatever is fine. So is short term. I might buy something after I sell my place in Portland. Who knows?" One step at a time.

Devon got to work. By the time he finished, I had an apartment in a building where several other players lived, and a lot of useful information, and the name of a reputable cross-country mover. Not that I'd be moving a lot.

I also got my credentials, which would enable me to use the training center, so I could stay in shape during the off-season.

After we finished, I wandered around a little. The facilities for the team seemed nice, and off-season access to the rink, gym, trainers, and physios was always a plus. We shared some facilities, like the gyms, with the Maimers, a skate smash team owned by the same family. The teams had their own spaces, too.

Yesterday, the nice rink manager had let me use a small rink reserved for professional practice. I'd been impressed—especially by the little pink-haired goalie. My guess was that she was local, maybe a recent draft pick, wanting to make a good impression when she met her team.

I found myself in a dining room for Knights' staff and players, the one I'd eaten in earlier. On the wall was a photo of a woman with dark, wavy hair, holding a mask and in full goalie gear. It was faded, the style of both the uniform and gear older. There was a little plaque underneath. Someone had hung a necklace made of pasta noodles from the corner of the frame. *Maria Barilla, first beta goalie in the PHL.*

Huh. Never heard of her. I snapped a picture and sent it to my friend Cooter–one of the Sasquatch's goalies and my best friend.

Cooter

All Hail the Queen of the Goalies. Where the fuck are you?

I took a picture of me in the Knights hat.

Cooter

Already?

Me

Why wait? Fishing trips are still on. Visit whenever.

Cooter

Are you not coming back?

Cooter and I had started with the Sasquatches together and had bonded over fishing and country music. I'd miss him.

Not that Cooter was in Portland right now. He was back on his family's horse ranch in the Appalachians, where he spent his off-season helping out and doing the books.

Me

I'll get my things once I sell the house.

Cooter

Does she know you moved?

Me

Keep those loose lips shut.

He sent a picture of himself holding his lips together.

Cooter

Maybe I should get in on that huge multi-team trade. I think Jersey needs a goalie. Then we can find the best honky-tonk in New York together.

A multi-team trade seemed like a nightmare, and I hoped he was kidding. It would be nice to be close to him, but the Sasquatches wanted to lose him even less than me. Not to mention Jersey seemed to go through a lot of goalies.

I ordered a car to take me to my new place. It was a sleek and modern building with a door-attendant and concierge. My floor even had a private elevator.

The one-bedroom was spacious and furnished. Devon had told me I could trade everything out through the furniture rental company. I took a bunch of pictures and measurements, so I could look at the website when I returned to the hotel.

The kitchen was pleasant, but definitely needed a few things. Not that I was much of a cook. The living room and dining room were open concept. I could fit an alpha-sized bed in the bedroom. Oh, and the view of the city was *spectacular*.

Morgan

Are you at Cooter's? We should talk.

Me

There's nothing to talk about. I wish you a happy life.

Not really. But after weeks of soul-searching, I knew I didn't want to reconcile. I didn't want to join her new pack. She'd torn my heart into a million little pieces, then ground them into the floor with her high heels.

I was ready to start over. This time, when my contract was up, I'd have more to show for it than an empty house and a broken heart.

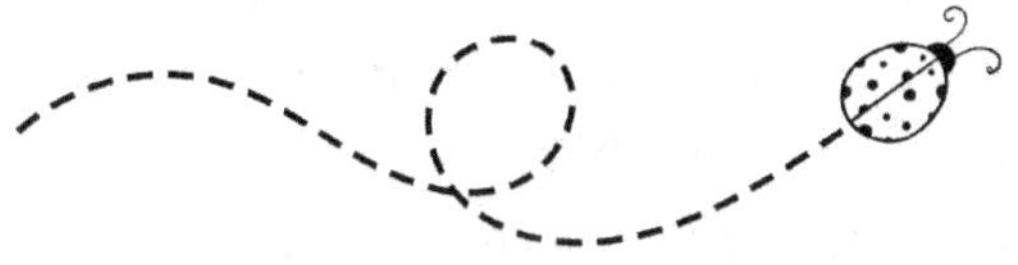

Chapter Five

GWEN

I sat on the subway, drowning in hopelessness. On Friday, Clark, Carlos, and Dimitri had spent the day feeding me, watching movies, and letting me cry. I'd spent most of Dimitri's party playing video games, getting too drunk, and had woken up on Clark's couch.

Yesterday, we'd cleaned my apartment, sorting through everything to see what was salvageable. They'd also bought me some basics, which had been sweet. Today, Clark had flown home, Dimitri was getting ready to leave on vacation, and Carlos had family things.

Leaving me on my own.

While I still had so much to do–like figuring out my life–I needed to get out of the apartment.

Austin's social media accounts had disappeared and his phone was disconnected. Did I even try to find him? At least to get the money he owed me? I'd spotted him quite a bit the past few months, as hockey finals, university finals, graduation, and everything else impacted his work schedule.

I'd been working overtime to make ends meet.

At least most of my tuition was paid for. Figuring out how to pay the rest of it would be enough.

Maybe? I didn't want to deal with him alone. If I was staying in the apartment for long, I'd change the locks.

Getting off the subway, I walked to the zoo. I hadn't been in a few days.

"Hey, Gwen, going to visit Marty?" the gate-guy asked as he scanned my pass on my phone.

"Yep," I nodded. Marty was a good listener.

Wishing I could justify buying a coffee from the cart, I walked around the zoo. The summer weekend made it crowded. Usually I came at odd times, bright and early after yoga in the park, between classes, right before closing. It was still nice—and calming—to visit all my animal friends.

I wandered my usual route, including the aviary and the reptile house. Finally, I ended up at the tiger enclosure. I'd always loved animals. My nonna had been a veterinarian. One of my cousins had taken over her practice. An aunt ran an animal sanctuary that Nonna and I would volunteer at. Also, I'd brought so many animals to the rink that the coaches made a rule about it.

Several people had gotten pets out of it. Marty was supposed to be *mine*. There'd been a big snowstorm in January. It had gotten bad quickly, and I'd been walking across campus to get to the subway before I got stuck there. Marty had been in a tree and I'd climbed up to get him, tucked him into my hoodie, and brought him home.

The little gold and white striped cat was so small and cute–and cold. Marty kept me company through the storm. Austin had been away with his team and had gotten stuck there when the airports closed. After we'd lost power, we used the gas oven for heat and stayed in the living room. I fed him kitten formula that Mrs. Jenkins had left over from fostering, and tiny little scraps of meat.

When Austin came back, he'd fallen in love with Marty, too. We'd decided to keep him, since pet rent was minimal.

Then I had to find out my kitten was a mini golden tiger cub that somehow escaped from the zoo when he'd been brought in from a raid. Ugh, not fair. Fail, kitten distribution system, utter and total *fail. No, do not recommend.*

Clark and Dimitri had gone with me to the zoo to give him back. The zoo had been excited and gave me the pass as a reward. It was sweet, but not the same.

I walked around to the viewing area on the side where the little tigers played. The keepers successfully integrated him with some cubs, and he was thriving.

Whistling, I called Marty, and he came bounding over to me and I played with him through the glass. I put up my hand, and he put his paw there.

Sometimes I wish I would have kept him. I mean, he was a *mini* tiger. Sure, he'd be a big cat, but tiny for a tiger. Who'd know?

No, it was the right thing to do. Animals were expensive to care for.

Still, I wish I had some Marty cuddles.

Trixie, one of the zookeepers, saw me and waved from the tiger side of the glass as she brought out some enrichment items. I stayed in the little nook against the glass and watched, the little tigers making me giggle.

Eventually, she finished and disappeared. A bit later, she came out to the viewing area. Trixie was a blond omega and worked with the mini tigers and tiger cubs. Omegas were great with predators, because they usually weren't seen as a threat—and many times got 'adopted' by alpha animals. She'd been kind about letting me have time with Marty and had even gotten me trained to play with the mini tigers in the playroom. Sometimes we took Marty for walks.

"Hi Gwen." She grinned. "Do you want some playtime?"

"Please?" My chest shuddered. I needed to tell him all my woes. He was a good listener, as were flowers and stray animals.

"Are you okay?" She eyed my forehead and bruises, then gave me a big hug, smelling of bubble gum and tiger.

"I broke up with Austin." It came out like a wail.

Her arms tightened. "It'll be okay. Tiger playtime will make it all better."

"I hope so." My heart ached. I still couldn't believe that he discarded me so easily for some deal he never mentioned, with people he hated.

That he'd *hurt* me.

We went into the playroom, which looked a bit like a kid's soft-play area, and had all sorts of toys and obstacles for the mini tigers. One wall was glass, so that people could watch the tigers play.

Trixie used her badge to get me in through the employee door, then used another door marked employee that opened into the tiger area, so she could get Marty.

"Marty," I squealed when he came out and ran toward me, straining against the leash.

Trixie unclipped the leash, and he leapt in happiness.

"I missed you so much. You won't believe what happened." I sniffed, picking him up and snuggling him. He was a golden tiger, so he didn't have any black stripes. Baby mini tigers also looked a little more like house cats than their bigger brethren.

Marty was so much bigger than when I'd found him. Not that he was nearly as large as he'd be if he were a regular tiger. Mini tigers were one of several wild animals genetically engineered to be house pets. While mini giraffes were a hit, mini tigers weren't what people expected and were ending up in zoos and rescues.

Obviously, people didn't do their research. I could take care of a mini tiger just fine. They didn't even get as big as malamutes.

As I played with Marty, I told him *everything* in Italian. It felt good to get it all out, and I knew he wouldn't judge me.

"What do I even do?" I told him, sniffing. "Do I drop out with two semesters left? If I had an agent, I'd call them up and see about going free agent now, but I don't even have that. I have nothing. Sure, I'll talk to Coach and financial aid tomorrow, and there might be a place for me at the townhouse my friend rents at. Still, how do I make it on my own here?" I felt so hopeless.

Marty gave me more snuggles as if to say *if you give up, he wins.*

"You're right; we don't let the assholes win. I'll crunch the numbers and make a plan," I agreed as we played with his favorite rope toy, Trixie watching us from the corner.

It's not like I had anyplace else to go. I sure wasn't going back to my dads. I *liked* New York. And my life. Yep. I'd rather starve than do that.

"Still, where did I go wrong, Marty? How could the person I'd loved for five years end up being like that?" Another sob wracked me.

Marty licked the tears off my face.

"Whatever happened, I'm pretty sure it wasn't your fault," Trixie said softly. "I get off at four. Do you need me to go with you to the police?"

I gave her a look, my heart skipping a beat, because I'd gotten *very* personal with Marty. "You speak Italian?"

"No. But I know what being hurt looks like. There's help if you need it." Her expression was kind.

"Thank you. Some people already talked to the police with me." Nothing was going to happen, considering Austin was an upstanding young alpha athlete with no record. Not that I wanted to blow up his life. But answers would be nice.

She gave me a look. "Are you sure?"

"I… I'll be okay. I just needed to talk through what to do next. It's a little scary." I nodded.

"It is," she agreed. "Especially when you're with someone for a long time and you suddenly realize that maybe you didn't know them at all."

I gulped. That's exactly what happened. "It's a lot to process."

"It is. Fortunately," she joined us and pet Marty, "this boy here is a good listener."

"That he is." I gave him extra pets.

"You can do this, Gwen. One step at a time." She squeezed my hand.

"Thanks." At least I had Marty.

She let me play with Marty for a long time. Finally, he had to go back. I gave her a hug.

My belly rumbled in hunger.

Austin also destroyed or had taken every bit of food in the house. While Dimitri had brought over some things, I'd need more than that. I'd eaten a lot of my meals at Tito's—where I no longer had a job.

One step at a time.

Leaving the zoo, I made my way to a little hole-in-the-wall Italian deli. It had red-checked tablecloths, pictures on the wall of famous people who'd eaten there, and the best pastrami sandwiches I'd ever had.

The deli always gave me free food. Probably because they knew I was friends with Lenny-the-Fence. Too bad I had nothing to sell him, I could use the money.

Even though it was a Saturday, guys in suits talked business and ate sandwiches.

"Who hurt you?" the older Italian woman I only knew as *Zia*, aunty, demanded from behind the counter.

"My ex," I sighed.

She leaned in. "Do you need my sons to take care of it?"

"It's fine. But thanks," I told her as I ordered my usual—a pastrami sandwich with extra pickles, fries, and a black and white cookie.

Her look grew skeptical as she got my cookie from the case of baked goods. "You let Zia know if you change your mind. You're not going back to him, right?"

"Never." I shook my head.

"Good. Sit." She handed me my cookie, and a bottled lemon soda I hadn't ordered.

I took a seat at my favorite corner spot that gave me a view of the bustling street. This area reminded me too much of home—and Nonna—so I didn't come here much. One of the good food banks was down the street.

Hmm. I checked my phone as I gobbled my cookie. The food bank was open today. Nice. The campus food pantry was closed on weekends during the summer, and I didn't have summer meal privileges in the dining hall. But I did have Knights' dining room privileges at the rink—and I got fed on shift, though it was more snacks than food. Okay, I'd use the meal boards more and go back to a regular food bank rotation. Yeah, I could make this work.

She brought me my sandwich and fries. "This is going to be your year. I can feel it."

"Thank you, I hope so," I told her. Zia knew all about my dreams of playing pro hockey. I dug into my sandwich, which always had the perfect ratio of meat to mustard.

After this, I'd visit the food bank. Then, I'd curl up on the couch with the laptop Clark lent me and figure things out.

Tony was right. I needed to focus on classes, hockey, and myself. If I was going to do that, I needed to see how much that would cost.

A good soothing spreadsheet would do the trick. I may have supported Austin's big dumb ass for all these years. He may have broken my heart. But I wouldn't let that stop me from reaching my dreams.

You're a fucking nothing who will never fucking make it.

I took a bite of pickle.

Yeah, we'd see about that.

Chapter Six

TENZIN

A feeling of calmness came over me when I arrived at the training center Monday morning. There was nothing quite like being on the ice to soothe a ragged soul.

The small rink was occupied. A machine rapidly fired pucks, and a goalie in full-and ratty-gear went after them with a vengeance. Cooter called that setting *"death wish."* The small goalie thwacked the pucks away with their stick and caught them with their catching glove over and over again.

It was mesmerizing to watch her—I was almost certain the goalie was female. There was some excellent technique there, too. She struggled with her glove-side.

Still, she attacked everything with a ferocity that made me worry. Cooter only set the puck machine to *death wish* when something was wrong.

The machine buzzed, and the pucks stopped. The little goalie slid into the splits on the ice with a sigh, leaning back into a stretch. She took off her catching glove, blocker, and mask. A pale pink ponytail tumbled out.

Oh. It was *her*. The goalie I'd seen the other day. Olive skin glistened with sweat. Short nails, painted purple with sparkles, reached for a towel, which she mopped her face with. Her nose, which winked with a piercing, was a bit crooked, and long dark lashes rimmed hazel eyes. An angry gash marred her forehead.

Tilting her head back, she took a long drink from her sticker-covered water bottle, which said *NYIT Hockey* on it. Bruises marred her neck and face, which made my hands fist. My alpha didn't like the idea of someone hurting her.

Her hazel eyes widened as she noticed me. "Shit. I didn't see you. Sorry." She scrambled up off the ice. "I didn't mean to interrupt. Tell me to leave, even if it's mid-workout. I don't mind."

"Are you alright?" I skated over to her.

"Me?" She picked up, then dropped her water bottle, then bent down to get it, and dropped her mask, like she was nervous. Her scent grew sour.

"My friend only uses that setting on the puck machine when something's wrong." I skated closer to her. Her scent was minty and dewy, fresh like an herb garden in the morning–not peppermint candy.

"It's been a shitty few days," she sighed. Her hockey skates–and she wore hockey skates, *not* goalie skates–looked like the end was nigh.

"I... I understand. I've had a few days like that myself." Over the weekend, I'd been setting up utilities, transferring accounts, getting a new driver's license, selling what I wasn't bringing with me, and all the other things that came with a cross-country move.

Each task was a nail in the coffin of my old life.

"Your boyfriend and you broke up after you spent *years* supporting his big dumb ass? I don't want that fucker back, but it still hurts. I... I never saw it coming." She frowned at me, absently running her fingers along the cut on her forehead, her scent going salty with sadness.

Had he done that? My heart went out to her.

"My girlfriend decided to have my friends' baby behind my back and was upset that I left, instead of wanting to play happy pack with them." That was the crux of it. I was the one who ruined everything by overreacting.

Jeez, Tenzie, it's not like you didn't want a pack–or that we don't spend any time with them. Why are you making such a big deal about it? It's perfect.

"I'm sorry. Need me to help you get your shit back? People helped me, I'm happy to return the favor." The young woman held up her stick.

She was a foot shorter than me, but the fact that she offered to help me–a stranger–meant everything.

"Thanks. It's been a little bit now, but I had to do some things this weekend that made everything feel so... final. Not that I want her back either, but..." I raked my hair with my hand. "I thought she was the one. After we broke up, I may have pretended that a target was her face and thrown axes at it."

Then I may have gotten drunk with Cooter and belted sad country songs in his backyard.

She pressed her lips together, suppressing her smile. "I might have pretended the puck was my ex's head."

"Good choice. Feel better?"

"A little." She gave me a shy smile.

"You struggle with your glove-side. Want me to shoot a few at you?" I offered.

"You don't have to." She shook her head. "Also, I don't know if Tony told you, but you *can* ask me to leave. They only let me use this rink if I'm not a bother."

"I'm fine with it."

I shot some pucks at her and we ran a couple of drills.

While she was a little short for a PHL goalie, she was *fast*. An alarm chirped.

She sighed. "This has been fun, but I have to go to work."

"Oh. What do you do?" My head cocked. "Summer job? I remember those days. Mostly I waited tables."

"I've done plenty of that. Today I'm wrangling little goalies." She laughed as she did a few stretches. "Later, I'm either on skate rental or at the snack bar."

"You work at the rink." I nodded, her privileges making sense. "You play for NYIT?"

She nodded. "Goalie."

I laughed. "I was thinking center. Hi, I'm Tenzin."

"Gwen. Seriously, I can practice at other times if this is yours. Since I couldn't sleep I thought I'd work some anger out so I don't make any kids cry today. It's not their fault I made shit life choices." Gwen looked away, her voice bitter.

"Sometimes we don't know they're shit choices until they are. It's like biting into a candy where you think it's one flavor, then realize it's another." My voice softened, because I knew how she felt.

I'd wondered for weeks what I did wrong, what I could have done differently. If I should just stop *being difficult*, make up with everyone, form a pack with them like they wanted, and go on with our lives.

She sucked in a breath. "That's a good one. I'm just feeling sorry for myself."

"Something I know well. I'll see you tomorrow, if you'd like? We don't have to talk. I... I recently moved here and I don't have any practice buddies yet," I offered tentatively, not wanting to come on too strong, but at the same time yearning for some human contact.

It had been a lonely weekend. Something about her called to me.

No. It was just my loneliness talking.

"I... I'd like that." Her head ducked as she stood. With a wave, she grabbed her things and left the small rink.

And I returned to practicing. Alone.

Every morning, I met with Gwen. We'd shoot some pucks, run a few drills, and do a little footwork. After she left to tend to her baby goalies, I finished on the ice, then went upstairs to do land drills, work out, maybe have some lunch and use their yoga studio. I hadn't run into any other Knights yet, but I'd met a couple of rowdy skate smashers who made cardio a little more amusing.

Gwen said little when we practiced, but what she didn't say spoke volumes. Rink gossip filled in the rest. Gwen Di Rossi was a university student who recently broke up with her long-time boyfriend who she'd put through university. She'd been found *passed out* on the ice, bleeding.

Gwen had led *two* different hockey teams to their respective collegiate national championships–and was talented enough to be part of the Knights' goalie development program. Which, according to Cooter, was a big deal. The Sasquatches didn't have that program.

Some of the upstairs rooms looked out onto the ice, and I'd seen her teaching young goalies land drills, coaching them on the ice, and being silly with them. She seemed like she could use a friend.

Or I could be projecting.

In the afternoons, I worked toward making my apartment a home and moving over from the hotel. Slowly changing out the furniture. Buying what I needed–like an extra-long alpha-sized bed. I explored grocery stores and outdoor markets, as well as made lists of the places I'd like to visit.

Yesterday, I'd spent the afternoon at an art museum, taking my time to savor the paintings. I'd enjoyed exploring the different exhibits without having to worry about anyone being bored. Then I'd gone to a night market and perused the stalls. It had been wonderful.

Until I'd gone home to an empty apartment that lacked all the charm and comfort I was used to. I *missed* my place. Seeing animals on my lawn. Having hiking trails in my backyard.

Perhaps I needed the bustle of the city to shake things up.

"Tomorrow's Saturday. Do you have any plans? Maybe since you don't have camp, we could get coffee or breakfast after our workout?" I asked as Gwen and I finished up what was quickly becoming our morning routine.

"Um, I just broke up with my boyfriend. I'm not ready," she blurted, her minty scent going salty.

Embarrassment coated me. Of course she'd think that.

"Oh, me too. I don't even have the nerve to tell her I moved. It's just..." My brows furrowed as I searched for the right words. "I moved here without knowing many people. While I enjoy doing things on my own, I didn't think it would be this lonely."

Her look softened. "I... I can see that."

"This is my awkward attempt at making friends. Usually I get adopted by extroverts." I laughed. That's how I'd ended up with Cooter as a friend. My heart twisted. It was also how I'd become friends with the Lewises–the throuple currently forming a pack with my pregnant ex.

She snorted. "Friends are good. I suck at it, too. But I'm trying. Yesterday I went to happy hour with my co-workers instead of working out."

"You work out after running drills with children all day?" My eyebrows rose. They worked those kids hard–and we put in a good morning workout.

"This is my last year on a university team. I have to bring it if I want a chance at going pro after graduation." She sighed.

"So, breakfast? Coffee? My treat?" I offered. "We don't have to work out first. Rest is good. Or we could go to a museum? The park? You've lived here for a few years, you probably know all sorts of places."

Gwen's head ducked, her minty scent flaring with anxiety. "I... I know who you are. The last thing I want is for you to think I'm using you."

"Maybe I'm using *you*? After all, you must know a bunch of the Knights," I countered, disliking her anxiousness.

"I don't know very many well, but I can introduce you to a few. Carlos is the only one in town right now. He's a winger. Dimitri will be back in a week or two. He plays defense like you." Her smile grew shy. "Clark's a center, but he returned home for the summer."

"I'd love to meet your friends." I smiled.

"I'd love to get coffee. I don't remember when I've last just sat in a cafe like I have no cares, while sipping a latte and eating an overpriced muffin. But this is a busy weekend. After work I have to go to campus and handle stuff. Then I'm closing the snack bar at the rink. Tomorrow I have more stuff to take care of."

She made a face. "I'm working at the rink snack bar again in the afternoon, then I'm at the rental counter for blackout skate. Sunday morning I'm playing tennis. I'm also teaching a couple of private goalie lessons. Oh, and Carlos is making me go to his mom's for dinner."

"What is blackout skate?" I blinked.

"Public skate, but in the dark with blackout lights, glow sticks, and warehouse music." She laughed. "It's fun. You should come. Do you play tennis?"

I shook my head. "Never tried it. Do you play golf or like art museums?"

"My ex played golf, but I never learned." Her head tilted in thought. "I like history and science museums. But I don't know much about art. I do like Dumas, mostly his ice skater and dancer paintings."

"The romantic era of tea-time Britain did have some lovely work," I told her. They were sweet paintings.

Her alarm beeped and she sighed. "Time to go."

"Could I give you my number? That way, if you have some time over the weekend, we can have that coffee. Or if you want someone to shoot pucks or lift weights with. We don't have to talk. Sometimes it's nice to be alone together." Inwardly, I cringed at how desperate I sounded.

"Okay." She handed me her phone, and I put my number in it, as she did a few stretches.

"If I don't hear from you this weekend, I'll see you next week?" I gave back her phone. "I... I'm not hitting on you. Promise. We could be lonely hockey players together during a long summer. We could hit some pucks, see some museums, try some food, and wander the city."

Did she like country music?

She bit her lower lip. "That sounds fun. I've lived here for four years and have barely seen anything. See you later."

Grabbing her stuff, she left, and I returned to my workout, hoping she'd text me.

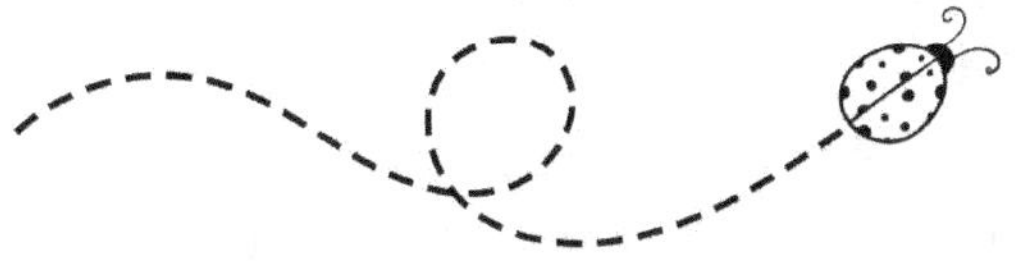

Chapter Seven

GWEN

"It's good, right?" I chewed on my lower lip as the landlord looked over my apartment. I needed every penny of my deposit back.

Thanks to Austin, I had barely anything to move out, just a couple of things I could salvage, some basics the guys had gotten me, and a few items I'd lifted from the campus lost and found.

"It looks good. I'm sorry I couldn't let you stay any longer. You were a good tenant, and I had no idea you didn't know that he'd given notice. I figured you'd both graduated and were moving," he told me.

"I appreciate you giving me the time you did."

As soon as I'd left, Austin had texted the landlord and said we'd be out in a week. Knotwaffle. The landlord found someone almost immediately and had already signed papers with them by the time I'd reached out.

After we finished the inspection, I grabbed my duffle bag, and a box, then went down the hall.

Mrs. Jenkins opened the door in her usual marabou robe. Today's was black. "You have a safe place to go?"

"Yeah."

"Did they catch him?" A cigarette dangled from her red lips.

"Not yet." The police were basically like, "*Um, we can't find him*".

Austin had disappeared. He'd left the state. None of his friends knew where he was. He was barely searchable online anymore as Austin Blake and I didn't know his real name.

Honestly, I'd decided that I didn't need an apology and I could live without an explanation, or the money he owed me, if it meant I'd never see him again.

"Thanks for everything." I waved. My heart broke and a tear rolled down my cheek as I left the building and walked to the subway station, like I was going to work and not leaving forever.

I hoped Austin's dad ran a pig farm.

At least he hadn't stuck me with many utility bills.

However, he'd done something much worse. Something that derailed my whole tentative plan I'd built this week.

I'd been feeling hopeful because the financial aid office and Coach Hirata at NYIT had helped me find a little extra money. One of my NYIT teammates had an open bed in a townhouse a bunch of them rented, too.

Sure, I'd be in a cramped place full of athletes, but it might be doable if I was frugal. I'd have to work my ass off this summer, and I'd have to work a lot during the year. At least my scholarship included a meal plan during the school year, and the team fed us a lot.

Everything looked like it would work out.

Until yesterday, when the business office dropped a bomb that left me bawling.

Austin's bank had canceled *every single one* of the tuition payments he'd made. I didn't know he could even do that. Now I owed them *everything.* He had to do the one petty thing that would hurt me the most.

The business office had been sympathetic to my tears and given me until the start of the school year, which was in early September. Still, there was no way I could rent a place right now–even in a house full of people–*and* pay that now-owed tuition.

I sniffed. If Austin hadn't promised to pay for this year, I never would have chosen to transfer to NYIT.

Dropping out was the obvious answer. Realistically, it would be better for me to stay and play my last year. I'd focus, find an agent, win another title for NYIT, and finish my degree.

Somehow.

Leaving the subway, I hurried down the street, running late for my shift. It was a good thing Tony said I could store my stuff at the rink. After years of working there, I knew all the good places. My community college team had practiced and had our games there, which was how I'd gotten to know Tony.

My Knights badge would get me even better places, safer places, as well as food and showers. Coach Kirov had given me summer access, and I knew where Chef kept the snacks.

Tony hadn't said I *couldn't* store *myself* there. I spent so much time at the rink no one would notice. I'd put in even more time there instead of picking up another waitressing job.

Slipping in through the back door, I made my way to the staff locker room. I shoved my bag in my locker and hid the box in the supply closet with the other few things I'd already stashed. Then put on my rink uniform.

One thing I'd also done this past week was a lot of soul searching. Like what would my nonna advise?

The last time I saw her she said, *"Even when you spread your wings, don't forget your roots. They don't stifle you, they just lead you home when you're lost"*.

That's what I needed to do; find my way home on the ice and go back to my roots. Because I felt lost. Adrift. I'd gotten so wrapped up in Austin, and everything else, that I'd forgotten what mattered most.

You were good once. Austin was right. Sure, stats didn't lie, but I'd buried a lot of what had once made me special out of fear.

It was time to find it again. Find her. *Bring the sauce,* as my nonna's neighbors always told me–that thing that made you special on the ice.

"You're late." Tony eyed me as I clocked in.

"Sorry." I hustled out to the snack bar.

Yeah, I'd find it. Right after work.

In the breakroom, I stuffed nachos in my face, replying to Carlos that yes, I was going to his mom's for dinner tomorrow. I loved Carlos' mom; she made the best enchiladas. Often, she brought them to games for me when I was on EBUG duty.

Since PHL teams usually only had two goalies, our job was to step in for *either* team should both of their goalies end up being sick, hurt, or otherwise unable to play. The Knights had three or four EBUGs that rotated, because we all played for our own teams, and one of us needed to be present at every home game. An EBUG going into play rarely happened. In my two years with the team, I'd never gone in.

Still, it was fun, and I learned a lot.

Usually, the EBUG on duty sat up in the press box, but they let me sit in the family section with the MASOs. The *mates and significant others.* While being in the press box was an experience, none of the MASOs were trying to pinch my ass, or making uncomfortable comments about how they could *help me with my career.*

Also, it was fun to get to know the players' families.

"Everything went okay yesterday at the financial aid office? Your team won the *championships.* You think they'd find more money for you?" Tony came over to me as I finished eating.

I took a sip of lime soda as I kept my emotions calm, so he didn't smell the lie. Alphas had much better noses than betas. He didn't need to know what happened with my tuition.

"They found some, which helps. Coach mentioned reaching out to alumni, but I'm not counting on that. They are getting me a new laptop though." I couldn't use Clark's forever.

"Good. What about gear?" he prodded.

"The company that sponsors our team is replacing my gear that my ex destroyed." I liked their hockey skates well enough, but I was *very* particular about my goalie skates.

Also, I wasn't a huge fan of how that company's goalie gear fit me. Which was why Austin had gotten me goalie pads from Canadian Hockey Supply for my birthday–the ones he'd destroyed.

But hey, it was free and I wasn't in a place where I could afford to be picky.

Part of why I was going over to Carlos' mom's was that he was going to help me try to get Austin's graffiti off my good goalie mask.

"What about housing? Still not sure how you didn't qualify for a student loan." Tony frowned.

It had to do with everything done to protect me back when I was a teenager, and possibly because I was a dual-citizen. Everything was legal, but sometimes it flagged weird. It had taken some work to get my credit union account. Maybe if I called the loan place like I had the bank...

"I'm trying to move in with some of my teammates," I replied.

He stayed there, eying me. "The Yeti's been hanging around all week. You think maybe the Knights are thinking of him to fill Elias Royce's place?"

"He would be a good choice." I shrugged. Given Tenzin told me he'd *moved* to New York, I guessed that's exactly what happened. But he hadn't offered the information up and I didn't want to pry.

I returned to work, switching from selling nachos and slushies to glow sticks and skate rentals. Blackout skate was always a good time, attracting a lot of teenagers and college students. The music was always fantastic–one of our frequent DJs did the music for all the Manhattan Maimer games.

After the initial rush for skate rentals, I scrolled on my phone, looking at all the fun things everyone was doing over the summer, while once again, I worked my ass off. Clark was at a fair. My friend Mercy was in London with some of her siblings. Even my hockey teammates that were still in town were going to a warehouse party tonight.

Jealousy spread through me. I wanted to go to a party.

Texting Tenzin was tempting. He seemed like a nice guy and I enjoyed our practices. The internet called him *stoic*. To me, he seemed quiet and shy. Something about him felt *safe*. Which was why I'd even consider going to coffee with an alpha I didn't know well.

But I didn't text him. Instead, I sent a silly picture to Clark, since he'd sent me a picture of a hay bale with a bow on it earlier, along with the caption *hay girl*.

"I can wear my own skates?" Tenzin stood there, dressed casually, eying the rows of rental skates, his hockey skates over his broad shoulder.

"Tenzin. What are you doing here?" I couldn't help but grin. He'd come.

"I had a burning desire to eat nachos and skate in the dark." He grinned back.

"Well, this is the place. Yes, you can use your own skates. You do have to wear things that glow in order to go on the ice though." I pointed to my glow necklace.

He bought one and put it on, then struck a pose. "I'm amazing."

"Too bad you don't play tennis." I grinned. That would be something we could do together.

Tenzin laughed. "Why tennis?"

"It's good for goalies." It was a fun way to work on hand-eye coordination and watching the ball. I guess golf was the same.

"Hmm, we'll see," he teased as he texted someone.

"Who are you texting?" You never knew with hockey players.

"Cooter says, *Yes, it's great for goalies, which is why I don't do it.*" Tenzin laughed.

A couple of teenagers, wearing black-light-conducive hoodies with ears on them, came up to the counter, and got skates and glow lights from me.

"What does he do then?" My guess was that it was Cooter Brown, the goalie for the Sasquatches.

"Are you sure you want to know that? Cooter's something else," Tenzin told me, waving at a little girl who was watching him.

"Yeah, I do." I was always interested in what other goalies did to improve during the off-season. Like Molly Crewe, the current shortest PHL goalie, who played for the Belugas, cross-trained through rock climbing.

"I'm not reading this out loud." Tenzin put his hand to his face and showed me Cooter's reply.

Cooter

Hookers and blow

I laughed. "Sure. Is he paying?"

Tenzin froze, phone in hand.

"I'm not flirting with him, and that's not my thing. Never tried either." I put my hands up in surrender, cheeks burning. Why did I say that?

"I'm hesitating because there's a sixty-three percent chance that if I text him that, when I get home they will be in my living room even though he doesn't have my new address. That's just how he is. Also, he's teasing. He actually swears by naked moon yoga, country line dancing, axe throwing, and fishing."

He leaned in and whispered, "Goalies are weird."

I couldn't help but laugh. "Sometimes I do yoga in the park."

"I know tennis is good for hockey players. But I never learned," he confessed. "All my friends play golf."

"I learned tennis as a kid, mostly to annoy my sister, who was fantastic, though I usually played with my mom." A little pang shot through my heart. My sister had been as good at tennis as I was at hockey. Better probably. She was now mated with kids like a good little omega. Though she also *loved* her job. I hadn't talked to any of my siblings in a long time.

Tenzin sent Cooter a text.

Tenzin

I'm going to tell your wife.

"Cooter's wife is beautiful, right? Super smart. Nice." Every PHL goalie I knew that was in a relationship had a partner who was smoking hot and majorly accomplished.

Cooter

Who do you think pays?

"Cooter doesn't have a wife. We made her up. If she was real, oh, the things we'd tell her," he laughed. "We had the rookies going for almost the entire season last year. Got them convinced she was this smart, pretty woman who could wrestle a bear, catch fish with her hands, scale walls barefoot, and swear with the best of them."

"Sounds like a woman I'd like to know." I laughed.

"Do you like line dancing?" His head ducked, and I realized there was a twang to his voice, like he'd lived in the south once.

I blinked. Line dancing? "I've never tried. I'm not sure you can do that in New York."

A family came over and I helped them get skates and glow sticks. When I finished, Tenzin was still there.

"Don't you want to skate?" Not that I minded him hanging out with me.

"Mostly I came for the company. While I had a great day, I came home and suddenly I didn't want to be alone. I'm not getting you in trouble now, am I?" He looked over at the busy rink.

Aww.

"It'll be fine, Tens," I assured. "No one will care as long as I do my job. Can I call you Tens?"

He smiled. "Sure. Not many people call me that anymore."

"Oh good, I wanted to check in case your ex called you that." I got some more glow ears out from under the counter.

"Is there anything I shouldn't call you?" he asked me.

I thought for a moment. "I don't like being called *Wendel*. Austin's, I mean, my ex's, friends always called me that. They're asshats. Most UNYC hockey players are."

Also, the nickname *Wendel* was dumb. I wasn't a Gwendolyn.

"That's not where you go, right?" Tenzin leaned up against the end counter, so he wasn't blocking it.

"No. My ex went to UNYC. I go to NYIT, who has a rivalry with them." The local state university versus the old fancy private one.

The main reason Austin pushed me to transfer to NYIT was *because* it was so prestigious. I didn't care, but Austin seemed to think it would help me in the future.

Tenzin nodded. "I attended Crestdale."

"Crestdale? Color me fancy," I grinned. Crestdale was a prestigious, but bohemian private university on the west coast over in the Bay Area. Their mascot was an avocado, and they threw fake rats onto the ice every time their hockey team scored.

"Was your major designation studies or mid-century literature?" I joked. It was a *humie,* a humanities-based university, versus a *techie* like my school, which was science and technology-based.

"Film. With a double minor in marketing and graphic arts," he laughed.

"You want to make movies?" That wasn't something I expected. Language, law, or diplomacy maybe.

A couple of kids came over and bought glow ears. I made a mental note to make sure we ordered more. Ha! Here, Tony thought they wouldn't sell.

"Nature documentaries," he replied. "After I retire from hockey, I want to travel all over the world and hike, fish and document all of the beautiful places out there."

"That sounds *amazing.* I'd love to travel one day." I'd traveled some with my family when I was little, but that was a long time ago.

"What do you study?" he asked.

"I'm a forensic accounting major." I straighten up the counter.

He blinked. "Accounting. NYIT is a science school, right?"

"Yep. No, they don't have a business school. It's part of the math department. A strange little subprogram that is forensic accountants, actuaries, and data scientists." It was delightfully weird, and I loved it.

Last year, a theoretical mathematician came to talk to us about making a virtual supercollider.

"You keep the books for dead people?" His eyebrows rose.

"The kind of accounting that puts corrupt business people in jail, when they're able to otherwise cover their crimes. One day, when I retire from hockey, I want to join the Bureau of Investigation." Where I'd put away rich, untouchable alphaholes.

We were basically alone now, everyone out on the ice or in the snack bar, as the lights and lasers lit up the dark rink and music made my bones thump.

"Um, are you in New York for obvious reasons?" I whispered.

"My ex hates New York so she'll never come visit me. She wants to be friends. I don't." He flinched, and I felt that.

"You don't owe her that," I assured.

We continued to talk, mostly about hockey and places we'd like to visit here in the city. Together, we compiled a list of restaurants, attractions, and activities.

"Have you been to the Natural History Museum?" he asked, as we divided the list into sections, adding in some suggestions from Cooter, that might be bars, and restaurants from another friend.

"When I was little. My grandparents lived upstate, and I stayed with them a lot, and even lived with them for a while. We'd occasionally come into the city." Like to see a Knights game. "They passed away when I was in high school."

Car accident. Or so the police told me.

Tenzin's brows furrowed. "My parents died when I was thirteen. I moved across the world to live with my much older sister. We had no idea what to do with each other. But we're good friends now."

"What does she think of your move here?" I asked.

"She suggested it. Well, not New York, but that I move and start over."

Desiree came over to me, sweaty and panting from ice duty. She eyed Tenzin. "My turn. One of Austin's friends?"

"One of mine." I didn't like Desiree. The omega was part of the UNYC figure skating team and semi-dating one of Austin's friends.

Her eyes rode over him as she let herself behind the counter, her sugary scent cloying. "Do you even have friends that don't play hockey, Wendel?"

"No." I shook my head, trying not to roll my eyes.

"Why are you even working here tonight? Don't you usually work at Tito's with Austin on summer weekends?" She sniffed, taking off her figure skates.

I took my hockey skates out from under the counter, which needed to last until my university got me new ones. "I don't work at Tito's anymore."

She smirked. "They finally fired you. Wow! Is Austin working tonight?"

"Don't know. Don't care." I laced up my right skate, trying to hide my anger. *Finally fire me?* I was a good server and my co-workers were pissed since I was always willing to sub for people if I was available.

Her look went to one of mock concern. "Oh. My. Goodness. Did you and Austin break up? Haven't you been together since high school? But did you really think once the Aces signed him he'd stay with you? I mean, you know he's going to marry a posh omega from some fancy omega academy. He mentioned that to Windy."

"Good for him." I wasn't sure about that. An omega, sure. One from a top omega academy? It depended on who his family was and whether or not he was hiding a pack, or potential pack, from me, too. I started on my left skate.

Omegas didn't have to attend omega academies. The top ones were competitive with elite universities and conservatories. These omegas weren't just mating top packs after graduation, they were also going into exclusive graduate programs, or taking positions with prestigious companies.

Some of them were so accomplished that they were named *omegas of note.* Competition for an omega like that was fierce. My mom had been one of those omegas once.

Desiree laughed as she stood, fluffing her hair. "It's okay to be jealous. Not everyone can be an omega. Pity he didn't even think enough of you to have you in his pack."

"Don't want to be an omega and I want *nothing* to do with Austin, who, by the way, did *not* get signed by the Aces," I replied, getting to my feet, and putting my whistle around my neck.

I had four perfect omega sisters and zero desire to go through all that bullshit. *Do not recommend.*

Desiree huffed. "It's that attitude that lost him. That and you don't even care about your appearance. Your hair is fried and your roots? Disastrous. What happened to your forehead? You could at least hide it with some makeup before work."

I spun around. "I dumped *him* when he threw the fucking skate I bought him at my head. He also ruined all my shit when we broke up. And no, I didn't do *anything* to make him do it and I didn't leave him because he didn't get signed. None of this is my fault."

"Oh." She frowned a little.

I left the counter and turned the corner where I sat down on a bench and sobbed. The gravity of being truly alone, with no safety net, weighed on me.

"He hurt you." Tenzin's voice grew rough as he sat next to me, his citrusy-yet-woodsy scent wrapping around me. It was like going for a walk in a fruit grove at sunset.

"He'd never done that before, and he never will again," I sobbed.

"I'm so sorry he did that. I'm glad you're done with him. You deserve better."

Did I really? I wiped the tears off my face with the hem of my work shirt. Sometimes I wondered. Given everything in my past, it would make sense if I never got a love of my life. However, Tenzin seemed like such a nice guy.

"I need to get to the ice. You... you can come with me if you like." I sniffed, my nose stuffy with sadness.

He stood and held out his hand. "I'd love that."

I hesitated, because you didn't just let strange alphas touch you. But I closed my smaller hand around his large one. He helped me up, and we made our way onto the ice.

The music was loud, which wasn't conducive to talking, but people were still laughing and having fun. Clothes glowed under the black-light, as the lights, glow sticks, and lasers lit up the rink.

The outer rink was meant for everyone to skate around clockwise. The center was mostly figure skaters showing off, even though they were supposed to keep the tricks to a minimum during nights like this given it was *dark*.

Immediately, people started dancing as the song changed to one made popular by the Manhattan Maimers. I put my whistle between my lips, directing people who were trying to do the full routine, to go to the middle, so no one crashed into them.

Skate smash was like team speed skating in a circular loop where you could physically stop other skaters from getting ahead–and getting ahead scored points. They also did fun routines on the ice before games and dance battled with the other team.

People liked to learn the routines. A couple of Maimers had shown me some of theirs. However, the main part of the rink during blackout skate was not the place to do them. Because, injuries.

Blowing my whistle again, I moved some kids out of the way before teenagers crashed into them.

The night continued. Finally, a group of teenagers pleaded with me to let them have the ice to do one of the skate smash dances. Since it was near the end, I cleared it with the manager on duty and the DJ made an announcement.

"You might want to clear the ice. I'm going to stay on, since I know this one," I told Tenzin. It was a really fun mix.

The people who knew the dance took to the ice. The music started and everyone began the routine. It wasn't nearly as cohesive as when the Maimers did it, because they all had specific roles, while this was more of a free-for-all. I did the routine as well, keeping an eye out for crashes, since this one had a couple of jumps.

The song finished, and everyone returned to the ice for the final few songs. Tenzin came back on and stood in the center with me, and we took a couple of laps. The night finished and we cleared everyone off the ice.

Fatigue pressed on me, but it was well after midnight. I helped Desiree take all the rental skates back, then clean and sanitize them.

"You looked good out there, doing the dance in *hockey* skates." Desiree frowned, like it shouldn't be possible.

I shrugged. "I like to mess around on the ice sometimes."

Okay, I'd done some competitive figure skating back in the day. While I liked it, I liked hockey more.

The DJ played a few songs she knew we liked for us to clean up by. The ice resurfacer was going and my other co-workers gathered trash and urged people to return their skates and leave.

"Are you dating *already*? He's on your team?" Desiree looked over at Tenzin.

"It wouldn't be any of your business if I was. But no, he's my friend. You *can* be friends with alphas." I rolled my eyes as I put aside a pair of skates that needed sharpening.

We finished that task and I inventoried the glow sticks.

Tenzin had his skates over his shoulder. "This was fun. Thanks for inviting me. Are you here for much longer? I don't know about you, but I'm exhausted."

"I'm almost done. Might get in some practice if I'm up for it. Want to stay? Or... we could get that coffee?" I offered, inwardly wincing at how needy I sounded. Sure, I was tired, but I suddenly didn't want to be alone.

Conflict flickered across his face. "I'd love to, but I'm so tired I might fall asleep on the subway and miss my stop."

Real. I'd done that before.

"Oh. Another time then." I tried to hide my disappointment.

"I promise to find the best muffins in the city for you. Maybe after you get off of camp on Monday?" he offered.

"I'm working here Monday night, but I definitely can fit in coffee after camp." I'd need the caffeine.

"You work a lot here. I understand needing to work through university. I did. But is that even legal?" He frowned.

I nodded. "Camp isn't run by the rink. Also, I need all the hours I can get given I was fired from my job at Tito's. It's a bar the Knights like."

"Um, did your ex destroy your goalie skates or do you not like them?" he asked. "I've only ever seen you in hockey skates."

"I wear hockey skates a lot at the rink and when teaching kids who might not have them. My ex destroyed my backup goalie skates and my good gear. My good goalie skates were toast after winning the division championship for my university. I was saving for a new pair, because I'm picky, but I spent that money on a pair of skates for Austin." I rubbed the cut on my forehead again.

"Which do you like? Curious if it's the brand Cooter likes."

I got out my phone and pulled up the website for Thunderbolt. "These are what I usually get. I've worn them for years. I sort of want that new model. There's also this one from Bowerman that I'd love to try. At the same time, I'm not sure I want to spend that sort of money and risk not liking them."

They were a more upscale company than the hockey brands I preferred. But not as expensive as what I'd gotten Austin.

"I'm hoping to save up before the season starts, but I might just have to use perfectly good free skates that my team will provide me with, even if they're not what I prefer. Listen to me, I sound so spoiled." I laughed.

He grinned. "You're allowed to be particular about your gear. Yes, you like the same brand Cooter does, just a different model."

"I have tiny narrow feet. Cooter probably doesn't," I replied.

"They're boats," he laughed. "Anyhow, thank you so much for the invitation. See you Monday morning."

My heart twinged a little as he left. I finished up, helping in other areas, since I needed the hours and had nowhere else to be.

Afterwards, I got my stuff and went to the small rink to run drills. The rink was quiet, just some pair skaters practicing in the main rink. Lights shined up in the executive offices on the third floor. Someone was working late.

The lights were off by the time I'd finished, so I headed upstairs, and got in a land workout, then lifted some weights in the small weight room. I hit the showers in the small upstairs staff locker room, then found the never-used storage closet I'd picked out as a sleeping spot.

There were a bunch of old cardboard cutouts of the team in there, which blocked off part of the closet, making a nice hidey-hole.

I made a bed out of old stadium blankets and cushions I'd found in another closet. It wasn't that comfortable, but it was only the first night.

Still...

I could reach out to my oldest brother. He'd help me in a moment. But if I did, I risked him telling the dads.

No. It was better to be free and sleep in a closet than involve my family.

Instead, I texted Tenzin.

Me

This is Gwen. Thanks for keeping me company tonight.

It was nice. I was looking forward to seeing who he deemed having the best muffins in the city.

Clark had sent a bunch of videos on insta-chat, mostly chronicling his day, what he fixed, what he ate. At one point, his little sister bombed the video and made faces.

A new video popped up. "Look, Ladybug."

The video moved and an expanse of stars filled the screen.

"There you are." His finger pointed, then a highlighter circled a group of stars.

I peered at the video, replaying it to get a closer look. I sent a new one, careful so my surroundings weren't obvious. "What is that?"

He sent me another video. "It's you. It's called the golden beetle, but I'd like to think it's the *ladybug*."

I replied. "You're so silly, Clark. The stars sure are pretty. Go to sleep. Where are you?"

"It's not as late here," he laughed, sending a new video. "I'm on the roof of the barn." The camera spun around, showing me his parent's home. "Good night, Gweny. Sweet dreams."

My body yearned for sleep—and I was playing tennis with Carlos in the morning. I'd found a racket in the gym lost and found when I was last on campus.

Usually I'd listen to forensic accounting podcasts before bed. Some of them were quite interesting, especially the *true story* ones, where they detailed how companies and powerful people had been brought down.

Instead, I found the playlist I'd been listening to all week. It was one my friend Mercy had up on Musify. She had the best stuff, including a lot of good songs I'd never heard of. This playlist was called *My big sister's sad girl playlist Number 2.*

I was a sad girl.

Shutting off the light of the storeroom, I put on the music, curled up in my little makeshift bed, and cried myself to sleep.

Chapter Eight

GWEN

I ducked into a takeout café. It was cute and friendly, with simple offerings at reasonable prices. What I liked most was the meal board. There were a handful of places like this around the city.

People could pay for a meal and pin it on the board for someone else to have. If there was a meal available, you took it off the board, brought it to the register, and it was yours. The first thing I ever did when I got a windfall tip was to buy something for as many boards as I could.

Meals also could go quickly, which was why I was looking now, so I could pocket it, then return after coffee and grab something for dinner on my way back to the rink. While I got food at the rink, it wasn't enough.

I didn't feel comfortable sneaking into the Knight's kitchen at the training center and making myself an actual meal, though I did grab snacks.

The place where the board had been was now a painting. Looking around, I didn't spy it anywhere else. I went up to the register, since they weren't busy.

"Um, did you move the meal board behind the register?" I bit my lower lip. The coffee shop had done that.

The woman, who I recognized, gave me a sympathetic look. "We got a new manager, and he got rid of it. Want me to see if there's any messed up orders in the back?"

I shook my head. "It's fine."

If it was anything like Tito's, they got to eat the messed up orders. I didn't want to take food from anyone.

"Do you want me to buy you something?" A man came up behind me. I recognized him vaguely, like he was a regular or something.

"Thanks, but I'm fine. I get to eat at work later tonight. I'm just tired of hot dogs and nachos." I grinned at him, then at the worker.

The worker grinned back. "I understand. Are you close? Maybe we could trade?"

"I work at the ice rink, which is a little far. Thanks anyway, and sorry for holding up the line." I waved and hurried down the street. It was too bad they'd gotten rid of it.

However, I was curious about where Tenzin was taking me today. He'd told me to meet him in front of a department store. Maybe we were going to a hidden coffee shop. I'd gone to hidden bars before with my hockey team. It was a fun thing to do when we were at away games.

Tenzin waved at me, dressed nicely in khakis and a polo. I wore shorts and a tank-top that I'd thrown on after camp, my burgundy *NYIT Hockey* hoodie around my waist. I should hit the thrift stores and get a couple of sundresses or rompers for when we visited museums.

"Hi!" I waved.

"Shall we?" he asked. I nodded and followed him *into* Hardwicks. It was a *very* fancy department store that had been here for close to two centuries.

"Are we going to the food hall?" I perked as we went down the escalator. Sometimes I'd splurge and buy treats here. It was the best for making picnics.

He shook his head. "We can walk through after if you'd like. My sister wants a bear wearing a Hardwicks shirt."

"I'm so curious." I'd never really explored beyond the food hall, the holiday room, and bathrooms, because I couldn't afford to shop here.

The entire store was beautiful, with plush carpets, wood walls, and chandeliers. It smelled faintly of winter and happiness. We stopped in front of some sort of dining room. Roses papered the walls, which were hung with mirrors and paintings. A *harpist* sat in the corner, playing soft music. Well-dressed people sat at tables, eating food off silver trays and sipping tea from delicate floral cups. A brass sign said *The Rose Room.*

"If this isn't what you were thinking of, we can leave. Confession? I have no idea if this is a good place or not. Over the weekend, every time someone asked me if I was the Yeti, I asked them where I could find good muffins. This one got the most enthusiastic recommendations," he told me, as he gave the woman at the host stand his name.

"This place is so pretty." I bit my lower lip, feeling a little underdressed. We needed *reservations?* What sort of coffee shop was this?

The host showed us to a corner table. Tenzin pulled out my chair and pushed it in. My head ducked at his care. He sat, looking a little large for the table and chair, like he was sitting at a child's table playing tea party.

I glanced at the menu—and the prices. No, this wasn't a coffee shop; it was a fancy tea house. The sort where you had tiny food off tiered trays, like rich omegas in a historical drama.

Tenzin leaned in. "Apparently, the muffin flights are *amazing*. Get whatever you want."

"Muffin *flight*? Like a little tasting tray of muffins? Oh, yes, please. I love it. No one has ever taken me to a place like this before." Aww. He picked this place for the muffins.

My mom and sisters liked places like this. I'd always been on strict nutrition plans due to figure skating and didn't get to gorge on carbs. At least not in front of my parents. Being with my grandparents was a whole different story. My nonna was all about the pasta.

"If this isn't satisfactory, we can go somewhere else." He twisted in his seat, his citrus scent turning anxious.

"Tens, I can get a latte the size of my face and a tray full of muffins. It's *amazing*," I assured. Everything looked *delicious*.

A server about my age, in a crisp uniform, came over to take our order.

"I'll have a latte and a muffin flight," I told her, the trays full of delectable morsels making my mouth water.

"I'll have a jasmine tea and a muffin flight, and a mini dessert tower for the table," Tenzin replied. "Thank you."

Our drinks came first, and my giant latte had *art* in the foam—a rose.

I started to take a picture, then paused.

"If you're taking a picture for your social media, I won't judge. I'm going to send a picture of the muffin flight to my sister," Tenzin told me.

"I haven't posted on my social media since the breakup," I sighed. "What do I even do? Post I broke up? Take years of pictures of him off? Delete it and start over?"

"I haven't posted much since my breakup either. I never announced that we weren't together anymore, but I took most pictures of her off." He took a sip of tea.

"My friend Valya keeps telling me that she's taking me for a *single girl glow-up* when she gets back from vacation. Maybe I should let her, then post that and leave it." I took a sip of my latte.

"That seems sound. *Let her?* Are spa days not your idea of a good time?" He gave me a quizzical look as the server brought our muffin flights, which were cute trays with five mini muffins on each one.

"More like out of the budget. She's like *no, my brother will get it for us.* Which is sweet, but it seems almost wasteful with everything I need. Though a glow-up would be fun. I should update my look. Especially since I should get serious on social media if I'm going to get an agent this year."

Also, I'd changed my hair from pink to blue in February, but Austin hadn't like it and wanted me to change it back. I'd wrecked my hair going pink again.

I ended up taking a picture of the tray and my coffee and posting it with *nom nom* as the caption.

Tenzin took a bite of the first muffin and nodded. "Extraordinary. You need an agent?"

I tried the first muffin and blueberries exploded across my tongue, mixing perfectly with the little sugar granules on top. "Oh yes, this was the best idea. A few agents approached me when NYIT won our division finals this year, but I never followed up."

When I'd won the finals with my community college the same thing had happened. Austin told me to ignore them. Stupidly, I'd listened.

But not so much time had passed that I'd wrecked my chances with this batch. Maybe.

"I can help you create a professional account. We'll start with whatever platform you like most. I can edit a couple highlight reels from your games–I'm guessing they're on the university website? Think of one or two things you might like to share besides hockey. Something that makes you stand out. For example, I like to post pictures of nature. Cooter's is full of fish. Real fish. Fish tanks. Gummy fish. Fish toys." He got out his phone and started making a list.

I finished my muffin. "That would be amazing, but you don't have to help me."

Something that made me stand out? Not only did I not like to stand out, I was too busy working and studying. Of course, pictures of studying in stadiums had made Mercy's big sister hugely popular.

"That's my background. Also, it would give me something to do besides practice hockey and visit museums," he replied.

"Fair. I'd like that. There's no way I could pay you. If you're editing videos for me, that's a lot of work." I picked up the next muffin, which was white chocolate raspberry with a little white chocolate curl on top.

"Accompany me to some museums and we'll call it even. I'm happy to help. Also, finals weren't that long ago. Make a list of those contacts and we'll see who to follow up with," he told me, making some notes on his phone.

I polished off that raspberry muffin and washed it down with a sip of latte. Perfection. The next one was chocolate chunk. "I... I'd appreciate all the help I can get, since I have to do this all by myself now."

While I handled household finances and logistics, the hockey side had always been Austin's realm.

"It can be daunting. I'm with a smaller agency, but it works for me." His head cocked, a lock of hair falling in his dark eyes. "I'm not sure my agent even reps goalies, though she's not taking clients. She just had a baby."

He pushed his fancy phone over, and there was a little squishy baby in a black and silver Knights onesie.

"Aww. A Knights onesie?" My eyebrows rose.

"I'm joining your friends at the Knights. It's finalized, but not announced to the press." He, too, took a bite of the chocolate chip muffin.

"That's exciting. I promise I'll introduce you to the players I know." Yep, he'd make an excellent addition to the team with Elias gone.

"Do you practice with the team during the season? The Sasquatches don't have a program like yours. How does it work?" Curiosity tinged his voice.

"We only practice with the entire team occasionally. We practice with the goalies more, and sometimes watch game videos with them and go over strategy. Us EBUGs also have our own practices with one of the Knights' coaches, too. Some years they let us participate in extra stuff like power skating and yoga. Our universities don't allow us to miss class, practice, or games for Knights' stuff without permission.

"The coaches are great with feedback, and the goalies are kind. We can use the facilities and sometimes get to help out or attend other things. But Coach Kirov believes in the program, not all the teams are like that." I picked up the next muffin, which was apple cinnamon.

"It sounds wonderful. So your plan is to get representation, go free agent after graduation, and get signed?" He took another sip of tea.

"Yep. The Knights are the dream, but I'm not picky–farm team, overseas, really, I'd go anywhere." Okay, except Canada and the Pacific Northwest. "I know given my size and designation, I'm not a standout, so I'll take what I can get."

"You're as tall as Molly Crewe with the Belugas, aren't you?" Tenzin took another sip of tea.

She was the other omega goalie in the PHL. Omegas weren't common in professional hockey–or most contact sports.

"I'm an inch taller. But Molly's the exception, not the rule. Goalies our size aren't common anymore. You have to be very special." Which was why I needed to rediscover that secret sauce that once made me stand out.

Make them look. Make them reconsider. Make them regret.

Like Maria Barilla did when they told her that professional hockey was too rough for betas. Oh, the teams that turned her down regretted that. The Knights built a legacy based on the chance they gave her.

"Challenge accepted." He finished his last muffin. "People were wary of me because of my size. I'm *large* and they worried I wouldn't be able to maneuver as well. So, I made videos of my best moves to catchy music. That was my first video project."

The server came back over and took our empty trays, refilled our drinks, and brought us a tiered tray of tiny desserts.

I took a picture and sent it to Clark, since he was always sending me pictures of his mom's pies.

"This is beautiful. Thank you. Thank you for doing something so kind for me. For offering to help me. Practice with me. You barely know me and you're being so nice." Tears pricked my eyes.

"He wasn't kind to you, was he? Your ex." Tenzin frowned.

"Oh, he was. One thing I loved was that he made me think I was worthy even though I'm just a beta. A few hours before we broke up, he baked me *brownies* and got my favorite takeout. I... I don't understand how he could do this." I sobbed into my mug.

"Gwen, hey, it's okay. Do you want to talk about it?" he offered.

"Could I?" I wiped my eyes with the napkin and sniffed. I told Tenzin everything as we demolished the dessert tower–from meeting Austin in junior hockey back in high school, to going to get my stuff and finding him gone. Though I left out a few things, like him taking back the tuition money and me living in the closet.

"That was the worst part, I think." I grabbed the last cookie on our almost empty tower. "Him destroying the photo of my mom. What did I miss? What did I do wrong? I was going to marry him. Form a pack. Play hockey." A sob ripped from my throat.

"He's not worth your tears. Do you think he's crying over you right now?" Tenzin's voice turned growly.

"No. He's probably banging the omega he was promised to, while learning the ropes at his daddy's company." I sniffed. I still hoped it was something where he had to get his hands dirty.

"Don't give him your tears–or your time," he told me. "Don't let him live rent free in your head. You're a smart, sweet person who knows her way around a goal. You did nothing wrong. He held you back for too long. You might have thought you were flying together, but you were being dragged, going where he wanted on his timing. Now you're free."

I sucked in a breath as I wiped my tears with my napkin.

"Freedom can be a little scary at first, but just wait until you soar. You're going to accomplish so much," he told me.

"I could?" I drained the last of my latte.

The best revenge is to thrive.

"You will. You'll see. It's okay to be sad. It's okay to take time to heal, to figure things out. We'll work hard this summer. We'll see the city and get your socials set up. When the season starts, you'll hit the ice ready. You're up for that, right?" He finished his tea.

Was I? What else did I have to do this summer? Might as well work on hockey *and* myself.

"Put me in, Coach." I might be a sad girl, but this sad girl was ready to soar.

Chapter Nine

TENZIN

"This place is amazing," I told Gwen, as she dragged me through the massive food hall at Hardwicks. It was a bit like a luxury indoor food market, with everyone having a permanent stall.

They had so many things, from fresh baked bread, to imported chocolates, to fancy cheese. There were also sandwiches, hot foods, salads, and so many other things.

We passed a bunch of roast chickens and I turned to her. "Do you have dinner covered?"

"I'll get dinner at the rink." There was something about her expression, the wistful way she gazed at things...

"Do you want a treat for later?" I worried about her not eating enough, given the calories she expended playing hockey with the children all day. The dinner options at the rink were pizza, hot dogs, fries, and nachos.

Her head ducked. Yes, she wanted something.

"What do you want? We can always split it?" I offered, trying to determine the root of her hesitancy.

Gwen bit her lower lip. "Maybe?"

We ended up with some fancy trail mix, tiny packets of nut butter, gourmet crackers, and sour candies. Not dinner, but a start.

I passed a case of truffles. Oh. I should get a raspberry one.

No. I stopped myself, my heart speeding a little.

"Are you okay, Tens?" Gwen stood close to me, there was worry in her soft minty scent.

"I... I was about to get some for Morgan. But there's no Morgan." My voice shook a little. "She loved dark chocolate raspberry truffles. I'd always pick some up for her when I was traveling, or even just out. She's a med student and always could use a treat."

"Want to tell me about it?" Gwen offered as we left the food hall.

"There's not much to tell. I met Morgan at the noodle shop where I often picked up food. She liked to study there. We started talking and began dating. Last year she moved in. It was so nice coming home to someone. Also, she's so busy with med school and her rotations that it was hard to see her during the season, given my own schedule." We'd had a lot in common, too, like a love of nature.

We wandered through the next section, which was all holiday decorations–for *every* holiday.

"Were you going to marry her–or mate her? Was she an omega?" Gwen picked up a bear in a pumpkin outfit, then set it down.

"Beta. We'd talked about mating after she finished medical school, and starting a pack and a family. But later, because her career is important to her. I did my best to support her. It was a surprise when she told me she was pregnant and wanted to keep the baby and join a pack." I grimaced, because the idea of being a dad overjoyed me.

Gwen sucked in a breath as we wandered out of the holiday section and into an area full of gift books and other such things. "It wasn't your baby."

"The Lewises were the first friends I made when I moved to Portland to be a Sasquatch." I picked up a book of nature photos and leafed through it. "Jacen was my real estate agent. He helped me rent my first place, then buy my house. He invited me over for dinner and his throuple adopted me. His alpha is a doctor. Their omega is an interior decorator. I was over all the time, and they adored Morgan. Jacen was one of my best friends."

I sighed and closed the book. At least I had Cooter.

"Oh no." Gwen looked stricken.

"Morgan loved decorating, so when she moved in, I hired their omega and the two of them became close. I'm gone so much during the season, it was a relief that she had more than the dog for company, though her studies kept her busy." I leaned against the bookcase.

"You have a dog?" Gwen brightened. "We had a dog when I was a kid."

"She took the dog." My head bowed. "I can't care for a dog with my schedule. Turns out, while I was on the road, she was growing *very* close to the Lewises. She let me think the baby was mine. I was excited, and planned a romantic trip where we could mate, and a party for us after. Then, Jacen and Ilya, their alpha, ambushed me, asking for us to form a pack with them. That it would be best for Morgan to have support, and their omega, who's also pregnant, could have company. I was ready to accept. They were my dearest friends outside Coot. Jacen let it slip that the baby was his and the whole story came tumbling out.

"It started out innocently enough. Their omega went into heat unexpectedly. Morgan was over and got swept up into it. Instead of them talking to me about it, they kept it a secret—and continued their relationship. The four of them kept up the pretense with me that they were just friends, and Morgan continued to make me think I was enough for her." That was the rub–the lies.

"Tens. I... I'm so sorry," Gwen put a hand on my arm.

"Morgan confirmed it was true. She was lonely, and they were there for her. Though, she also insisted she needed me." I walked through the store, not knowing where I was going.

"So, she was like, *whoops, I fell on his dick and got preggers. Let's move in with them and raise the baby together*?" Gwen trotted to keep up with my longer stride.

"Pretty much. The fact I didn't want that baffled Morgan." My throat grew tight. "I felt betrayed, and they told me it was wrong for me to feel that way. I thought about it for weeks. In the end, I just couldn't get over the lies. Now I'm here. She and the dog moved in with them."

We were now in the home section, full of pillows and blankets.

Gwen had tears in her eyes. "I'm sorry. Your best friends, too. Your feelings are valid."

"If they'd come to me, been open, I would have been for it. Instead, they lied. I hate liars." I grimaced again, my voice going sharp with pain and anguish.

Gwen jumped, dropping a purple pillow shaped like a heart.

"Hey, it's okay," I soothed, putting out calming pheromones, even though it was a bit of an overstep.

I was probably triggering her, given her ex's lies. Picking up the pillow, I gave it back.

"As long as you're not living a double life, you're fine," I joked. Morgan had been. A life with me when I was home and a life with them when I was on the road.

Gwen's head bowed as she held the pillow to her chest, shivering as she took in a breath. "I'm not living a double life. But I left a life behind after my mom died. My dads are assholes who didn't like me playing hockey."

I wanted to bundle her in my arms and hold her. But I wasn't sure she'd accept my touch so soon. Still, the alpha in me hated that I made her upset.

"When you moved away to play junior hockey after your grandparents died?" The few things she'd said fit together. There were still people who thought only alphas should play the rougher sports, like hockey and rugby.

She absently ran her fingers over the stitches on her forehead. "Yeah. My name was changed legally. Mostly I try to not talk about things instead of lying. But..."

I came up next to her. "That's different."

"Lies to protect yourself still can hurt people." Her voice turned bitter, and she looked away.

"Keeping secrets for safety is something I understand, and I appreciate you sharing that with me." My heart broke for her as I moved to meet her gaze.

"Austin didn't know much about my past. He got his jock in a twist when he found out Gwen wasn't the name I was born with. Ironic, considering his name isn't Austin. One time we were dancing at a club and ran into someone from my past who knew my old name. It was one of those weird things." Her scent took on a bit of burnt sugar, fear.

"It happens. My sister's a singer. When I was a teenager, I'd go on the road with her during the summer. It's always funny when I'm out with the hockey team and people are *wait, aren't you Zaya's little brother, the one who'd wear the dinosaur costume and shoot T-shirts into the crowd?*" I offered, trying to soothe her fears before I hugged her to my chest and never let her go.

She let out a little chuckle. "I need photos."

"Maybe this summer we'll hunt her down and she'll show you all the pictures. You're no-contact with your family?" I asked.

"I... I wanted to keep in contact with some of my siblings, but I can't do that. It's all or nothing. I get it if this is a deal breaker for you. I'll miss our practices." She put the pillow back and her head hung.

The hopelessness in her face, her voice, made my heart break even more. Something about her brought out all of my protective instincts.

"Changing your name is pretty normal. I mean, Cooter changed his name to Cooter when he was nineteen." I hated how defeated she looked.

"Cooter is his legal name and not his nickname?" She blinked.

"Yes. At Crestdale, half my class changed their name to something having to do with nature. My sister changed her last name when she became a singer, and I changed my name to match hers when I was living with her because it made things less complicated. Also, people go no-contact with family members," I added, thinking of those who'd stopped talking to Zaya and me after our parents died.

"True. I don't really tell people stuff like that. You're easy to talk to." She shuddered a little, still looking scared and vulnerable.

"I'll keep your secrets." I wanted to make her happy, protect her, soothe her fragile soul. It went beyond the normal alpha need too. Something pulled me to her, and it differed greatly from how I'd been drawn to Morgan.

"You're so nice and I'm sorry she lied to you." Gwen's arms wrapped around herself.

"I appreciate you trusting me. Should we go find some bears to hug?" I offered, wishing we were at the point in our friendship where I could hold her.

We set off in search of a teddy bear for my sister. Zaya collected them. It was the least I could do. She put her music career in a holding pattern to get me through high school. Our hard work and sacrifice paid off. Now, we both played for sold-out crowds.

There was a whole little area of Hardwicks merchandise, including a display of bears in an assortment of sizes.

"These are so soft." Gwen rubbed a small bear on her cheek, a look of bliss on her face.

"Do you want one, too?" I offered, choosing a medium-sized dark brown bear in a green sweater for Zaya.

"I'm good." With reluctance, she put it down.

"Gwen, do you want a bear? If I offer to buy it for you, I mean it. I'm not a starving student. It's not a hardship. Talk to me?"

Gwen pressed her lips together, brows knitting in thought. I gave her an unamused look.

"Or is there something else you'd like?" I offered, recalling the food hall. "Something you need? Something you want? Either here or elsewhere."

If her ex ruined all her things, there was most likely something she was doing without.

She was quiet for a moment. "You would, wouldn't you? We've known each other for like a week."

I nodded and paid for the bear. "People helped me out in university and high school. Now I can pay it back. Clothes? Makeup? Those goalie skates you're saving for. Practical, ridiculous, whatever you want."

While I didn't want to push, I wanted to give her some small happiness. I took the bag with the bear and we left the register.

Her head ducked as we walked through the sumptuous store. "The guys are going to get me some clothes and shoes. Until then, I can get by fine with what I have or hit a vintage store, or something. Carlos' friend is re-painting my goalie mask. Clark said he'd get me what my school didn't equipment wise."

"So you're going to get him to buy you the goalie skates you want?" I prodded. I think the problem here was that she didn't like asking for help.

She shrugged. "I... I don't want to be a bother. I'll probably just make do with what my school gives me until I can afford what I want."

There it was. She *wanted* help. She didn't want to *bother* people by asking for it.

"Gwen, Clark came to find you at the rink in the middle of the night. I haven't met him, but I'm pretty sure if he offers to get you something, he means it. He's probably going to ask his sponsor for what he needs." I wasn't sure if that was true, but it might make her feel better.

She laughed. "His sponsor makes boxers."

I had one of those. Also, I might have asked my rep at Bowerman this morning about getting her a pair of goalie skates. While the company she liked didn't sponsor me, the company that made that model she wanted to try *did.*

"Don't be afraid to ask for help." My alpha hated that she was so hurt, so used and wounded by that ex of hers. If I ever saw him, I'd punch him. Then when the media storm hit, I'd tell them *exactly* what sort of alpha he was.

Gwen was sweet and kind. Hardworking and dedicated. She deserved an alpha that would support and cherish her.

"I'm okay right now. Please don't buy me skates, Tens. The ones I like are expensive," she told me.

I gave her a look. "Do you know how much I make?"

"More than a rookie." Her lips pressed together, fighting a smile. An alarm beeped on her phone. "I have to head back to the rink, but thank you for the wonderful afternoon and the treats."

"Let me walk you to the subway stop." I'd go with her to the rink, but I didn't want to spook her.

After I saw her off at the station, I got out my phone and checked my email. They were shipping the skates tomorrow. Good thing I caught her size one day. They were excited she wanted to try them out.

Gwen

I had fun, thank you.

Me

I did as well. We should do it again, try another place.

Gwen

Sounds good. Let's find the best muffins in the city. My favorite is blueberry.

Me

Me, too. I like that idea a lot.

There was a lot to like about Gwen. It was in her smile, her easy nature, her drive, her fierceness in the net, the way she worked with kids. If my heart wasn't so broken by Morgan and the Lewises, it would be easy to fall for her. Hard.

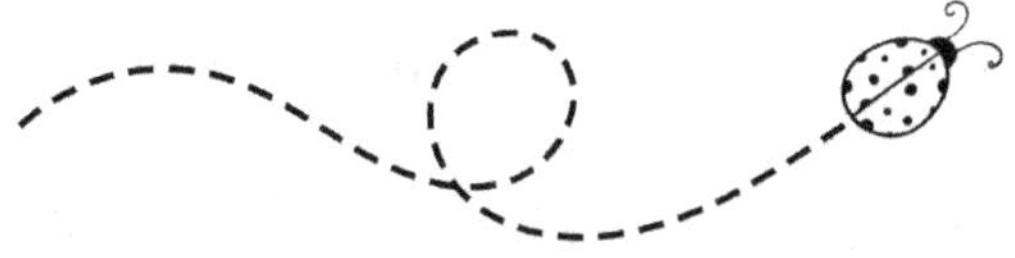

Chapter Ten

GWEN

"Tens, this is incredible." I watched the video he'd made, with clips of my games from this past season set to music, along with my stats. It was a work of art. Much nicer than anything Austin ever had.

"Thanks. I admit, I went through a few versions. Cooter liked this one best." He gave me a shy smile.

I'd finished my shift at the rink and now we were at a fancy rooftop coffee place. All week we'd been building my socials. We'd also gone to a museum and seen a traveling exhibit featuring paintings by Dumas. My favorite wasn't there, but it was still fun. We'd tried two different coffee places. Both had delicious muffins, but didn't top the muffin flight at the Rose Room.

"We'll pin it up at the top so it's easy to find. I'll make another of the season before, since you won that team a title as well. Few people can boast leading two teams to their respective division's national championships," he told me.

My cheeks warmed. "I'm just doing what I do."

Since the other title was 'just' community college league, it was often dismissed.

There was a giant electronic billboard on the building facing us. Clark, holding a cologne bottle, filled the screen. I took out my phone and insta-chatted it to him.

"Did you know you have fan accounts?" Tenzin turned his laptop around.

"My host mom from junior hockey runs *Ladybug Spotting*." I laughed. It was filled mostly with pictures of me in the stands at Knights games that she took off the television.

"There are others, too. Also, you made the sports news a few times during playoffs? Goalie-in-waiting?" He pulled up an article.

"For games, we sit in the stands and watch. If someone gets injured, we'll go down to the equipment office, get partially dressed out, and wait, just in case. We only get half-dressed because we could end up going in for either team. A reporter found me hanging out, and we got to talking. She saw me again several times throughout the season. Then we had playoff-agedon." I grimaced and took another sip of coffee.

While I'd been excited for the Knights to go all the way and win the finals, it had been a rough journey.

"There were so many injuries and illnesses that it made me wonder if we'd make it through the playoffs. During the playoffs, I ended up in the office, partially dressed out for *every single game I was on duty for*, though I never went in. She and some of the reporters had a little fun with it," I told him. It was cute.

"Was that disappointing, never getting to play?" He took a sip of tea.

"Not really, since that meant my friends were hurt or sick. It would be amazing, though. Well, except for the finals. That would be nerve-wracking," I admitted.

My phone buzzed.

JP

Are you coming to my wedding?

Me

I don't know. I'd like to, but it's in *Canada*.

I played it off like it was distance, not fear. Jean-Paul–one of the Knights' goalies–and his fiancée Celine were from Quebec.

JP

We will protect you from whatever it is here that scares you. I need you for the goalie dance.

Me

Goalie dance?

I blinked. What in the what, what? However, I liked how he just rolled with my fear of Canada and didn't make fun of me for it.

If only he could protect me from what scared me there.

JP

For Celine. We need an even number.

The idea of us doing a dance at the wedding for Celine made me grin.

JP

If it's the cost, I'll get your train ticket. Carlos or Clark might let you stay with them.

A train ticket *would* help. The wedding wasn't until late August, so I had time to save up a little for food. If the guys actually got me some clothes, I might be able to get a dress that would work for the wedding.

JP

Come on. It'll be fun.

Tenzin looked over at me. "Everything okay?"

"I'm being pressured to participate in an all-goalie dance at a wedding." I laughed.

"That sounds amazing." His eyes gleamed as he chuckled. "Are you going to do it?"

I considered this. It was Quebec, not Vancouver. Also, given my single status, me sharing a room with someone else wouldn't be an issue.

"I think so. It'll be hysterical, I'm sure." I could only think of the bro-nanigans JP would concoct. He was offering the ticket, so it was okay to take it, right?

Me

A train ticket would help. Thank you. I'm in.

JP

Great. Let Celine know. Also, sorry about the breakup. As someone who wouldn't have made it without a supportive partner, I'm sorry he was shitty and bailed before he could hold up his end.

He and Celine had met when they were at university. Also, JP knew about the breakup? Ugh, hockey players were such gossips.

Me

Thanks

I got into my email and found the wedding information and let Celine know I was going.

My phone lit up.

Ladybug has been added to Goalie Dance Chat.

JP

Ladybug's in

Dean

YAY!

Me

I let Celine know.

JP

Très bon. I'll send videos.

Me

Merci

I was better at Italian than French, though my extensive privately tutored education had included it when I was young.

Goalie dance? That would be worth the trip.

I realized I was leaning against Tenzin and I sat up. "Sorry, I didn't mean to use you as a backrest."

"It's fine." His voice was soft. "I don't mind. Also, you were with an alpha for so long, from such a young age. Your body is probably missing the contact."

Oh. I didn't even think of that. That could be why I missed snuggles and hugs.

Tenzin and I worked a little longer. He yawned.

"Sorry, I think I'm going to go to bed. Would you like me to order you a car? It's late," he offered.

"I'm fine. Thank you so much for all your help. It looks great." I set off for the subway and returned to the rink, hitting a late-night cafe on the way back that discounted their grab-and-go stuff drastically after a certain time.

One of the security guards saw me in the halls. "Working late?"

"Forgot something." I slipped upstairs, knowing how to avoid the cameras at night.

I showered and changed, then went into my closet. Putting on my headphones and queuing Mercy's sad girl playlist, I scrolled through social media, as I ate my chicken wrap.

Clark had game night with his family. Dimitri's vacation looked incredible. My teammates and classmates were mostly working or with family, but still having a good time.

And I was sleeping in a closet.

I tried to sleep. My little bed wasn't very comfortable. Also, I didn't feel that safe, even though I knew I was. This was a locked floor, used only by the Maimers and Knights. No one was up here this time of night.

Taking out my phone, I started to text Clark, like I had a million times, and ask if I could crash at his place while he was out of town. There was no way I could afford to be his roommate, but maybe he'd let me couch surf for free for a couple of weeks?

Like every other time, I didn't. Instead, I texted him inane things like always.

Me

Tried more muffins at the rooftop bar. Tens is making me highlight videos.

Clark

It's nice that you have Tens to hang out with. Where'd you meet him again?

Me

He's defense.

I wasn't sure if I could start telling my friends who he was. After all, there'd been no announcement for a reason.

Clark

Got it. Also, a film major? Send them to me?

Me

Yep. Sent

I added the link.

Clark

Can't wait to watch. Today I fixed two tractors. One of my moms made an apple pie.

Pie. My mouth watered.

Me

Are you going to JP's wedding? I'm being forced to do a goalie dance.

Okay, I was excited about the goalie dance.

Clark

I am. Do you want me to ask Dimitri if there's room for you? He got a villa or something, we're sharing.

Again, did I take the offer? But I couldn't go without a place to stay.

Me

If there's room for me, I'd like that, thanks. But I don't think I can afford wherever they're staying.

I hadn't really paid attention to where it was.

It's fine. Are you doing okay? I'm here if you need me.

I hesitated. Was this where I asked him about his guest room? No. I think he was talking about emotional needs.

Thanks for checking in. I'm doing okay.

I listened to my favorite accounting podcast. Still, I couldn't sleep. So I snuck down to the main floor and got my stuff out of my locker, then went to the small rink.

Which I'd been doing a lot this week.

Back to basics. I ran through everything that my nonna's neighbors had taught me, trying to harness the sauce. *You were good once.*

And I'd be good again.

Make them look. Make them regret.

Oh, I would. Because I was going to thrive. Soar.

When I finished, I was tired, but not sleepy. A song I liked came on over the sad girl playlist.

Taking off my pads, I skated, letting the music wash over me. It had been a while since I'd done this. The moves came back easily. It wasn't like I never figure skated after I stopped competing.

I just did everything in hockey skates.

At some point, I picked up my stick, making it part of my routine. It was a bit of silliness I'd done with my host sister back in junior hockey. Her drill team performed on the ice with pom-poms, flags, and hockey sticks before hockey games and during intermission. She now skated with a traveling show.

I skated to song after song, letting go of everything—my sadness, my stress. Everything floated away until there was nothing but me, the ice, and the music.

Finally, I was home.

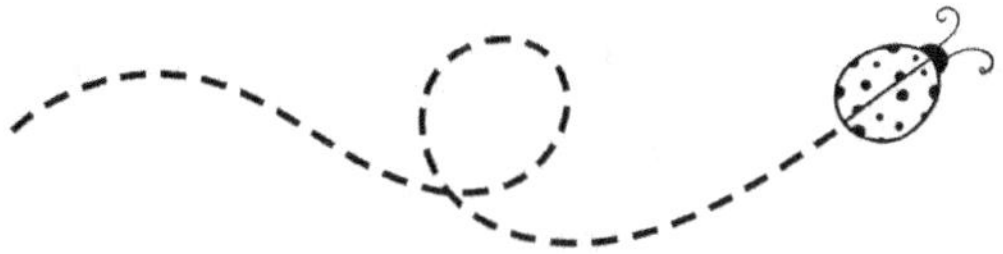

Chapter Eleven

TENZIN

"Tens, where are we?" Gwen looked around the honky-tonk I'd brought her to. The dim place smelled of sweat, wood, and beer, making me homesick for all the places like this I'd gone to in high school, and during breaks when I was at university to support my older sister.

"It's a bar, Firecracker." The endearment just slipped out. That's what she was. A little pink spitfire.

Every day she smiled a little more, glowed a little brighter, ducked her head a little less. The real her was starting to shine through. We'd gone to dinner at a place on our list—a hole in the wall with amazing food recommended to me by my friend that lived here.

I led her to the wooden bar, which was busy, but not completely crowded. Country music played on a jukebox. People sat at tables talking and drinking. There was a small stage and dance floor, with some instruments being set up.

"I've never been to a bar like this. Mostly, we go to sports bars, like Tito's or Marabou Mike's. Unless it's a birthday and we go someplace fancy like a rooftop bar or a club, someone has a hookup to, or the Arctic Toilet, or something."

She looked cute in a yellow sundress and some canvas slip-ons. Her hair was up in a messy bun, with a few pink strands coming down in wisps, revealing the shaved parts that had grown out, but not enough to put up.

"What do you want to drink?" I wondered what she liked.

She shrugged. "Beer's fine."

Did she order beer because she liked it, or because it was cheaper? I was fine with beer myself. I didn't have a huge tolerance for alcohol, anyway. We ordered two from the bartender.

"There's music?" She eyed the musicians as they took the stage and warmed up.

"I didn't bring you here for the beer." The band was decent, covering well-known country songs.

"You like country music?" She nodded. "You know, before the breakup, I wouldn't say I liked country, but after listening to *mad girl revenge music,* which is mostly country songs about property damage, I can see the appeal. Both to the music and dumping your ex's truck in the lake."

"That happened to Cooter once." I laughed. Actually, that song was *about* Cooter. I regretted ever introducing them. But we were young dumbasses.

We found a high-top. There were enough boots and Cowboy hats to make me think of wearing mine next time. How would she look in a Cowboy hat and boots?

"Are we here for the band or the vibes?" She took a sip of beer.

"I wanted to see if you liked country music. I enjoy it and bars like this. If you do too, well, that's one more thing we can do together." I liked spending time with her; it made life here less lonely.

She nodded. "Okay, but you could have just asked. Not that I'm complaining."

"Asking and experiencing are two different things." Something I knew firsthand. I wasn't happy when my sister said I'd have to come with her to a lot of her band stuff–until I heard the music.

"It's fun." Gwen smiled and took another drink of beer.

The band opened with a song I loved and couples started dancing. Standing, I held out a hand. "Dance with me."

"I don't know how to dance to music like this." She ducked her head, self-conscious.

"It's a two-step, not a line dance. Though we can do that, too, if you want." Part of me relaxed as she took my hand.

"Line dancing. Like hats and boots and everything?" She let me lead her onto the floor.

"Absolutely. Do you know how cute boots and hats can look with sundresses?" I positioned her hands, our bodies not quite touching.

At some point, we should go to a fair and hear my sister play. Gwen could wear some boots and a hat, we could ride some rides, pet some cows, and eat some food *not* on a PHL-approved nutrition list.

Gwen thought for a moment. "I could make that look cute."

Yes, she could. Did I get her pink boots to go with her hair?

I taught her the moves and after a couple of songs, she was laughing and twirling with the best of them.

A song came on, and she closed her eyes, spinning and smiling. She gave a laugh, and opening her eyes, took my hand. Her laughter made everything better.

We got some water when the music shifted.

"What do you think?" I asked. She seemed to be having fun. I was enjoying myself immensely.

Gwen nodded. "I could be persuaded to do this again."

A song from my sister's band came on, and people started line dancing.

"Would you like to line dance?" I gestured to the crowd.

"Maybe." Gwen eyed everyone dancing in unison. "You did this a lot back in Portland?"

I nodded as I took a drink of water. "Yes. And at university, and even with my sister when I was in high school back in Nashville. Cooter's *very* good at it. There's this place by his ranch that is amazing."

"Why doesn't it surprise me that Cooter likes line dancing?" She held up her phone and took a picture of us. "We should send it to him."

My phone beeped as the picture of us appeared and I sent it to Cooter.

Me

We tried the bar you recommended. We're having fun.

Cooter

Dance with Babybug for me.

Oh, I would. She had a good sense of rhythm and caught on fast. When did he start calling her *Babybug?*

"We're going on a couple of fishing trips this summer. One's in a couple of weeks," I told her. "I also have to go back to Portland soon, because the house sold."

Morgan was *pissed* about the house sale. So was Jacen, given I'd used his biggest competitor as my realtor. So far, the news of me being traded to the Knights hadn't broken.

It was only a matter of time before someone figured it out.

The music changed again and couples took to the floor.

"Dance with me?" She gazed at me through veiled lashes.

How could I say no to that? I took her hand in mine and led her back out to the floor. Yes, she was going to need some boots. Good thing I knew her size.

Chapter Twelve

GWEN

Yawning, I trudged down the hallway of the training complex, coming from the Knights' dining room. I had a tumbler of coffee in one hand and an apple in the other. I couldn't sleep.

Chef didn't mind when I made myself some coffee and grabbed a piece of fruit. I planned on heading down to the rink to practice a little before Tenzin arrived.

"Oh, sorry." An alpha in a suit nearly bumped into me.

"Me, too. I was lost in thought. Sorry." I wasn't expecting anyone to be here yet. Not even the cleaning staff. I eyed him warily, because I'd never seen this man. He was in his mid-thirties, broad and tall, but not distinguishing so, and probably not as fit as he once was.

"Are you supposed to be up here? Also, what are you doing here so early?" He eyed my sweatpants and *NYIT Hockey* hoodie.

"Early goalie gets the puck?" Shit. He was most likely someone who shouldn't be seeing me up here. New office staff maybe? Though it's not like he saw me coming out of the showers.

He nodded. "Goalie. Got it. Do you know how to work the coffee machine in the kitchen? I'm not usually here this early, but there's a lot to learn. Sorry, I'm Constantine, the new assistant GM."

"Morning, Ladybug." The janitor waved, pushing his cart.

"Morning, Ralph." I waved back.

Constantine jerked his head toward the dining room. "About that coffee lesson?"

"Sure." In a strange moment, I showed the new assistant GM how to use Chef's fancy coffee maker, and where the cookies were kept.

"Thanks," he told me.

I waved, then left the kitchen.

Downstairs, the small rink sat empty. I finished my apple, then ran through some basics. Every day I felt a little more confident, a little more connected to my roots. To what had made me the player I was as a kid. My old host mom had even found some footage from junior hockey for me to review.

Clark sent me a picture of his breakfast. Farm life had early wake-ups. I sent him a picture of me on the ice.

There was still time before Tenzin came, so I put on my headphones, grabbed my stick, and skated to a song from the sad girl playlist that I'd roughly choreographed. Not only was it flowing and lyrical, but the words called to me.

Clearly, Austin never thought about *us*. Just *him*. His education. His career.

Whatever. I didn't need him to be happy. Every day I was less sad about the breakup and finding more joy in the little things.

Like learning about art with Tenzin, going dancing, and eating muffins.

There was a lot to like about Tenzin. Like how he always treated me with so much care. He also tipped his servers well. One thing that mildly annoyed me about Austin was that despite being a bartender, he didn't tip well and didn't like it when I did.

I don't know how I'd have gotten through the past year without big tips. Most of them were from people who knew me.

As the music played through my headphones, I skated my heart out, jumping and twirling, all while holding a hockey stick, because I was silly like that. When the song finished, I did it again, tweaking and adding to the choreography.

I played the song one more time, putting my heart into every move, every jump, every spin, every twirl of my stick.

When I stopped, Tenzin stood there, watching.

"That was incredible." He beamed at me.

My cheeks burned as I plopped down on the ice. "I was just messing around."

"I've never seen anyone figure skate like that in hockey skates–or holding a hockey stick," he told me.

"Lots of people figure skate in hockey skates." Okay, it was more of a Canadian alpha thing. My last coach had mostly trained alphas. I was there because they were mated to two former PHL players and lived next door to my nonna. Also, they knew I'd rather play hockey, but had to please my dads.

"If this is something you do a lot, it might be fun to put on your social media," he offered. "That thing that sets you apart. You could wear something that matches the song or theme. I could bring out my good camera, maybe a light or two. Think about it. I'm guessing you figure skated when you were young."

"Yep. Hockey has my heart, though. Are we going to practice now?"

"Let's go. But wait..." Grinning like a goofball, he pulled something out of his bag.

"Tens, this better not be what I think it is." I eyed the box in his hand. My muscles ached from all the figure skating.

"I didn't buy them—I got them from my rep. Yes, I checked, and it doesn't violate any NACA rules, since they gave them to *me* and they come out of my allotment." He held it out.

The National Association of Collegiate Athletes had very strict rules and was the reason us EBUGs got paid in tickets, snacks, and merch.

I bit my lower lip. "I don't want to deny you skates when you need them."

He must go through a lot of pairs, too, and didn't need to resort to all sorts of measures to make them last longer.

"Don't worry about that, just try them. This way, if you don't like them, you didn't pay for them, and you can keep saving for what you want." His look grew expectant.

While part of me hesitated to accept them, he did tell me if he offered, he meant it—and he listened to me and followed my requests.

I opened the box to reveal the state-of-the-art new model goalie skates from Bowerman that I'd been curious about. "Tens, they're beautiful. Thank you."

My heart filled up. They were even my size. I didn't ask how he knew—he was observant like that.

"Try them out?" he offered.

"I might as well break them in. Thank you." My throat swelled at the gesture.

I put them on, and even with them not being broken in or even touching the ice, I knew. I was ruined.

"Let's go." I skated out on the ice. Oooh, I was going to want these always.

We did our usual workout.

As we finished, Tenzin wiped sweat off his forehead. "Do they live up to the hype?"

"I love them. Once they're broken in and sharpened the way I like they'll be perfect. You're creating a monster. Thank you so much. It was so nice of you that I have no words." I took them off and put them in my bag.

For a moment, he looked a little sad. "You deserve the tools you need. I'm happy to get them for you."

"Well, thanks."

"Anytime. Should we go up and get some breakfast?" he asked.

Since I had dining room privileges, we'd been grabbing a breakfast sandwich before camp. Also, Chef would make me a sack lunch to eat with my campers. Which was nice, since I no longer had a kitchen to make myself one. Sure, I could run up and grab whatever they were serving, but my campers might be sad to see me with a tasty hot lunch while they had brought-from-home sandwiches.

"Think about what I said about the videos?" he added as we headed toward the elevator.

"Yeah, I will." Put videos of me figure skating online? I didn't know about that. Maybe I'd just stick to pictures of muffins.

It *was* something different. Not to mention it opened up other silliness. Like doing Maimers dances while holding a hockey stick. Taking dances from social media and doing them on skates.

Hmm. I'd have to think about it. Skating like that felt good. I just wasn't sure if I wanted to share it with the world.

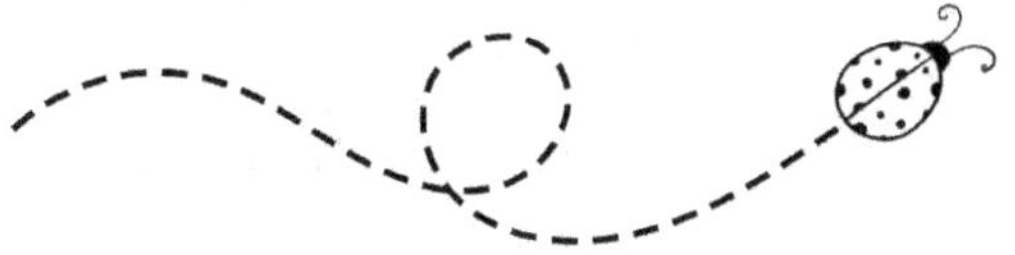

Chapter Thirteen

TENZIN

My phone rang. Morgan's name flashed across the screen. Again. I ignored it again as I sat at the table, working on editing another video for Gwen. There were no texts, just calls. A chill swept through me. What if something was wrong?

Against my better judgment, I answered it. "Morgan?"

"Tenzie. There you are." Her voice turned scolding.

"Is everything okay? You had a scan today?" Even though I shouldn't, I did read the inane update texts she and Jacen sent me.

"I did. It's a girl." Her voice softened.

My heart broke. A girl.

"Anything else?" I now knew a little more than I had the night that Jacen had told me he was the father.

It had been too early to do a paternity test; he was guessing. The two of us *had* been having unprotected sex the entire time she'd removed her birth control implant and was taking fertility enhancers in hopes she would get pregnant during one of Imogen's heats, so they could be pregnant together, and I hadn't been on birth control.

"I don't want to do a paternity test. It's all our baby." Her voice grew hard.

"I didn't ask." Not now, not ever.

She sighed. "If I did, and it's yours, will you come home? We miss you. I get it. We messed up. We weren't trying to hurt you, but we did and we're sorry."

Wow. That was a *huge* admission. Had she done that earlier, it would have changed everything.

Too late.

"You did. All four of you." I missed them, too. But I wasn't going to tell her that.

"Tenzie, we're sorry. What we did was wrong. We should have communicated and it won't happen again. What else do you want?" she pleaded.

"Nothing." I exhaled sharply. At one point, I'd really wanted to hear that. "I won't come home and play happy pack if the baby is mine. But I will do my duty as a father."

"I don't want your money," she spat.

"I was speaking more of knowing her. Taking her fishing, teaching her hockey. I won't fight you for her, but I'd definitely help support her." Perhaps a college fund or trust if Morgan didn't want support payments. We could go on fun holidays, and perhaps my next team would be closer and I could be more present.

"Oh. I could absolutely see you wearing her in an infant carrier, while teaching her how to fish." Morgan sighed. "Baby Bean is fine. I... I don't know if I want the test. I do want you to come home though."

"The house is sold. I'll be there next weekend to take care of some things."

"Where did you move to?" Curiosity tinged her voice.

There it was. "It doesn't matter."

"Please tell me you didn't quit hockey and move to New York like some bohemian filmmaker? I don't want to be the reason you leave hockey."

"I didn't quit hockey." My eyebrows furrowed. How did she know I was in New York?

She sighed in relief. "So you'll be back when the season starts? You just needed some time away to look at art? I can respect that. Are you moving in with Cooter?"

Did she not know New York had hockey? She was never interested in the nuances of the sport. Though she'd come to games and cheer for me. They all had. Jacen loved watching hockey.

"How do you know I'm in New York looking at art?" I frowned.

"People take pictures of you and put them online. Who's the pink-haired girl with the nose ring? She's an art student? I was never artsy enough for you." There was a hint of jealousy in her voice.

Woah. I took a deep breath, suppressing a growl of annoyance.

"She's not a film student and I'm not seeing her. She's a hockey player, showing me around the city, and knows nothing about art," I explained. There were pictures of us online?

"You took her dancing." Morgan sounded like she was pouting. She loved dancing. Not to country music–formal dancing. I learned the dances because it made her happy.

I sighed. "Is there anything you need from me?"

"Come home?" The whine in her voice tugged at my alpha nature.

It was too late for that.

"Things can't go back to how they were. I'm sorry. There's nothing you, or anyone, can do to fix it. We're over and I'm moving on with my life." I ended the call, my shoulders slumping. I'd told her this many times, but this time it felt so final.

Yet it was. I was tired of her acting like I'd changed my mind if she nagged me enough. Taking my phone, I did something I should have done long ago, and I blocked her.

Taking a deep breath, I emailed my lawyer, just in case.

Emotion exploded in my chest. It wasn't sadness. It was relief.

I checked the time and closed my laptop. Yes, it was time to move on. First step, meeting some fellow Knights.

"Hey, Tens." Gwen grabbed my hand, dragging me into the large workout room at the training center, which reeked of sweaty alpha. She was wearing leggings and a sports bra, showing off her muscles—and her ribs.

Worry about her not eating enough to compensate for all the calories she burned tugged at me again. Nachos and hot dogs weren't a nutritious dinner. She probably wasn't cooking for herself either. Cooking for one was lonely.

Would it be strange to invite her over? I had no idea how to take care of her without making it weird. But I itched to.

"Hi, Firecracker." I sensed the room change as we entered. But I was a large alpha, who was often called *stoic* and not known to them.

"This is Carlos, and that's Dimitri," Gwen introduced. "This is my friend Tens. I first met Carlos when we played together in community college. Dimitri is back from vacation."

"Hey, man." A nice-looking Hispanic guy, a couple inches taller than Gwen, and a little younger than me, who was shirtless and holding a weight, waved with his free hand. Carlos Rodriguez was a forward, a left winger. He often acted as agitator, riling up the other team's players—and was good at it.

He was a kappa, which would make things interesting. I'd played with a kappa on the Sasquatches. Well, we'd thought Ellie was a kappa until she came out as a gamma in support of Grif Graf last season. She was still as chaotic as fuck, and I'd miss her.

Carlos looked me up and down. "Mariquita." He gave her a look. "You failed to say your friend Tens is the *Yeti.*"

A large Russian guy with piercing blue eyes and messy dark hair joined us. Also shirtless, he had a couple of tattoos. Arms crossed over his chest, the alpha blatantly sized me up, eyes squinting slightly. He was shorter than me by a few inches, but imposing.

Yes, Dimitri Belikov, alpha defender. I'd been trying to learn the roster, but I already knew of many of them from when the Sasquatches had played the Knights in the championship finals.

"Tenzin. Nice to meet you." I nodded.

"This is Tens. Nia's over there." Gwen waved to a muscular brown-skinned woman on the bike, her dark hair in Bantu knots.

"Hey, Tens." Her eyebrows rose as she waved. She was one of their forwards.

"Bozh'ya Korovka, you should return him to where you found him before the Sasquatches get mad. He's not a racoon in a bucket." Amusement tinged Dimitri's Russian accent, his face remaining in an almost-scowl.

"Raccoon in a bucket?" Yes, she was a firecracker, wasn't she?

"That was one time." Her eyes rolled.

"You came onto the ice with a cat in your shirt," Carlos teased.

"Don't forget the puppy," Nia said. "Seriously, she walked into the locker room holding a lost puppy. Pupper says hi by the way."

"Nia and her pack kept the puppy Gwen found when she couldn't find the owner," Carlos explained.

"It wasn't a cat. It was a baby *tiger* the zoo lost." Dimitri's arms remained crossed, looking like an unwelcoming wall, except for the slight fondness in his gaze. Like she was an annoying little sister he cared about.

Gwen huffed. "Looked like a kitten to me when I climbed up during a storm to get him out of the tree, and the zoo was happy I returned him. He's a *mini* tiger and I would have made a great tiger mom." She looked around. "Carlos, is Lucky around or is he still with Grif? I never thought to ask you earlier."

Lucky?

Carlos grinned. "Oh, I stole Lucky from the wedding. He's staying with me while they're traveling. Grif hasn't even noticed. Lucky likes to stay home and play with my nephews a lot. But I brought him today. Right now he's napping on the yoga ball."

"Oh, there he is. I'll pet him later. I could use some cat snuggles," she replied.

There was nothing on the yoga ball. My eyebrows rose. "Lucky is a pet?"

"Lucky is Grif Graf's imaginary cat," Dimitri replied.

What?

Gwen giggled. "It's sort of a joke. Just don't sit on him or feed him cheese and you're fine."

Well, then. Cooter and I did make up a wife.

"We're getting a Yeti." Dimitri's gaze focused on me again. "Vickers and Yeti. Good choices. We'll have powerful defenses."

I'd seen that in the sports news. The Knights had traded another one of their defenders for Shawn Vickers. I knew him a little. He'd played for the Sharks.

Nia looked over. "Oh, shit. Welcome."

"It's not common knowledge, but yes." It was a little strange and uncomfortable. Meeting new teammates always was.

Gwen shot Dimitri a smug look. "See, we get to keep him."

"Fine. Let's workout," Dimitri huffed in fond annoyance.

Yes, Gwen was the little sister of the team, clearly.

Dimitri was a quiet one, who mostly hummed under his breath absently. Carlos and Nia kept up a steady stream of chatter, giving us all the gossip. Like how a forward named Anders was trying to get to the Motor City Gears through that multi-team trade Cooter was talking about. Or how the Knights had a new assistant general manager. They speculated on Bunty retiring. I also heard recounts of everyone's vacations.

Gwen stayed quiet, other than to shrug and say she was teaching hockey camp most of the summer and hoped someone named Castle got moved up to the Knights from their farm team.

"Valya says she needs all of next weekend for shopping," Dimitri told Gwen.

Gwen laughed. "Yeah, no. Your sister gets Saturday morning. I'm working Saturday and Sunday night at the rink, Sunday I'm playing tennis with Carlos in the morning and in the afternoon I teach goalie lessons."

"I'm having a party next Saturday," Dimitri replied. He turned to me. "You should come."

"Thank you, but I have to go to Portland that weekend." Pity. I'd rather spend time with Gwen.

"I can try to trade some shifts around, so I can give her all of Saturday and come to the party. That's all I can do, other than if I cancel playing tennis." Gwen grinned at Carlos.

"You work too much," Dimitri replied, with the air of someone who'd never lived on instant noodles.

She did. Gwen wasn't working late tonight, so we were going to try another country bar on the list. I'd noticed that she was getting touch starved. Taking her dancing was a way to touch her without it being weird.

Gwen scowled. "I have bills to pay, Belikov."

"Why did you want to come to New York, Tens?" Carlos asked, changing the subject. "Or did you not have a choice?"

"I needed a change," I said honestly.

"From Portland? I mean, I love New York, but it's beautiful there." Nia looked skeptical.

Ugh. It was only a matter of time before the gossip hit. "I broke up with my girlfriend. It was bad. I was ready to go anywhere. She hates New York, which is a plus."

"Got it. Tens is a raccoon in a bucket." Carlos looked at me and nodded.

Gwen flipped him off. "It was *once*."

"I dub thee *bucket*." Carlos took a foam roller and waved it around like a sword.

Bucket?

We worked out a little longer, then Gwen got up to go to the bathroom. Dimitri looked at me and Carlos expectantly.

"How is she really?" Dimitri said gruffly.

Nia shook her head. "Poor Ladybug. She and Austin were together longer than I've been mated. Is that why she's going shopping with your sister, Dimitri? Distraction?"

"Austin destroyed her things. She doesn't like asking for help. Valya will make her get clothes. Because no one can say no to Valya." Dimitri nodded.

"That's an excellent plan," I told them.

"What happened to her forehead? That scar," Nia asked. She wasn't an alpha, but I couldn't remember what she was. Delta maybe? They had a lot of alpha characteristics.

"Austin. Asshole," Dimitri grunted.

Her look turned fierce. "Did you beat the shit out of him?"

"He disappeared before we—or the police—could get to him." Carlos scowled. "Don't worry, if we ever find him again, we'll take care of it."

Good. I'd be happy to help.

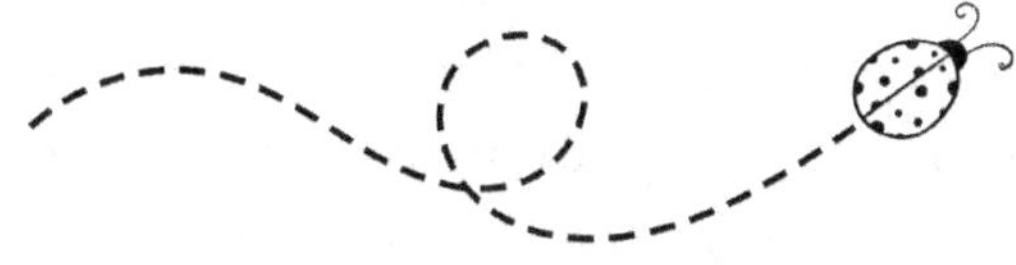

Chapter Fourteen

GWEN

S cratches woke me up. A rat maybe? Certainly it wasn't Lucky-the-imaginary-cat.

Rolling over, I turned on my phone light. It continued to move. But not fast. Getting up from my blanket bed, I looked over among the cardboard cutouts.

Staring at me was some sort of small, *beautiful,* black and orange lizard. He looked made of beads.

A quick photo search told me that he was *not* native to New York. I didn't know how he got here.

Getting a popcorn bucket from another closet, I made him a little home with a water dish and fed him a few tidbits the internet told me he'd eat.

"There you go. I'm going to call you, *Gary.*" After my favorite grandpa who'd passed away in a car accident along with my nonna and other grandparents. They were my mom's parents, and I'd loved them fiercely.

Using the computer and printer in the small conference room, I made a couple of flyers and put them up around the rink. If no one claimed him soon, I'd take him to the reptile people at the zoo when I went to visit Marty.

I was up and ready to go, despite the early hour. So, like I'd been doing, I grabbed some coffee and an apple, did the land drills my nonna's neighbor had taught me, then made my way to the ice.

Time to bring the sauce.

Finished with my workout, I laid down on the ice, reviewing the footage I'd taken of myself using a stand I'd found upstairs.

I got an alert from insta-chat, not from Clark the early bird, but *Mercy.* While she'd been posting pictures of her adventures abroad, I hadn't heard from her specifically.

"Oh my fuck, Gwenifer, are you fucking okay?" she drawled on the video she sent. Mercy wasn't a hockey player. She was a skate smasher and had lived in the south before being drafted by the Maimers.

Her brown hair was loose, something I didn't see much, since she wore her hair in Dutch braids constantly during the season.

"You've been listening to the sad girl playlist over and over and not the good one, the weird one. You don't respond to your messages on Musify. What. Is. Wrong?" she demanded.

For some reason, she called me *Gwenifer.* Which was pretty funny. I also didn't know you could message people on Musify, where I listened to the playlist. Sometimes she made me feel old, given she was barely eighteen.

If I had a younger sister, I'd want one just like her.

"How do you know I've been listening to it?" I insta-chatted her back. *The weird one?* I *loved* every song on there.

She answered immediately.

"I finally checked my metrics. I haven't been online much, because we've been traveling. Now what's going on?" Her tan face was full of worry.

I made another message. "I broke up with Austin." Absently, I rubbed my forehead. "It's been rough."

"I'm sorry. I know you loved him. If he broke up with you because he got signed, I'll take the ultra-bullet to Philly and kick his ass," she replied immediately. "Or hold him down while you beat the shit out of him."

I'd love to see that. Mercy was an alpha, but a baby alpha, only recently awakened and still learning to handle her alphaness. However, she was strong and muscular. Skate smashers were as athletic and fit as hockey players. She was also a crusher, which was the most violent of the three positions.

Yeah, she could probably hold her own against Austin. She knew all sorts of neat moves from her team and her sister's packmates. The skate smashers always let me join them in the weight room and sometimes taught me things.

Yeah, I'd like to punch my ex.

"I broke up with *him*." I gave her the short version.

"I've been a shitty friend and haven't been around. Promise I'll make it up to you when I get back," she told me.

"I'm happy you're seeing your family and having a great time." It would be nice to take off and see the siblings I liked. But that took money, and well, talking to them.

We chatted a little longer. I took off my goalie skates and put my hockey skates on. I'd been considering Tenzin's idea to put my silly routines on the internet. It would be fun. I had a few ideas.

My headphones had broken, so I'd been using a small speaker I'd borrowed from the little weight room. Positioning the stand and my phone, I did a couple of moves, figuring out how to stay in the frame.

Mask in hand, I did a few moves, including a layback spin, and a couple jumps, then ended with a sit spin.

Laying back down on the ice, I watched it, adding a couple of simple effects in the app. That sort of sucked, but it was a start. I sent it to Clark to get his opinion.

"Are you dead? Should I call Steve?" a sweet, female voice said.

"I'll get off. Whoops. I'm so sorry." I scrambled up from the ice. Steve? Who was Steve?

"You are one of Steve's, right? One of the goalie interns?" The small, red-headed omega in figure skates, a hoodie, and beanie stared at me with big green eyes.

Oh, that Steve. I never thought of Coach Atkins, the head coach for the Knights, as *Steve.* Sometimes we explained the goalie development program as *goalie interns.*

"Hi, Cait. Um, yes, please tell Coach Atkins I've been working so hard in the off-season that I'm dead." I grinned. Coach Atkins' omega was half of one of the most beloved figure skating pairs ever. She was very busy coaching skating, but sometimes she came to the Knights' games and sat in the family section.

Her head cocked. "Why were you figure skating with hockey equipment? I was spying. One of my pairs canceled, and I was bored."

"Being silly. It's just something I do for fun sometimes. My friend wants me to put them up online, so I was feeling out some stuff." I was a little embarrassed that she'd seen me do that.

"Go on then. I have time." She leaned against the glass and took a sip of her water bottle.

"Um, sure. I mean, yes, Coach." What else could I say?

I did the routine, then stopped and looked at her, nerves bouncing around. This had been choreographed haphazardly, and my technique was no longer perfect.

"You were one of Klavdiya's? Because, wow, those jumps." She eyed me and took another sip of water.

"Vail Russo," I told her a little too quickly. I'd hated skating for Klavdiya and it irked me that you could still see her in my technique.

"Oh. You're one of theirs? I didn't know they trained betas. Huh. I've never met you." She frowned.

"I stopped in high school. Anyway, I was always running off to play hockey with their mates." Those had been a good few years, living with my grandparents, playing hockey, training with Vail, and living my best life away from my dads.

When my mom got sick again, I came home. After she passed away, everything went to shit.

"Oh, right. They have two retired hockey players as mates." Cait nodded. "I forgot that. Why figure skate if you wanted to play hockey, or could you not decide?"

"My dads thought it would make me an omega if they forced me to learn all the things my omega sisters did. Didn't work." I grinned, but that grin hid pain. Because of their disappointment and their expectations; not to mention the expectations of others.

"Oh." Her face softened. "I had a student like that once. Watch your knees. Also, your prop is messing with your momentum on the turn. You might want to change the placement." She waved at the ice. "From the triple. No music."

Cait ran me through the routine over and over, critiquing my technique, fixing the choreography, and working my ass off. Sweat ran down my face and my calves burned.

Then we ran through another one of my potential routines. By then, Connor, the other half of her pair, who was also in Coach Atkins' pack, had joined her. Both of them were changing my choreography, and telling me to tuck my chin, extend my leg, and watch my elbows.

"Good job. You should put them up. Remember what I told you." Cait patted me on the shoulder.

"Yes, Coach." I wiped my face with the hem of my T-shirt. "Thanks for the lesson. I appreciate it."

I knew how much a session like that cost.

"Happy to help," Cait told me. "Please, let me know when you put up the videos, and I'll repost."

"Really? Thank you so much. Both of you."

"You're going to put it up? I'm proud of you." Tenzin stood there in his hockey skates. "Let me know when you want to film it."

How long had Tenzin been there? He was *proud* of me? Aww. My whole body got warm and fuzzy.

"Thanks." I smiled at him. "I think I will."

Chapter Fifteen

TENZIN

"One... two... three." I snapped the picture on Gwen's phone, which was worse for wear.

"Thanks, Tens." She rolled out of the headstand.

We'd finished yoga in the park. It was a lot less intense than what I did with Cooter. Gwen put our mats in the basket and waved to the instructor, who taught at her university.

"Can we have coffee at the zoo?" She was on her phone posting the photo, a tote bag slung over her bare shoulder, as she shoved her feet into some slip-ons.

"Zoo? Okay. I haven't been there yet." I put on my shoes.

"You can meet my tiger." She took my hand and pulled me across the park.

Ah, yes, the tiger she'd found. I liked that she was becoming more comfortable with me. She gave me focus, which soothed some of those alpha instincts left raw by my ex.

"Is the zoo even open this early?" I asked as we approached the gates.

"With a pass like mine, yes. My treat. I get guests. The pass was my reward for returning Marty. It's a nice place to go when I need a moment." She scanned her phone on the turnstile.

We got coffee and muffins from a cart, and I followed her as she bounced about the zoo, giving me a mini tour. I loved how happy she looked.

Leaning against the rail of the tiger enclosure, we sipped our coffees as she named every one. Finally, she led me around to a viewing area with glass. There was a sign about mini tigers and how they didn't make good pets.

She crouched down and put a hand on the glass, making an odd little whistle. A moment later, a young tiger bounded over, trying to nuzzle and lick the glass. He was an interesting-looking tiger, with no black stripes, just white and orange.

"Hi, Marty." Gwen's entire face lit up. "Marty, this is Tens. Tens, this is Marty." Her shoulders fell. "I wish I could have kept him."

"It's nice to meet you, Marty," I said to the tiger, imagining her watching TV with him in her lap or taking him for morning runs.

Some kids came over and she taught them how to play with Marty through the glass. A zookeeper walked through the inside of the enclosure and waved at Gwen. A few moments later, the zookeeper disappeared, then joined us.

"Hi, Gwen. Are you doing okay today?" She was a middle-aged omega with blonde hair in a braid.

"Hi Trixie, I'm okay. Hey, this is my friend Tens. The one I was telling you about. Can we bring Marty out for a walk today, please?" Gwen batted her eyes.

"Sorry, Gwen. Not today." She gave her a fond look. "I can get you some playtime. Your friend will have to stay out here so Marty doesn't get territorial."

"Great. I'll meet you at the playroom." Gwen took my hand.

"De-scent yourself well," Trixie called.

"You get to play with the tiger?" one kid breathed.

"I've been trained to play with the mini tigers. I've known Marty since he was a baby." Gwen led me over to another viewing area. Instead of the enclosure, it was a little room with toys. "Sit here. I won't play long."

"It's fine. Take your time." I took a seat on the bench as she disappeared, leaving me with her tote bag.

A few moments later, she appeared through the glass, as did Trixie, who had Marty on a leash. I watched Gwen pet Marty, fed him treats, snuggled with him, and played games like he was a cat.

Trixie was right there with him, and the two of them were having a conversation. A bunch of children watched excitedly. I took some pictures and sent them to Cooter.

Me

She's certified to play with baby tigers.

Cooter

She would absolutely wrestle a bear.

Me

If she hasn't already.

"How much did you have to pay for her to have that experience?" an alpha dad asked me. "One of my kids loves anything dangerous. She was keeping a *possum* under her bed."

"Gwen had a racoon in a bucket." I chuckled, still unsure what the story was. "She rescued Marty when he was a baby, so she gets special privileges."

The alpha smiled and shook his head. "She rescued a tiger? Have fun with that."

I heard some noises, like something from her tote was rustling. Did I even want to know? My phone buzzed.

Eats

> **Back in town. Going to my sister's pack's farm later. Any interest?**

He added a link to a summer farm party. Oooh, live music, barbecue, beer, berry picking, hayrides, and dancing? Too bad she had to work tonight. Eats was the one person I knew in New York. While we weren't really close, we went way back.

Another zookeeper clipped the leash to Marty and took him away. A few moments later, she came back out with Trixie, smelling like a tiger.

"Thanks, Trixie. Oh, do you know anyone at the reptile house?" She asked, then gave her a hug.

"I do. Why?" Trixie eyed Gwen as she got a popcorn pail out of her tote.

It rustled again, and I saw a shadow.

"I found this little guy at the rink. I put up signs, but no one called me. Since he's illegal to keep as a pet in New York, I thought I'd bring him here." Gwen took the lid off the pail.

Inside was a small orange and black lizard that stuck out its tongue in an annoyed gesture.

"Gwen. You found him at the *rink?*" A fond, exasperated look crossed the omega's face.

"In a storeroom. I've only had him a couple of days while I looked for his owner. I've been feeding him like the internet said." She handed Trixie the pail.

Trixie got out her walkie talkie. "Taking ten and going to the reptile house."

"Um, why?" a voice echoed.

"Gwen found an endangered venomous lizard." Trixie shook her head.

Laughter echoed over the walkie. "See you when you get back."

"You found all the animals as a child, didn't you?" I said as we followed Trixie out of the tiger area.

Gwen nodded. "My nonna's wasn't quite a farm, but there was land, a pond, and lots of wildlife. Nonna was a vet and taught me so much about animals. She wouldn't let me keep the wolf cub after her leg healed though. We used to volunteer at an animal sanctuary my aunt runs, too." She sighed. "I miss having pets."

"One day," Trixie assured her. "Animals love you."

"Yeah." Her scent turned salty with sadness. "Does Cooter have a pet armadillo?"

"No, but Cooter's family has a horse ranch where he spends the off-season," I told her.

"That sounds fun. I never learned to ride a horse."

We entered a building that said *Reptile House.* My nose scrunched at the potent smells, my alpha nose overly sensitive sometimes. Trixie led us through a door that said *staff only.*

"Lan," she called. "I've got something for you."

A beta with a beard came out. "For me?"

Trixie showed him the lizard in the bucket. "Gwen found him at the ice rink. It's not ours, is it?"

He shook his head. "No. Let's check this little guy out. *You,* little lizard, should not be running wild at an *ice* rink."

"His name is Gary," Gwen replied.

Of course it was.

The beta inspected the lizard, giving him a thorough checkup. "He's in good health. I'm going to call around and see who might have lost him. This little guy is protected and probably belongs to someone. If they call you looking for him, have them call us. If they have a permit, it won't be a problem giving him back. Thanks, Gwen."

We left and walked around the zoo. She held my hand. "Um, someone wants to trade shifts with me and take mine tonight. Want to go dancing?"

I squeezed her hand. "Absolutely, Firecracker. Would you like to go on a little day trip? I have a vehicle now."

The pickup truck I'd leased was better suited to Portland than here. But I liked trucks. Sure, there was great transportation here, but having my own vehicle would be useful. Also, I should get her out of the city for a bit. It would be nice to see Eats.

"That sounds great. Should I change? Do I have time to shower and throw in some laundry?" she asked.

"Plenty. Do what you need. I'll work on finishing editing the video from yesterday, so you can put it up." Yesterday we'd filmed the first of her figure skating videos. "I'll pick you up?"

She nodded. "You can pick me up by the rink?"

"Sure." I lived by the rink, anyway. "Wear one of your sundresses?"

I had the shoes covered. This was going to be fun.

Chapter Sixteen

GWEN

The sweet-tartness of sun-ripened blackberries exploded over my tongue, and my eyes closed as I savored the taste of summer. My head lolled back. "Mmmm."

Tenzin had driven me to a farm to go *berry picking*. It was so delightfully wholesome. His friend's sister's pack owned this place, and we were meeting up with said friend.

Tenzin gave me some tan Cowboy boots, which I was wearing right now with the blue denim sundress I'd picked up at a vintage store after camp one day with Bonnie.

Around us, children ran and played.

Picking another off the vine, I turned. "Taste." Before he could do anything, I shoved the berry into his mouth. "So good, right?"

"Delicious." Tenzin smiled as he methodically put berries in the basket, getting the ones too high for me to reach.

After we finished, we explored the farm; him carrying the basket. There was a beautiful grove of apple trees, and I immediately scrambled up into the branches.

Everything looked better from a tree.

His phone rang, and he sighed. "I have to take it. It's my realtor."

"Okay. I'm going to hit the restroom." I climbed down, found the bathroom and re-fixed my hair. It was awkward, the roots and my undercut growing out, and it was damaged. I'd get it fixed when I went to the salon and shopping with Valya.

I had no idea where I'd put everything, and my coach at NYIT wanted me to get my hockey gear and new laptop. Would Clark let me keep stuff at his place? He hadn't mentioned me staying there since I'd been homeless.

It was hard to ask. Also, I didn't know when I'd be able to get everything. My financial prognosis wasn't looking good.

Realistically, I could work my ass off, and after I paid off tuition, I could move in with a bunch of my teammates. I'd have to live in the closet at the rink until tuition was paid off–and continue to work hard all school year to make rent. There'd be little left over to replace anything I lost or for fun.

Or I could live in a closet at the rink until graduation, work enough for essentials after I paid off tuition, and focus on hockey and classwork.

Realistically, that would be the best plan. The closet had no rent or utilities, warm showers, access to snacks, and free laundry.

Sure, when the season started, it might get a little harder to hide. But I had months to find a better spot. No fancy alumni donor had come through, and I got discouraged trying to call the student loan place and work through things.

So that's what I'd do, even if I really didn't enjoy living there. It's not like I could ask Clark to keep my ass for free for the *entire* school year.

And I still wasn't desperate enough to ask my family for help. Nope, nope.

When I came out of the bathroom, I didn't see Tens. I hopped on some hay bales, both because it was fun, and to see if I could spy a giant alpha in Cowboy boots and jeans.

"Gwenifer!" someone bellowed.

I turned and saw Mercy Thorne running toward me.

"You're back!" I couldn't help but grin.

"Briefly. My sister's pack is dragging me to their cabin and I have to go to Rockland and see my other sister and then I'm going to alpha camp. I thought the off-season was going to be restful. But I miss my family."

Mercy's long brown hair was loose, under a straw Cowboy hat. She had on shorts, a tank-top, and canvas slip-ons.

"You should see your family," I told her. Also, alpha camp was exactly as it sounded, a place where young alphas went to learn shit and network. My brothers had all gone to very fancy alpha camps.

I could see the skate smash skate tattoo on her ankle. She'd gotten it when she'd awakened as an alpha. We'd gone together, and she'd gotten me a little ladybug tattoo on my ankle, which had been one of the sweetest things anyone had ever done for me.

She'd also had a *tattoo artist* at her excellent eighteenth party and I'd gotten a tattoo of a hockey stick on my other ankle.

"How the fuck are you doing?" Mercy eyed me.

"I'm okay."

"I'll kick his ass if you want me to." She slung an arm around me. "Have you seen the mini cows? Who are you here with?"

"Mini cows?" I perked. "Oooh, I want to see. I'm here with my friend Tens. But I lost him. Why are you here?"

"This is AJ's sister's farm." Mercy kicked a rock, and it skittered across the dirt path.

I'd met him several times. He was in finance and interesting to talk to. Mercy lived with her older sister Verity and her pack—several of which played for the Knights.

We entered the petting zoo. Mercy waved at someone, and before I knew it, I was on a hay bale, with a rabbit on my lap, while petting a mini cow, wearing a bro-tank. Ahhh, much better. I snapped a picture of me and the cow and sent it to Tenzin so he knew where I was.

The fur of the rabbit was so soft. "Hey, so Tens and I made this video for my new fancy professional social media channel. Can you tell me if it's any good?"

I was second guessing myself, mostly because of the raw emotion in my skating. It was like I was doing the routine naked and posting it would be akin to laying myself bare for all the world to see.

"Um, fuck yeah." Her eyes sparkled. She was great at going viral. She looked at it. "Shitballs, this is fucking cool. While I knew you could skate, I had no idea you could skate like *that*," Mercy breathed as she watched the video of me skating.

I looked at Mercy. "So you like? I should post?"

"Yes. You should do more. You could totally take skate smash dances and do them with a hockey stick." Mercy nodded, still petting Clara the mini cow.

"Absolutely," I replied. "Thanks."

"Of course, that's what friends do. I'll be gone more, but I'm here if you need me. Also, I know how to get rid of bodies," Mercy added.

I laughed, because I could see that. Southern girls were built differently.

"What do you need?" she added, as we took pictures of us with Clara, the mini cow. "Are you waitressing somewhere else? You know I'm a good tipper."

That she was.

"I'm worried about tuition. I'm just working at the rink right now, but maybe I should get another waitressing job." I told her what Austin did. "I didn't even know you could reverse bank charges like that."

Her spiced plum scent grew spicier with anger. "That asshole. Maybe your department has ideas? Do you have any research Compass BioTek would want? I have an in and they pay people for that."

"Not that sort of mathematician," I laughed. Three of her siblings did stuff for them.

A shadow fell over us.

"Ladybug!" Dean grinned, green eyes sparkling. He was well over six feet and positively *giant* for an omega. His strawberry-blond hair had grown long in the off-season, and he had a scruffy goatee instead of being clean-shaven. He was a goalie for the Knights.

"Hey, Double D. Hi, Team Mom." I grinned back.

Verity, also known as *Team Mom* by the skate smashers, was with him. She was around the rink *a lot,* because she had to be Mercy's responsible adult before Mercy had turned eighteen.

She was striking, with long, thick dark hair, golden skin, and blue-green eyes, and leaned on her pink forearm crutch. Verity was tall, even for an alpha female, and willowy.

"I'm excited to be included in the goalie dance for JP's wedding," I added to Dean. I'd been learning it from the videos.

"It's going to be so much fun," Dean agreed.

"Are you and JP recovered enough to do that choreography?" I frowned. Both of them had been nursing injuries during the playoffs. A couple of times they had to bring up a goalie from their farm team to help.

Dean nodded. "We'll be good to go."

"How are you going to get your hair done at spa day with Valya? New status, new hair." Mercy was friends with Dimitri's sister, too.

"I was thinking of cutting it shorter since it's so damaged. Maybe dark purple? I never did a breakup post. Maybe I'll just post an *after* of my *single girl glow-up* and leave it like that." I'd been deleting the more couple-y pics of us off of my social media.

Five years was a lot.

"Great idea. I might join you for shopping. Nothing fits right," Mercy told me.

In these past few months Mercy had gotten *tall* and broad, hitting that last growth spurt now that she'd come fully into her designation as an alpha.

"Oh, hey, Ladybug." Jonas appeared. "Dark purple would be nice. So would a dark blue. Like ink. Sorry about the breakup." The alpha's eyes fell on my forehead. "That asshole didn't deserve you. Are you here alone?"

He was a little taller than Dean, and broader. The Asian defender had lots of piercings and tattoos, also *blue* hair. Jonas was in a pack with Dean and Verity.

I shook my head, seeing the text that Tenzin had found his friend and was on his way. "I'm here with my friend, Tens."

Jonas smirked, absently petting Clara the cow. "Oh, right. Your new racoon in a bucket."

"Who has a racoon in a bucket?" Griffin 'Grif Graf' McGraff joined them. He had red hair and a bushy beard. The star forward was bigger and taller than everyone else, standing six-foot-six.

He'd also pretended to be a beta until last year, when he'd been outed as an omega. While there were a couple of omega goalies, there hadn't been omega forwards in the PHL—especially an enforcer like Grif. Technically, Anders was the enforcer now.

"Ladybug," Jonas replied.

"Congrats on the wedding. The pictures were beautiful," I told Grif and Verity.

Grif and Verity had met on an airplane like they were in a rom-com. Verity had marrïed Grif in a field of omega lilies on a Greek island this summer, so she could have the fantasy wedding of her dreams, followed by a huge-ass bonding party to celebrate their pack.

My phone buzzed with a message.

Unknown

You found my lizard? I saw your posters.

Me

I did! I couldn't take care of him any longer, so I brought him to the reptile house at the zoo at the park. Call them and they'll give him back.

Unknown

Thank you. He's a slippery one.

Oh good, the owner had seen my signs.

"Grif, do you know Carlos has had Lucky since the wedding?" I asked. Grif had come to the Knights with his imaginary cat, but Carlos stole him an awful lot—and liked to blame things on him. Like farts.

Grif chucked. "Absolutely. I get pictures and videos."

Nothing like getting a picture of an imaginary cat riding a mechanical bull—or getting a lap dance.

"Should we get some ice cream? It's so hot." Verity fanned herself with a manicured hand.

"Sounds good to me." Ice cream made everything better.

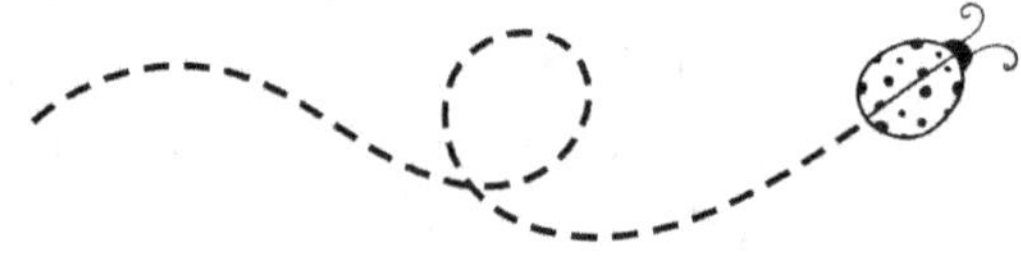

Chapter Seventeen

TENZIN

I finished up the call and put the berries in my truck. My realtor had needed to go over a few things, which was a relief. I'd been afraid that Morgan and Jacen were making trouble.

"There you are," AJ, or *Eats,* as I'd called him when we were younger, stood there in the parking lot, wearing khakis, a polo, and loafers, with a fancy watch on his wrist. He was an alpha, athletic, with dark hair, a goatee, brown eyes, and golden skin. AJ had been a pro hockey player but had to retire after a career-ending injury and now worked at a prestigious finance firm.

"I hope you don't mind, but I brought a friend. We went berry picking." Which had been fun. Gwen sent me another picture of her with a little cow and I let her know I was on the way.

"Do I get to meet your med student?" he asked as we walked back toward the farm and festivities.

A pang struck my heart. It had been a while since we'd caught up.

"We broke up, which was why I moved to the Knights." I sighed, giving him the short version of my breakup as we walked through the little farm.

"Sorry to hear that. The Knights are decent people. Well, the three in my pack are," he told me.

"Where do you need to be? My friend is at the petting zoo," I told him.

"My pack, too. Stupid mini cows. Seriously, they might be adorable, but they're not smart and always get stuck." He laughed.

We grabbed some beers and got caught up. The petting zoo was a fenced-in area full of hay bales and small animals. Gwen sat at the far end feeding a tiny cow ice cream.

She looked up at me and beamed. "Hi, Tens. Team Mom got me ice cream."

"Hi Gwen." I realized she wasn't alone. There was a stocky teenager and a lithe, dark-haired woman I didn't know with her, as well as three large hockey players I recognized.

AJ started laughing. "Your friend is Gwen. Why does that not surprise me? Tens, this is my pack—my mates Verity and Grif, my packmates Jonas and Dean, and Verity's little sister Mercy. Everyone, this is my friend Tens. I've known him since he was in high school."

Oh. Of course, Gwen would know them if they were Knights. "Gwen, this is my friend, Eats. I see you've met his pack."

She beamed at me. "I might know these people. This is my friend Tens."

"Is this Bucket?" Dean Donovon's face broke out into a giant grin.

While I didn't know the omega goalie well, he was well-liked and respected. He was the shortest of the four guys.

"Yes. I don't have to give him back. I get to keep him." She looked smug.

Bucket was sticking, wasn't it? It wasn't like I had much of a choice. Also, my alpha liked her saying she was keeping me.

Gwen had gone back to talking to Mercy.

"Do I ever get to hear the racoon in a bucket story?" I was quite curious.

"There's not much to it. One night, when she was working late at Tito's, she took out the trash, caught a little raccoon in a bucket, brought it inside, and wanted to keep it. We weren't there, but Dimitri and Carlos were," Dean replied.

"How do you two know each other? *Eats?*" Grif asked.

I turned to AJ. "As in, *AJ eats everything*. Eats, you never told them about the summer you ran away to be a Cowboy?"

It had been quite a sight, this rich kid from New York City trying to make it in rodeo. The circuit he followed mimicked the fair circuit my sister's band was doing. Since it was summer, I was dragged along from fair to fair. Endless fair food and rides wasn't the worst way to spend a summer. AJ and I had become friends and stayed in loose touch.

"You a Cowboy? That's an incredibly sexy thought." Verity put an arm around him.

AJ laughed. "Tens, have you told them about all the summers you spent in a dinosaur costume, shooting T-shirts from a cannon, with your sister's band?"

"I know about it, but I haven't seen pictures." Gwen looked up from her phone.

"That sounds epic. Rodeo? You were a clown?" Mercy added.

"Bullfighter. Then I broke my collarbone, got yelled at by my agent, hockey coach, and dad, and never went back. Tens and I still keep in touch," AJ replied.

"So this is your pack. Congrats." My heart squeezed, but I'd get one, eventually. I was twenty-seven and not getting any younger.

I'd watched as many of my teammates had packed up and started families.

Gwen pet the tiny cow, giving it a fond look. "Tens, I want one."

"Of course you do," I replied, coming closer. "Where would you keep her?"

"At your place?" Her face perked up.

I shook my head. "It's a no pets building."

"Boo. I'm telling Cooter's wife on you." She made a face. Gwen opened insta-chat on her phone and made a video of her and the cow. "Cooter, Tens won't let me get one. They're so cute. Please tell your wife on him for me. Thank you."

She sent the video and shot me a smug look. Cooter added her on insta-chat?

AJ's eyebrows rose. "Cooter? Like the goalie for the Sasquatches?"

"He has a *wife*?" Dean blinked.

"It's a joke. Not sure I should have introduced Gwen and Cooter. I feel like it will end with the two of them in a pickup truck, with some strippers and baby goats in the back, going ninety through a cornfield at two in the morning, while the police chase them." I laughed. Mercy and Gwen had their heads together again as they looked at their phones.

"That is an oddly specific story," Verity replied, giving AJ a look.

"Yeah, that's not how the story went." AJ laughed.

"Well, that's about how it would go with them. I met her tiger today." I chuckled.

Grif laughed. "We've all met Marty."

"Oooh, he replied." Gwen beamed at me.

"It's not going to be the answer you like," I warned. Cooter *hated* cows.

"No can do, Babybug," Cooter drawled in his thick Appalachian accent. "If the wife knew about these tiny cows, she'd want one. Then I'd have a house cow sleeping in my bed. I hate cows. They're hell spawn." He shuddered. "I'm glad you're at a farm. It's good for you. Be good now."

"Unfair. I'm telling Clark on the both of you." Gwen's face fell, and she pouted. She made another video with the cow. "Clark, I'm at a farm and I want a mini cow. Tens won't let me have one. Can I have one? Please?"

Gwen pouted again and sent the video, then shot me another one of those adorable expectant looks that made me want to give her everything.

"Would you like to go on a hayride?" I offered. "I also found axe throwing. We could do that after, then eat? The music should start by then. Unless you're hungry now?"

"Sounds good." Gwen hopped up and looked at me like I hung the moon.

"Ooh, I want to go on a hayride." Mercy hopped up off a hay bale too.

We found the hayride and our group loaded up on the trailer with hay bales.

"Clark replied." Gwen leaned up against me. She played the video. A nice-looking man about her age, wearing a straw hat, appeared on screen.

"I hope you're having fun at the farm." He beamed. "You can absolutely have a mini cow. But, you have to keep it at my parents' place and my baby sister will adopt it. Miss you!"

"Now we're in for it. Clark just told her she could have a cow." Dean chuckled. "Have you met Clark yet?"

"Not yet. Carlos, Dimitri, and Nia, though." I realized two things. Clark had a giant crush on Gwen, and she had no idea.

I'd also seen Clark bare-ass naked. More than once.

We were sponsored by the same boxer company and had done a calendar shoot together last year. It was about time to do it again, too.

The hayride took us around the farm. Gwen continued to lean against me, probably not even knowing what she was doing.

Our group got off the hayride and walked to the axe throwing booth.

Getting our axes and a quick safety lesson, we headed over to the area. I helped Gwen with her grip when it was her turn. "Focus," I told her.

She got it right in the middle and did a little dance. "I did it."

"Yes, you did. Feel better?" I couldn't help but grin.

She smiled. "Thanks. So much better."

"Let's get food and find a table." Gwen took off running.

Mercy, the brunette teenager, gave me an expectant look. "You hurt her and I will break your stick. Understood?"

Without waiting for me to answer, she ran off to join Gwen.

Well, then.

"Be gentle with Ladybug?" Dean turned to me.

AJ's eyebrows rose. "The *Yeti* is literally letting her drag him around the city, eating muffins. How much gentler can he be?"

"Gwen has been very kind to me, introducing me to my new city. It's an excellent distraction for us both." My voice lowered. "Her ex crushed her in so many ways. I enjoy seeing her happy."

Mercy and Gwen were now talking to some little girls that looked a bit like AJ.

We got our barbecue and sat down, the music already in full swing. Mostly it was young couples and packs with small children. More than one parent danced with a child and little kids twirled around on the dance floor together to the lively tunes. People also danced with each other, and my heart twisted seeing such deep love on display.

Gwen squinted at her barbeque brisket, ribs, and corn. "I thought we were having burgers."

"Try it," I told her. "It's pretty good, too."

"As good as Cooter's?" Gwen asked, picking up a rib.

I laughed. "If it was, I'd *never* tell."

By the way Gwen devoured everything, I think she liked it.

"Hold up. Your nose must have been hungry." Taking my thumb, I brushed the sauce off of her nose.

The music changed and Gwen beamed. "Dance with me, Big Guy."

"Absolutely." I let her drag me onto the floor and I twirled her around.

The music changed to a line dance I'd taught her, and we did it together, her confidence shining, as she kicked up her cute little boots, and laughed. Mercy, Verity, AJ, and Dean joined us on the floor.

We danced and danced until sweat drenched us, and I was a little out of breath. "Do you want something to drink?"

"Beer me, please," she said and nodded.

"Nice moves, Bucket." Mercy nodded. She turned to Gwen. "My other big sister knows all sorts of obscure line dances. Let me teach you this one she showed me when we were in Greece. I still wish you would have come with us."

Her look went wistful. "Me, too."

I got us each a beer and came back to the table. Mercy, Gwen, and Verity were doing some dance I'd never seen before.

"You still have your moves," I said to AJ, as I took a pull of my beer.

"So do you. Has she met your sister yet?" AJ asked.

I shook my head. "Not yet. But I think Zaya will like her."

"She's kind and works her ass off. Zaya will appreciate it. We're heading out to our cabin, but I'm here if you need me," AJ told me.

"Thanks." I sighed. "I'm hoping I made the right choice by leaving Portland. They twisted me up so badly there's no way I could stay."

"Everyone's going to think you're after a championship," he told me.

"There are worse reasons to change teams."

AJ's eyes focused on the three ladies as they kicked and turned. "True. I've never seen her look so happy."

"Gwen is fun to be around. It's comfortable, like I've known her for years instead of weeks. She's so different from Morgan, too." I got out my phone and snapped a few more pictures of her, as if by doing so I could save some of her joy for later.

"Both are driven women who know what they want, and are determined to get it, but..." I shook my head. "It's not their age difference. Maybe the way they approach the world? Gwen is cautious until she isn't. That's when she really shines."

We talked some more, enjoying the night as it cooled off and the stars came out.

"Your sister's farm is nice. This was a good choice," I told AJ. This was exactly what I needed–a little slice of comfort. Some farm animals, good food and music, and beer with decent company.

I'd absolutely do this again.

Gwen came back off the floor. Her hair was stuck to her shiny face. She grabbed her beer and drained the entire thing.

"That was refreshing. Thanks." She held out her hand. "Can we get some apple cider donuts, then dance some more?"

"We can do whatever you want, Firecracker," I told her. "We've got all night."

Chapter Eighteen

CLARK

"What do you think of this for your cow's house?" I swiped the screen of my tablet, brought up a sketch I'd made and sent it to Gwen on insta-chat. It was a tiny pink cow complete with flower boxes.

It wouldn't take that much time to build and the materials would be easy enough to get. I had a two-year degree in architecture and had been looking to transfer to a state university, but instead got signed by the Knights.

Mostly, I wanted to build better barns, plan efficient farming communities, and keep small farms alive and well.

"I think it should be pinker." Gwen looked like she might be on the ice. It seemed like she often went there at night after she got off work and I worried about her getting back to her place alone so late.

I made a few changes to my sketch as I sat at the kitchen table and sent it back. "Better?"

The kitchen was one of my favorite places to be, reminding me of years of doing homework, working on projects, and playing board games. It wasn't a modern fancy kitchen. But it was home and literally filled with generations of memories.

We didn't have an actual working farm anymore, just the orchards, animals, a large garden, and the tractor and small engine repair businesses.

Our family didn't have a lot, but we usually had enough. Not to mention, I was determined to do everything I could to make everyone's lives easier.

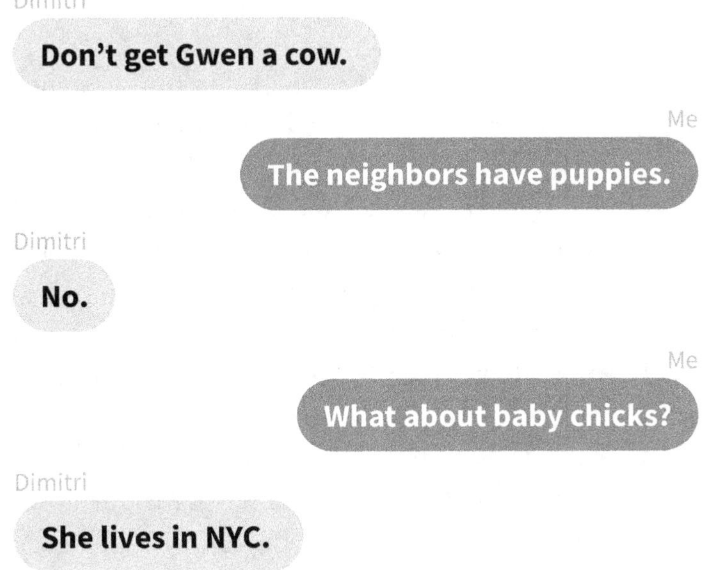

I sent him a picture of some baby bunnies my sister's friend's rabbit had.

Dimitri

Then get her a stuffie.

I sent him an annoyed picture of me.

"What are you doing in here?" One of my moms, Ma, came into the kitchen.

I had three dads, two moms, and six siblings. I was the second oldest. My grandparents lived in a house across the way with my aunts and their two kids. My uncle and his pack and kids lived in a house on the far side of the property.

"Insta-chatting Gwen and texting Dimitri." I studied the sketch. It needed something. Maybe a tiny hayloft?

Currently, the living room was full of siblings and parents watching extreme boxing.

Ma opened the wooden cupboard. "I don't understand how sending each other short videos can be a conversation. Just call her."

"Call her?" I laughed as I added the hayloft to the design. "Our conversations can go on for days like this. If we get busy, you don't need to hang up, you just answer whenever."

An alert showed me that Gwen had replied.

"Much better." Gwen twirled around on the ice, making the camera spin.

I sent Gwen the new sketch. "Wait, there's more."

"Okay. Still building the mini cow barn?" Ma got down the popcorn popper.

Mmmm. There was nothing quite like fresh popped popcorn. We always grew some gourmet popping corn and dried it for the year.

"I like that. It needs a flower box!" Gwen laughed again.

I loved her laugh and how free she looked when laughing.

"I'm going to finish practicing. Chat you later," she added.

I turned to Ma. "I was thinking of putting it back by the chicken coop."

Ma was a beta, brown-haired and stocky, from generations of beta farmers that had settled here long ago, looking for the freedom and independence they didn't have in their home countries because of their designation. This was her family's farm that they'd had for a long time. She was a social worker and worked mostly with teenagers.

She gave me a look as she filled the air popper up with popcorn. "You're actually building a barn here and getting her a mini cow? I thought you were joking."

"I mean, if she wants me to, I will." It wouldn't come to that much and I could handle the upkeep costs, so it wouldn't be a burden. I'd bribe my littlest sister to handle the chores. "It makes her happy. Look at the cow-house I designed, Ma."

"It's very cute, Sweetie. You did a great job." She admired the sketch. "It makes her happy *talking* about it. But would a mini cow she'll never see truly make her happy? The girl needs so many other things more. Didn't she lose everything in the breakup *and* is going into her last year of university?"

I nodded. "Dimitri's getting her some clothes this weekend."

My mom gave me a bone-chilling mom-stare. "She's only now getting clothes? Hasn't it been a month?"

"I got her some stuff before I left. When we were at that used bookstore, I found beautiful versions of her favorite series that he ruined." I'd give them to her when I saw her next.

"While sweet, she can't wear books."

I frowned. "She wears mostly workout clothes, and her university hoodie, and her work uniform. She got some sundresses and someone got her Cowboy boots. I mean, if she needed things sooner, she'd ask one of us, right?"

All those pictures of Gwen from the farm were too cute. Her picking berries. In a tree. On a hayride. Throwing axes.

"Would she now?" My mom made an annoyed noise as she melted the butter, the *pop pop* of the kernels filling the air.

My frown deepened. "Why wouldn't she ask? We're friends."

"Not everyone grows up in a home where it's okay to ask to have their needs met." She grabbed the salt as the plastic popcorn bowl continued to fill with white fluffy kernels.

"Ma, she's not one of your teenagers." The words troubled me. She *would* tell me if she needed something, right? Gwen seemed to be doing okay.

"She could be. Something about her cries *former runaway*. Look, maybe she's doing great, but perhaps she doesn't know how to ask you, or understand that you mean it. She's a beta girl, and sometimes they have trouble advocating for themselves, not wanting to bother people with their needs–*especially* alphas."

Ma tossed the popcorn with the melted butter and salt.

"Oh. I... I never thought about it that way." Because Gwen seemed to be fearless. Still, I'd seen other sides of her. The Gwen that kept her head down to not 'annoy' the players that weren't goalies. The Gwen that made herself small in Austin's shadow. The Gwen who stuffed food in her pockets when she thought no one was looking.

"You can't assume someone will always tell you what they need. That doesn't mean you need to guess either. As an alpha, it's your job to ask, offer, watch, and most importantly, make sure those you care about feel *safe* asking for your help. And that they know it's genuine and you'll follow through. You care about her, right? I've only met her a few times, but she seems like a sweet girl."

Ma put the salt away, then came over and stroked my hair, like I was still a boy.

"Of course I care about her. I... I had no idea. What did I miss?" The idea that she might not feel safe asking for my help hurt my heart. From the moment I met her, I cared about her so fucking much.

Last summer, the EBUGs were helping at developmental camp. I was a scared farm kid who'd just been signed, hoping I didn't screw up my big chance at being a pro hockey player. She was this teasing pink ray of sunshine. There was something about her that called to me, made me want to be her friend.

Okay, there was something about her that made me want to be *much* more than friends. Back then, she'd been very taken.

Ma hugged me. "Hey, you'll figure it out, Sweetie. Make sure you *follow through*. Let her know she can trust you. Things are still rough for her, so be a good friend, check in with her, and make sure she gets what she needs. It's probably not a cow."

"What about a kitten from under the barn?" My pre-teen sister, Tess, bounded into the kitchen. Her hair was in two long braids, her nose full of freckles.

"Ooh, I should bring Gwen a kitten. That's exactly what she needs. She was so upset when she had to give the kitten she found in a tree back to the zoo, since it was really a tiger. She's been feeling alone, and a kitten will help with that." It also wasn't any of the ideas Dimitri had shot down. I stood and turned to my sister. "Are they weaned? Help me pick out a kitten for Gwen?"

Ma put her head in her hands. "I'm pretty sure Gwen doesn't need a kitten right now."

"You sound like Dimitri. Think of how happy she'd be if I showed up with one." All I wanted was to make her happy. To see her smile. To have her eyes light up with unbridled joy.

"Come on, let's go eat this popcorn while it's hot." Ma's look and tone were no nonsense.

"Yes, Ma." I could always sneak a look at the kittens later.

Chapter Nineteen

Gwen

"That's it, like that," I coached one of my tiny goalies. This week had been exhausting, because I was with the littlest of our hockey campers, mostly four and five-year-olds.

"Mariquita!" Carlos called from the stands nearest our group.

We were working in small groups on different parts of the ice. Bonnie had her group skating through cones, which were nearly as funny as my babies in full goalie gear.

"Why did he call you ladybug in Spanish?" one of my little goalies asked, as I kept running them through the drills.

"Ladybug is one of my nicknames," I explained.

Carlos came onto the ice with his stick and skated over to us. "Can I join in?"

My campers all stared at him, slack-jawed. Oh, he had no idea what he'd done.

"You're Little Brother Carlito," one of them breathed, like Carlos was one of the most famous people in the world.

Another turned to me, eyes big. "Little Brother is going to play hockey with us?"

"Yes. And if you can show me that you can be good listeners, we'll all play *Puck, Puck, Goose* together after we finish," I told them. That game was a favorite and made a great reward.

"Ladybug." Clark picked me up and spun me around.

"Clark!" I hugged him tight.

"I watch Monstruo Lane all the time," another said, as they crowded around Carlos.

"I thought you weren't coming back until Sunday?" I laughed as Clark put me down. It was nice to see him. Tenzin had left for Portland yesterday, then was going fishing with Cooter. I'd gotten some texts, but it wasn't the same.

"My agent wanted to have lunch with me today. I'm doing another calendar shoot, which is exciting, since we already shot a TV ad campaign and some billboards." He gave me a boyish grin, a sports strap attached to his black nerdy glasses. When he played games, he usually wore contacts.

"That's great," I told him. "Want to visit Marty with me tomorrow morning?"

"I'd love that," he beamed. Marty adored him.

One kid started singing Little Brother Carlito's signature song, which was a song in Spanish about cookies.

"I didn't realize you had tinys this week." Carlos got down on their level and sang with them.

Carlos was a semi-regular character in an educational bi-lingual children's show. He played the younger brother of a blue monster named Anita, who was his actual older sister, wearing a fuzzy blue suit.

The show filmed during the summer, so there wasn't any conflict with hockey. Carlos didn't wear a furry costume, he was just himself, because families came in all flavors. For some reason, he wasn't often recognized in the hockey world, except by his tiniest fans and their parents–though the cookie song played when he scored a goal.

The two of them helped me run drills. Then each of my baby goalies got to work on blocking them, hitting the gentlest shots ever from Clark and Carlos. We finished up with *Puck, Puck, Goose.* When we finished, Carlos and Clark helped me send them all off.

"Dimitri's waiting for us upstairs," Carlos told us, checking his phone, when the last one had been picked up.

"Go on up, let me clean up and clock out and I'll join you," I said to the guys.

Bonnie and I helped the other counselors clear the ice of cones, nets, and other training gear.

"We're meeting up tonight at Marabou Mike's, *come,*" Bonnie said as we finished putting everything away.

"Possibly. I might bring tagalongs," I replied. The guys would want dinner at some point. Marabou Mike's was cheaper than Tito's and had a better happy hour.

"Please, bring Little Brother Carlito." Bonnie laughed. "I had no idea Carlos Rodriguez, the forward, played that character."

"Most people don't." I grinned.

I went upstairs to the team area, excited to catch up with Clark. Maybe I'd ask him if I could keep some things at his place. I'd gotten another message from my coach at NYIT that my laptop and hockey things were in her office and I needed to get them.

Maybe I'd find the confidence to ask Clark if I could stay the rest of the summer. I mean, I could be house-sitting? That was a thing people did.

"Ladybug, hi." Constantine, the assistant GM, came around the corner. "Just the person I wanted to see. Come." He ushered me into the dining room, which was empty.

"Um, is everything okay?" My belly tightened. I hoped they weren't getting rid of the EBUG program or decided I couldn't stay for a third year.

"Thank you for finding my lizard. I didn't secure the lid to his tank, and he escaped while I was off," Constantine told me.

"Oh, Gary's yours." Relief sluiced over me. "Hopefully, I didn't get you in trouble by turning him into the zoo. I couldn't take care of him any longer."

"I have a permit for him. His name's Maddox, and you can visit him any time in my office. The reptile keeper spoke highly of you." Constantine smiled.

Our new assistant GM had a permit for a rare poisonous pet? Amazing.

"Wait, you have a poisonous lizard named *Maddox?* Like in Doom Squad?" They were the arch nemeses of the Defender League.

"Indeed. Listen, Gwen. You... you can't sleep here. It's not safe." His voice got soft, his scent filling with concern. "I know you're feeling very unsafe after your breakup. I'm so happy the Knights make you feel secure. But if legal found out you were living here..."

Fear shot through me. My knees trembled. "Please, don't fire me."

Caught. I thought my hiding place was good. While I couldn't be fired for just any reason, this was possibly violating the honor code or something.

"What? No. Of course not. Devon will be back on Monday and I'm sure he can help you find a place with good security. Does one of your friends live in a secure building? I know you're trying to not bring trouble to their doorstep, and a hotel probably doesn't have enough security to make you feel safe, but you can't stay in the closet."

His brow stayed furrowed with concern.

Yeah, I couldn't afford any place Devon would find me, or a hotel. Did Constantine think I was an actual paid member of the team? It wouldn't be the first time. Usually they thought I worked in social media or was Ice Crew. At least Constantine figured I was staying at the rink, because it was secure and not because I was broke.

"Ladybug, why are you staying in a closet?" Clark asked.

I turned around and saw his puzzled and concerned face. My eyes welled up with tears. "I can explain."

"Oh, hi. We haven't met yet. I'm Constantine, the new assistant GM," Constantine greeted.

"Clark. Forward. Hey, it's okay, Gweny. I'm here. We'll get it all sorted, okay?" Clark wrapped an arm around me, enveloping me with his hay and sunshine scent.

"Can I speak with her?" Constantine asked.

Clark frowned. "Of course. I'll be right outside."

"Are you okay with him? I don't know who might be friends with your ex or who you feel safe with other than the Yeti?" Constantine asked me, eyeing the now empty doorway.

"Clark's safe. Thank you so much for checking." That extra bit of concern warmed me.

"Don't worry, you're not in trouble. I want you to be safe. You just have to be safe somewhere else. If you need me to call hotels for you, let me know," he told me.

"Thanks. I... I'll talk to Clark first. I appreciate it." It seemed like Constantine was sincere. Also, he had a point about legal. I hadn't considered that. They were scary.

Constantine left. I took a deep breath, my belly in knots, and walked into the hall where Clark leaned against the wall on his phone, a worried look on his face.

"Clark, can I stay in your guest room, maybe house sit for the rest of the off-season?" I blurted. "To be honest, I can't pay rent and I don't know when I'll move out, even after classes start, because things are fucked right now. But the closet is uncomfortable and, well, I can't stay there anymore, and it doesn't have room for my things, anyway."

I braced myself for him to be mad or to say no, but I had to lay it all out there.

"Of course you can stay in my guest room. House sitting would be great. I don't need you to pay rent or anything. You don't need to worry about it. Stay as long as you need, even after the season starts." He pulled me to him and I rested my head on his shoulder, which felt so natural.

"What if I need you to keep my broke ass all school year for free?" I couldn't look up at him. I was asking a lot.

But I needed it so badly. If he'd actually let me stay there, I had a huge chance of figuring out paying off tuition, and still being able to not have to overwork myself when classes started.

"Then I keep your broke ass all school year," he soothed. "I pay for a second bedroom regardless of whether anyone lives in it. Right now, the whole place is sitting empty. It might as well get used. I'm *so* proud of you for asking me, Gweny, and I'm sorry if you didn't feel comfortable asking me sooner. When I offered it to you before, I meant it. I should've followed up. I was going to check in with you while I was here and see what you needed."

Wow. I'd never heard an alpha speak like that before.

"I don't really need a mini cow." I looked up at him. The way he was holding me was comfortable. The thing I missed most about being in a relationship was cuddles.

"I know. It's been fun designing a cow-house though. I wanted to bring you a kitten, but Ma wouldn't let me." He grinned, revealing a dimple.

"Your cow-house is amazing. I feel you could sell those plans on the internet or something. Does your building allow cats?" I laughed. "I'd love a kitten. A *real* one."

"They're real." He gave me a dopey grin. "We don't have to tell. Come on, let's get your stuff moved into my place. Are we telling Carlos and Dimitri about all this?"

"I... I don't know." I didn't want anyone to be mad or disappointed. "You're going to let me move in. Just like that?"

"Yes. We've been friends for a year, and I trust you. You need help, and I want to help you, and I meant it when I offered." He gave me an earnest expression.

I looked away. "I... I don't want to be a bother."

While I didn't really know him to take people home, I didn't want to get in his way.

"Why would you be?" He gave me an earnest, puzzled look. "You're not a bother, Gwen. Your needs are valid."

They were? Tears pricked my eyes.

"Hey, I've got you." Clark pulled me to him as I cried all over his T-shirt.

My needs were valid. Shit.

"We'll get you all set up in your new room tonight. Tomorrow, you'll go shopping with Valya and get your new hair. On Sunday we'll go to Swoop and you can fill a cart with whatever you need. If you feel bad about it, I can give you a time limit and you can race through the store like you're on a game show."

He stroked my hair as he continued to hold me.

"Oh, I can? I always wanted to be on that show when I was a kid. Thank you for being kind." I sniffed. There was so much to love about Clark and I was happy he was in my life.

"Me, too. I'm not good at guessing, and I don't always remember to ask, so please tell me if you need help, Gweny." His scent grew concerned.

"It's hard." I gulped. "But I'll try."

"Good girl." He beamed.

Him calling me a *good girl* did something to me.

Dimitri joined us, frowning. "What's wrong?"

"Things aren't going as planned. She's going to stay with me for a while. Also, she's been storing her things in closets here, but has to move them out. I'm going to help her with that now. Maybe we can meet up at Tito's for dinner?" Clark gave me a look that clearly said, *I hope that's okay.*

"Good. You'll be safer at Clark's." Dimitri gave a nod of approval.

"I was going to meet some friends at Marabou Mike's later. They're all collegiate hockey players. Want to come?" I offered. "I haven't been to Tito's since I got fired."

My old boss had left me a couple of messages asking me to fill in out of desperation. I hadn't answered. He couldn't fire me for not coming on the day I'd specifically taken off, then turn around and ask me to help out. I felt bad for my co-workers, though.

"That sounds fun," Clark said.

"Need help?" Dimitri offered.

"We'll let you know if we do," Clark told him. "Come on, let's get everything gathered. and I'll get us a car. I took the subway here, not my bike."

I took him into the storeroom where I'd been sleeping. "Thanks for covering for me."

"I appreciate you trusting me." He looked around. "Oh, Ladybug. This can't be comfortable."

Something about his sad puppy look cut deeper than any alpha growl ever could. I hated disappointing him like that and I crumpled inside.

"It's not. So many times when I texted you late at night, I was trying to bring myself to ask if I could stay with you. But it's such a big ask." I hiccupped as I gathered my things.

Clark stacked cushions and folded blankets. "You'll be much more comfortable with me. Tell me what's going on? Did the place with your friends not work out?"

The entire story tumbled out, like Austin's bank reversing the charges and how I'd tried and failed to figure out a way to fix it, to my tireless calculations and my grand plan to live here until graduation. It was such a relief to tell someone. It had been weighing so heavily on my soul.

"I can't believe that knothead did that," he told me, his scent turning spicy with anger. "You literally supported him for years and the one year he was supposed to support you, he broke his word."

"He sure knew how to make it hurt." I sniffed, as I gave the closet a once over, moving a few things, so it was like I never lived here, other than my scent. I'd grab some de-scenter from the cleaning closet and give it a spray. Okay, I should wash the blankets too. But I'd do that later.

"Pity you don't have your deal in writing," he added.

"Oh, I do. I'm an accounting major. I document the shit out of everything. Even if we could find him, I'm not sure I want to go after him. I'm done with all that." I sighed.

"We'll get this figured out. I want you to be safe. I want you to not be stressed out, so you can focus on classes and hockey," he told me. "This is your year, and it's going to be great."

"I appreciate your confidence in me." Having a place to live would be a tremendous relief.

We got the rest of my stuff and lugged it out to the street and into a waiting car.

"I have to say, the idea of living in the closet is brilliant. Free utilities and laundry, good security, and access to the kitchen," he told me as the car drove away from the training center.

"It was. Pity I was foiled." Worry that I'd get in trouble nagged at me, but I'd like to think I could trust Constantine.

"Question. Austin was supposed to pay your tuition this year. How did you do it last year? Life-changing tip? Big win at the casino? Sold a kidney? An extra scholarship?" Clark asked.

"When I was at community college, I had a few other scholarships, the kind that aren't tied to your school. Those all had dried up by the time I transferred to NYIT." There'd been some rough semesters.

I winced. "I have some aid from NYIT, but it doesn't cover everything. So, I sold my signed Maria Barilla rookie card. I've sold most of my collection over the years. That one hurt the most, because the card meant so much to me. It was also worth a lot."

She'd given it to me herself.

"Gweny." His hand went to his heart. "I'm so sorry. I know how much you admire her. Do you want me to get you one?"

"No, you goofball." I play-shoved him. "I want you to keep my ass and take me to Swoop and let me race down the aisles."

That was going to be fun. Swoop was one of those discount stores where you could get pretty much everything you needed in one *swoop*.

"Okay." He nodded.

We arrived at his building and went up to his floor.

Clark's place was immaculate and smelled a little stale. The living room was the focal point with a giant alpha-sized couch, a video game chair, a coffee table, and a big TV. The dining room table was small and glass. It was a good-sized two-bedroom apartment.

"There's my room." He pointed to a door that was cracked open. "Here's yours."

The room was set up like a basic, pleasant guest room, with a comfortable-looking bed, a dresser, a desk, and an *incredible* view of the city. There were also a bunch of weights, some resistance bands on the chair.

"I'll move my stuff. We can go to Home Things, too. Tonight, tomorrow, Sunday, whenever. Then you can choose sheets, towels and pillows, all that. We'll either order a car or borrow Dimitri's." He put my bags on the chair.

"Clark. Thank you. Thank you so fucking much." I set the box on the desk and wrapped my arms around him. It was a lot. Oh, maybe Home Things had a coupon.

"You're so fucking welcome, Ladybug." He squeezed me tight. "That's what friends are for. Also, I found beautiful editions of the Intrepid Space Explorer Series for you. They won't replace the ones he ruined, but they're nice."

"You did? Thank you." I brightened. He remembered? Those books had meant a lot to me in my teenage years and one of the few things I'd brought with me when my name had been changed and I'd been hidden. They were my comfort books.

"What's in the box? Not trying to pry, but it's pretty." He eyed the carved wooden box I'd put on the desk. It was a decent size; a little larger than a box of skates.

"Something I found after you helped me clean everything up. I figured Austin took it out of spite." Which was weird. Wrecking everything in here would hurt me a lot.

Not as much as losing my only picture of my mom though.

I opened the metal latches on the box my host dad in Rockland had made me when I graduated high school.

"It's my hockey box. Here's my ring I got for winning the NYIT championship this year." I handed him the little velvet box. Because of NACA rules, they weren't very expensive. The golden ring sparkled with maroon and gold stones–the Kings' colors and had our logo and the year. My name and position was inscribed on the inside.

"That is so cool," Clark said. "I have one from my community college division win."

"Me, too." We'd won our respective community college divisions the same year. I handed him that box, too. That ring was much nicer. My community college wasn't under NACA rules. The alumni association had gone wild, springing for nice rings and an amazing party.

"I wonder what the Knights' championship rings will look like," he added. Since the Knights had won the PHL championship they'd get rings when the team had a dinner for them in the fall, when the team officially got the championship cup for the year.

Though the cup had been taking turns with the members of the team. Carlos had posted pictures of Lucky in it when it was his turn. Clark had taken it for a ride on a tractor.

"I have my jerseys from both those wins, too," I added. Signed by the team. I brought those out, along with my other team jerseys, most signed, from high school, junior hockey, and the youth international team I'd played on one summer.

There was also the shirt I'd gotten the time I'd attended a developmental camp for the Mexico City Tigres–and one from a high school camp the Rockland Daredevils ran. I also had some signed pucks; including a couple from before I'd been Gwen that I couldn't bear to leave behind.

"Is this Callahan?" He held up a signed Knights puck.

I nodded. He was almost as good as Maria Barilla and had been a Knight, too. "My nonna and her neighbors brought me to games sometimes."

"I'm so happy your ex didn't ruin your special mementos. We could always display things if you want." He looked at the bare walls.

Display things? Was I staying? Though I wouldn't be mad if he kept my broke ass all year.

"Why don't I help you put everything away before we go eat?" he offered.

"Thank you. I have the best friends."

For that, I was grateful.

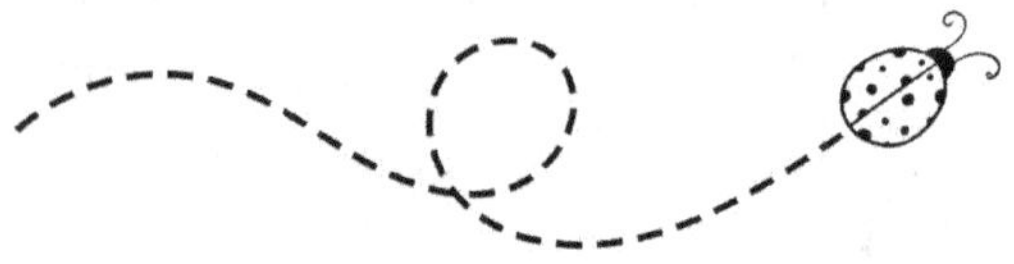

Chapter Twenty

GWEN

I smoothed my hands over the lavender beaded dress, which had a high slit, a low back, and vintage feel, as I swished back and forth, getting a look at myself in the full-length mirror. Yeah, I looked cute.

My hair caught my eye. The stylist had given me a chin-length fluffy cut, which had been dyed amethyst purple, and a little layered to help my undercut grow out. I wasn't sure if it was the retro way she'd styled it, or how they'd waxed my eyebrows and done my makeup, but I looked a lot like my nonna when she was young.

I wasn't sure how that made me feel. Part of me still feared being noticed. Still, I wasn't going to make it as a hockey player if I didn't put myself out there. I had to step into the light and hope my dads didn't notice me, until I was too big to mess with.

Of course, I was flattering myself. The dads probably knew exactly where I was. Hopefully, they'd continue to leave me alone so I could live my life. I texted Clark a picture.

Me

What do you think? A possibility for the wedding?

Clark

The dress matches your hair. I like it.

I also sent one to Tenzin, since I missed him. He and Cooter were catching salmon or something.

Tenzin

Very nice.

"Gwen, are you coming out?" Valya called from the other side of the dressing room door.

I came out of the dressing room, into the private lounge area of the *very* fancy shopping boutique that Valya had brought me to. It was the kind where you lounged on chaises and drank champagne while eating cookies as the assistants brought things for you to try on. My mother and sisters loved places like this. I wasn't into the fuss. But the person who worked here was Valya's friend.

"I don't know what you think I do all day, but I don't need clothes like this." I laughed, as I showed her the sparkly purple gown which had a high slit and a low back. "All I do is go to work, class, and hockey practice. Don't need an evening gown for any of those."

Valya wore a flowing red dress that made her look like an omega from a fairytale, with her pale skin, red lips, petite and delicate frame, and her long, dark, straight hair. She attended Posey Academy, which had once been Miss Posey's School for Elite Omegas.

Where my mother had gone.

"You could wear evening gowns to those things, depending on what you're trying to accomplish," the sales omega, who's name was Jolette, said. She attended the same omega school Valya did and sang in the choir with her.

I started laughing. "Could you imagine the coaches' faces?"

Valya took a sip of champagne. She looked me up and down. "You need nice things, for JP's wedding, to meet agents and sponsors, and to go to parties, so you can meet new and better alphas. You don't want to date a hockey player; they are big dumb-dumbs."

Mercy, who'd shown up right after we'd arrived, laughed. "They are big dumb-dumbs. But as someone who lives with my sister's four big dumb-dumbs, I can see the appeal. I don't think I want to date a professional athlete, though. Their schedules are too demanding."

Skate smasher schedules were as busy as hockey players.

"Are you still planning on moving out now that you're eighteen?" I asked.

It was a pretty dress. I could wear it to the fancy party the Knights hosted to raise money for their youth hockey program.

"I don't know." Mercy frowned. "It's not awful living in a giant penthouse with my sister and her dudes for free. I think I'll stay there and save up, so I can buy a cute townhouse and restore it."

"That seems like a good idea. I mean, free rent? That's a gift." One I was grateful for. Last night, after we'd all had dinner at Marabou Mike's, we'd hung out at Clark's and played video games. This morning, Clark *made me breakfast.*

Yeah, I could make living in Clark's guest room work. Also, I was fairly certain Tenzin lived across the hall. That would be a nice bonus.

"Here, try on these." Valya piled some things into my arms.

I went into the dressing room, took off the dress and tried on another. "Question. What would I have to talk about if I dated someone who didn't play hockey?"

"Common interests and hobbies, world events?" Jolette offered from the other side of the door.

"Which would be hockey, activities hockey players enjoy, and what is going on around the world in hockey?" I replied as I shimmied into a pale blue dress.

Okay, I suppose I could date someone in the financial sector who enjoyed watching market news and listening to forensic accounting podcasts. They'd have to at least like *watching* hockey and maybe play in a finance bro rec league.

"Or just keep them pretty, silent, and good in bed." Valya laughed.

I chuckled, taking off the dress, because it didn't look right, and put on another. This one was strapless, dark blue, and hugged my hips, then flowed down. Wow, I looked like an old-fashioned movie star. I took another pic and sent it to both Tenzin and Clark.

Me

Would this be too fancy?

Clark

I'm not the person to ask. But I think you look beautiful.

Me

Awww, thanks.

He did? My heart fluttered a little at that.

Tenzin

You look lovely. It's so elegant.

Cooter votes for that one.

"What about Clark? He's good looking and really nice," Mercy called through the door.

I came out in the dark blue, flowing gown. "Clark?"

"Clark is a puppy. An energetic, happy puppy." Valya now wore a *stunning* navy dress.

"He has that golden retriever energy–very refreshing in an alpha." I twirled. "But I'm not interested in dating anyone right now." It would be easy to fall for Clark. His cheerfulness, kindness, and all-around good energy, made him beyond loveable. He was fun to do things with. We had a lot in common.

Also, he said I looked *pretty*.

I could fall for Tenzin, too.

"That dress does incredible things for your boobs. That's for JP's wedding?" Mercy wore a sparkly pantsuit.

I looked down at the bright blue dress. "I like how it makes me look like some retro bombshell. Isn't it too fancy? The purple one is nice, too."

"Not too fancy. This one for the wedding, purple for the party the night before. Your snowman–if you want a hockey player, that's who you should be with. Stoic, but considerate. Handsome, but kind. Rich, but thoughtful and supportive." Valya handed me some suits. "You could have Clark, too. Different people fill different needs. Maybe add Carlos, have an entire pack."

"I thought you said hockey players were big dumb-dumbs." I laughed.

"They are. *Smelly* dumb-dumbs. But if it works for you..." She held out her manicured hands in an empty gesture.

"Absolutely not interested in dating Carlos." While he was a dear friend, he was a trainwreck in the relationship department. "Also, I'm a beta. We don't get packs. We're part of packs."

But the idea of Clark *and* Tenzin? Or rather me between them? So sexy. I might not be ready to date, but a girl could dream.

Especially since my bathroom at Clark's had a *bathtub*. I hadn't had one of those in years.

I'd fall for them.

Fall into their beds.

"No negative talk. If you want, go for it. Everyone else can fuck themselves." Valya gave me a no-nonsense look. She was two years younger than me and six inches shorter. But she took absolutely no shit.

In New York, a pack had to have four members. Austin had wanted a pack and omega, so that was the future I'd seen for myself. But a throuple with two alphas? I could be persuaded.

Eventually.

"No Dimitri?" Mercy asked.

Valya shook her head. "He's the biggest of dumb-dumbs. I think there might be someone. But I don't know who."

"Huh. I... I'm curious about what it would be like to have a pack." My cheeks warmed, and I ducked my head as I headed back into the dressing room to put on this new pile.

While Austin satisfied me in bed, there were things I'd wanted to try that he wasn't interested in. I'd always wondered when we formed a pack if one or two of them might also be my lovers or mates beside Austin.

"Did you not have that lesson in school? My other big sister's mate is an advocate for the Omega Center, and he has access to every educational video ever made," Mercy said.

"She's talking about fucking." Valya laughed.

"I... I've never really dated anyone other than Austin. I'm not sure how dating multiple people or forming a pack would go." Looking at myself in the mirror, I grimaced. Ugh, I looked like I worked for my dads.

Hard nope. I couldn't get the suit off fast enough, and I put on another.

Ooh, this could work. I pulled on the jacket. Oooh, I looked like a powerful, sexy bitch in this feminine navy pantsuit.

"You look fucking hot in that," Mercy appraised when I came out. "You'll need a couple of suits and nice things. That's one thing I didn't truly understand when I got drafted. Fortunately, I have a Verity to dress me."

"She's always so put together. Valya, I'd much rather have regular clothes than evening gowns. I don't have any jeans, or skirts, or cute dresses, nice tops, dressy pants, or even pjs," I admitted.

"We'll make you so cute. Some of the outfits you still need for the wedding will work for less formal occasions, too. Let me make you a rack of casual outfits, and I'll be right back," Jolette told me.

I looked at Valya. "We can always go someplace else for regular clothes."

"Try. It's fun." Valya handed me more things.

I continued to try everything on, sending pictures to Clark and Tenzin, drinking more champagne, and eating all the cookies. The school outfits Jolette put together were super cute. It was like a whole different person looked back at me in the mirror. She was fierce, confident, and poised.

We helped Valya decide on dresses for the wedding and a couple of outfits for her choir's trip to Europe, and Mercy found some things for the upcoming season. The Maimers tended to wear flashier outfits to their games than hockey players. The sparkly suit she wore a lot last year was one of my favorites.

Jolette brought us some cake and coffee. While I could use some coffee, since I was feeling *fantastic* from all that champagne, I'd like some actual food.

"Okay, Jolette, bring everything we liked back out, so I can make my final choices." While I didn't need all those outfits and dresses, I'd like a few. Not only did I need clothes, but I felt *good* in them.

"It's fine. We'll now go to Beautyland for makeup. Your clothes will be delivered to Clark's." Valya stood.

"You got me *all* the clothes? That's too much, Valya." I didn't want to take advantage of Dimitri's kindness, since he was the one paying for all these clothes, our spa day, and whatever else Valya had planned.

"You have new hair, time for a new style. It's no problem." Valya went to the restroom.

"Don't worry, I'll organize everything by outfit with a list so you know how it goes together. Have so much fun at the wedding and you're going to look great when classes start." Jolette took our empty cups.

The bottom fell out of my stomach. I turned to Mercy and lowered my voice. "Did Valya just buy me *all* those clothes? I thought I was going to pick. I think she may have dropped more than I owe in tuition."

That was so much money.

"Probably." Mercy nodded. "However, she wanted to buy you *clothes*, so she did. Now you have a fucking amazing wardrobe."

"You're right." I took a deep breath.

"Also, Jolette works on commission. I think this is a ploy to both get you clothes and make sure Jolette has money for the choir trip," Mercy told me.

"That makes sense. It's just a lot of money for me. There's still so much I need. Like sports bras and some normal non-cute outfits. I mean, I guess I could get some of it when I go run down the aisles at Swoop with Clark. But I don't like Swoop's sports bras and I'd rather get some of the other things I need. Same with running down the aisle at Home Things with Carlos. Not that they sell bras either."

"What?" Mercy's eyebrows rose as she stuffed the last bit of cake in her mouth.

"Clark said he'd take me to Swoop and I could fill up a cart and he'd time me. I'm so excited." I laughed, my head still a little spinny. "Carlos said he'd do the same for Home Things."

He'd also brought me my fixed goalie mask, which looked *amazing.*

"That sounds like so much fun," Mercy agreed. "Look, let Valya buy you whatever she wants, okay? What are you doing tomorrow? Athlete's World on 8th has the best ladies' department. It's where I buy most of my non-fancy clothes. I'll time you. We could turn it into a silly video. Say you won a bet and have you with a tiny basket trying to put large things in it."

The ridiculousness of it, combined with the sugar and champagne, had me giggling so hard I fell off the couch.

"You don't need to buy me things." I frowned, still sitting on the plush carpet.

Mercy rolled her eyes. "You know I'm a professional athlete, too? I also signed a new contract, since I'm eighteen now. I make a little more and even got a re-signing bonus. So, I can get you some sports bras and workout shorts. I want to help, too. You were fucking there for me when I got my alpha and freaked the fuck out. Let me be there for you?"

Her sister and her pack had been away, because someone had a breakthrough heat. Mercy didn't understand what was happening. Because hockey was full of alphas, I'd been around a whole lot of teenage alphas awakening and knew what to do and how to reassure her.

"It sounds fun." A trip to the clothing department at Athlete's World would round things out. I might be able to get a couple of cooler weather things, too. It wouldn't be summer forever.

"Also, you don't work at a place where I can massively tip you anymore, so we'll just pretend it's that," she added.

"True." My eyes teared a little. Mercy had left me a giant tip when I needed it, more than once. "Why is everyone so nice to me?"

"We're your friends, you ding-dong. Also, I know how it feels to lose all your shit." Mercy handed me my purse and the bag from the salon. She swayed a little.

Her and Verity's place had flooded right before the snowstorm where I'd found Marty. It had forced them to move in with Verity's guys, which then had been her boyfriends, not mates.

"Thank you." I leaned my head on her shoulder. I'd figure out tuition, eventually.

"Hey, where are you living now? Valya said your things are being delivered to Clark's?" Mercy asked, as she grabbed the bag with the outfits she'd bought.

Valya came out of the bathroom and grabbed her purse. "Onward."

"I'm staying in Clark's guest room for now. I'm not sure about fall. The dorms are full up and sort of expensive. I could move in with a bunch of friends, but I might stay at Clark's until he evicts me." I followed Valya into the main part of the boutique.

Jolette waved. "Thanks ladies. See you at choir practice, Valya."

"That would give you a chance to save up," Mercy said as we exited the store into the bright, hot early August afternoon.

"True." A deposit was a lot.

"It's good you're living with Clark. Carlos thought you were living in a closet at the ice rink." Valya laughed as she flagged down a taxi.

I laughed as we all piled into the taxi. "Could you imagine?"

Chapter Twenty-One

CLARK

European warehouse music thumped all around me as I made my way into the kitchen of Dimitri's townhouse. Models took turns lying on the granite counter and doing shots off of each other's bare stomachs. While a couple of rugby players played cards at the kitchen table.

I grabbed a beer and went back out to the living room, where beautiful people dressed in nice clothes, danced, drank, and talked. Carlos made out with someone on the couch. A group of omegas held court in the corner, talking about whose daddies had a bigger yacht. A business deal was going on in the hall.

Outside in their tiny garden, a few people played with a miniature fútbol, including some hockey players that lived in New York in the summer, and trained with Dimitri and Carlos.

Dimitri's house parties always brought out the young and rich of New York. You never knew who'd show up. I'd found one of my sponsors this way. One moment, I was talking to a woman who was trying to come up with ideas to impress her dad. The next moment, we were in the bathroom, shooting a mock-up of an ad campaign for cologne. Now I was on giant billboards.

Also, the thrill of running into random famous people hadn't worn off after a year in New York City. However, I didn't spy the person I wanted to see.

I saw Carson though, an asshat who played for the Mexico City Tigres. He was hitting on some cute omegas, along with Mitchy, who played defense for the Knights. Carson and Mitchy were local, but spent most of the off-season in Toronto training.

"Clark!" a male voice called.

I turned around and saw a grinning, giant Swede. "Anders, back in town?"

"For Squire Camp." Anders nodded. It was the summer camp run by the Knights' youth program.

We found a quiet place and got caught up, as he'd been back in Sweden with his family. Last year we'd been rookies together.

"Any word on that trade?" It seemed like every time I turned on the sports news, that multi-team trade Anders was part of had gotten even more complicated.

"No. I really want to go to Motor City, too. Not that I don't like the Knights, but..." He shrugged.

"I get it. We're supposed to get another forward in that trade, I think?" I wasn't sure. Winston Royce, one of our forwards, had retired, along with his mate, Elias, who played defense.

"I think so. For defense, the Knights are getting Vickers and–get this–the Yeti." Anders took a sip of beer. "They traded Crowley for Vickers. I think the Yeti is supposed to replace Elias."

"What?" A weird feeling fluttered through me. I had a low-key crush on the Sasquatches' giant defender. It had all started when we'd done a calendar shoot together last year.

Though Crowley was an asshole that we'd acquired last season when they'd traded a rookie defender that didn't fit. I was glad he was gone; he liked to hassle Gwen.

"Rumor has it that the Yeti's sick of coming in second with the Sasquatches and wants a title." Anders checked his phone. "It's a sound move, even if he doesn't seem like any fun."

"He doesn't need to be fun, just do his job. He's a very good defender." The Yeti? On the Knights?

Something about the giant, stoic guy did it for me.

Almost as much as a little pink-haired goalie. Well, purple-haired now, judging from the pictures she'd sent me.

Not sure I should be into either of them. There were no rules saying I couldn't date them, I only had to fill out a form with HR. Though they didn't like players dating the EBUGs. I was also getting ahead of myself. After all, Gwen had a broken heart.

I needed to get laid. The problem with going back home was that anyone I might want to hook up with had expectations. Not to mention everything that had happened with my high school girlfriend.

Also, I'd recently turned twenty-one, and was going into my second year of pro hockey. While I wanted a relationship and family one day, now wasn't the right time.

Unless Gwen wanted it.

I pushed that thought back. Gwen would start her hockey career next year, and she most likely wouldn't be a Knight. It could take years for us to get to the same team. Did she even like me?

Still...

"You okay, man?" Anders asked.

"I was wondering about those omegas. Some of them are hot, but I'm not sure I want to mess with academy omegas," I deflected.

They would be a good distraction, but I also didn't want to hurt Gwen... just in case she liked me back.

"Just fuck betas." Anders laughed. "Speaking of hot betas..." His eyes traveled over to the doorway.

Valya and Gwen walked in. Gwen looked smoking hot in some little dress, with her new dark purple hair hanging in her smokey eyes.

"Not sure you want to do that," I muttered. Gwen was talking to Valya and hadn't noticed me.

"Oh?" He grinned. "Go for it. She's single now."

"Gwen's more than a one-night stand." I kept staring at her, willing her to notice me.

"What if she *wants* a one-night stand? She had the same boyfriend for years. She's probably itching to see what's out there," Anders challenged.

Considering I heard her crying in the middle of the night, probably not.

Dimitri stormed through the room, half-dragging Carson, the player from the Tigres. "You're not allowed in my house, you," he called him something in Russian.

Oooh, someone was in trouble. One didn't mess with Valya's friends without facing Dimitri's wrath.

"Dimitri, it was all in good fun," Mitchy protested, trailing after.

"You can stay," Dimitri replied. "He goes."

"Look man, I'm teasing you. I'm not going to fuck Gwen. Yeah, I don't need JP and Double D trying to kick my ass for hitting on her. I just think she's hot." Anders shrugged. "Maybe I'll try those models in the kitchen. Wanna come?"

"Did you and your girlfriend break up again?" I asked. She lived in Sweden.

He nodded. "Yeah."

Mitchy came over to us, sighing. "Dimitri is such a buzzkill."

"I have sisters. I can understand. How's everything going?" I asked. Mitchy was also a forward and had gone to rookie camp with Anders and me. He'd gone down to the Bantams. They'd brought him up when Sarah got too pregnant to play last season.

"Tonight would be a lot better if I scored." Mitchy made a face.

Gwen waved and came over to us.

I waved back. She looked *great,* and her outfit and makeup brought out her hazel eyes.

"You're such a fucking puppy, man." Anders laughed.

"Wait, is that *Ladybug?* Fuck me. Did her boyfriend get a big signing bonus?" Mitchy took a swig of beer.

I shook my head. "They broke up. This is the single girl glow-up."

"Oh, that thing when girls cut their hair after a breakup. Sucks they broke up. She looks great though." He eyed her appreciatively, and I tried not to growl at him.

"Hey, Clark, hey, Mitchy." Gwen joined us with a beer in her hand. "Motor City? Why, Anders? Why? They're the douchiest club in the entire PHL. Captained by the douche brothers and coached by King Douche himself." She made a face.

The Motor City Gears were owned by the Deloitte family, which was hockey royalty. Grandpappy Deloitte also owned Deloitte Automotive. One of his sons was general manager, while the other son coached, and his daughter ran operations.

Two of his grandsons co-captained the Gears, another was on defense, and his granddaughter was goalie. Yeah, *four* members of their family played for the team. While other relatives worked in different parts of the team or played hockey for other clubs–or helped run the car company.

They were a family of assholes. The kind who threw big charity balls for the poor, while lobbying for laws that would let them get away with paying their factory workers less.

The Deloitte brothers also played dirty and were giant trash talkers. I'd nearly broken an arm getting slammed into the boards by them.

"I'm a douche. Figured I should go where I belong." Anders grinned. "Douche or no, Coach Deloitte was once one of the top forwards in the PHL himself. I could learn a lot."

Gwen made a face.

"Yeah, but we won a championship, something they didn't," Mitchy replied.

I didn't really get along with Mitchy. He was arrogant and flaunted his wealth and privilege.

"Ladybug, are you going to any team camps this summer? This is your last year at university, right? Someone's got to be watching you after that playoff game with the six overtimes?" Anders asked.

"Haven't been invited to anything in a while. I went to Mexico City a couple of years ago. They were helpful, but they need me to be five-foot-ten and that's not going to happen. They called me Pequeña the entire time." She shrugged. "I wouldn't mind playing for the Tigres. I'll play for anyone, really. Well, except for the Belugas."

"Don't you admire Molly almost as much as Maria Barilla?" I took another pull of my beer. The Belugas were a decent team. Gwen was talented if you could look past her height and designation.

"Oh, I do. But I'd never move to Vancouver. I have a fear of Canada." She laughed. "So much that I'm still nervous about going to JP's wedding."

Oh, right? She'd told me that one night when we were drunk. I think one of her asshole dads was Canadian.

"You're afraid of *Canada*?" Mitchy snorted.

Anders gave him a look. "I'm afraid of Finland."

I knew that story and it was a whole separate thing.

"It'll be fine. I got everything sorted out today for the wedding," I told her. Well, Dimitri had planned most of it.

Anders' eyebrows rose. "You're going to JP's wedding together?"

"We're traveling on the ultra-bullet as a group. You're welcome to come with us," Gwen replied, her fingers absently running the scar on her forehead, which was still a little visible, even with makeup.

"I have my plane ticket booked," Anders replied.

"I'm taking the ultra-bullet from Toronto," Mitchy added.

Anders stood. "I'm going to head to the kitchen to talk to those models. Want to come, Mitchy?"

"Don't have to ask me twice." Mitchy hopped up, and they left the room.

"Your new hair looks nice," I added. The dark purple suited her. Her nails had been done and her outfit showed off her toned legs.

Her hand went to it. "Thanks."

"Did you have fun shopping?" I loved how she sent me all the pictures. I was saving all of them. Hmmm, would it be weird to make the one of her in the blue dress the wallpaper on my phone?

She dropped into Anders' spot. "Next time Valya wants to go shopping, I'm saying *no.* I don't care how many things she wants to get me. After dinner, she dragged me to *three more stores.* I'm exhausted."

"Shopping is hard work. Going to the store with my sisters is a serious affair," I agreed. Of course, we were also pretty far from a mall or even a big shopping center.

"The single girl glow-up was fun, and I... I posted it." She ducked her head. "That's all I'm going to put up regarding the breakup. I just felt like I should do something."

"I'm proud of you. How do you feel?" I'd seen the picture.

"Better. Like I'm ready to move past all this." She nodded.

Happiness burst inside me. Not in the sense of her wanting to date or anything like that. More like being proud of her for being ready to explore what life was like without him.

"Dance with me." Gwen took my hand and dragged me into the living room.

The music thumped so hard I felt it in my soul, and Carlos was nowhere to be seen. Gwen's eyes went half-lidded as she jumped and twirled to the music. I bopped along; I was never sure how to dance to music like this.

"Here." One of Valya's friends handed us shots.

Gwen toasted me with her shot glass, then downed it, and I did the same. We continued to dance, and do shots, and everything got pleasantly warm and buzzy.

"Ooh, I love this song." Gwen got close to me. Her body touched mine. That fresh minty scent of her invaded my nostrils, even though the house was thick with so many smells and pheromones, as some sort of banger in *French* came on.

I put my hands on her hips, drawing her close. The song dropped so hard I felt it in my balls and my body took over.

A sultry look crossed her face as she leaned in and out with the beat, tantalizing me with her scent, her body. She licked her lower lip, an almost *hungry* look in her gaze, as she entwined her fingers with mine and twirled around.

The alpha in me wanted this to be an invitation to throw her over my shoulder, take her upstairs, and fuck her until she screamed my name.

Another part warned to not read into this. Gwen was letting off steam. She was also a little drunk. I was *safe*. She trusted me.

The song ended, and another came on, but Gwen stopped dancing. Instead, she leaned on my chest. "Fuck, I'm hot."

Don't I know it?

Her hand was still entwined with mine. She was sweaty, which enhanced the scent of her arousal. At least she wasn't leaning on my hard-on.

"We can go outside," I told her.

"You have such pretty eyes." She tipped her head up as she gazed at me.

Her lips were so close. It would be so easy to kiss her…

"Gwen, come. I have someone you need to meet." Valya took Gwen's free hand, pulling her from me. Shooting me a giant smirk, she and Gwen left the room, dancing.

"Oof, cockblocked." Some guy I didn't know laughed. The alpha was tall, broad, and had those rich boy good looks. By his hands, he hadn't done any hard work in his life.

"Probably for the better. She's a little drunk, and she's not someone to take advantage of," I replied, fanning myself.

"Who is she? That omega she's with is *smoking*." His eyes flickered to the doorway she and Valya had left through.

"Valya, the omega, is Dimitri's sister. This is Dimitri's house," I added, since sometimes people came with friends and had no idea. "He's a defender for the Knights. Gwen's basically the little sister to half the Knights. You hurt her, they'll end you, after she's kicked you in the nuts."

I didn't want Double D kicking my ass because I kissed Gwen while she was drunk. No, if I ever kissed her, I wanted it to be consensual—and I wanted her to remember it.

"Yeah, you don't want to touch Belikov's siblings unless you have a death wish. He's a fucking asshole," another well-dressed man added, handing his friend a drink. "Probably rip your arms off."

The first man laughed. "If Belikov's an asshole, why are we at his party, Holden?"

"He throws good parties." Holden held up his glass. He also looked like an entitled rich boy, from his expensive shoes to the fancy watch on his wrist.

Dimitri came into the room and glanced at us. Holden held up his glass and smirked.

"Get out of my house, Hardwick," Dimitri growled. "Get laid elsewhere."

"You're no fun, Belikov. I'm here with my friends, not to annoy you or get laid." Holden Hardwick rolled his eyes.

Dimitri growled again. "Out or face the consequences. I already threw out one person tonight. I'm not afraid to throw you out as well."

"Fine. No one fun is here tonight, anyway." With a roll of his eyes, he and his friend left the room.

"Um, what was that?" Gwen joined us.

"Curing sick kids doesn't make him better than everyone," Dimitri fumed. "Fucking asshole alpha."

"Hardwick? Like the department store?" I added.

"Yes." Dimitri followed them to make sure they left.

"Clark, I'm ready to head home when you are. If you're not, I'll go play video games until you're ready to go," Gwen told me, still a little tipsy.

"I'm ready, but I'll play Go-goKart with you." In the kitchen, I grabbed us some waters, before heading downstairs to the game room. The models were now playing a drinking game with the Rugby players. Anders and Mitchy were nowhere to be seen.

Gwen hooked her arm through mine. None of those models compared—and well, I was pretty sure no one but Gwen would do.

Chapter Twenty-Two

GWEN

"Hey, Ladybug." Rusty, who was captain of the Manhattan Maimers, waved as she and a few others left the small rink at the training center. Her hair was bright red, and she had a lot of elaborate plant tattoos.

"Hi, Rusty!" It was Sunday afternoon. I was tired and a little hungover from Dimitri's party, which had been *exactly* what I needed. Well, except for the part where I nearly kissed Clark.

Would it be that bad? I mean, Clark was sweet, cute, kind...

I shook it off. Yeah, it was just me wanting to be dicked down. I wasn't nearly ready to date again.

But I could date Clark so easily. Tenzin, too. Valya's words about dating them both came back to me.

Hmmm. We'd see.

My phone beeped, and I got yet another picture of Tenzin with a large fish in a cheesy pose.

Me

It's such a big fish!

Tenzin

You should see the one that got away.

This is Cooter. Mine is bigger.

Putting away my phone with a snort, I took to the ice and got warmed up. Clark, Carlos, and Dimitri would be here shortly.

While I hadn't played tennis today, I'd gone to Athlete World with Mercy and Home Things with Carlos, then taught my goalie lessons. Now I had a bit of a break, until I did the evening shift at the rink.

"Get off the ice, Wendel. We're using it." Windy came onto the ice, wearing a Knights' T-shirt–as were the handful of people with him.

Prospect development camp started officially tomorrow. It was where a team gathered all their draft picks, those from their farm team, and those they might be watching, especially internationally, for a week of on and off-ice training. Austin had been to the Ace's camp many times.

Everyone got in this morning, and they were doing health assessments and tours. Coach Kirov had invited me to the barbecue they were having tonight, but I had work.

"Fuck off, Windy." I rolled my eyes. Windy was in his last year at UNYC, one of Austin's besties, and a Knights' draft pick. The alpha was about the same height and build as Austin, but had dark hair and eyes.

He was also a colossal knotwaffle.

"No, you fuck off, Wendel. You're only allowed to use this rink when your betters let you, and I say that you need to leave." Windy tried to swat my legs with his stick. I caught his stick with mine and twisted, knocking it out of his hands.

"Your name is Wendel?" a guy drawled. He had a baby face and was probably one of this year's draft picks.

"It's Gwen. Is Marlin here?" I asked, looking for someone I knew.

Everyone wore matching black and silver shirts and shorts. They all had their sticks and skates, and minimal gear.

I was wearing leggings, with a sports bra, and a crop-top I'd gotten today at Athlete's World that said *Puck Off*. I'd gotten a bunch of cute tanks and crop-tops.

"Marlin got traded to the Tsunamis," someone I didn't know replied. The Tsunamis were Hawai'i's team.

"Oh, I wanted my cards read, but good for him," I replied. Marlin had been an EBUG with the Knights my first year here. When he'd met Austin, he'd thrown the entire contents of a salt shaker on him. I'd brushed it off as general goalie weirdness, but maybe he was on to something.

"Leave, Wendel." Windy got in my face, and pushed me hard. I tumbled backward.

"Is there a problem here?" Dimitri growled, coming onto the ice with Clark, Carlos, and Anders.

"Gwen. Are you okay? Fuck off, Windy." Clark helped me up off the ice, concern on his face and in his hay and sunshine scent.

Right, they knew each other from last year's developmental camp and prospect tournaments. Windy didn't like that Clark not only was signed, but got a spot on the Knights' roster–while he'd been sent back to UNYC with no contract.

"That wasn't very nice," Clark snapped as Dimitri shoved Windy.

"Well, if she'd leave when she was told, I wouldn't have to make her." Windy made a face, moving to shove Dimitri back, then thinking better of it.

"Who says you get to tell Ladybug when to leave?" Jonas stood there with Grif and Dean, who was eating a snow cone.

Windy took a step back. "Tony only lets her use the rink when the professionals aren't."

"If I ever hear you talk to *anyone* the way you talked to Gwen, I'll have you tossed out of here so fast your balls will spin. And," Jonas gave Windy a shove. "You hit anyone again, you'll answer to me. We don't tolerate abusive alphaholes here on the Knights. That goes for all of you. Want to be a douche? Go play for Motor City."

"Also, EBUGs are still goalies. You touch the goalie, you will get your ass beat," Dean replied, taking another lick of his snow cone.

"Sorry?" the one with the drawl said.

"Hey, Coach said we we're on Rink B." Shauna Castle joined us. She waved at me, Grif, Dean, and Jonas. "Oh, hey guys. Now I want a fucking snow cone, Double D."

"They're delicious, you should get one." Dean toasted her with the cone.

I loved Castle. She was a forward, and tall, blonde, and muscular. We'd played against each other a bit in junior hockey. Also, she was a Bantam and had filled in a few times last year. She was friends with Carlos and some of the Maimers and occasionally popped up at Dimitri's parties.

"Hey, Castle. Okay, Rink B, six on six. Now," Jonas growled.

"I'll ref," Dean offered. "I think we're crashing Ladybug's practice party."

He gave them what was probably meant to be a menacing grin. Dean was a big, himbo goofball even when his lips weren't blue with snow cone.

"Why are you hesitating? Move," Jonas growled.

The developmental camp players left, hurrying over to Rink B.

"You sure?" I asked Dean.

"I have a snow cone. We were here to be a menace, because Mercy needed to practice some jumps." He shrugged. "Also, you get a taco for every shot you block."

"I do? Do I have to eat them all at once? I can't out-eat Dimitri in a taco eating contest." I always came in second. Sometimes third, depending on who joined in at Taco Hut for dollar tacos.

"Nope," Dean replied.

"Sounds good. Please bribe me with tacos." I grabbed my gear.

As we walked over to the ice, Jonas assigned everyone else a spot, and Grif went to go get his and Jonas' sticks.

Clark was center, Carlos left wing, Grif Graf right. Jonas and Dimitri were defense. Anders was on reserve. I threw on some gear. When I joined them on the ice, Dean was standing there in the middle, with a *whistle* and his snow cone.

Coach Steve Atkins appeared along with some of the other campers, who, like the ones positioned on the other side of Rink B, all wore their matchy-matchy developmental camp outfits.

"Double D, am I interrupting something?" Coach gave Dean an amused look. Coach Atkins was a big guy, and older, with graying hair, but still fit. He was a bit of a legend, having won several championships and *the Olympics.* Which was also where he'd met most of his pack.

"One of your hoodlums likes to mouth off. So we're going to see if they play as good as they talk, Coach," Jonas replied, giving Windy a hard stare.

"I want to make substitutions." Windy looked over at the other players.

"No." Jonas shook his head.

Coach's eyes fell on me. "If Dean's ref, who's in the net?"

"Ladybug," Jonas replied.

I skated back and forth, getting the crease ready, since the ice looked freshly resurfaced.

It wasn't a bad lineup. Unfortunately, Windy was good. Better than Austin. Coach had everyone not playing take a seat. Dean announced the rules, then he blew his whistle and we were off.

Over and over, I ignored Windy and blocked his shots. One from Castle got through, but that was after Grif had scored twice on their goalie. As much as I hated letting pucks in, I remembered what my nonna's neighbor had told me.

It's okay if you let one in sometimes, the trick is to let in less than the other goalie.

There was a lot of sweat and determined faces because, unlike a normal game, there were no line changes. It didn't bother me. I was a goalie and we played the whole fucking game. My team was up three to one. I'd blocked five shots.

Dean blew the whistle. "Time."

Windy didn't stop, going right for me, knocking Dimitri over, then he hit a slap shot, low and hard, right at me. This particular version wasn't legal in the PHL, but was in collegiate hockey.

Windy and Austin liked it because it meant the goalie had to drop to stop it. One advantage of being shorter was that I didn't have as far to go. I caught the puck in my glove.

Mine.

Windy palmed my mask with enough force to make me fall backward.

Dean blew his whistle again. "Foul on team hoodlum."

"Back off, Windy, you don't touch the fucking goalie. I should beat your ass for that." Jonas smacked him upside the head, while Dimitri helped me up.

"Windy, bench. That was uncalled for," Coach Atkins yelled, coming onto the ice. "Jonas is right, that *will* start a brawl. I see you do shit like that again and you'll be doing sprints until you puke." He looked at me. "Are you okay, Ladybug?"

"I'm good, Coach." I nodded, and I patted the goalpost. *Good post.*

Coach looked at Jonas. "Play another round? I want to give a few others a chance."

"Sure, we were going to play two periods anyway." Jonas nodded.

"We'll do three. Make whatever line changes you need." Coach switched around some players.

"AJ, want to play?" Jonas called. AJ sat in the bleachers with Verity and Mercy. There were a lot of people watching.

"I need a stick," AJ called.

"Take mine." Clark skated over, giving AJ his.

While AJ had to retire from the Biscayne Bay Hurricanes because of a knee injury, he was still a *really* good player. He sometimes filled in on one of the all-finance bro recreational league teams that practiced here. Myra, their goalie, was insane on the ice.

"Anders, can you take left wing?" Jonas asked. He looked at Dimitri, "Good?"

"Good." Dimitri nodded.

Jonas looked at me. "Is Bucket here?"

"Portland. And I'm good." I grinned. "I have five tacos."

Dean blew the whistle, and we started again. By the time the third period finished, I was drenched in sweat and had fourteen tacos. I'd let in one more puck. We won seven to two.

Coach looked at me. "Good job, Ladybug. Someone's been working hard this summer."

"Thanks." Wow, he noticed? That made me happy, because I'd been working my tits off. I gave the goalpost another pat for being such a good post.

"Everyone on the ice for drills, let's go. Knights, you can stay, too, if you want," Coach yelled.

"I'm staying." Mercy was on the ice in a red crop-top, red knee-socks, and white cargo shorts.

"Mercy, you don't even play hockey." Coach gave her a puzzled look.

"I don't play professional hockey. I know how to play." Her eyes rolled. "Also, we're doing *drills*."

"Who's that hot brunette? Those legs. I think I've seen her somewhere. Dimitri's parties?" Castle said softly to me.

"Mercy Thorne. Crusher for the Maimers. Her sister's mated to Jonas, Dean, and Grif," I whispered back. "She's single. However, she only just turned eighteen, and also lives with her sister and said hockey players. So far not allowed at Dimitri's parties."

"Mmmm. Sounds fun." Castle nodded. "You were good out there."

Coach blew his whistle. "Less talking."

Castle waved and skated off.

"Come on, let's go do goalie shit." Dean grabbed my arm and dragged me off the ice.

I waved to Clark, who'd joined the rest of our friends with Coach and the summer crew.

We found ourselves back on the small rink. I drained my water bottle. "I'd hoped *goalie shit* meant making ice cream sundaes in the kitchen."

"We can do that, after. You did such a good job that you get a lesson from me." Dean grinned. "No, seriously, you did good. But I think I can help you be better. I've been training with fucking *Callahan* a little this summer at the rink by our cabin."

"Put me in, Coach." I'd take any help he wanted to give me.

Dean worked me hard until I play-collapsed onto the ice, letting it cool me down.

"You're a fucking weirdo." Dean laughed as I made ice angels.

"Says the goalie," I laughed back, taking his hand and letting him help me up.

We took off our skates and snuck upstairs to the empty dining room. Slipping into the kitchen, we found the ice cream, and made ourselves some sundaes.

"Do you have an agent?" Dean asked as we sat on the counter and ate ice cream out of little plastic hockey helmets, since we couldn't find any bowls.

"No. But I've been making inquiries and sending my videos. I know I should have one by now. My ex always said I didn't need one yet. When I did, I'd sign with his, and if people wanted to get a hold of me, they'd talk to my coach."

I let the sugary goodness explode over my tongue. The ice cream was probably for Squire camp, but there was plenty of it.

"Who are you looking at?" He took a bite.

I told him about the ones I'd followed up with, a couple that had replied, and a few I was interested in. So far no takers, a lot of, "*Your stats are great, please tell me you're still growing.*" Yeah, I was twenty-two and a female beta. Five-foot-eight was as good as it was going to get—and I was lucky to be this tall.

Dean got out his phone. "I'm sending you my agent's contact info. Tonight you're going to email him that you're in your third year of the Knights' goalie development program, you're in your last year at NYIT, you've won two championships, and drop my name. Then add your video and your stats. Thank him and that's it. No fluff, just the facts. Can you do that?"

"I... I can. Thank you." Wow. "You're repped by Stu Thomas at Venture. He's one of the top agents in hockey." I wasn't sure if I wanted an agent like that, because would he have time for me?

"He is, and let me tell you, he saved my ass. When I was outed as an omega back when I was with the Aces, my career wouldn't have survived like it did without him. Same with Grif, when he was outed last year. Also, Stu was instrumental in helping with all the problems we had last season with Grif's old agent. An agent like

Stu can be the difference between your career tanking and thriving when your past comes back to haunt you," Dean told me.

I sucked in a breath. How did he know?

"I won't tell. Were you waiting for Austin to get signed, then you could mate and stay on the same team? I mean, I know that rule is only valid if both have contracts, but it's only a matter of time for you," Dean asked quietly.

Oh. *That's* what Dean thought my secret was? The PHL allowed mated alpha and omega players to stay together on the same team. Spouses didn't get that privilege. Packs only got it if they had a pack contract.

"Much to my ex's chagrin, I'm not an omega, Dean. Just a beta." I shrugged. "I'd be *tall* for a female omega."

Clearly, that had been Austin's plan. Also, my past could come back to haunt me at any time. It had once since I'd come to New York–it was only a matter of time before it happened again.

"Grif and I are tall omegas. So is Molly on the Belugas." His look was skeptical. "Still, email Stu. He probably won't email or call you back. I have to work on him. He thinks you're too short."

"Most teams do." I laughed. Sure, I'd do it. Maybe he'd pass me on to someone else in the agency.

Dean continued to give me pointers as we ate. We finished our ice cream. No one had found us yet. My phone was quiet, though I had to go to work soon, and should shower.

"Want to play ping-pong? Ping-pong is good for goalies." Dean hopped off the counter.

"Sure, I have a little time before I have to go to work." I slid off and rinsed off my helmet bowl. I could always go to work smelly. After all, I was just working in skate rental with Desiree.

Dean was winning when a bunch of the prospects came back up, heading straight for the drinks and snacks.

"I should probably get ready for work," I told Dean, well aware that Windy was trying to murder me with his eyes. "See you tomorrow."

I found the others in the main weight room.

"Where did you go?" Clark asked, as he benched some weights with Anders.

"Double D and I were doing goalie shit." I shrugged. Grif and Jonas were working out, too.

"Stacking pucks?" Anders laughed.

I scratched my nose with my middle finger.

Dimitri came in and went straight for Grif. "Here's your cat. Carlos left him at my party last night. He's still hungover."

"Of course he is. Fuck, Lucky. You need to go easy on the beer," Grif scolded as he took a handful of nothing.

"I think he was doing body shots with the models." I laughed.

"Is it time for work?" Clark asked. "I should be home by the time you get off. We're going to crash the barbeque, then head to Tito's or play video games at Dimitri's. Let me know if you want me to pick you up?"

"I'll be fine, but thanks." It was a sweet offer–and I did like riding on the back of his motorcycle.

Clark sat up and wiped his forehead with a towel. "If you change your mind, let me know."

The alarm beeped on my phone and I sighed. "See you tonight."

I'd rather go to the barbeque and hang out with them, but I'd taken last night off. While I might have clothes and other cute things, those wouldn't pay my tuition.

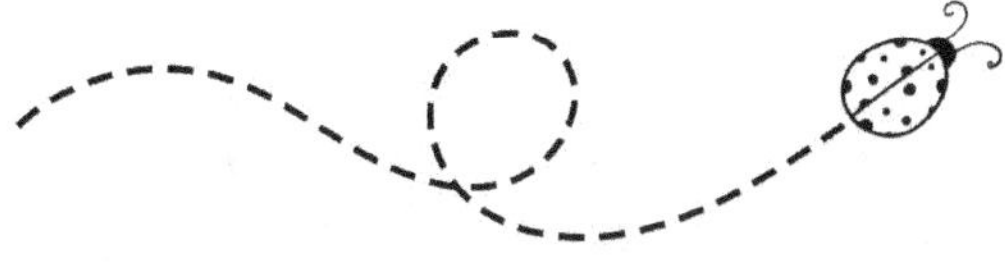

Chapter Twenty-Three

GWEN

"Move, move, move," Coach Hirata yelled, as we pushed weights across some turf in the area the NYIT hockey team used for off-ice conditioning. "Come on, you'd think you worked all day," she guffawed.

My university team had started formal pre-season conditioning and skills training, which was optional, since classes didn't start for a month and not everyone was local. Those of us who were in town were all working our asses off with day jobs and internships.

Hence her joke—and why practices were in the early evening, so we could work during the day, and those who also had evening jobs could still hit the night shift.

There's been informal conditioning and weight training sessions all summer, and while I'd made some, I hadn't gotten to that many, since they were often when I was working. Still, I was confident that Coach could see that I hadn't been slacking.

Today was the first day of Squire camp. It was the highlight of the Squire Foundation's youth program and why so many Knights were around. It was a hockey summer camp where the *Knights* were the counselors and coaches, and I'd been hired to help.

In the morning, we had younger kids. In the afternoon, the big kids came. These were advanced high schoolers–some were part of the Squire program, some were local junior hockey kids, and others were talented young players that had been invited.

We ran it like a mini version of developmental camp and worked their asses off.

Coach Hirata continued to run us through drills. Finally, she waved us off. "Hit the showers, then there's dinner for you. Make sure you take home leftovers and stuff your pockets."

Yes, please. I ate quickly, relishing the time with my teammates, but aware that I needed to get to the rink to work the evening shift.

"Di Rossi, can you stop by my office before you leave?" Coach asked.

"Yes, Coach." I stuffed a garlic knot in my face. The Knights always had things like salmon and grilled chicken, mushroom risotto, roasted vegetables, and spinach salad. Healthy, tasty food optimized for nutrition. But nothing beats a pasta dinner with garlic knots after a day of hard work.

"Oooh, you're in trouble." Maze laughed, dark eyes dancing. She was team captain and had just come back to town. She was one of my teammates who lived in the townhouse I'd looked into moving into.

"Naw. Coach is nice and found me new goalie pads to replace the ones Austin shredded when we broke up," I replied.

"What? Those were nice and that shit's expensive. We missed you at camp today," Bonnie told me. "Also, I don't like this rink as well as the training center."

They'd had to move that camp since the rink was busy with squire camp and developmental camp–and I wasn't working with them this week.

I finished up, threw a bunch of hydrogels and protein bars in my backpack, then ducked into Coach's office.

"Here's your laptop." Coach handed me a thin box.

"Thank you. I'm so relieved to have this." Now I could give Clark back his computer. I signed the receipt and lovingly tucked it into my backpack. Then I signed for everything else. Our sponsor had been generous, and I had a giant pile of things, which would take a bit of organizing to get back on the subway.

"You looked good out there. You've been working hard," Coach told me.

"Thanks. It's my last year and I plan on bringing it." Maybe I'd splurge and order a car, drop this all off at Clark's, then go to work. Oooh, I could also have the car take me to work, stash it, then bring it all back after my shift.

Yeah. I'd do that.

"Good. There's interest," she added. "Did you ever follow up on those agents that were interested in you after the playoffs?"

"Yes, Coach. I'm working on getting one. Teams are interested?" Hope sparked inside me. While I hoped teams were watching me from afar, *knowing* they were made a big difference.

She nodded. "One wanted to know if you'd grown."

"The Tigres?" I tried to stuff as much as I could into one equip- ment bag.

"Yes, I didn't realize Mexico City was watching you." She stud- ied me. But then she'd only been my coach for a year.

"I don't think I'll grow enough for them." This wasn't all going to fit in one bag, even if I took the skates out of the boxes. However, there were two bags.

"Show them wrong." Coach Hirata was a beta and had played for the Scorpions and the Dinosaurs. She understood what challenges I faced.

"Yes, Coach."

Make them look. Make them reconsider. Make them regret.

"I'm going to email you a practice plan for the rest of the season, so you can work on things we'll be focusing on when pre-season officially starts," she told me. "Also, I have some great news for you."

"You do?" I zipped up the bag, my heart thundering in my ears. I already got a laptop and gear, what else was there?

"The alumni donor came through." She beamed at me. "He and his pack were impressed and happy to cover everything. The money hit your student account today. I wanted to confirm it before I told you. I know you've been stressing out over this, so I'm happy we were able to get this resolved."

Joy bubbled inside me, mixing with relief in an effervescent cocktail of happiness. "The donor came through? Really? Tuition is covered and I'm okay? Who is it?"

NYIT Hockey had a number of distinguished alumni.

"They wish to be anonymous, but you should write them a thank you note. Bring it to me next practice and I'll make sure they get it," she told me.

"Of course." I'd be okay. Tuition was covered. I had a place to live. I had clothes, a laptop, and equipment. No more sobbing in my sleep, because I didn't know what I was going to do.

"Also, he told a few others about you and the business office has had people calling to put money on your student account. So now you'll have help with housing, living, and all that," she added. "You live off campus, right? I think they disperse funds a couple weeks into the school year."

"I do, thanks." Other people were putting money into my account? How sweet. Tomorrow I'd check up on that. For all I knew, it was just a couple hundred bucks, but hey, even that would help a lot.

Awkwardly, I grabbed all my stuff, and ordered a ride to the rink. When I got there, I rushed to the employee locker room, put on my uniform, stashed my things, and went to clock in.

"Cutting it close, again." Tony sat at his computer doing schedules.

"Sorry, Coach Hirata wanted to talk to me. The scholarship from the alumni came in. I'm set." I'd checked my email on the drive over. Sure enough, I had a fancy little award letter, and confirmation that my *entire* outstanding tuition had been paid in full.

"Great, because I don't know how much longer I can allow you to work as many hours as you want," Tony replied.

"Oh. People are complaining? I've tried to be willing to trade shifts when people ask, so no one gets mad." I'd hoped to keep overworking until classes started.

"There are these things called labor laws." His look went amused. "Also, I'm completely serious that you should work as little as possible this year. Focus on what's truly important."

"Let me crunch the numbers, but that might be doable." I left the office and got back to work. I couldn't wait to tell Clark.

Chapter Twenty-Four

CLARK

"Take that, Anders." I laughed, as Anders, Dimitri, Carlos, and I played Go-goKart in my living room. On my big TV, my little red go-kart slammed into his, making him spin off the track as I raced onward. The remains of our pizza and empty beer bottles sat on the coffee table.

"I don't know how Ladybug does it all day, work with the little children," Dimitri grumbled from his place on my couch. He'd worked camp with us.

"I love the afternoon group. Fuck, some of those kids can *play*," Anders replied.

They could. The morning group... Well, they made me laugh. They had fun. They *tried.*

"Those little ones she had last week were like herding cats. Where is Gwen? It's late." Carlos looked at his phone as he tried to play with one hand. Pretty sure he was texting his ex. Again.

"She's working the late shift all month. Her university coach started pre-season practices and held them in the late afternoon," I told them as I leaned back in my gaming chair. At least we weren't far from the training center. I worried about her coming back late at night alone.

Dimitri's go-kart *jumped* over me as he used a power-up. "She works too much."

"She's worried about paying her tuition." I frowned as my go-kart chased after him. "Does anyone know how much she owes?" A place like NYIT was probably much more than community college.

"Mercy does. Yesterday her and Team Mom asked me to contribute to get it paid. I threw some money on it." Anders' green go-kart caught up to me.

"I did, too. Gwen gets to keep anything extra to put toward living and shit. Though watching her race a shopping cart through Home Things was hysterical," Carlos replied.

It was hilarious. I still had to take her to Swoop, which I was looking forward to.

"Team Mom's organizing a fund for Ladybug? That's sweet. She didn't ask me to contribute." Which was weird, since I knew Team Mom. She'd helped me out a lot last season, when I was a rookie and learning to live on my own.

"Team Mom knows you're keeping Gwen's ass." Carlos laughed. "Just like she knows Dimitri dropped the GDP of a small nation on the shopping trip that Valya took Gwen on."

"Looking good is expensive." Dimitri shrugged. He came from money besides his high salary.

"Ladybug's staying here?" Anders smirked. We were almost at the end of the track. Dimitri was in the lead.

"She's *house-sitting*." Maybe I should have brought back a kitten–for me. Then Gwen would have a job to do. I didn't even have plants for her to water.

There was a bump at the door, then a shuffle. The door flew open. Ladybug stumbled in with her backpack, and two large equipment bags–one that said *NYIT Hockey* and one that said *Victory Sports.*

They were a company that made equipment for pretty much every sport and sponsored her university. She also had two goalie sticks.

"Hi." She waved and dropped her things by the kitchen island, then went right to the box on the coffee table. Her face fell when she saw it was empty.

"There's food for you in the fridge. Give me a second." I used a power up and raced after Dimitri, the end of the track in sight.

"It's fine. Thanks," she said.

Dimitri's go-kart shot flames at me, causing me to stall as he sailed over the finish line, getting first. Carlos sped past me, getting second place, but I finished before Anders.

When I looked up, Gwen was in the kitchen, microwaving the personal pizza I'd ordered for her. She was the only one of us who liked pineapple and ham.

"Did you rob Athlete's World?" Anders laughed.

"Coach Hirata did," she snorted. "Guess what?"

"What?" I asked. Her energy was electric and I couldn't help but get excited for her, whatever it was.

"Remember how Coach Hirata said they approached a couple of alumni about helping me out? Well, one of them came through. My tuition is paid for. I'm going to be okay." She grabbed a beer from the fridge and opened it.

"Ladybug, that's *amazing*." I vaulted up off the couch and entered the kitchen, so I could swing her around, her beer nearly spilling.

"Put me down, you goofball," she laughed.

"Never." I kept her up in the air. "Who was it?"

"Don't know. They want to be anonymous." She kicked her feet.

I put her down. "That is amazing. I'm so happy for you."

"Also, I guess some other people are putting money on my account, too. It's so nice that random people would do that." She got her mini pizza out of the microwave and took a bite. "So good."

The guys were whispering. All I caught was *AJ.*

Gwen plopped down on the arm of the sofa. "What about AJ? Oh. The donor is AJ. Shit. That makes sense. He attended NYIT before he played for the Hurricanes. He has ties to the Knights through his mates. Mercy knew about my tuition issues. Anonymous? What a drama queen." She laughed. "Wait..."

Her face was a study as she put it together.

Carlos grinned. "Yeah, Mercy and Team Mom have been asking us to contribute to your account. You might think you're 'just' an EBUG, but we do care about you, Mariquita."

"Awww, you all are the best." Her hand went to her heart and her eyes teared. "Fuck." Gwen wiped her eyes with the back of her hand.

Carlos' phone buzzed. He glanced at it. "Well, I'm out of here."

"Don't meet her. It's a bad idea." Gwen shook her head.

"What? I'm not meeting anyone." Carlos feigned innocence.

"He's been texting her all night," Dimitri tattled.

Carlos hopped up off the couch. "Who? Just texting my boy Dusty."

"Mmm hmmm." Gwen rolled her eyes. "Be safe. Don't trip and fall into her bed."

I wasn't sure what the deal was between Carlos and his ex. But I knew she came to town every few months, and it inevitably ended up with him hungover and full of regret. Once Dimitri had to bail his ass out of jail, which had gotten us all punished with sprints by Coach. I did know he had a long-time friend named Dusty.

"I'll make good choices." With a wave, Carlos left.

Right after Dimitri and Anders went home as well. Anders was staying in Dimitri's guest room for the duration of Squire camp, then heading back to Sweden.

"Can we watch a movie?" Gwen grabbed another beer from the fridge. She held one up and I nodded.

"Sure. What do you want to watch?" I turned on the TV.

"Anything. I'm too happy to sleep." She plopped down on the couch next to me, really close. "Oh, sorry." Gwen scooted over and handed me my beer.

I grabbed the blanket off the back of the couch that my mom made and covered us.

"Does someone need a cuddle?" I teased. Oh, I'd cuddle her as much as she wanted. I couldn't get Dimitri's party out of my head, where I'd come so close to kissing her.

"Why do I miss being hugged?" Gwen snuggled into me, tucking her bare feet under her.

"Tens didn't give you enough hugs when I was gone?" I joked. After I said that, I felt a little weird.

I pushed that away. *No, no jealousy of her other friends.* I hadn't even met him yet.

"Tens and I aren't hugging friends—or snuggling on the couch. Not yet anyway. I miss him though. We've been looking for the best muffins in the city. We also go country line dancing. It's fun." She looked up at me. "You should come."

"You can do that here? It's popular at home, but not something I'm into. I'll go with you if you want, and I'll snuggle you all you need." Yeah, not a hardship.

"I hope you and Tens will be friends." She rested her head on my chest, her muscular body feeling so right, as she practically melted into me.

I stroked her hair as I started the movie. "I'm sure we will."

As long as he wasn't an asshole, or mean to her, I'd be friends with whoever she wanted.

Chapter Twenty-Five

Gwen

"**Y**ou picked it up so quickly. It's going to be so fucking cute. I've got the perfect outfit for you, too," Mercy told me, as she taught me one of last year's Maimer dance battle routines, on the small rink.

"Thanks. I'm really surprised they're letting you use a Bro Ken song, though. I love his music, but it's not always family-friendly." Learning the dance-battles was always so much fun.

"Me, too. But it's a fun one, and well, they're trying to get him to sing at one of the games. I guess he's from here?" She shrugged.

"He is. You should ask Carlos, they're friends. He's brought him to Dimitri's parties before." Though Dimitri didn't like it because shenanigans always ensued. Like the hot tub catching fire.

"Okay. Sounds good. Um, did you compete in ice skating under a different name? I wanted to see little you in a sparkly outfit, but I couldn't find you," Mercy asked.

"I did. It drives Desiree nuts, since she can't figure it out and wants to see if I was good or not." I laughed. "I was average. But I had cute costumes."

"That's good. Verity's outfits were hideous when she and Creed pair skated in middle school." Mercy gave me a sly look. "Can I try to find you?"

I bit my lower lip. "For your and Team Mom's personal amusement only? There are... reasons."

"Yeah, totally. I get it." Mercy smiled. "Are you still good?"

"Still good. Thanks for checking. I like living with Clark, it's fun," I told her.

Mercy and I finished up and I headed upstairs. There was a ton of laughter coming from the dining room. I peeked in and saw Castle playing ping-pong with Dean.

I quickly got changed and grabbed my backpack. Constantine's office was open, and I knocked on his door.

He looked up from his desk. "Ladybug. Everything going okay?"

"Yeah. I caught some crickets and brought them for Maddox." There was a big, beautiful enclosure for the lizard along one wall, complete with a miniature Doom Squad headquarters.

"He'd love that."

I opened the top of the tank. "Hi, Maddox."

"Having fun with Squire camp?" Constantine asked as he worked.

"I am." I opened the plastic container I'd put the crickets in and let them go. I'd caught them on campus.

"Have you thought of coaching when you're done with hockey? You have a gift."

"Me?" I put the lid back on, making sure it was secure. "Um, no. It's fun, but my background is in accounting. I always figured I'd work for the Bureau of Investigation as a forensic accountant."

So that I could take down the untouchables that hurt people. First up, the prime ministers of Canada.

Constantine beamed. "You're a numbers person, too?"

"Yep. I know you can't tell me, but I hope you move up Castle," I told him.

He nodded. "Bunty wants someone from the Scorpions. But I'm impressed with her. I noticed you and that Windy guy clash."

"Sorry. Not trying to be unprofessional. He's friends with my ex." My head ducked.

"Got it. You've been with us a couple of years, right?" he asked.

I nodded. "This will be my third season."

"Terrific. It looks like they haven't gotten to you yet. Since I have the list in front of me, I might as well add you. Did you want a ring or pendant?" He looked up at me.

I had no idea what he was talking about. Probably some new swag the players were getting in their welcome back goodie bags. Last year, they had golf and tennis accessories. Carlos had given me his racquet cover, which had been destroyed when Austin ruined my racquet.

"I don't know?" I didn't expect to actually get one, but Knights' jewelry would be fun. Sometimes the MASOs ordered cute stuff, like earrings and bracelets. They'd had matching jackets for play-offs.

"Ring. You want a ring. Do you know your ring size? Devon has the sizer." He typed on his computer.

"Um, yeah, I do." Because we'd been sized for our NYIT championship rings. I gave it to him and he added it to the sheet. "Thanks. Anyway, I have to go. See you later." I waved and left.

Clark was in one of the workout rooms with one of the trainers.

"We're going to Tito's. Come? You're not working tonight, right?" Clark asked as he did his exercises.

"Not working tonight." I should make an appointment with the physio. I liked the ones here more than at NYIT. My hip had been bothering me, but I'd broken it when I was in high school and it happened sometimes.

"Okay, then, after Tito's, do you want to go to the movies? Since you're not working?" He grinned.

I sucked in a breath. "I haven't been to the movies in so long. Can we get fancy popcorn?"

He nodded. "Yes. We can even put chocolate candies in it."

"I'm so there." Though he had me at popcorn.

I found Dean and his pack over by the bar at Tito's. This included Team Mom and AJ, who wore a suit and looked like he'd just got off work.

"Hey, Ladybug, great job today," Dean praised. "You're so good with those kids."

"Thanks."

"Do I have you this semester?" Verity asked me. In addition to getting her PhD she taught some classes. Last semester I'd been in her plant mythology class with a bunch of my teammates.

"Nope. It's all stuff for my major, pity." It had been a fun class. I turned to AJ. I'd given Coach Hirata the thank you note for him at practice yesterday. "Thanks, AJ."

"For what?" He kept his face passive.

"For being amazing." I turned back to Verity. "And thank *you*."

She gave me a hug. "Anytime. It was all Mercy's idea. Are you okay now?"

"I am, thanks. Especially since Tony's cutting my hours at the rink." I made a face.

"Why?" Dean frowned.

"Something about how much I can legally work. Laws, am I right?" I rolled my eyes. I understood wanting to protect people from being *forced* to work a lot, but I *wanted* to work a lot. There wasn't much summer left.

AJ chuckled. "Oh, yes, those pesky labor laws."

"Oh, I remember that. It gets hard to work, go to practice, and class, but shit's expensive." Grif made a face.

I waved and joined everyone. We finished up and I followed Clark to his motorcycle. He handed me his blue helmet with the Captain Everything shield on it.

"I'll leave my keys with you. You can take it whenever you want. I'll show you how to drive it." Clark climbed on and I took my place behind him.

"I can't even legally drive a car, let alone a motorcycle," I admitted, wrapping my arms around his waist. "Never needed to."

"We should work on that. It's good to at least have one," he told me.

"True. I know the basics. Here you have to go to driving school and I could never afford extras like that," I told him. Okay, also, I was sort of afraid to drive after my grandparents died in a car accident.

We zoomed through the streets and I sucked in a breath as we pulled into the underground lot of an entertainment plaza.

"We're going to the fancy theater?" I took off his helmet. It had big seats, and they brought you food while you watched the movie, like it was a restaurant.

"Yep. They have the best selection of fancy popcorn. Later, if you want, we'll go to Swoop and get you what you need, since I leave Saturday night?" he asked. "Will you be okay? I'll be gone for two weeks. But I'll be back in time for us to attend JP's wedding."

"Go, spend more time with your family. I'll be fine on my own."
Also, Tenzin came back on Sunday. We took the elevator to theatre
level.

I leaned my head on his shoulder. "Also, feel free to bring back a
kitten."

His look grew mischievous. "I just might."

Chapter Twenty-Six

GWEN

Clark's place was empty when I got back from going out with Castle and a few others that were here for developmental camp. Their mini-tournament had gone well, and tomorrow they'd all go home. Hopefully, I'd see some of them for rookie camp in September.

The door rang. It was my dinner–the tacos that Dean owed me. Well, three of them. He'd put money on a food delivery app for me and we had very different ideas of what tacos cost. That was okay though. This way I could get an entire taco dinner. If you asked for an extra tortilla, you could use the rice and beans to make a burrito to have the next day.

Curling up in a blanket, I ate my tacos and watched a movie. This was... nice.

My phone buzzed with a text.

It's back to school time. Got anything for me? I'll be in town soon.

How nice of him to check. He was my brother's best friend and the one I'd sold my jewelry and hockey cards to.

I'm good this year. Got a scholarship.

Good for you. I'll still buy you a pastrami sandwich.

I thought for a moment. All I had left was a couple of pieces of jewelry Austin had given me that I'd been wearing, or had fixed the best I could from Austin's smashing. It wasn't valuable, but I think I'd sell it on principle.

I broke up with my boyfriend. Might sell what he gave me.

You know where to find me. Sorry about the boyfriend.

That might be a good, cathartic thing. The zoo had a program where you could name a mouse after your ex and have it fed to a snake. I could do that with the money.

My phone rang with a video call. I paused the movie. "Hey, Big Guy."

"Hi, Firecracker. Where are you?" Tenzin's face filled the screen. He'd gotten some sun and needed to shave.

"Oh, right. I had to move out of my place, so I'm house sitting for Clark for the rest of the off-season. I might even be in your building." We hadn't talked much while he was away, mostly texts and pictures.

"Well, that could be fun. I'd love to share some of this fish we caught with you. I'm not much of a chef, but I can cook fish," he told me.

"No, that sounds great. My work schedule isn't as hectic, so I'll have a couple more evenings to do things–like cook and go dancing. Maybe go to another museum or two?" Seeing him on my phone made me realize exactly how much I missed him.

Though spending time with Clark had been so much fun. I needed them to get along.

He grinned. "That sounds perfect."

"Hey, Babybug." Cooter stole his phone. His beard was crazy, as was his hair.

I talked to them for a while, then finished my movie. I started a bubble bath, lighting some candles I'd gotten on my trip through Swoop. The bathroom now had cute towels, a fun rug, other decorations, and *all sorts* of bubble bath and other products.

Tonight I was horny as fuck and needed to take care of business. Bathtubs were very good for that. While the tub filled, I put away my leftovers, cleaned up a little, and noted a few things I wanted to get food-wise for the week.

Turning off the water and the light, I removed my clothes. I sunk into the warm bubbles, relishing the sensation, leaning against the bath pillow.

This. This was it. I sighed.

Closing my eyes, I ran my hands over my body, one sliding between my thighs. One thing I missed about having a boyfriend was the living dildo attachment.

As I touched myself, I kept seeing Tenzin's face. I had to admit, he was really cute, with a *nice* body. That man probably knew how to please a woman. What would it be like for those big hands to cup my breasts, rub my clit? How would his face feel between my thighs? He probably had a massive dick, too.

My breath shortened into pants as I imagined that my fingers were his cock. His knot would feel incredible, too. Yes, Tenzin's knot in my pussy.

And Clark's in my ass.

While it had initially been difficult to take a knot, years of being with an alpha had trained my pussy well. She missed knots. A lot.

Out of nowhere, I imagined two sets of hands on my body, Tenzin's *and* Clark's. A moan escaped my lips as I could almost hear Clark say, *"that's it, take it like a good girl"*, as he slid his cock into my ass, my pussy already filled with Tenzin's.

Pleasure spiked through me over and over as I pretended I was between the two of them, both of them kissing me, fucking me, and telling me over and over that I was a good girl.

Mmmm. Something about that got me off. My ex had never called me a *good girl* in bed. I'd never had any dick but my ex's, let alone two in me at once.

My pussy clenched as I came hard all over my hand, the water sloshing onto the floor. Ooh, that was exactly what I needed.

I stood and showered off the bubbles, then washed my hair as the water drained. Where had that bit with Tenzin *and* Clark come from? Not that I minded. I found the idea of being between them incredibly sexy ever since Valya had brought it up.

Clark was beautiful. He was sweet. There was a lot to like about him. Especially if paired with Tenzin. The two of them balanced each other out. Tenzin was calm, Clark was excitable.

Mmmm, I'd be having this fantasy again. Still, that's all it was. A *fantasy*. While there was so much I loved about both of them, they hadn't even met each other yet. Who knew if they'd even get along?

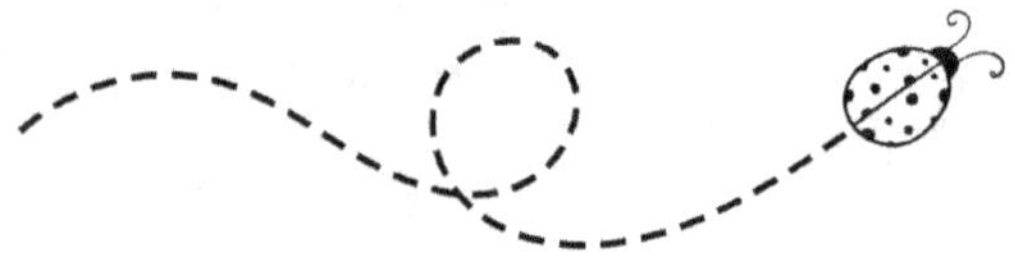

Chapter Twenty-Seven

TENZIN

"T his one?" I held up a straw Cowboy hat from the massive rack in front of me. "Or this one?" I held up a white one that I'd been carrying around the store we'd stopped at, on our way to the airport.

"This one." Cooter held up a brown one with a heart pattern woven into it and a little silver heart on it.

"Hmmm. It would go with the boots she already has."

Cooter grinned at me. "You miss her."

"Yes. I didn't expect to miss her this much. Not that I haven't had fun with you." We'd been fishing for salmon.

"Well, how can I compare with Babybug?" Cooter laughed. "I should get her a present. Not here. I'll make her one." He toyed with the necklace he had around his neck–a penis bone from a raccoon on a leather cord that he wore for luck.

I wasn't sure what Gwen would make of that.

It had been a great few days. I was so much freer and lighter with the house being settled, Morgan and Jacen behind me, and knowing there was a little firecracker waiting for me in New York.

Not to mention the fishing had been terrific.

"Are you going to date her?" Cooter asked, as I paid for the hat.

"I don't think she's ready." I took the bag, and we got into our rental, which was filled with fishing poles and gear. "I'm not ready. While I adore her, what is the point of starting something if next year she could go literally anywhere?"

Cooter got into the driver's seat. "Um, because it would be better to be with her for a year than not at all? Not to mention long-distance relationships exist. Also, isn't she the Knights' EBUG? Doesn't that mean she gets a shot next year?"

"I don't think it works like that. I'm not sure who else is looking at her," I replied as we drove off.

"Mexico City, even if they think she's too short. The Hawai'i Tsunamis, who were scouting someone else during that playoff game where her team won the championship–that game where during the sixth round of overtime they dropped the second fucking puck. Though they just brought on a new goalie. The Rockland Daredevils have been keeping an eye on her since she played junior hockey. Oh, and the Quebec Étoiles. I'm not sure what the story is there," Cooter replied as we drove to the airport.

"How do you even know this?" They were all pretty decent teams.

"I asked. Might be some others, but contrary to popular belief I don't know everyone. If she goes to the Tsunamis, we're spending off-seasons with her there. Heard the boar hunting is *insane*, not to mention it's a fucking island. Fishing should be great." He turned the music up a little.

They were all so *far*. Why couldn't she go to Jersey? We could live together if she played for Jersey. We could make Philly or Boston work too and just commute on the ultra-bullet.

But Hawai'i? Mexico City? Rockland? We *could* make Quebec work. They were at least in the same conference.

"I don't even know if she wants a relationship. Or me?" I shrugged.

Cooter snorted. "Babybug likes you. You just need to heal her tender little heart some more. Also, don't not try just 'cause you're afraid."

"If I have her, I'll want to keep her. The last thing I'd ever want is to prevent her from having the career she deserves though. She's only twenty-two," I blurted, my cheeks warming, as a sad boy country song came on the radio.

"You have it so fucking bad," Cooter chuckled. "You're only twenty-seven. Promise me if she wants a relationship, you don't throw it all away 'cause she might end up on some other team. You're overthinking this."

"True." I sighed. "There's a lot to like about her. What if I mess it up? I'm having such a good time being friends."

He chuckled again. "Then be friends. Dance with her. Feed her muffins. I have a feeling Gwen knows exactly what she wants."

It was late as I dragged my things down the hallway. Fatigue from the flight pressed down on me. Also, I had a lot of shit—all my fishing poles and gear, which had been at Cooter's place in Portland, a couple of suitcases, a cooler full of frozen salmon, and her hat.

As I unlocked my door, the one across from me opened.

"Hey there, Big Guy. So you *do* live across from Clark." Gwen stood there in a pair of blue satiny pants with stars on them and a tank-top with a matching star.

I opened the door, then turned around, keeping it ajar with my foot.

"Firecracker." I couldn't help but grin. "Did you just get off work?"

"Yep." She grinned. While she'd been working tonight, it hadn't been that really late shift she often had. That shift always worried me.

"Come over in fifteen minutes?" My belly fluttered a little. Her new hairstyle suited her.

"Sounds good. Do you have everything?" She eyed all my stuff.

"I've got it." I pushed everything inside the door and it closed behind me.

Quickly, I started a load of clothes in the washer off the kitchen. The poles and gear went into the corner of the living room. I dragged my suitcases into the bedroom, then I tossed the fish in my empty freezer, and put the cooler in the sink.

Then I jumped into the shower. The doorbell rang as I got out. Shit. I slid on some shorts, toweled off my hair, and grabbed the bag with the hat in it, dropping it on the coffee table as I opened the door.

"Sorry," I told her.

"I could've given you longer," she laughed.

"Come in. I was going to make some tea." My heart beat like a nervous teenager as I ushered her in.

"I'd love that. Tens, you're ripped." She joined me in the kitchen and looked me up and down, appreciatively.

Looking down, I realized I wasn't wearing a shirt. "Occupational hazard."

Gwen laughed again. How I'd missed that laugh. I started the kettle, then got out two mugs and a wooden box full of tea.

"Pick one." I handed it to her.

She looked a little different, and it wasn't only the hair. There was something about her that looked more relaxed. Happier. Not to mention some of the thinness had disappeared from her face. Some of the shadows had disappeared from her eyes as well.

An elaborate spine tattoo peaked out from her tank-top. She had a ladybug tattoo on one ankle and a hockey stick on the other.

I had a tattoo of two fish on my bicep, Cooter had a matching one. Also, I had a yeti face on my shoulder that I'd gotten as a rookie and had been drunk as fuck.

"Clark isn't going to miss you, is he? He's back?" I tried to bite back the jealousy. Was he the cause of all these changes?

"He flew back home yesterday, but he'll return in a few weeks. I can't wait for you two to meet. He's letting me stay in his guest room. Which is such a relief. My housing situation got messed up, but it's fine now." She bit her lower lip.

"I'm glad to hear that." I took the tea bag she picked and added it to a mug. Guest room. That must be the two-bedroom side of the building.

"What about when classes start? Are you moving into the dorms?" I asked. "I have a truck, so I can help you move."

She shook her head. "Housing is full. I could join the waitlist, but Clark says I can stay as long as I want. Knowing you live across the hall makes that *very* attractive."

I poured the tea. We sat down on the couch and she caught me up on her week, telling me about Squire camp, shopping, her university practices restarting, and so much more.

It made me realize a few things. Gwen had been keeping a lot from me—and rightfully so. We didn't know each other well yet. She'd been struggling to figure out how to pay tuition and worried about where she'd live.

"Things are good now." Gwen smiled. "I never would have thought the Knights–and the Maimers–would come through for me like that."

"How could they not? You're one of them. What do you still need?" I asked, glad she had the big things figured out.

"Eventually, a new backpack and some stuff for my classes. I have a few more weeks. But enough about me. I want to hear about fishing." She finished her tea.

I told her all about our trip, showing her pictures. "I've got a freezer full of salmon now. One night this week I'll make you dinner?"

"I'd like that. Can we go dancing again? I missed that." She gave me one of her shy smiles.

"Absolutely. Before I forget, I got you a present." I gave her the bag.

"Tens. You got me a hat." Gwen put it on her head, smiling bright as the sun. "I love it."

The sight of her in those pajamas, that showed the outlines of her nipples, her bare feet, and the hat made my groin tighten. She looked kissable. Lickable. Fuckable.

Yeah, I'd missed her so fucking much when I'd been gone.

"My sister is going to be playing a fair down south in a few weeks. I think we can take the ultra-bullet," I told her.

"I'd love that. Oh, I can't wait to meet her and hear her band."

My sister was *so* curious. I wasn't sure what they'd make of each other. Hopefully, it would be good.

"Hey, this is so stupid, since I have camp in the morning, but do you want to watch a movie?" Her look grew shy as she bit her lower lip.

"That sounds perfect. Should I get us a snack? I only have a few things that I'd bought for the plane. I need to go shopping." In the fridge, I found a couple beers, and I put some snacks on a tray. She might not have tried any of them.

"What are these flavors of chips? Crayfish? Cumin Lamb? Red Meat?" Gwen curiously read the packages.

"I like the spicy flavor best, but I ate them on the plane. Also, these are some of my favorite cookies." I pushed the box toward her. "They're matcha." There was also a bag of salted plums and some jelly snacks.

"Oh, I've had these cookies before." She opened the box and ate one. "Mmmm."

We put on a movie, and I had fun getting her to try all the different flavors. When the movie ended, she looked about ready to pass out on my couch.

"You should go to bed," I told her. "Are we back to our normal routine? It's okay if your new living situation changes things."

"It changes nothing other than you can take the subway with me in the mornings. I'd like that." Her smile melted my heart.

"I'd like that a lot." I was looking forward to getting back to our routine.

Cooter was absolutely right. I might not be ready to date again, but if Gwen wanted me, I'd be powerless to stop it.

How I hoped that one day I should be so lucky.

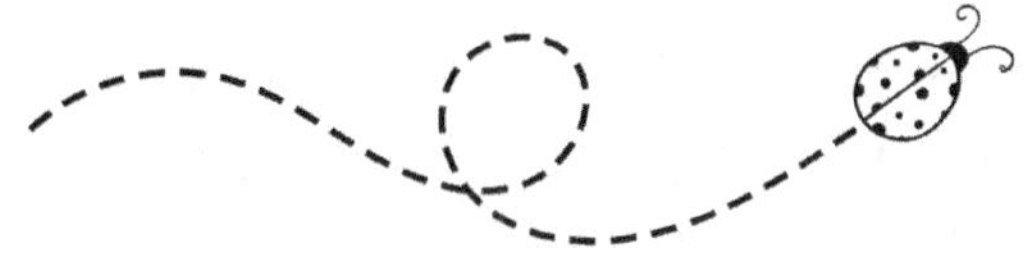

Chapter Twenty-Eight

GWEN

Tenzin twirled me around as we danced to the live music at the bar he'd first taken me to. The past two weeks have been fun. We'd fallen back into our normal routine with a few slight changes.

In the mornings, we'd take the subway together to the rink, or walk if it was a nice day. If we walked, we usually picked up coffee and muffins. We'd practice together on the ice, then eat breakfast upstairs. Then I'd go to work, and he'd practice more, before doing whatever he needed to do that day. He met up with AJ for lunch a few times as well and played golf with him once.

After work, if it wasn't a practice day for NYIT, we'd go upstairs to do conditioning, strength training, or land drills, often with Carlos and Dimitri. Sometimes we'd go to Tito's after, or to Dimitri's. A couple of times we'd all gone to Carlos' mom's.

If I had practice for NYIT, I'd often end up either going to Tenzin's and we'd cook together, or we'd meet and wander the outdoor market, trying new things, or maybe check a new restaurant off the list. Sometimes we worked on my social media, or he'd help me in my agent search. Over the weekend, we'd gone to yoga in the park, more museums, and visited Marty.

Tenzin and I also made more videos of me figure skating with hockey sticks.

The music changed, but the two of us continued to dance in the crowded bar. I'd met with a campus therapist today to try to handle my shit regarding Austin. This was our second meeting and so far she was fine, and not pushy, which was good, since I didn't want to talk about my family—something they always wanted to do.

Why wasn't *"I don't talk to my dads, because they're assholes"*, enough?

That was partially why I'd asked to go dancing, a fun reward. I was also horny as fuck. Again. I'd have to start putting music on when I took baths, since in three days Clark would come back. Couldn't have him hearing me taking care of business.

We danced until the band stopped for the evening, sweat running down our backs. I took his hand, and we walked to the subway. He looked at our hands, but said nothing, just gave it a squeeze.

What was I doing? But, I enjoyed holding his hand. I liked dancing with him. It was nice sitting close enough to touch him while we were on the couch.

Yes, I wanted to be touched. But I wanted to be touched by *Tenzin.*

Okay, I wanted to be touched by Clark, too. But Clark wasn't here. Yet.

I wanted them both. Though I still wasn't ready for that. Which meant I shouldn't be holding Tenzin's hand. Or leaning my head on his shoulder when I danced.

But I liked it. It felt right, and Tenzin hadn't complained. Again, *what was I doing?*

We went back to the building and walked to our doors. It was fun living across from him.

"Come over in twenty? Though I'm out of beer," he offered.

"I've got some. I did a grocery order today," I told him. Clark let me use his grocery delivery membership, and it was quite convenient. I had to admit, walking through markets with Tenzin, picking out fresh produce, and trying new things, was awfully fun, though.

I slipped into the apartment and took a shower, washed off the bar, and changed into some sweats and a T-shirt. My phone buzzed with a video call.

"Hi Clark. I haven't burned down your place yet." I plopped down on my bed, a pillow falling off onto the floor.

"Good. Question, do you want a kitten? They're weaned now, have gotten shots, and are so adorable." Clark held up a little white kitten.

"Oooh. I do. How much trouble will we get in for having an illegal kitten?" There were more on his lap. They were all either white or white and black. Clark being covered in kittens was the cutest thing ever. I took a screenshot and immediately made it my lock screen.

"If we get in trouble, we'll move somewhere pet friendly? We could call this one, Snowball." He rubbed his cheek against the snow-white kitten in his hands.

"Clark, you do not need to bring Gwen a pet. How many times do I need to tell you?" a female voice yelled from off screen.

"But we want one, Ma," he yelled back.

I laughed, as I hung partway off the bed, trying to get the pillow. "My nonna had cats. At home we had a dog."

The dog actually belonged to the youngest of my three brothers. Though out of all my siblings, I'd been closest to my oldest brother.

I'd been missing those two, and one of my sisters. But I had to be strong. There was no guarantee that my dads would stay out of my life if I started talking to my family again.

It was better this way.

Besides, I'm sure they were too busy with their important, grown-up lives.

"I feel like with our schedules, a cat would be better," Clark replied. "Also, easier to hide since we don't have to walk them. One day. We'll get a big dog?"

"Like malamute big." I put the pillow back. "Until then, yes, a little fluff ball will do. Hi, Snowball."

We talked for a few more moments, then he hung up. I couldn't wait for him to come back.

I grabbed two beers and slid on my flip-flops. Tenzin thought me walking across the hall barefoot was weird.

He let me in, I left my shoes by the door, and we settled on the couch with our beers. Tonight he had more chips for me to try. We watched the evening news, since I enjoyed knowing what was happening in the world.

Beers and snacks finished, Tenzin made us some tea, and we turned on the show. It was this Chinese drama, about an omega prince, who had an arranged marriage to a lady alpha general, even though the prince already had *three* beta wives.

I liked the relationship between the beta wives and the general, because the general was kind to them and protected them. It had subtitles, but I didn't mind.

We watched an episode while we drank our tea though I wasn't quite curled up in him the way I did with Clark.

The episode ended and Tenzin paused it. "Another?"

I looked at my phone. "We've been going to bed so late."

"Mmm hmmm, given you usually didn't hit the ice *after* you got off work?" Tenzin gave me a measured look. "You have a point. See you in the morning?"

"Are you still up for morning yoga in the park and a trip to see Marty before I hit the drop-in workout at my university?" I offered. I needed to see the NYIT physio after the workout, as the Knights' physio had been off.

"Then we'll go to music in the park? I'll bring the picnic if you bring the blanket?" he offered.

"Perfect. Good night, Big Guy."

"Why are you crying? I'm here now. We're finally together." He looked genuinely perplexed as I sobbed in the four-poster bed he'd tied me to.

"Let me go, I'm not your mate." I sniffed, fighting against the bonds.

He'd found me. He'd fucking found me after all this time. How? I had a new name, a new look, and it had been years.

"But I am." He sat down next to me and ran his fingers through my hair. I flinched at his touch. "Hey, none of that. I know you don't feel it yet. You will. We'll make a magnificent home together, you'll see. You're my match."

"Please don't." My belly clenched, because I knew what he meant by that.

I wasn't his true mate. I was just a beta. Even if I wasn't, we weren't soul mates—scent matches. I was merely the focus of his obsession.

Dumbass spoiled, entitled, rich, alpha brat.

"Don't be afraid. Don't you want to be with me forever?"

My dream twisted as his old-money, good looks faded into Austin's.

Austin sneered at me, eyes full of malice. There was a skate blade in his hand. "No? You're just a no good beta bitch, aren't you?"

The blade came down, biting into my neck as I screamed.

I sat up with a start, sweat running down my back, heart pounding. This was the third time this week I'd had some variation of this nightmare. Now they were back with Austin, who hadn't even been there. Even the fairy lights from Home Things couldn't keep them away.

My room felt suffocating, so I went to the kitchen and got a glass of water, the tile cool under my feet, the darkness now familiar.

"He can't get you," I muttered as I leaned against the counter, drinking my water, my hands still shaking, sloshing liquid on my tank-top. "It was years ago. He's gone. You're safe."

The feeling of being smothered, the terror, didn't stop. It was like he lurked in the shadows, even though that was impossible.

Before I could stop myself, I grabbed my phone, shoved my feet into my flip-flops, darted across the hall, and knocked on Tenzin's door, shaking, my mouth dry.

The door flew open and a shirtless Tenzin stood there. "What's wrong?"

I'd never heard such fierceness in his voice before. My arms wrapped around that bare, muscular chest, and I cried for everything I lost because of that spoiled, selfish man.

"Hey, it's okay, I've got you." His arms wrapped around me as he brought me inside and closed the door.

I slipped off my shoes and kicked them toward the rack by the door.

"What happened?" His voice was softer, but still reverberated with alpha authority.

"I had a nightmare." I winced. It sounded so childish when I said it out loud.

"Okay. Do you want to talk about it?" Tenzin's hand smoothed my hair.

"Absolutely not. If I don't talk about it, it never happened." I sniffed. Dealing with that time in my life hurt too much. So I ignored it.

"That's not healthy, but I won't make you talk about it tonight. What do you need?"

What do you need? Those four words catapulted me back to being a teenager, lying in bed with my mom, when she was too sick to move, and I had a broken hip, as we watched movies. One of my dads would come in and check on her. Mom was their omega, the love of their life. While they could be giant alphaholes, they'd do anything for her.

Her death had broken them.

I cried harder. My relationship with that time in my life was complicated, too.

Tenzin picked me up, and we sat on the couch in the dark living room. He pulled the blanket off the back and covered us with it. I nestled into his warm, hard body, letting his earthy, citrusy scent comfort me.

"You're safe. No one can hurt you here," Tenzin whispered as he stroked my hair.

It was so kind, so tender. It would be so easy to fall in love with him. Part of me really wanted to. Not just because being with someone filled the gaping wound in my soul that would never fully close.

As I drifted off to sleep, I wondered if he and Clark would still care about me if they knew I'd killed a man.

Chapter Twenty-Nine

CLARK

It was *early* in New York as the car stopped in front of my building. I got my stuff and went in, waving to the doorman. My place was quiet when I slipped inside, piling my bags in the living room.

"Gwen?" I called. It was about the time she got up in the mornings, so I didn't feel too bad about looking for her.

The bedroom door stood open, but her room was empty, her fairy lights still on, the sheets and pillows in disarray. It reeked of fear and sweat, like something bad had happened. Fear balled in the pit of my stomach.

"Gwen?" Where was she?

I opened the location app on my phone. We shared our locations with each other for safety. She was in the building?

Oh. Right. Her hockey friend, Tens, lived in the building. Must be a rich boy, considering he lived *here* and had a *truck*. I'd gone to community college and lived at home, borrowing my grandparents' car, or taking the bus.

I'd stayed local, partly because of money, partly because my family needed me. Also, if I'd gone away everyone would assume I was running away from what had happened with my high school girlfriend.

My stomach twisted more. Was Gwen seeing him? Had I missed my chance?

The front door opened, and I headed back into the living room as a barefoot Gwen in her pajamas walked in.

"Clark, you're back early. It's only Saturday." She threw herself into my arms, the look on her face bringing me joy.

"Hi, Gweny." I swung her around, holding her tight, relieved she was happy at my appearance.

I put her down, but held onto her. Another alpha's scent coated her, which made my belly clench with jealousy. At the same time, something about the woodsy yet citrusy scent turned me on.

"Where did you go?" The fear, anxiety, and tears underneath the other scents all made me worry.

"I was at Tens' place." She shrugged.

"Oh." My heart fell.

"None of that." Gwen's look turned fierce.

I shook my head, swallowing the bitter taste in my throat. "You're an adult. You can do what you want."

"I had a nightmare. A bad one." Her face buried in my chest, though my arms went slack. "I couldn't sleep. He held me on the couch and I cried myself to sleep. I didn't fuck him. I'm not ready to date—and he's not either."

My arms wrapped around her. "I'm so sorry you had a nightmare. If you want to talk about it, I'm here. Also... you can have sex with whoever you like. Also, fucking and dating can be different things. I also understand not being ready for that. I'm happy you have a friend like Tens to go to when I'm not here."

It was hard to say, but true. Ugh, I wanted to punch him. Cuddling Gwen was *my* job.

She clung to me like a burr. "Change of plans? Though I'm so glad you're back."

"Yeah. I have a meeting tonight. If all goes well, maybe I'll have a new sponsor," I told her, unable to hide my excitement.

"I'm so happy for you. I'm going to make some coffee. Want some?" She padded over to the kitchen.

"Please?" I plopped down on a stool at the breakfast bar, then texted Ma, letting her know I'd gotten in safely.

Gwen started the coffee.

"Apparently the Knights are getting the Yeti? Shit, he's imposing, but I get this sense that he's a good dude." I changed the subject to something neutral. "He's also so sexy. I mean, I work with some good-looking people, but something about him sort of does it for me."

Not quite as much as her.

"Have you met him?" Gwen leaned against the counter as the scent of coffee filled my kitchen.

"We did the calendar shoot together last year. He was that guy–the one that walked in on me, *twice,* while I was changing," I admitted. "I think I still have a crush on him."

"That's the guy?" She got down two mugs. "If you feel something, go for it. He's nice."

"You've met him?" Hmmm. She'd look cute between the two of us. I'd be fine with that if he was good to her and into it.

"I have." Her eyebrows waggled.

He probably already moved here, and she'd met him at the rink.

Someone knocked on the door. Maybe she ordered groceries?

I opened the door and there, filling my doorway, was a six-foot-eight, *shirtless* Asian guy, with a tattoo of a fish on his bicep, holding a pair of purple flip-flops.

All sorts of butterflies filled my stomach.

Why was a shirtless Yeti at my door so early on a Saturday morning?

Hot damn, that was one good looking wall of muscle.

"Oh, Clark, you're back." He gave me a shy smile. "Gwen must be so excited. Gwen, you forgot your shoes," the Yeti called over my shoulder.

"You didn't need to bring them back. I could have gotten them next time. But thanks." She took the flip-flops from him, giving him a fond look, and put them by the door.

Wait? What? Jealousy shot through me, because of the way she looked at him—and the way he looked at her.

I'd just confessed to her that I liked him. Confusion also bubbled to the surface, since she'd told me to go for it. It was obvious there could easily be more between them.

"Tens, this is Clark, forward for the Knights. Clark, this is Tenzin, the Knights' new defenseman." Gwen slipped an arm around my waist, which settled something in me.

The hurt look in the Yeti's eyes, the spicy edge to his scent, put me on edge. *Tens.* Tenzin. Gwen's rich friend that she'd been spending so much time with wasn't some spoiled classmate.

He was my team's new defenseman.

Which she'd failed to mention, as had Carlos and Dimitri, who'd both met him. Shit. She was friends with the guy I was crushing on.

He was crushing on her. I was crushing on her...

Tension filled the room, and a growl came from my chest. Tenzin huffed at me, nostrils flaring.

"No. None of that. I will absolutely not tolerate it. You both mean so much to me, more than I can say. So, I need you to cut out the alpha posturing and get right to being friends with each other. Or more than friends. I don't mind that. Both of you are very loveable in your own ways." Her voice broke as she took her free arm and put it around his waist, too, so she was holding both of us.

She did not say that. My face burned with embarrassment.

"Okay, Gweny. I'm sure Tens and I will be great friends." I gave her a little squeeze.

Tenzin nodded. "I'm looking forward to getting to know him."

"Good. The idea of you not getting along makes me want to vomit." Gwen shook a little as she looked from me to him, a pleading in her hazel eyes. "I... I need you both so bad. I'm not ready, but I need you both."

She pulled us close, until we sandwiched her between us, sideways, so she wasn't facing either of us.

Tenzin was *right there.*

"Not ready for us to be friends?" I blinked, not understanding, as my mind struggled to comprehend that her friend Tens was the Yeti.

Gwen turned to me, tipping her face up. Her lips grazed mine as she kissed me, soft and sweet. It was more than a peck, but not a full on tongue kiss. "We're already friends. I have a crush on you, you big dumb-dumb."

Shit. She liked me back! I couldn't help but grin as giddiness filled me. Gwen liked me. And that kiss...

That sweet kiss. I wanted some more. Gwen needed me. If I was a puppy, my tail would wag so hard, I'd sprain it.

She turned to Tens, who had a startled look on his face. Rising on her toes, she grabbed his head, pulled it down, and kissed him. His eyes widened, but he didn't push her away. His arm tightened around her, as I got hit with a whiff of arousal.

Seeing them kiss was sexy, and I was glad she'd positioned herself in a way where my hard-on wasn't digging into her.

"I'm crushing on you, too," she told Tenzin, breaking off the kiss. Her eyes teared. "I know it's unfair to ask you to wait for me, but I want you to. I'll try not to take too long. In the meantime, please be friends with each other—or more. I can't choose between you. It's not me being some fickle, indecisive beta. I truly need you both. Um, I really hope you both like me back. I'll be so embarrassed if you don't, and I could have just ruined everything."

Those tear-filled hazel eyes pleaded with us again. She'd taken a risk. After all, she lived with me and she hung out with Tens a lot.

"Gweny, I'm here. I like you back so much and have for some time. I've waited this long, so I can wait a little longer." Wiping away her tears, I ran my hand down her face.

She wanted both of us? I could deal with that if Tenzin was as nice of a guy as he was hot. There was something about the way he smelled...

Tens gulped, tension in his face, as he gazed at Gwen. "You're easy to fall for, Firecracker. Take as long as you need. By the time you're ready, maybe I'll be, too."

"Um, I need to get dressed if we're still going to make it to yoga in the park. Tens was coming with me. You're welcome to come too, Clark. We're going to the zoo after. You can see Marty. He misses you."

Without looking at either of us, she ducked out from between us and darted into her room, the door closing behind her.

Leaving me standing in the living room with a half-naked Yeti.

"Well, that was unexpected," I breathed. She liked me back. Such a relief.

Tenzin's eyebrows rose. "You didn't know she liked you?"

I shook my head. "No idea. I've liked her for a year. You okay, man? You like her back, right?"

"There's so much to like about her. I just don't know if I can give her what she wants." His eyes flickered over to her closed door.

"Oh." I deflated and looked away. "I... I'll step back for you."

Because I couldn't fight him for her. Tenzin was bigger, stronger, richer.

More ripped.

He shook his head. "That's not what I meant. Next year she'll be off with whatever team signs her. I don't know if I can be with her, knowing I'll have to give her up."

"Give her up? Do you honestly think that you have to quit her when she goes pro? Do you not do long distances?" I looked up at him, confused.

"I... I could. But the last thing I want to do is hold her back. She's so young." His look grew wistful.

"Young? She's a year older than me." An angry yowl came from by my suitcase. "Oh, shit, Snowball."

I went to the plush, soft sided cat carrier I'd gotten and retrieved a pissed off white kitten. "Sorry, Snowball. I got wrapped up in everything. Welcome to your new home."

"Isn't our building no pets?" Tenzin eyed the kitten cautiously.

"You won't tell, right?" I grinned. "Oh, are you allergic?"

"No. I've never been much of a cat person." He stared at her as she squirmed in my arms. "I should get dressed."

With that, the Yeti left my living room.

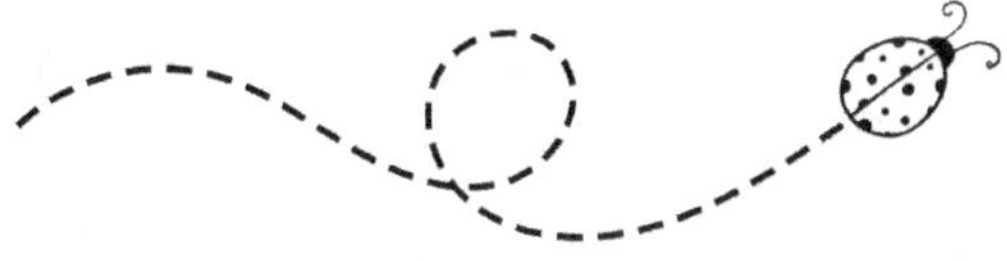

Chapter Thirty

GWEN

What had I done? Leaning against my closed door, I bent down and hyperventilated. The taste of Clark and Tenzin still lingered on my lips. I just told them I liked them. When had it gone from bathtub lust to *wait for me? I want a relationship with you both?*

It was true. I wanted to be with both of them.

Clark's kiss had been eager. Tenzin's tentative, but sweet.

I craved more...

Could the three of us even make a functional relationship? What did I know about being with more than one guy?

I took a super quick shower, mostly to wash off the stink of my nightmare, which still clung to my skin. There was a knock on the door right as I'd pulled on some leggings, with a sports bra, and a tank-top.

"Come in?" My heart pounded.

The door opened and Clark slipped in, wearing workout clothes and holding a little white kitten.

"Meet Snowball. I have her litter box set up in my bathroom, and her food and water in the kitchen by the washer. Tomorrow we can go to the pet store and get her some toys. Maybe order a cat tree?" He held out the little kitty.

"Hi, Snowball." I bundled the tiny, soft thing into my arms and she sniffed me curiously. My heart melted.

Clark beamed as he got closer to me. "My sisters, um, also told me I should finally tell you that I like you and I'm willing to wait."

His cheeks pinked, and something about his eager, but bashful expression made me want to kiss him.

Instead, I planted a kiss on Snowball's furry head. "Your sisters are smart."

He got us a cat. She was perfect, small and fluffy.

And he liked me back.

Wait, finally? How long had he liked me?

"The idea of you two being jealous of each other made my stomach churn. Would you be okay if I liked you both?" I scratched Snowball's little head.

"Yes, I'd be okay with you liking my crush. But did you have to say you're fine with us liking each other out loud like that? I mean, he might not like me. We don't even know each other." His embarrassment was evident. Also cute.

"I'm okay with it. I might want to watch sometimes. The idea of you two kissing gives me a lady boner," I admitted. So did the idea of me being smooshed between them.

Clark's face brightened. "I enjoyed seeing him kiss you. Why didn't you tell me that your friend Tens was the Yeti?"

"It started off innocently. He'd signed with the Knights, but wasn't ready to make it public due to his ex. Then it just became funny. You should have seen Carlos' face." I laughed.

"I can imagine," he replied.

"As for the kiss, I can't believe I did that." I ducked my head, focusing on Snowball.

Clark's arm slipped around my waist. "I'm happy you did. Like I said, I can wait. I'll work on getting to know Tens. I can't promise we'll end up lovers. But can you imagine being railed by him?"

I looked up into his eyes, framed by his black glasses. "I have imagined that. Usually you're railing me together."

His eyes looked like they'd bulge out of their sockets. "Gweny."

"I'm sad, not dead."

"You're still sad?" His hand smoothed my hair.

"Not about my ex. It's more like I'm mourning the time I lost and the decisions I made, because I didn't realize we were only playing house. I thought we were actually building our lives together." I leaned into his touch. It was more than that, but it was a good start.

His forehead tipped to mine. "I'm right here. So, is this good for yoga in the park?"

"Your outfit is great. I'm going to throw my bedding in to wash while we're out. My room smells weird from the nightmare." If I could smell it, Clark *definitely* could.

I put Snowball down, tossed everything in the washer, drank my coffee, then grabbed my stuff. There was a knock on the door.

Tenzin stood there, dressed in a T-shirt advertising fishing gear and workout shorts.

"I... I hope I didn't freak you out," I told him, belly twisting.

"Only a little?" Tenzin admitted.

"We can forget it happened for now. Bring it back up when we're ready?" I offered.

He nodded. "I'd like that."

Me, too, Tens, me, too.

"Hydrosteel might sponsor you? That's great," Tenzin said as we sipped our coffees and walked around the zoo after yoga in the park.

"They'd make a great sponsor. I hope they sign you. I like the blue hydrogels," I replied. Which were little squeezy packets of electrolyte gels and one of the company's many sports hydration products.

"Hopefully tonight's event will go okay." Clark nodded. "I'm helping my family upgrade their business and paying for my siblings' educations. Another sponsor would be helpful."

Tenzin nodded. "Your family fixes farm machinery?"

"Yep. We have the family tractor repair business, and a small engine repair shop that is mostly the domain of my teen sisters with a little oversight from one of my grandfathers." His eyes lit up. "One of my sisters holds the state title in chainsaw carving."

"Sounds fun," Tenzin replied. "I attended high school in Nashville. It was a shock to move there from the Himalayas. But I loved it. One of my favorite things was going to fairs, where chainsaw carving isn't uncommon."

"You grew up in the Himalayas? I didn't know that." Clark blinked.

I liked seeing them get along.

"That's why they call me the Yeti," Tenzin explained. "Most of my parents were scientists, working at a research station there. They met at university. Though one of my moms was a mountain guide."

"I saw that ad from the Yeti Soap Co. The one with you in the shower." I waggled my eyebrows.

Tenzin laughed. "I didn't know that was out."

"Oooh, I like their shower gel. Some of my parents met at the university. Ma was studying social work. My dads were all studying business and engineering," Clark replied. "Ma dropped out when one of my grandmas died. Grandma was an omega and everything went into a tailspin. My dads helped Ma out, and, well, never left the farm. Everyone finished their education eventually. They found Mom at a mixer at the Omega Center."

Packs could go to shit when their omegas died. I'd seen firsthand what my mom's death did to my dads. In some ways, it was better that my nonna and her pack died all together.

"What about you? I know your dads are assholes, but the few times you've mentioned your mom, you seem like you really loved her," Tenzin asked me.

I sighed as I led them toward the tiger enclosure. "Yeah, I miss her so much. She attended Posey, an omega school here in New York, and was in the choir. She met one of my dads at a reception after one of her concerts. He chased her around the world, running into her *on accident*. Babo's a hopeless romantic." I rolled my eyes.

"He introduced her to his pack, and eventually, she graduated and moved to live with them, mated them, and had the eight of us. They loved her a lot and I'll admit some of their assholery is directly connected to losing her. I just don't like it focused on me, even if I'm the baby of the family."

"That makes sense." Tenzin squeezed my hand.

"Where did you live when you weren't with your nonna upstate?" Clark asked.

"Vancouver. That's why I'd never play for the Belugas and also, why I'm afraid of Canada. I know Quebec is on the other side of the country, but what if I run into someone I know and they tell the dads they saw me?" Fear shot through me.

Clark put an arm around me, snuggling me to him. "I won't let anyone hurt you."

"You're an adult, you have nothing to fear from them," Tenzin assured.

I took a deep breath, enjoying the safety of his embrace. "I'll keep telling myself that."

"Um, are you doing the calendar again for Bare Armor?" Clark didn't meet Tenzin's eyes, as we leaned against the outer rail of the tiger enclosure.

"I am. Will I see you there this week?" Tenzin replied. "It should be fun."

"Maybe you'll be roommates." I grinned. "And there will only be one bed."

Clark laughed. "Sorry, but Gwen thinks we should hook up."

Tenzin got that deer-in-the-headlights look. "I... I'm not ready for any of that."

"Sorry. Keep it in your head, Gweny." Clark bumped my hip with his. "You can tell me when we're alone," he whispered.

I couldn't help but giggle and I took both their hands. "Now let's go see Marty. Maybe today we can take him for a walk."

Chapter Thirty-One

CLARK

"You know, when you said we were going clubbing with the Yeti, this was *not* what I expected," Carlos whispered as we sat at a high-top, in a honky-tonk bar, that seemed *very* out of place in New York City.

It felt a lot like the dive-bar in town my parents liked to go dancing at on Saturday nights.

Everything with Hydrosteel had gone well. Today, I'd successfully signed with them and we'd gone out to Tito's to celebrate. When Gwen wanted to go dancing with Tenzin and me, Carlos and Dimitri asked to come with us.

Here we were.

"Tens is into it." I took a sip of beer as I watched her two-step with Tenzin. They were cute in their hats and boots as he twirled her around the dance floor. While I knew a few line dances, I didn't know how to do *this*.

"Well, Lucky likes country bars. We'll send Grif a pic." Carlos tipped his beer like he was giving the cat some and snapped a photo.

I found the whole imaginary cat thing a little weird, but it wasn't the strangest thing I'd encountered playing hockey.

The song ended and people started a line dance that was common at weddings back home, so I dragged Carlos out and joined them.

Gwen waved at me as she kicked, turned, and stomped. Tenzin looked relaxed and at home. It made me very curious about all the time he spent in bars with his sister, while he was in high school. Maybe she was a bartender, and he sat in the corner doing his homework, while she worked, like Ma's friend's kid.

After a few dances, we all came back to the table to drink some water and get more beers. The music changed as Gwen twirled around, closing her eyes, holding her beer. "I love this song," she squealed.

It was one of those revenge songs, this one about throwing your ex's truck in the lake, and it had a good beat. This version seemed to be sped up with a thumpy warehouse track to it. Apparently, it had a dance. A bunch of women came onto the floor and did a modified version of another I knew.

Gwen's cheeks were flushed as she set her beer on the table and took my hand, dragging me out to the floor.

Tenzin shot me an amused look, toasting me with his beer, as I took the floor with her. Without bumping into too many people, I managed to figure out the dance, mostly. We did a few others, our friends joining us. Everything then slowed down for a two-step.

Gwen took my hand. "Dance with me."

Oh, how I wanted to. I shook my head. "Gweny, I have no idea how to do that."

"I'll dance with you, Bozh'ya Korovka." Dimitri took her hand and swept her off her feet.

Leaving me in the dust.

"How does he do that? I swear the man didn't even know what country music was when we walked in here," I muttered.

Tenzin stood at my side. "Come."

Without waiting for me, he turned and left the dance floor. I followed him to a place near the back by some pool tables.

"I'll teach you. You be Gwen, so you can understand how to lead her." Tenzin took my hands and put one on his hip, the other on his shoulder. His hands weren't baby smooth, but they weren't rough either. They were also *large.*

You know what they say about large hands.

"Her hands go on you like this. Yours would go like this." He placed his hands on me, pulling me close, but not incredibly so.

I could feel the heat of his body through his button-down shirt, his jeans, and smell his heady citrusy scent, as he led me through the very basic steps.

"Now, to get fancy, here are a few things she likes." Tenzin showed me how to twirl her and a few other moves.

I tried to pay attention. After all, it was kind of him to teach me to dance, so I could go out there with Gwen. It grew difficult to focus though, because his intent teaching face was sexy.

Would he look like that during sex?

Not to mention we were a good height for dancing together. His scent was so enticing, and I could only imagine what sort of muscles those clothes hid.

My low-key crush on the Yeti had been growing.

It was easy to pretend he was dancing with me, whirling me around the floor, us on a date, rather than him teaching me to dance, so I could make Gwen happy.

If we were going to do this eventually, the three of us, I think I'd like to have a piece of him, too.

Well, if he liked me back. Yet there was *something* between us. I could feel it.

"You're doing so good. You're going to look great with her," he praised, as he twirled me out, then pulled me back in.

Distracted at the thought of him kissing me, I nearly hit his chest. I looked up into his eyes. His lips were right there. What if I kissed him?

"Yes, like that." Tenzin's voice grew breathy, his lips close to my ear.

My breath caught in my chest, as the bar and music faded away, until it was only us.

Kiss him.

"There you are," Carlos said, breaking the moment, and we practically popped apart.

"I was teaching him to dance so Dimitri doesn't steal her all night." Tenzin looked at me and smiled. "You'll do great. I'll get her more water. She's had quite a few beers."

Tenzin left, and I scanned the bar for Gwen, my heart pounding in my ears.

"Um, what was *that?*" Carlos smirked as we returned to our table.

Yeah, what was that?

"He was teaching me to dance." My voice was tight. Why did he have to interrupt us? What would have happened?

"Yes, and I didn't fall into my ex's bed the last time I saw her." His smirk grew.

I itched to smack that smirk off his face. "You didn't have to do that."

Carlos's eyes widened. "You like him? I thought you liked Gwen."

Whoops. I wasn't sure I wanted my teammates to know I was crushing on our newest member.

"Shit, you *do!*" He grinned. Then he glanced at the dance floor. "Does she know?"

"Yes. Why can't I like both?" I kept my eyes on the floor as Gwen laughed and danced.

"You can." Carlos shrugged. "I just haven't known you to like anyone and now you like *two* people?"

"I wasn't ready for a relationship." It had taken me a long time to get over my high school girlfriend, and the guilt I'd felt, even though it wasn't my fault. My college boyfriend broke up with me when I'd gotten signed by the Knights. Last year, I focused on my career.

Now I might be ready for something.

Carlos looked over at Tenzin and Dimitri, who were near the bar, talking. "Gwen *and* Tens? I mean, you and Gwen make sense. But Bucket? Huh. Gwen brings something out in him. Like who'd have thought he was such a beast on the dance floor?"

Or make jeans and a Cowboy hat look so delightful? I didn't have a fancy hat and boots like he and Gwen did, but maybe I'd ask Ma to send mine along, with some more pickles and the jam Gwen liked.

"Um, don't tell? Please? I mean, I have no idea about any of this." I finished my now-warm, half-full beer.

"Of course not, man. I think he's still broken up over whatever happened in Portland." Carlos signaled the waitress for more beer.

"I think so too." I'd gotten the gist of it from Gwen. "Should I be worried about starting something with her, given who knows where she'll be next year?" I wasn't concerned, but Tenzin was.

Carlos shook his head. "No. Also, this is Gwen. What she wants, she gets."

Tenzin and Dimitri came back with beers and waters for everyone. He didn't meet my gaze, instead looking at the dance floor.

"She's a good dancer," I said, not knowing what else to say.

"She is. She comes to dance class with me sometimes." Dimitri drank his beer.

Dimitri attended dance classes? Well, he was very graceful on the ice.

Tenzin held up the glass of water and gestured for her to come join us.

A breathless Gwen came off the dance floor and took the water from him, gulping it down. "Thanks."

The music changed, and she looked up at me with those enormous hazel eyes, her lashes a bit sparkly. "Dance with me, Clark? I don't care if you step on my feet."

Tenzin gave me a look that said *you've got this.*

"You're sure about that? I wouldn't want to hurt your toes." I stood and took her hand as her eyes lit up.

"Absolutely." She led me to the floor, her smile giving me confidence.

"I'm not very good at this." I positioned her hands on me, the way Tenzin had, a shiver going up my spine as I remembered his touch.

Gwen smiled at me as we danced. "I don't care. I just want to dance with you."

What she wants, she gets. True. Gweny had me wrapped around her tight. Tenzin smiled at me as we danced past.

Would it be too much to hope the same for him?

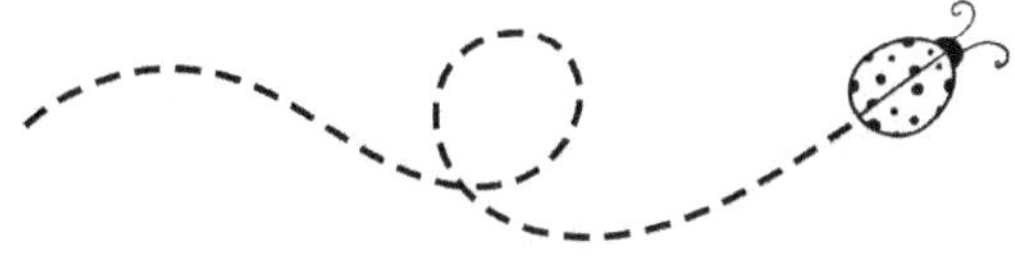

Chapter Thirty-Two

CLARK

"**G**ood morning, Tenzin." I waved as the car we were sharing to the airport pulled up. It wasn't even light yet, but we had an early flight to get to the photo shoot for the Bare Armor calendar.

Tenzin gave me a nod. He might not be a morning person.

We put our bags in the trunk and got in.

"This should be fun," I told him, excitement bubbling inside me. "I haven't been to too many places." We were going to an island off the southern coast.

Tenzin nodded, taking a sip of whatever was in his tumbler. Tea most likely. "It should be nice."

We checked in with the Bare Armor PR person. It looked like we were all on the same flight and sleepy patrons waiting for their flights were checking us all out. We were a good-looking group, all of us wearing suits.

I went to ask Tenzin if he wanted to go to the coffee stand, but he was sitting already, reading a book on national parks.

As I walked to the cart, I texted Gwen.

Me

What kind of tea does Tenzin like?

Gwen

Jasmine

I got myself a coffee and a croissant, then got Tenzin a jasmine tea and a tiny blueberry muffin. He liked muffins, right? After all, that was his and Gwen's thing, trying muffins at different places across the city. She'd post pictures of them.

Tenzin was still reading when I returned. He looked up when I stood in front of him.

"Here." I offered it to him, belly churning. Was this even a good idea? Yes, it was, since I was being *kind*.

"Thank you." His eyes brightened a little.

"Um, I wasn't sure if you like muffins, well, I mean, you do, right?" Why was this so awkward?

"I do." He took a sip of his tea and his eyebrows rose as if to ask how I knew what to get.

"I asked Gwen." I ducked my head.

Tenzin gave me a nod of thanks and picked up his book.

The flight attendant called for first class and we boarded. I found myself next to Tenzin. The seats weren't as comfy and spacious as the Knights' private plane, but were still big enough for most alphas. Tenzin looked uncomfortable, but then he was a big boy.

He had his book out. "Thank you again. The muffin was the perfect size. You got the blueberry with the little sugars on it. It's my favorite. But don't feel you have to do things like that for me."

The praise made a very different type of warmth flow through me. "You do such a good job of taking care of Gwen. Who takes care of you?"

His head cocked. "I'm an alpha. I take care of people."

"Same. Hey, do you like the beach? I hope we get to spend some time there." I'd only been a couple of times.

Maybe I'd take my family on a vacation next off-season. The problem was that hockey off-season was high-season for my parents.

"I enjoy going to places I've never been," he told me, as people continued to board. "I'd like to get some good photos."

"That sounds nice. I'd like to see the stars there. It's fun looking for the same constellations in different places. I've never been good at photographing them, though," I replied.

Tenzin nodded. "Photographing the sky is an art."

I got out my Game Buddy. "Do you play video games?"

He shook his head. "Not really. Your tie is crooked."

Tenzin straightened my tie, making me once again very aware of him. Of his touch. The muscles in his face. His citrus scent that wasn't quite lemon or lime.

"There. That's a very interesting tie pattern." He brushed my suit with his hands.

"Oh, Gwen got it for me. It's like the wallpaper in the waiting room of the Defender League headquarters in the movies. The tie tack is their symbol. I have a matching pocket square, but I'm not really a pocket square guy. I used it to make wallpaper on my bookshelf for my Defender League figures," I told him. "Do you like those movies?"

My dad taught me to read using the comics, and I still found them and graphic novels easier than books.

The flight attendant brought us drinks. Tenzin blinked a little, like he had no idea what I was saying.

"I love Professor Weird," he finally told me. "That latest movie with the multiverse was a mind-fuck."

"I know, right? The multiverse is trippy." Of course, his favorite Defender League character was Professor Weird, who was one of the more obscure characters. Gwen loved Aquatica, who was an underwater badass. I liked Captain Everything, given he was cheerful and always did what he thought was right.

He eyed the tie. "Gwen got it for you?"

"She got my name in the team holiday gift exchange last year." My cheeks burned. "Since we wear suits, she thought I'd like it." I loved it.

"You looked good out there, dancing with her," he added, gazing at me.

"It was fun. Don't feel you need to include me in all the special things you and Gwen do together. It's okay for us to do different things with her," I told him. "Like outdoor yoga–or that show you watch. You can keep those. Though I will totally join you at the zoo for Marty visits."

His head cocked. "Is it the show itself or the subtitles?"

My breath caught in my chest. "The subtitles. How... how did you know?"

"Cooter is dyslexic. He prefers dubbing to subtitles. I'm unsure if there's a dubbed version of this one. When we start a new show, I can look for a dubbed version?" he offered.

"That would be nice, but again, you and Gwen should have your things. I don't want to encroach." I was amazed that he guessed, since it wasn't something I told people. It was why I preferred comics to books.

"We have lots of things. I don't mind sharing. Do you like art?" he asked.

"I like art museums in the sense that they tend to have interesting architecture," I replied. They could keep art museums, too.

"Yes. You're an engineer. She told me all about the cow-house you designed. I can't believe you got her a cat." He shook his head.

"I figured that if I got a cat, it would give her a task to do while house-sitting and make her feel better about not paying rent."

He nodded. "Ah, yes, I see. That is a sound plan."

"Also, Snowball is so cute," I gushed. "Here's a picture of her sleeping on Gwen." I showed him the photo I'd taken through her open door the other day.

One thing Gwen had gotten on her trip to Home Things was a net canopy with fairy lights. Most everything was in different shades of purple. She looked like a sleeping princess.

"You're a good friend to her. I hope you know that," he told me.

There was something in the way he looked at me that made me all gooey inside.

"I just treat people the way I like to be treated." I gazed at him right back, hoping he knew that he was included in that sentiment. Something about him awakened instincts in me I'd never felt.

It went beyond crushing on him. It was a sense of rightness. Of belonging.

"Good."

The air whooshed out of my lungs as he said that.

"I didn't mean to keep walking in on you. Last time we did the shoot. It was an accident, not some weird flex or power play." His voice was quiet.

"It's fine." My heart fluttered a little, since I hadn't expected him to bring that up.

I knew it was an accident. They had us changing in these little pop-up tents and it was hard to know if they were occupied.

"Did you like what you saw?" It came out in a bare whisper and I didn't look at him.

"Yes."

He liked what he saw? Mmmm. I couldn't wait to tell Gwen.

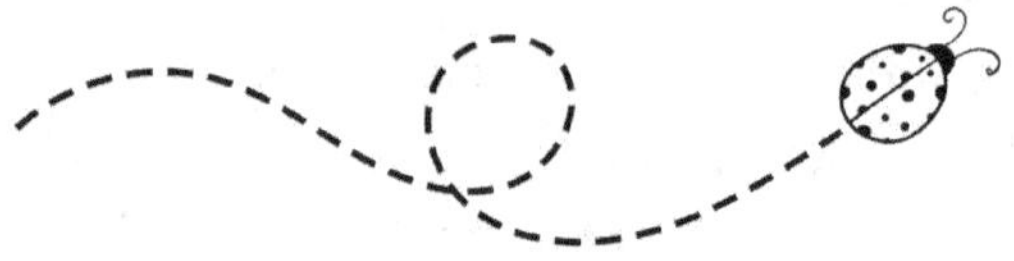

Chapter Thirty-Three

GWEN

Restarting the music, I ran through the wedding dance routine one more time in the dance room. The Maimers used it to learn their dance battle numbers before they hit the ice. The Knights also used it for yoga class.

Tens and Clark had left this morning to go to some tropical island for their underwear calendar. Carlos had to go shoot for Monstruo Lane and Dimitri needed to do things. So I was working on the dance we were doing for Celine at JP's wedding.

Yeah, this was going to be fun. *Hard.* But fun. I couldn't wait.

I took a quick shower and changed into one of my cute, but not too fancy, outfits that Valya had gotten me, then fixed my makeup.

Grabbing my backpack, I walked past Constantine's door, but it was closed. I could give Maddox crickets tomorrow.

I took the subway back toward my old neighborhood. So many complicated feelings washed over me as I stood in front of Chello's. I hadn't been here since the day I picked up takeout before Austin and I broke up.

I can do this.

Inside, I saw Lenny already sitting at a table. I let the hostess know and joined him.

"Buttons." Lenny grinned. His nose was more crooked than mine, and there was a scar on his olive jaw, from when he went cliff diving. Long black hair was up in a ponytail, and he wore a suit that could have paid my rent in my old place for months.

I'd known him my whole life. When I was little I thought he *was* one of my brothers because he and my oldest brother were always together. When he wasn't around I just figured he was at work or something.

"Hey, Lenny." I put my backpack on the empty chair.

The alpha looked around. "Low-brow Italian hole-in-the-wall? I was expecting a pastrami sandwich."

"If I freak out, we'll go to the deli. I need to do this. This used to be my favorite place. Last time I ate it was when Austin and I broke up." I took a deep breath.

He leaned across the table and swept my bangs away, which I'd gotten to help hide the scar.

His boney face clouded. "Who hurt you?"

"Austin." I opened the menu and was catapulted to the last time Austin and I were here in person. He'd taken me here after NYIT had won the national championships for our division. I'd worn a cute dress, he'd worn a suit.

Even though we'd been over-dressed for this place, we acted like we were going to a top restaurant. The staff had been kind to us and gave us a free glass of wine.

I sniffed and put the menu down. Maybe this was a bad idea.

"You okay? Want me to take care of him?" His dark brown eyes met mine over the menu.

I shook my head, tears running down my face. "Ugh, I spent so many years on him. I don't want to think it was a waste, but…"

"Oh, Buttons." He pushed my napkin toward me. "You were young. Young, dumb, and in love. A lot has happened to you. For you, Austin was safe and I'm sure this has cut deep. We don't have to eat here. However, I admire you trying to conquer this, instead of pretending it didn't happen."

I glared at him. He shrugged as the server took our drink orders. I ordered a glass of wine. Lenny ordered one too.

"Do I order what I always order, or something new?" I studied the menu. I could do this.

"You could always order for the both of us, then if one dish makes you cry, we'll trade," he told me. "I'm proud of you."

"It's been almost two months. He hurt me. Shouldn't I be over it?" I sniffed. "Why am I like this?"

"Grief is a process. Yes, you can experience grief when a relationship ends–and you can mourn the relationship and not the person." His expression softened. "Five years is a *huge* part of your life."

That made sense. "The things I miss most aren't really *him*. It's the things he did. It's cuddles. It's having someone to talk to at the end of the day."

"Get a roommate and a dog. That's what I did." His eyes went a little glassy. Lenny's fiancée had left him years ago and I'm not sure he ever got over it.

I nodded. "I moved in with my friend and his cat."

"Also, Buttons–and I say this because I care about you–you know why you're like this, and you know how to fix it." While his voice was gentle, eyes full of care, the words stung.

I flinched. "Fuck you."

If I didn't think about it, it never happened.

The server brought our wine and a basket of bread, eyes wide. "Should I come back?"

"Order before you get hangry," Lenny told me, his alpha voice no-nonsense.

I sighed. "Fine. We'll have the stuffed mushrooms to start. I'll have the house salad, he'll have the minestrone soup. I'll have eggplant parmesan with spaghetti. He'll have chicken fettuccine."

There. I always wanted to order the eggplant, but never did since it was expensive. Usually, I ordered the fettuccine, with no chicken, because it was cheaper.

"Very good." The server scurried off.

Lenny shook his head. "I worry about you."

"Don't." I looked away. "Um, I'm seeing a therapist again."

"Good. You do know that no one believes you, about you stopping because the insurance didn't cover it." His look grew smug.

I scratched my nose with my middle finger. "You're not telling them you saw me, right?"

"Your dads? No. Matty, yes—but only that I saw you, and that you're okay."

The second part was most likely a partial lie, but I was a beta, so I couldn't smell them. I was sort of okay with him telling my oldest brother about me. As long as no one came for me.

"Matty's the only one who knows I see you sometimes. But if your dads ever ask me directly, I won't be able to lie to them." He took a piece of bread and dipped it in olive oil.

That I believed.

"Do you want to talk about Austin? Last time I saw you, you were hopeful about hockey finals and Austin getting signed." He held up his half-eaten bread. "This is good."

"I guess." I gave him the short version as I ate too much bread and drank my wine.

"So he disappeared? He owes you money. He hurt you. I'll find him and he'll pay." His look grew intense.

"Alphas like Austin get away with everything, you know that." I pressed back memories of another entitled alpha that got away with too much, until it was too late.

"We don't have to let law enforcement handle it." He cracked his knuckles. "That only complicates things."

I rolled my eyes at his alpha posturing. Part of me was honored he'd make such an offer. At the same time, fear struck me. Acting against people could have *very* unexpected repercussions.

"I don't know who he actually is. While I hope his family runs a pig farm or a plumbing service, it could be someone we don't want to mess with." I shook my head.

Lenny looked unimpressed. "I don't care who he is. If you want to know, I'll find out. It doesn't mean we have to act, but it's an option. No one is going to hurt you. Never again."

I scowled, not liking that he kept bringing that up. "No one can make promises like that."

The server took away the empty appetizer platter and brought my salad and his soup.

He took a sip of soup. "Not your nonna's, but not bad."

"This place reminds me of her. The sauce is not as tasty as hers, but still good," I admitted, taking a bite of salad. "Enough about me. What's new with you?"

Lenny caught me up on his antics. Some of which might be true. Though I wasn't sure about him being chased across Paris by super model spies in sports cars. But who knew? Besides restoring paintings, he was a procurer of things and information. Which was why I fenced shit through him.

Our dinner came, and I gazed at my eggplant parmesan, then at his chicken fettuccine.

"What do you think, Buttons?" he asked.

"I can do this." I took a bite of the eggplant, the deliciousness of the sauce making me dance in my chair.

Lenny grinned. "Now that's a good sign. Last year of university? I'm proud of you. Not to mention, unlike your brothers, you got into a top school all on your own."

"I'd never thought about it that way." My three alpha brothers were pretty smart and hardworking. As I tore through my dinner, he asked me about classes, hockey, and the like.

"Do you want news about any of your siblings?" he offered.

I shook my head. "I... I don't think so."

Lenny frowned. "Okay. Do you ever listen to true crime forensic accounting podcasts?"

"Are you talking about JoeCountant and Its Accrual World? That is Joe, right?" I'd know my brother's voice anywhere. "That is so weird that he does those, but fascinating."

They were great podcasts and my classmates loved them.

"I think he does it for you, hoping you're out there listening. He pulled away a lot after you left. Not to mention he *is* an accountant." He took a bite of his food.

"Oh." My heart swelled. Joe was the youngest of my three older brothers. He did them for me? That was a very Joe thing. Like hanging up fairy lights in my bathroom, because I was afraid of the dark, but didn't want to be teased for having a nightlight.

I wished I could have a relationship with my siblings without worrying about the dads.

Over dessert, I got out the jewelry from Austin and pushed it across the table. "All proceeds will buy mice that the zoo will name after Austin and feed to snakes."

I couldn't wait.

"That's *amazing.*" Lenny looked over the small pile. "This is shit. Glad you're okay with tuition, since this won't buy much of anything." He gave me a look. "Are you sure you're okay?"

"Ugh. I don't need anyone's money. Didn't I make that clear? I'm *fine.* Tuition is covered. I have a place to live and a job. Now I

can finish my last year myself. I like my life, thank you very much."
My jaw set.

If I gave in the slightest bit...

"Good for you. Personally, I'm proud of you for doing your own thing." He took the jewelry and got out his phone. "It's not much, but it should buy some mice."

A notification showed that he'd overpaid me. It was going to the zoo, so whatever. "It's a pleasure doing business with you."

His look softened. "Always."

We left and talked about nothing until his car came.

"Do you need a ride?" he asked.

"I'm good, thank you. Thanks for dinner." I was working a late shift at the rink tonight.

Today made me feel a lot lighter. I'd made progress today. Between eating at Chello's and selling the last link I had to him, I felt ready to put Austin behind me.

In the staff locker room, I put on my uniform. I clocked in, then took my place at the snack bar. Yeah, I was feeling much better.

After I got off work, I was going online and buying some mice with Austin's name on them.

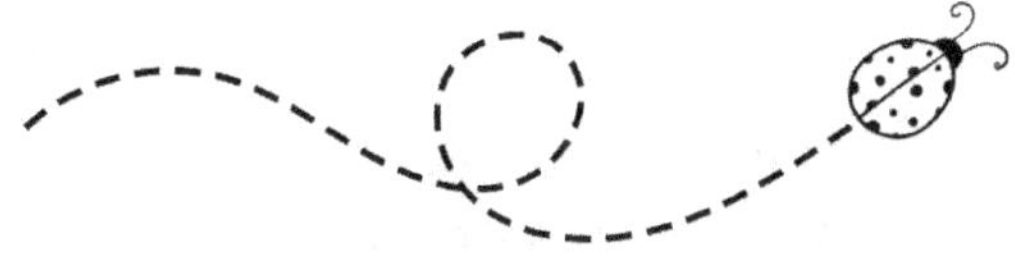

Chapter Thirty-Four

TENZIN

All around me, people laughed, chatted, and drank as music played in the background. The ballroom at the beachfront hotel we'd been put up in was filled with posters advertising Bare Armor. As nice as the party was, after a long day of photo shoots, I was done with people.

My phone buzzed, and I slipped outside. The summer air was warm and humid, but better than inside. I walked along the patio, until the noise of the ballroom gave way to sounds of the night. Leaning against the metal fence that separated the resort from the beach, I checked my phone.

I missed Gwen so much. But tomorrow afternoon we'd head back to New York. On Sunday, we'd go to the fair and see my sister's band play. Should I ask Clark to come with us? He was high energy and cheerful, but there was something about him.

It wasn't just how physically attractive he was. Or that he was kind to Gwen. We didn't have that much in common, other than hockey and similar taste in music. Still…

He felt right. They both did.

"There you are." Clark bounded over to me.

"You found me. Did you want to go for a walk? I'm done with the party." I looked back at the lights, music drifting toward us.

"I'd like that." Clark gave me a shy smile.

He and Gwen were good together. Both of them were cheerful rays of sunshine. She was the morning sun, and he was mid-day.

They were closer to the same age too. He didn't seem phased by her going off at the end of the season.

If only I could be like him.

We walked in silence, following the railing of the hotel, until it led to a gate to the beach. As we trudged through the sand, Clark took off his shoes and socks, then ran with abandon.

He was so carefree, and I loved that about him. I took some pictures of him running in the moonlight. Yes, I could use a little more sunshine in my life.

"Tag." Clark touched my shoulder, and took off running across the beach, dropping his socks and shoes. When he noticed I wasn't following him, he turned around, running backwards, arms out. "Come get me."

What a loaded statement.

"Come on," he teased. "You're it."

He wanted to be chased, did he? Maybe it was time to see if what I'd felt when we'd danced in the bar was real.

Without saying a word, I took off my socks and shoes, and put them neatly on the sand. I took off after him with a little growl.

"Shit, man." Clark laughed as he changed angles, heading toward the water, trying to avoid me.

I raced after him, trying not to let the thoughts of what I might like to do with him when I caught him slow me down. Usually, I wasn't playing tag for innocent funsies.

No, I played for another sort of amusement.

He turned again, and I dove, tackling him to the sand. My hands pinned his shoulders to the ground as I straddled him.

Chest heaving a little, I bent forward, my face hovering close to his. "Caught."

Clark's breath quickened, and I felt him harden under me. Oooh, he *liked* that.

I could imagine it now–chasing him, catching him, stripping off his clothes, and tying his wrists with his tie or my belt.

Making him scream my name as he came.

His scent, like a field of freshly mowed grass in the summer, flared with desire.

"You caught me. I... I'm at your mercy." Clark's eyes sparkled in the moonlight.

What was I doing? I let go and got off of him. "Are you okay? Apologies for being overzealous. I think we play tag differently."

He looked up at me, still lying back in the sand. "I think I like this type of tag."

For a moment we said nothing, listening to the lapping waves of the ocean, and looking up at the stars. Even with the lights from the resort, a vast expanse of twinkling stars filled the sky.

"When did you get a tattoo?" I finally asked. I'd noticed a small one on his leg and I didn't remember it before.

"Have you met Gwen's friend Mercy yet? She had a tattoo artist at her birthday party, though it's the artist Gwen used for hers on her back. Anyway, I got Captain Everything's shield. I'd always wanted one and it was free," he told me.

"I've met Mercy. That sounds like some party," I told him, looking up at the stars.

"It was." His voice was soft as he turned his head to face me. "Hey, I understand if you're not ready for more yet. I'll wait for you, just like Gwen."

"Why?" I looked for different constellations in the sky. Why would they wait?

"Because you're kind. Because you're smart. Because we like lots of the same things. Because you look hot in a pair of jeans. Because you care for Gwen as much as I do. Because you play hockey with such intensity and I can't wait to see how that plays out in other ways. Because I wanted you from the moment you walked in on me last year, and getting to know you the past few days has only increased my crush from low-key to major."

His look grew coy. "Need me to go on?"

I sucked in a breath and turned to face him. "Thank you."

He'd look so good on his knees. Clark also took direction well, I noticed that when we were dancing.

Clark started pointing out constellations in the night sky, some of them I knew, and some I didn't—and some he had different names for. Like the one he called *ladybug*.

Yes, this was nice, indeed.

"I... I'm in year two of a two-year contract," Clark said softly. "I could be traded at any time. That doesn't mean I don't want whatever the three of us are, for however long we can do it. Life is so fleeting; you can blink and it's gone. I'd rather have Gwen for a season, then kiss her and wish her the best, than not have her at all. That's all I want to do—love her and support her... I'd do the same for you."

My heart pounded. The three of us already had the potential to be so comfortable together. Logistically difficult, but still comfortable. Dancing. Watching movies. Playing hockey.

"We'll wait. Give us a chance, Tens? Please?" His voice was breathy, eyes on the stars.

"Okay." I wanted to. Wanted them.

Clark reached over and squeezed my hand. "Good."

Chapter Thirty-Five

TENZIN

"That was delicious," Gwen told me as she finished her funnel cake. Powdered sugar covered her face. She threw the paper tray in the trash bin. It was one of my favorites, especially with whipped cream and strawberries.

The fair was busy, as children ran around excitedly, people ate and chatted, and the sounds and smells of my teenage years surrounded us. The mid-August heat pressed down on us, the breeze easing it only slightly. I should have worn short sleeves.

"You have powdered sugar on your nose." I reached over and brushed her soft skin with my thumb. Her eyes closed as she leaned into me. Last night she'd needed so many snuggles that I'd fallen asleep on their couch with the two of them. At least Clark had a long and *wide*, comfy alpha-sized couch.

Gwen required a lot of love and care. Especially if she was going to successfully transition from being a student that hid in the shadows to a professional athlete. I could do that.

"Let's ride some rides?" Clark suggested, holding the stuffie he'd won for Gwen.

"I'd like to ride the bubble wheel." Gwen pointed to a sky wheel made up of little bubbles, that looked like the passenger could see out, but you couldn't see in.

That had potential. We passed a fun house. Using my phone, I bought us some ride credits.

"Firecracker, can I chase you through the funhouse?" I whispered, pulling her close.

"What do you get if you catch me?" Her voice became breathy as her minty scent flared with desire.

I nuzzled her soft cheek with my nose. "A kiss."

More, actually. I could smell her desire and I needed her to relax before my alpha took over and decided the best way to settle her was to sit her on my cock.

After that moment with Clark, I realized I did want them. I just needed to move slowly. And start with her. Put her needs above mine.

Right now, she needed to come.

"You want her alone?" Clark asked, biting his lower lip. He might sense it, too.

"Please. Meet us by the exit?" I bribed the ride operator to let us go in alone and give us a little extra time before he let in more people, but it wasn't popular like some of the other rides.

Taking her hand, we walked in, surrounded by mirrors and tilted floors. I leaned in and whispered one word in her ear. "Run."

Gwen took off running. She wore that white sundress—a bold choice for a fair—along with her boots and hat.

While I was aware our alone time in the funhouse was finite, I wasn't in too much of a hurry, as I followed the sounds of her boots. Suddenly, they stopped.

"Are you hiding from me, Firecracker? We're playing tag, not hide and seek." I rounded the corner and caught a bit of white fabric as she disappeared. Picking up the pace, I continued until mirrors surrounded us. She squeaked, then ran, but got disoriented by all the mirrors.

I got no fear from her minty scent, only desire.

In a few steps, I closed the gap between us and grabbed her by the waist. "Caught you."

"I concede." She turned to face me, tipped up her head, and *booped* me on the nose with her finger, nails painted sparkly pink.

Leaning down, I gave her a sweet peck on her lips. Sure, she got caught, but I needed to be gentle with her. I pressed her into the mirror, making sure one of my thighs was between her legs as I devoured her mouth.

One of my hands ran down her body, toying with her nipples through the thin fabric. I'd been wanting to do this for some time. We hadn't done more than snuggle.

Gwen ground into me, hard, as her hands cupped my ass, pulling me into her as she got me in just the right place for maximum friction.

"Good girl," I murmured, as one hand worked under her dress. "Take what you need. My firecracker needs to pop so badly."

Ooof. That was cringy. She kept kissing me, rubbing herself on my thigh. Her panties grew damp as I caressed her through the fabric. Releasing her lips, I sucked on her neck.

Her breath caught and her chest shook.

"Let go and come for me like a good girl," I growled. She ground against me hard one more time, then an orgasm shuddered through her body.

"Tens," she breathed, as she looked up at me in a way that made my heart explode.

I bundled her in my arms, her body still pressed between me and the mirror. "That's my girl. You're going to feel so much better now."

Also, I selfishly did this so I didn't lose control.

For a long moment, I held her in silence, peppering her head with tiny kisses, as I took in her heady scent. "Are you okay? I didn't push you, did I?"

"It was perfect," she sighed. "I've been wanting you to touch me for so long."

"I enjoyed touching you. We should go." I kissed her nose. My dick was hard, but this was about making *her* feel better.

If at some point she asked for more, I wouldn't say no.

Chapter Thirty-Six

CLARK

S till holding onto his hand, she took mine when they exited the funhouse. Cheeks flushed, she smelled of arousal.

Tens also looked smug. When he asked to go into the funhouse with her alone, I knew he had something planned.

Had he chased her? Mmmm. I'd let him chase me through a funhouse–and happily take the consequences when I got caught.

"What next?" I asked her. Maybe I could kiss her on something.

"Bubble wheel!" Gwen skipped toward it, pulling us along.

Oh, yeah, that was a great ride for kissing.

We got into the bubble wheel line. When it was our turn, the three of us squished into a bench seat. The door shut, enclosing us in a bubble that had windows where we could see out, but there was only a small window you could see in as the wheel of individual bubbles went round and round.

Tens' hand caressed her bare thigh, pushing her white dress up a bit. "Do you need Clark to make you come too?"

Her lips parted, as did her legs, and her eyes blew out with desire. "Yes, please."

"You made her come?" I tucked the stuffie in my backpack.

"She got caught. I think our sweet girl needs to come again." His hand worked up under her dress.

The tiny car filled with her arousal as her eyes went half-lidded.

My eyebrows rose. "You want me to fuck her on the ride?"

"Yes," she gasped as he touched her. "Take me while he watches? I can take a knot, but I don't think we have time for that."

"Are you sure, Gweny? I didn't think our first time would be on a carnival ride? Though I've always wanted to do this." I took a condom out of my wallet. The bubble wheel was a pretty commonplace to have shenanigans, since we could see out, but others couldn't see in.

"Oh, so sure." She unzipped my pants and took my hard and ready cock out.

Gwen gasped. My eyes were on Tenzin, who eyed my piercing appreciatively.

"Clark. You bejeweled your dick." Gwen licked her lips suggestively.

"So, um, I was sort of hazed. Carlos and Dimitri brought me to the piercing shop at our first away game last year. They told me everyone had piercings down there and I had to get one, too. I just hadn't seen them, because they took them out for hockey. Um... yeah, the other rookies got tattoos, and I ended up with that."

I'd been pissed about it at first, but it was more about being tricked, than the actual piercing. The looks in their eyes made it all worth it.

She put a hand to her mouth. "That was you. Hey, it's okay, I like it."

"It's all yours, Sweetheart," I told her. His, too, if he wanted it.

Tenzin continued to play with her under her dress, but his eyes were on my dick.

So hot.

I rolled the condom over my cock and held out my arms. "Okay. Gweny, does someone need to come?"

After all, cuddling her was my job. If she needed a full body cuddle on a carnival ride, who was I to deny her? I didn't need to knot her to make her happy.

She climbed onto my lap, straddling me as she sank down on my length. "Please. I... I need you. I missed you so much. Both of you."

Mmmm, that felt good.

"We missed you, too, Firecracker." Tenzin got close to us. "We're right here." He ran his hands over her body, cupping her breasts, playing with her still hard nipples through the fabric.

I smashed my mouth to hers, one hand supporting her back, as she rose and fell on my dick. Her moans filled the bubble, as did the scent of our desire.

"That's it, Firecracker. Take what you need from him. That's a good girl," he murmured, kissing her neck.

Oooh, that turned me on.

"Take me good, Sweetheart," I told her, relishing how warm and sweet her pussy felt. "I'm not going to last long." Also, I didn't know how long we had. We didn't need to get caught going at it on a carnival ride.

"I'm close," she gasped.

Reaching down, I rubbed her little bud.

Her pussy fluttered around me as she moaned and collapsed onto my shoulder. I let myself come, wishing I was filling her up. *Another time.*

"You came so good in my arms. Think how good you'll come one day when I tongue your pussy," I whispered.

"That sounds nice." Her eyes closed. "I feel better. Who knew I needed to be chased through a fun house, then ride Clark on the bubble wheel?"

"You were both so beautiful," Tenzin told me as I pulled off the condom.

I had no idea what to do with it, so I tied it off and wrapped it in a tissue, then put it in my backpack.

"Are you next?" She gazed at Tenzin.

The ride slowed as they started dropping everyone off.

"Another time, Firecracker." Tenzin gave her a kiss.

We got off the ride. "I'm going to use the bathroom," I told them, leaving to deal with the condom. Shit. I'd just fucked her on a ride like a horny teenager. Amazing.

When I came back out, I found her petting the baby goats at one of the animal exhibitions.

"No, you can't have a baby goat," Tenzin told her fondly.

Her eyes rolled. "You're no fun."

"I'm lots of fun." He grabbed her ass and she squealed.

Shaking her ass at me, she bounded over to play with some rabbits.

"Are you okay? Did I push you too hard?" Tenzin asked me.

"I've never done anything like that before. It was fun." I looked at her talking to some kids as she pet the rabbits. "She seems much more relaxed."

"She does." He nodded.

"Are you okay?" I eyed the hard-on in his jeans. He looked good in that green button-down, with his hat and boots.

His eyes flickered over to her. "I'll live. I needed her to feel better before my alpha went unhinged at her need."

"Fair. What time is the concert? We should feed her first." Apparently, the reason we'd taken the ultra-bullet to the *South,* to go to a fair, was because his sister's band was playing. I had no idea what sort of music she played or who her band was.

"Yes, let's do that." He waved her over. "Come on, Firecracker, let's get some supper."

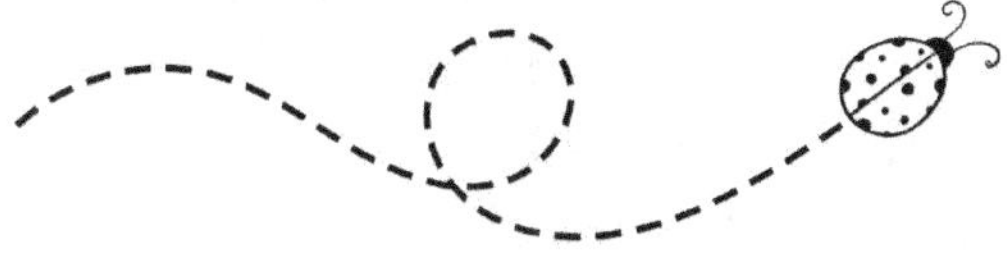

Chapter Thirty-Seven

TENZIN

We got some food and sat down at a shady picnic table. Gwen eyed the paper boats of ribs, chicken, brisket, corn, and biscuits. Several people stared at us. It could be because we were hockey players. Also, Clark and Gwen were adorable together. Those glasses of his really did it for me. That short-sleeved blue shirt looked nice on him.

She leaned on his shoulder, probably needing the extra touch after being fucked. I hadn't expected that; I was going to get her to ride his leg. It was beautiful. Though all this was a bit fast.

Gwen took a sip of iced tea and made a face. "Why is my tea sweet?"

"We're in the South, Firecracker. Now eat some barbecue." And hopefully not get food on her pretty white dress.

We finished our meal and Clark went to grab us beers.

Gwen leaned into me. "Are you okay? I liked being with you in the funhouse."

"I did as well. It's all a little fast though," I admitted. "But if you need to feel better, I want to be here for you."

Yes, if she needed me, I'd be inside her in a moment.

She gave me a kiss. "I can go slow. I get it. My hormones got the best of me, but you two made me feel so good. I liked you watching us. Um, I'm not sure how this all works."

"I liked watching you," I growled into her neck. "You don't need my permission to fuck him. Also, there's no score. It's not your job to see to my needs, it's my responsibility to see to *yours*."

"Okay." She leaned into me and I wrapped my arms around her.

It would be so easy to fall into whatever this was head first. Common sense urged me to take it slow, at least finish healing from Morgan.

"Let's go." Clark appeared with the beers.

We made our way over to the outdoor amphitheater. I got out our passes and hung them around everyone's neck, then led us down to the VIP area.

Clark looked at his pass, giddiness covering his face. "Your sister's in *this* band? You're shitting my dick."

"No beans. Better than a blowjob from a dinosaur, right?" Gwen put her arm around him.

What? Sometimes they made me feel so *old*.

While the venue had seats, there was also a lawn filled with people having picnics, a pit area so people could dance, and a VIP area with cabanas, food, and drinks.

"Tenzin." Cash waved from the VIP area the band reserved for staff and family.

We entered the area and the slight omega male, dressed in white from head to toe, gave me a hug.

"Cash, this is Gwen and Clark, this is Cash, Zaya's omega," I introduced.

Gwen waved. "Hi."

"Hi, Sugar." Cash gave her a big smile. Like my sister, he was in his late-thirties, and very good looking, though in that soft omega way. His dark hair was back in a tail.

"It's very nice to meet you. You're not in the band?" Clark asked, pushing his glasses back up his nose.

"I'm a costumer. Zaya and I met when she needed to be dressed for an award show. I do all the costumes for the band," Cash said. "What do you do? Farm boy, right?"

Clark's cheeks pinked. "Only in summer. In the cold season, I play hockey."

Cash gave him an appreciative nod. He was a huge flirt. "Another hockey boy. Oh, and you, Sugar," his eyes focused on Gwen, "they're both yours. Good for you. You're a skater, aren't you, with those legs?"

"Cash, stop, they're not used to you." I laughed. He could be a lot.

Gwen ducked her head. "Hockey player. I think I'll keep them."

My heart grew three sizes as she said that. We got food and took our seats. Cash and I caught up as the opening act played.

"I've got the dinosaur costume if you want it for the last song, maybe? Shoot some T–shirts?" Cash took a sip of whiskey.

"You should absolutely do it," one of the band's assistants said. She looked at us. "I might have T-shirt cannons for all of you."

"Oooh. We should," Gwen said. She leaned over me. "Cash, do you have pictures of teenage Tenzin?"

I pulled her to me and growled in her ear. "If you see them, you need to stop using *better than a blowjob from a dinosaur.*"

I'd spent a lot of time in that dinosaur costume.

She giggled. "I suppose."

He showed her some pictures of me. A song Gwen liked came on. She took Clark's hand and dragged him off.

Cash gave me a smug look. "You go to New York and get yourself a pack in a couple of weeks? Gwen is *delicious*. You should get her a different hat for that dress."

"Cooter picked it out." Pack? There definitely was a pull between the three of us. Was I ready for a pack? No. No, I wasn't.

Were they my pack? Or at least the start of it?

I think they were.

Cash started laughing. "Cooter's not dating any more singers, is he?"

I laughed. "After having two different ones make post-breakup songs about him, I think he's done."

"The kids miss you. I'm sorry they're not here for this," he told me.

"Me, too," I replied, as he showed me a bunch of pictures. Most I'd already gotten from Zaya.

The opening act finished, and more people came by to say hello. My sister and her band, *The Lonely Cowgirl Club,* came on, opening strong with *The Stars and Me,* which was one of their most popular songs.

Clark and Gwen dragged me up toward the front of the stage and I found myself line dancing.

A song perfect for two stepping started, and I took Gwen's hand and danced with her, careful of everyone else. Clark watched us, a hungry look in his eyes. I spun her out, but instead of bringing her back in, Clark grabbed her hand and spun her into him, taking over. They looked beautiful among the lights and hay bales.

I glanced up at my sister, who smirked from her place onstage.

"Come on, we need you," the band's assistant finally said at the end of their set, bringing the three of us backstage. I put on an inflatable dinosaur costume and Gwen and Clark were taught how to use a T-shirt cannon.

"We should shoot snacks, like Team Mom does at the Maimer's games," Gwen said.

"That sounds perfect for festivals," the young assistant said.

That sounded dangerous.

The band played their last song, then left the stage, the crowd shouting *one more song.*

"You in a dinosaur costume always amuses me," Zaya said, holding her guitar, sweat dripping down her face. My alpha big sister looked so much like our mother, with her long, dark hair and striking features.

"It was your idea." Okay, it was because I'd lost a bet. At fourteen, I thought I knew everything. Not to mention, Nashville was so strange compared to our life in the mountains.

"Most of the good ideas are." She laughed.

Like she pushed me to keep up with hockey and did everything she could to support me in it, even if it was costly and took a lot of time.

Zaya gave me a little push. "Now get out there."

"Come on, we've got to get them to yell louder," I told Gwen and Clark.

As soon as I walked onto the stage, the heat of the lights brought me back to the very first time I'd done this. Once I even got Cooter on stage with me in an inflatable unicorn costume.

The crowd went wild. From offstage, Zaya played a little tune, and I danced around as Clark and Gwen shot T-shirts at the crowd. The music got louder and louder as the tune continued, then turned into the song everyone wanted to hear.

The band came bounding back on, playing *Reasons I Hate My Family,* a very fun, silly song. I continued to dance around, and Gwen and Clark shot shirts at the crowd, until they were out, then traded them for more.

"Thanks for coming out. Special thanks to our helpers and my baby brother, Tenzin, who is in the dinosaur costume," Zaya shouted as the song ended.

I got Gwen and Clark's hands, then dragged them off the stage, while my sister and her band finished their bows and I got out of the costume.

"That was *amazing*. My sisters can't believe I'm here." Clark grinned.

The band came off stage and my sweaty sister wrapped her arms around me. "Tenny."

"Hey, Zaya. I finally made it." I hugged her back. Usually I came to more concerts, but this summer had been weird.

Her eyes danced. "New York looks good on you."

Did it?

Zaya grinned. "Let me get cleaned up. While I've heard all about Gwen, I need to know about glasses guy."

We ended up at a bar given the fair was closing for the night. Gwen danced with Clark and Cash. I sat with my big sister, as I told her all about the two of them.

"Okay, so what's the problem, then? You're twenty-seven. That's not a bad time to get packed up," she told me.

"It's fast." I took a sip of beer.

She looked at Cash as he twirled Gwen. "It can happen quickly."

"Yeah, but Cash is an omega." I was grasping here. "You'd been with your band for a while." Not all her band members were in her pack, but some were.

Zaya frowned. "Gwen's not a tall omega on suppressants?"

I shook my head. "No. She's incredible, though."

"Huh. No doubt she's remarkable. Still, love can be fast, Tenny. Sometimes you need to take risks," she goaded. She was the risk taker, not me.

"I know. But Clark or I could be traded at any time. Gwen could end up anywhere next year," I confessed. "Cooter says I'm overthinking."

"You are. You'd be a dumbass not to go after them, simply because you're afraid they'll end up somewhere else. If you feel like they're your pack, you need to act on it somehow, so you don't lose them. Even if you're not ready for everything. You're an alpha. Your job is to support her, Tenny. Support her career, support her dreams, support her love. Keep lines of communication open and see what *she* wants. It was pretty clear from onstage that she's madly in love with both of you," Zaya told me. "You three are adorable together."

Your job is to support her.

Zaya was right. With everything in Gwen's life, that was really the best thing I could do for her. Support her. Love her. Care for her. I watched as Clark took Gwen in his arms and they swayed to the music.

No, I didn't want to lose them.

"Also, he's not going anywhere. Even if he's traded, he's yours. If he was an omega, I'd tell you to lock it down quick." She grinned.

I'd told her that in regard to Cash.

"What you have with them is so different from Morgan. It's palpable. Do it. When Gwen comes to you, excited that she got signed to France or whatever, swing her around, tell her how proud of her you are, take her to dinner, then have a talk about what you three look like while she's abroad. While things might be a little different, I'm pretty sure she's not going to break it off," Zaya told me. "Same thing if you or he gets traded. Sure, shit happens, and Morgan fucked you up. But this..."

She gestured to Clark and Gwen, who were now being silly, spinning each other around. "This is real, Tenny. You might have to go with the flow, but you've got this. You've found two sweet hockey players that are going to run you ragged, but are worth it."

I laughed. "They're very high energy."

"Just love and support them, and they'll do that for you in return. I'm so glad you moved to New York and found them." She smirked and finished her beer.

"Well, you did tell me it was time for a change." I didn't think it would look like them. Yet here I was.

And happier for it.

Zaya grinned. "As your big sister, I'm always right."

Chapter Thirty-Eight

GWEN

"Thanks for dinner and a movie." I squeezed Clark's hand as we left the fancy movie theatre. Not only did we get the good popcorn with chocolate candies, but we'd ordered wings, beer, and pizza, since this was the place that brought you dinner while you watched the movie.

The space adventure movie we'd watched had been good, too. Tenzin had a sponsor thing, and I didn't have to work, so the two of us had gone out.

"Anytime. Do you need anything for when classes start? Backpack, books?" Clark draped an arm around me as we entered the outdoor plaza of the entertainment complex. The night air was warm but not awful and a lot of people were out tonight.

He was wearing jeans and a T-shirt. I had on my blue denim sundress.

"Tens is getting me a backpack. I could use some pens and stuff." My eyes fell on the big bookstore across the plaza. "I have books for class. But I *am* out of books to read."

Verity would loan me all the smutty books I wanted. But I was in the mood for a good high fantasy with a million unpronounceable names. Or possibly an epic space story with explosions. Jonas had some, but he didn't loan out his books. Everything I wanted from the library had long hold lists.

Clark's hand went to his mouth in mock horror. "That won't do. To the bookstore."

Tugging on my hand, we ran across the plaza like a couple of goofballs. My hand was still in his as we burst inside. He dragged me over to the fancy stationery section, grabbing a basket.

"Get whatever you need for class first, then you can get some books." He picked up a pen with a pompom on the end and booped my nose with it.

I laughed. "You'll actually buy me books? How many books?"

I'd been joking. Still, even one book would be nice. After I got my scholarship distribution, I should go to my favorite used bookstore to recoup some of what Austin destroyed.

Clark considered this. "Seven."

"Seven?"

What?

"Is that not enough? I don't know what series you're reading right now." He held up a pencil pouch with Aquatica from the Defender League on it and put it in the basket. "You should get this."

A woman looking at cards glanced over at him, then to me. "He's a keeper."

"He is." I giggled, then wrapped my arms around him. "I'm keeping you."

Clark set down the basket and picked me up off the ground. "Okay."

He put me down and scampered off. I perused the ultra-cute and slightly-overpriced stationery section. I'd planned on just going to Swoop. Everything here was so freaking cute. I could let him buy me cute school supplies, right? Just a couple of things.

I mean, I needed that Aquatica pencil pouch.

But I wouldn't let him buy me seven books. Four. Yeah, that was good. I did have to think about getting everything back on his motorcycle.

Some star-shaped paperclips and a pack of dragon erasers went into the basket.

Five books. And no more. I took the paperclips out.

I looked at two different packages of gel pens. Since I had all the cute outfits for class, I should get cute pens.

A display full of space books caught my eye as I added the matching pack of highlighters. Pondering my basket, I put back one pack of pens. No need to be greedy.

"Here you go." Clark bounded over and shoved a bubble tea in my hand.

"Thanks." I took a sip. "You remembered I like brown sugar milk tea."

"Of course I did." His brown eyes sparkled through his black-framed glasses. "I remember everything about you."

My pussy clenched. "If you keep talking like that..."

"Like what, Ladybug?" He got close to me, scent flaring with desire. Then he took a loud slurp of his own bubble tea. "I'm going to look at comics." Clark scampered back off.

I chuckled as I wandered over to the display. Oooh, the author of the Intrepid Space Explorer books had a new series? Space *Romantasy?* Yes, please.

As I sipped my tea, I pursued the shelves, looking at all the new releases. When had I last bought new books? My birthday maybe? With a gift card?

Clark came up behind me and wrapped his arms around my waist as he slipped a graphic novel, some comics, and a Professor Weird sticker into the basket.

"Hi." I leaned into him. "Professor Weird?"

"That's Tens' favorite. His water bottle is naked. We should fix that." He nodded sagely.

"Oh, we should." I stroked the spine of the book, then put it back. You couldn't have a naked water bottle.

Clark eyed the basket. "There's only five."

"They're *hardcovers*. Two are special editions with sprayed edges." I chewed on my lower lip. I had quite the haul here. Maybe I should put one back? Especially since I got some cute school supplies?

"Get the books, Gweny." His voice grew rumbly as he buried his face in my neck.

"It's fine, really." I couldn't bring myself to get seven.

"Okay. We can always get more later." He wrapped his arms around me. "I'll carry it." Taking the basket from me, Clark headed toward the register.

I followed.

"Are you sure?" He smoothed my hair, which was a little crazy today with the humidity.

"I am. Thank you." I tucked myself under his arm as we checked out.

The total made me suck in a breath.

"I know. We work hard, so we're allowed to get treats some-times," he told me as we paid for our things.

His arm stayed around me as we walked through the plaza, finishing our bubble teas, him carrying our bag.

Shit. He'd bought me books. If I hadn't already decided I want-ed something with Clark, this would tip me over.

"Anything else you need?" He tossed our empty cups into the garbage.

"I'm good, thank you." I squeezed his hand.

He tucked everything into his backpack and we went into the parking garage. Putting on his helmet, I got on behind him and wrapped my arms around his waist.

The area of the parking garage our floor used was empty. Including Tenzin's truck.

"Thank you again," I told him as I took off the helmet.

"Any time." Clark leaned in and kissed me, tasting of milk tea.

Heat flared between us as I pressed into him. His hand moved under my sundress.

"Sit on the seat, Gweny." His eyes gleamed.

"What?" I looked up at him as he worked my panties off.

"I need some dessert. Now be a good girl and sit on the seat and spread your pussy wide." His voice went rumbly.

I'd never heard him speak like that, and I didn't move. Because I liked it.

His look softened. "Hey, you can say *no*. You can *always* say no. I don't want to push you. I was being silly. Isn't buying a girl books and bubble tea, then eating her out on your motorcycle sort of a universal girl fantasy? If you're not ready, it's okay. I just want to take care of you. Apologies if I misunderstood."

"Please have me for dessert." I sucked in a breath as I climbed onto the motorcycle, spreading my legs wide for him. *It's my fantasy now.*

He set everything down, then *got on his knees* in front of me.

Mmmm, an alpha on their knees? So incredibly sexy.

"Look at you, with your legs spread so wide and ready for me." Clark stroked my bare thighs, re-positioning them. "Such a good, good girl."

That dirty talk was hot.

Clark buried his head in my pussy, a hand on each thigh. His tongue caressed my inner folds. A gasp escaped my lips as the motorcycle moved back and I grabbed onto it, bracing for a fall.

One hand moved behind my back. He gazed up at me. "You won't fall. I've got you. Now, where was I…"

He attacked my pussy like I was a delicious dessert and he hadn't eaten all day. One of my hands fisted his hair, more to hold on than to guide him. Another moan left my lips as he rolled my clit with his tongue.

Mmmm, he didn't need any guidance.

Not to mention I'd never been eaten out in a parking garage where anyone could come in. The very thought heightened *everything*.

Mmmm, I wouldn't mind if Tenzin came home and saw this.

"You taste so good, Gweny. Best dessert ever," he murmured into my pussy, one hand stroking my leg.

Closing my eyes, I let the sensation overwhelm me as the motorcycle rocked gently. His mouth got a good spot, and I gasped, getting closer to my release.

"Come whenever you want. I love making you feel good," he added, his tongue flicking my clit.

"Clark," I squealed, my head lolling backwards, which made the bike rock more.

His grip on my back and thigh tightened. "I've got you. Let go."

Yes, Alpha.

"There, right there," I gasped, my chest shaking.

"There?" He flicked my clit with his tongue. "Or there?" Clark licked little circles around it.

Pleasure pulsed through me and I gasped again. "Both."

"What about this?" He nibbled my clit.

My pussy spasmed, and an orgasm flooded my body. The motorcycle rocked again. Standing, he caught me in his arms.

"I've got you, Gweny. Are you okay?" Clark's muscular arms wrapped around me.

"That felt so good." Arousal tinged his hay and sunshine scent and I buried my head in his chest.

I'd never heard of that fantasy before, but I wouldn't mind acting out this one again. Not at all.

Chapter Thirty-Nine

TENZIN

I drove my truck into our section of the parking garage. Clark was beside his motorcycle and Gwen had her arms around him.

My heart. I'd gotten pictures of them on their movie and bookstore date. It looked much more fun than dinner with my sponsors from Bowerman. But I had to keep the sponsors happy. They wanted to do a photoshoot with me in a couple months to promote a new line.

The car door shut as I got out, slinging a duffle of gifts from my sponsors over my shoulder. Gwen looked up.

"Tens, you're back." Her face lit up.

The closer I got to them, the more I could smell them—and their arousal. I was happy they had each other.

"Hi, Firecracker." Without thinking, I kissed her forehead.

She beamed.

"Hi, Tens." Clark's look was a bit jealous.

"Your hair is all messy." I smoothed it back for him. "Just got back from the movies?"

A pair of panties lay on the cement next to a backpack and a helmet.

"Yep." Gwen slid down to the ground. "Your meeting went well?"

"It did. Do you two want to come up and watch something?" I offered. "Clark, my sister recommended a show for us. It's dubbed and about superheroes. Do you want to try it?"

The last thing I wanted was for him to think I didn't care about him simply because I wasn't ready to get physical. I enjoyed spending time with them. We'd been practicing together, visiting Marty, and having a good time. Gwen had finished camp and now only had work.

Clark and I had even gone on some *Art and Architecture* walks while she was at her NYIT practices.

"That sounds great." Clark picked up his backpack, which seemed heavy, and headed toward the elevator.

Gwen grabbed the helmet. Her scent flared with embarrassment as she saw her panties on the ground and she swiped them up, then shoved them in her purse.

I kissed the top of her head. "There's nothing to be embarrassed about. Just be careful about being in public. Your career doesn't need a sex tape scandal."

"True." The embarrassment in her scent grew as her head ducked.

I pulled her to me as we joined Clark, who held the elevator.

She leaned into me, eyes half-closed. Gwen's body tucked itself so well into mine. I loved how she was comfortable with me now.

"Do you only have one helmet?" I eyed the helmet in her hand, which was blue with Captain Everything's symbol on it.

"Yeah, I need to get Gwen one. I have her wear mine. In New York City, alphas are exempt from helmet laws." Clark shifted the weight of the backpack.

That was a dumb rule. Sure, alphas might be a little stronger, a little faster, heal a little quicker, but they didn't have tougher heads.

A little growl rumbled in my chest. "It's bad enough you ride that. You *both* need helmets."

Also, she was wearing a dress. Was that safe?

Clark smirked as the elevator opened. "Yes, Alpha."

I growled again. Gwen giggled.

Those two.

"What's in that backpack?" I grabbed it from him. *Ooof.*

"He bought me books." Gwen laughed as she punched the code into their door. "We'll meet you in twenty minutes?"

"I'm proud of you for letting him buy you books." I opened my door and went inside. Slinging the duffle onto the couch, I took a quick shower and put on something more comfortable than the suit I'd been wearing.

I started the tea and got out some snacks. Given I was leaving soon, I didn't have much.

Oh, her backpack. When we'd gone backpack shopping, they'd been out of the one she wanted and it had come today.

There was a knock on the door as I set everything on the table.

"Come in; your backpack came." I eyed her bare feet. She was going to catch a cold, always running around barefoot like that. Her hair was wet, and she wore those star pajamas with the thin tank-top.

"Oh, thank you." She beamed as she opened the box to reveal the black leather backpack she'd wanted. Gwen hugged me. "Thank you, Tens."

"You're welcome." I settled down on the couch with them, Gwen in the middle. It wasn't as long or wide as theirs.

"Oh, I got this for you at the bookstore." Clark fished something out of his shorts pocket. His hair was also wet. At least he wore flip-flops, which he kicked off by my door.

He handed me a sticker with Professor Weird on it, looking proud.

"Thank you. It was so thoughtful to think of me," I told him. A sticker? What did I do with a sticker?

"It's for your water bottle, given it's naked," he told me.

"Oh, I see." It seemed silly to put stickers on laptops and water bottles, but it was kind of him.

Grabbing the remote, I turned on the TV. I'd miss them while I was gone. I was going to visit Cooter on his ranch before we attended a bonding party for one of our teammates, and I was his plus-one to a wedding for his university friend. After that, we had our last fishing trip of the off-season.

Then the season would start. Something I was looking forward to.

We watched a couple of episodes of the new show and ate our snacks. It wasn't my style, but Clark and Gwen got into it.

Finally, Gwen yawned. "If we're going to practice in the morning, I should go to bed."

"Good night, Firecracker." I hugged her, then looked at Clark. "See you in the morning."

"Good night, Tens." Clark grabbed her backpack. With a wave, the two of them left.

I cleaned up, then grabbed my laptop. I ordered her a motorcycle helmet to be sent directly to her, since I'd be gone.

If anything happened to them...

The very thought made me sick. I hadn't known them for very long, but I'd be absolutely devastated if they got hurt.

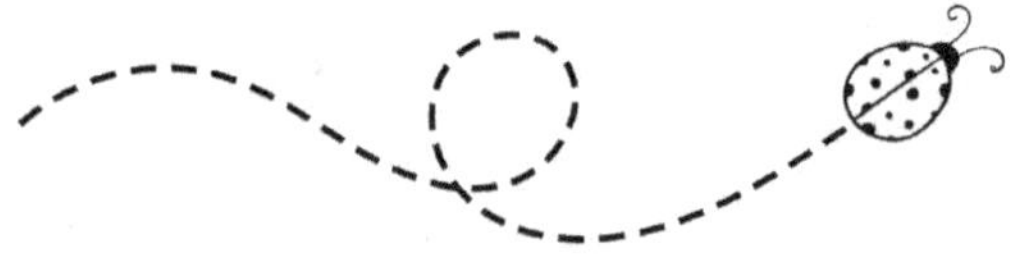

Chapter Forty

GWEN

The energy in the premium ultra-bullet car was electric, since nearly all of us were on our way to Montreal for Jean-Paul and Celine's wedding. Or rather, their multi-day marital spectacular, filled with activities, dinners, and parties.

Betas couldn't bond with each other the way alphas and omegas could, so weddings were a huge part of beta culture. They weren't always fancy or expensive, but they were usually a big deal. Not only for the couple, but for their family and community.

Jean-Paul and Celine's was no exception.

Tenzin was off with Cooter, going to his ranch, hitting a couple of weddings, then going on one last fishing trip before pre-season began.

Shit, I missed him. At least I had Clark with me.

My summer was officially at an end. On Tuesday, classes started, as did official NYIT hockey practices. I was ready for my last year; I was all paid up and had the classes I wanted.

This was going to be a great year. I was going to soar.

Thrive.

Succeed.

Nerves bounced around inside me as the train sped closer to our destination. I was going back to Canada. That was *a lot,* even after talking with my therapist about it.

I'd also paid zero attention to where exactly we were going, letting the guys organize it. For all I knew, the wedding was at a castle, which would be so very Celine.

It'll be okay. You'll be in Quebec. It'll be fine.

"Are you okay?" Clark asked, pulling me closer to him.

"Nervous." I took a deep breath. "It'll be okay, right?"

"When were you last back? Was it when your mom died?" Clark stroked my hair.

"I..." My chest shook. It was during one of the times I didn't like to think about.

"You don't have to talk about it," he told me, holding me tight.

"Last time I was in Vancouver, I literally climbed out of my bedroom window, in the middle of the night, after leaving my dads a *fuck you* letter," I admitted. Not my finest moment, but I had to get out of there.

"You're going to be fine. Besides, you're going to *love* where we're going." Clark gave me a boyish smile. "I've got you."

"Okay." I put my head on his shoulder. "I... I've been to Canada since then, but it was only Toronto for pre-season hockey with NYIT." Which felt different, since it was only a couple of hours. We'd be here for *days.*

What if the dads found me and tried to keep me like last time?

Dean gave me a silly look from across the aisle as if to say, *oh, that's how it is.* I scratched my nose with my middle finger.

Clark was mine. I was keeping him. Tenzin, too.

There was an announcement that we were at the Canadian border, and to get out our IDs.

My heart sped up. What if the dads had done something to my record? Or what if they were tracking it? They knew this name. Really, I should have changed it again. But I liked my life. Starting over would mean giving up my hockey dreams. I'd already had to fight for them once.

"Whoa, are you okay?" Clark's brows furrowed.

"Yeah." I gulped as I got out my phone and pulled up my ID.

Two people in uniform came through, scanning everyone's IDs. One scanned Clark's ID, and it turned green. "Enjoy your trip," she told him.

She scanned mine. I held my breath, waiting for it to beep and alert her that I was a runaway or wanted, or something. It turned green, and I exhaled.

"Welcome home." She went on to the next person.

He turned to me. "You're Canadian. Right. I forgot."

My ex always did, too.

The train continued on, and we all disembarked in Montreal, got our luggage, and Dean led us to a waiting bus, while holding a little Knights' flag like he was leading a tour.

We got on the bus, which I presumed took us to the hotel. Celine had rented the castle, didn't she? An exiled omega princess had built it. I'd toured it once as a child. A wedding there would be beautiful. I just adored castle weddings.

One day...

Dean stood as the bus drove away, holding his phone. "This bus is going to Jean-Paul and Celine's wedding. If you're not going there, you're in the wrong place."

Everyone laughed.

"JP wanted me to read some notices. First, they speak French here, so don't be surprised that things are in *French*," Dean said. "Second, the really attractive flight attendants are Celine's co-workers and friends. Don't break any hearts, or Celine will hit you with her purse."

That elicited chuckles and a few people looked at Carlos. Celine was one of those ladies who liked large purses. She also loved the gym, so that would *hurt.*

"Third, we don't have the whole place to ourselves, and there's another big party, so please be courteous. Fourth, it's a nature park. There are going to be animals everywhere. Be cautious, especially when walking across the park at night, drunk, so you're not eaten by a deer. And..." Dean started laughing. "JP wrote, "*Will someone please check Ladybug's bags before you depart, so she doesn't take any animals home?*"

The entire bus broke out in laughter. Including me.

"I'm not going to steal a baby deer," I told him. Wait, we were going to a nature park? While that sounded amazing, something wiggled in the back of my mind. Maybe I should have paid more attention to where we were going.

Nia laughed, her hair now in short braids. "Of course not. You'll steal a baby wolf cub and pretend it's a dog."

"Then you'll cry when it eats your cat," Dimitri added.

"I mean, I did want to keep the wounded wolf my nonna and I nursed back to health," I shrugged. I'd be a great wolf mom.

"Who got Ladybug a cat?" Dean shot me a look.

"Clark," Carlos blabbed. "But it's actually a cat and not a tiger. Do you think Lucky will like Snowball?"

I pondered this. "Absolutely."

Carlos' mom was cat-sitting for me.

Dean read a few more things, then sat down.

"I think I've been here?" I murmured to Clark. "That awkward moment when you can't remember and there's no one to text and ask." I looked at pictures online. Would Lenny know?

No, I wouldn't ask him, just so he wouldn't tell my brother.

"It seems like a great place for a family vacation," Clark agreed, leaning over to look at my phone.

His closeness was comforting and not only because I liked cuddles. Being with him made me feel like myself. That real self that I'd been trying to poke out.

We drove through the gates of the wilderness park. As soon as I saw the sign, the memories hit me like a puck to the face. The place was beautiful, filled with trails, deer, wolves, rabbits, foxes, bison, and many other animals. There was a drive-through path, a learning barn, hiking trails, a tree top adventure place, picnic areas, a lake, and streams.

By the time we pulled up to the sprawling wooden lodge, I knew exactly where we were. Dread lumped in my belly.

"Are you okay, Ladybug?" Dean asked as we got off the bus.

"What happens if the park doesn't let me stay?" I'd had a different name, but I'd be mortified if I had to go back to New York in disgrace.

"What did you do?" Dean laughed.

"My brother's mating ceremony was here. I tried to take home an arctic fox that I'd befriended." If it wasn't for my sister Maricella, I'd have succeeded. I'd had a plan. My nonna was a vet. My aunt ran an animal refuge. It wasn't like I was going to keep the fox in my room.

Okay, much or often.

Clark draped an arm around my shoulders. "It'll be okay, Gweny."

He went over to check in. I used the bathroom, then returned to the lobby. The opulent wooden lodge was as I remembered.

Clark bounded over to me. "I have our key code and schedules. Dimitri booked a wolf villa that you, me, him, Carlos, and Valya are sharing. Like it's in the wolf area and you can watch them through enormous windows."

"Oooh. That sounds amazing." I remembered the wolves.

We set off in golf carts, and I looked over my schedule. Everyone's was a little different; like I had goalie dance practice shortly. We passed the opulent chalets where I was pretty sure I'd stayed as a kid.

Not that the villas were dumpy. No, they were adorable three-bedroom suites with balconies and full kitchens.

Valya got her own room, Carlos and Dimitri were sharing one, and Clark and I had the other.

"Oh no, there is only one bed. Whatever will you do?" Carlos laughed as he showed us a room with a wolf view and one enormous bed.

"Fuck you, Carlos." I laughed, giving him a playful shove.

"What? Not me." Carlos knocked me with his hip.

It was a lovely room, with a fireplace and a couch. Obviously, these villas were meant for families, and this was the parents' room. Carlos and Dimitri had *bunk beds*.

"Are you going to be okay?" Clark asked me as we brought in our suitcases.

"I'm okay sharing a bed with you, Clark." I began hanging up my dresses.

It had been a few days since he'd eaten me out on his motorcycle and I think I was ready for more. Okay, my head was ready for more. My lady parts had been wanting more, since the moment I'd gotten off the motorcycle.

"I won't make any moves unless you ask." Clark put his arms around me.

"What if I ask?" My chest shook a little. "We're in Canada and this is a big step for me. I might need all the snuggles?" I might need some full body snuggles later. Not to mention I liked the two times we'd been together.

"My snuggles are all yours, including the full body naked ones." He scooped me up and spun me around, and I could feel the heat between us.

There was only one bed. Poor me.

"Non, non, turn faster," JP scolded, as we practiced the goalie dance, in a ballroom, in the main lodge.

This was the *silliest* thing I'd ever experienced. It was just what you'd expect at a goalie wedding–a bunch of goalies dancing around to a medley of sexy club songs. The choreography was *fantastic*, and we had custom jerseys that said *Team Trembley* on them.

We also seemed to be short a dancer. I never had figured out who everyone was on the group chat. It wasn't only me, Dean, and JP. Coach Kirov was there, as were other goalie friends of JP's.

We did the routine again. Coach Kirov kept complaining that she wasn't as young as we were. Not that she was old.

Much of the choreography hinged on the fact that goalies were a flexible bunch. Timing was also key.

"Double D, non, you go left, not right, Peter will go right," JP directed.

"Who is Peter and where is he?" Dean looked around.

"Peter has another wedding, but he'll be here tomorrow." JP shrugged. "We played together at university."

Well, it was the season for hockey weddings.

We finished the practice, as a few other players and people I didn't know came in for another dance rehearsal. This one was all JP's attendants, which were usually your siblings, cousins, and besties.

I found Clark with Anders and a few others drinking beer and eating snacks on the bar patio. Clark held out his beer. Taking a swig, I grabbed a chicken wing as he pulled me onto his lap.

"Anders, any word? Are you leaving us for the Gears?" I took another wing.

"The trade has stalled. Or at least that's what it feels like." Anders' shoulders slumped.

"At least it hasn't fallen through," Clark replied, putting an arm around me.

Coach Kirov came over to us. "Ladybug, do you have a moment?"

"Aways," I told her, hoping this was a good talk, and not a bad one.

We went to the bar and got some beers.

"You're not firing me, right?" I bit my lower lip. I always felt like I was in trouble when someone asked to talk.

Coach laughed. She was a big Russian alpha who'd played in the Olympics more than once. She was here with her pack and kids. Today her blonde hair was up in a high messy bun instead of the usual bun braid she wore to the rink. Coach Kirov was good friends with my coach at community college. Before I became an EBUG, I'd babysit for Coach K. Sometimes I still did.

"You're senior EBUG this year. This means you get to help with the schedules. I'll send you the game schedule for the year, and the practice schedules for September and October, so you can start working on things. I'll give you the contact info for the new one. Let me know if we need a fourth," she told me.

We might. Weekend games were the worst, since so many collegiate teams played then.

Coach took a sip of her beer. "I hear you've been working hard all summer. The new assistant GM thought you were on the team. He took *emergency backup goalie* to mean, as he put it, the *understudy goalie*. He came from a big theater company on the west coast, but he's a wiz with budgets." Her look was thoughtful, not teasing.

"I mean, we sort of are?" I laughed. Constantine didn't seem to know much about hockey. But then a business was a business.

"Also, put me in, Coach. NYIT doesn't penalize scholarship athletes who leave before graduation to take a contract. Just call my agent," I teased, feeling a little bold. Not that we needed a goalie.

JP and Dean played tandem, switching off. They had us EBUGs if there was an issue during the games and could always bring someone up temporarily from their farm team.

"If you don't have an agent, you should get one," she added. "I'll help you the best I can, but you know there's a good chance you'll end up overseas. There are lots of teams in Europe that aren't afraid of short betas, if they have a save rate like yours."

"Working on the agent. I'm not afraid of playing overseas or in the minors," I replied. A couple of agents wanted to see me play when the season started.

She nodded. "That's what I like to hear. I know you don't shy away from hard work."

We talked for a while longer, mostly ideas for the EBUG program for the coming year. I hadn't realized I'd be a senior EBUG. Even though I had seniority, I figured Ty would appoint himself, given he was an alpha dude.

JP came over to us and grabbed my hand. "Coach, I need her. Come, Ladybug. We have things to do."

I waved to Coach and let JP drag me off.

Things to do involved folding paper airplanes to be thrown as JP and Celine ran down the aisle as a married couple.

"Hey, are you with Clark? I thought you were into Bucket," Dean asked as he folded a blue piece of paper.

"Who's *Bucket?*" JP waggled his eyebrows as he threw an airplane at Nia.

"Oh, right, JP hasn't met Bucket." Nia laughed. "Bucket is Ladybug's new rescue."

I put my carefully folded plane in the basket. "Why can't I like both?"

"You can," Nia assured me. "Double D's being nosey."

I got a picture of Tenzin on the beach.

Tenzin

Did you make it to Montreal okay?

Me

No international incidents. How's the beach wedding?

Tenzin

Warm and sunny.

Me

There are animals here. Miss you.

Tenzin

Miss you too, Firecracker.

I sent a picture of myself folding airplanes. I also sent one to Cooter with the caption *goalie wedding*. One day I hoped to meet him.

We were almost done when my phone buzzed.

Valya

Come back, I need to do your makeup before the welcome reception.

"Valya has summoned me. See you soon." I waved.

The lodge lobby was full of people carrying flowers and pillars. Memories of coming here with my family hit me, one after another, as I left the lodge and walked toward the villa. My big sister thwarting my attempts to bring home an arctic fox aside, it had been a fun trip. Being here made me miss Matty and my dads *a lot*.

"There you are," Valya said as I walked into the villa. "Get dressed, then I'll do your makeup."

"Sure." I entered our empty room. Outside the window, I saw some wolves running by. I took a quick look at my schedule again. There was a *welcome reception* followed by a *hockey bus,* which looked like my entire night.

I was in Canada. For a wedding. Shit. I grabbed a beer out of the mini fridge and downed it. Hopefully, we were going bar hopping on that hockey bus.

Chapter Forty-One

CLARK

I came out of the bedroom and into the living room. Gwen sat on the wooden floor, holding a beer, watching the wolves play through the gigantic windows.

"What do you think?" I turned around for her, modeling the puppy onesie. At the welcome reception, everyone had grabbed a bag with their name on it, that had instructions for their evening activity. Mine had told me to put on the onesie and a red wristband, then to go to the lobby at seven. This was so exciting.

"You look adorable." Gwen was wearing something red with black spots... oh, she was a ladybug. Of course!

"We're being pranked, right?" Carlos came down the stairs, wearing a blue furry onesie.

"No. This will be fun." Dimitri joined us, his onesie resembling a tuxedo.

We got in the golf cart and Dimitri drove us to the lodge. Gwen was quiet, still drinking her beer. Valya was going to the family bonfire.

I put my arm around Gwen. "I'll protect you."

"What's wrong?" Dimitri demanded as he drove the golf cart.

Gwen sighed. "Being back in Canada is a lot. I didn't realize we were going to a place I've been to before. I'll be fine."

I gave her a little squeeze. I'd take care of her.

We parked and went into the lobby of the lodge, which was *full* of people in onesies. JP was dressed like a shark, and Celine was a hot pink unicorn pegasus, and they got our attention.

"Look for the bus that matches your wristband," JP said in English. "If you're not wearing a onesie, you won't be allowed on the bus. Feel free to watch a movie under the stars and have a bonfire with the families." He translated it into French.

We got onto a bus with a disco ball and a full bar in it. It wasn't only Knights, but Jean-Paul's hockey friends from other teams, brothers, friends from childhood and university, and his pregnant sister, who was dressed like a kangaroo, complete with a stuffed kangaroo in the pocket.

"I like Lucky's costume," Carlos told Grif. "The sparkles bring out his eyes."

We pulled up to a building that said *Ice Kart*. We filed inside, Gwen staying close to me, looking around warily, like her dads could appear around the corner at any time.

"There are prizes for the winners," JP's sister told us. "This was the place where JP and Celine came on one of their early dates."

Ice go-karts? Yes, please. I sent Tenzin a picture of me. Oh, how I missed him.

"I'm going to win. Lucky rides with me," Carlos said, pretending to snatch Lucky from Grif and taking off.

"You, win?" I grinned as I chased after him. "Not if I do."

Yeah, this was going to be fun.

"Should someone cut Ladybug off?" JP looked concerned as Gwen danced with Celine and a bunch of her friends, while holding a drink that *glowed*.

Gwen was a silly drunk. While she'd done nothing but laugh and twirl, it was better to stop her before she tripped over something and got hurt.

After the ice carts, where Carlos and I hadn't won any prizes, we'd gone to the pizza arcade where JP and Celine had met. I'd won enough tickets to get Gwen a blinking necklace, which she now wore.

Both groups had come together at a dance club they liked, where they'd reserved the entire VIP area. Plenty of people were watching, since we were all still wearing our onesies.

"She's staying with us, so I'll take care of her," I assured.

"Gwen's not okay?" Jean-Paul looked worried.

"She's been through a lot, but it'll be fine." I didn't want to say anything that might be a secret.

He nodded. "Ah, yes, she thought Austin was going to propose. I remember her telling Celine. I forgot. If we find him, he'll pay for breaking her heart."

Oh yeah, he would.

I came over to Gwen as she spun around, giggling.

"Dance with me," she laughed, nearly spilling her drink.

"Sure. Let's put this down." I put her drink aside, took both her hands, and danced around with her, keeping it silly. I wasn't sure if she'd want the entire team to see her sexy dance with me.

We danced for a while, then I dragged her to a couch and got her to sit down and drink some water. She leaned her head on my shoulder and I stroked her hair. Carlos and Dimitri danced with a couple of flight attendants dressed like fairytale creatures.

I got a bunch of water in her, and we danced some more. By the time JP got us all back on the bus, she was only a bit tipsy.

We didn't go directly back to the resort. We *all* stopped for food, and Gwen devoured some sort of French fry concoction, which probably absorbed a lot of the booze.

Finally, we returned to the lodge and took the golf carts back to the villa.

"Go shower first," I told Gwen when we got back to the room.

"Okay." She kissed my cheek. "That's for making sure I didn't do anything stupid. I... I know I shouldn't have had that much to drink, it's just..."

"It's okay." I pulled her to my chest and held her close. She smelled like a bar. "Lots of people had a little too much. I know you have so many feelings. I'm right here."

Gwen looked up at me and kissed me on the nose. "Thank you."

She went into the bathroom and closed the door. I responded to some texts from Tenzin as she showered.

Dimitri stood in the doorway and knocked on the open door. He handed me some vitamin shots and hydrogels. "For both of you. They were in a basket left for us on the kitchen table. We've got beer and snacks if you're hungry."

"Thanks, man." I left them for Gwen, then went back out to the living room and got some water. Carlos and Dimitri were eating snacks from a basket.

Yeah, I wouldn't mind a snack.

"That is amazing." I grabbed a bag of chips, and we sat and watched the wolves through the window for a while.

When I returned to the bedroom, I found Gwen passed out in the center of the bed, wearing nothing but one of *my* T-shirts. The alpha part of me liked the way my clothes looked on her.

The hydrogels and vitamin shots were all gone except for one of each, like she was making sure there was some for me. Awww.

I downed them, showered, put on some pajama pants, and got into bed. Immediately, she rolled toward me like a heat-seeking missile, burying herself in my side.

"I've got you, Gwen." I turned out the light and snuggled her tight, wishing I could hold her like this every night.

Chapter Forty-Two

GWEN

My head thudded, but not as much as it could, considering how much I drank last night, which had been a great time. I was so grateful Clark was there to make sure I didn't do anything stupid.

Lunch and mani-pedis with the MASOs helped a lot too. It had been fun to spend time with them all, especially Celine before her wedding, and Janessa, given her mates Elias and Winston had just retired from the team and they'd moved away. The MASOs included me in things sometimes.

I set off across the lobby, so I could meet Clark by the lake where the animal tour was departing from. The lobby bustled with people checking in and out, and vendors bringing in things for events.

An older woman walked by and I frowned. Did I know her? Shrugging, I walked past the check-in desk toward the door that led to the porch that looked out to the lake.

"Buttons?" a male voice said.

Oh shit. My belly twisted as we made eye contact. My ID had been flagged and now someone had come to fetch me like a lost puppy.

That was part of the problem–my family still thought I was a teenager

Putting my head down, I ignored the voice and hurried out the door of the lodge.

"Buttons, please wait," the male voice called.

I shook my head and kept walking, past the people on the porch, watching the deer on the lawn or enjoying a snack. *Almost to the steps.*

"Please. Buttons, Gwen," Matty called as I rushed down the steps.

I turned around, and there stood my older brother, alone. He still looked the way I remembered, only he now had a beard. Dark hair. Olive skin. Hazel eyes. The two of us looked the most alike of me and my siblings. While he wasn't wearing a suit, he was dressed nicely and his watch could pay my tuition.

Anger bubbled up inside of me. It also *hurt.* Matty was my favorite brother. He attended university and law school locally, so he'd lived at home, and stayed in the area after. Some of my favorite memories were of doing things with his pack.

Unlike some of my sisters, his omega always made sure I was included.

"I don't know how you found me, but I'm *not* going back with you to Vancouver," I snarled, careful not to yell, since there were people around. "The dads can fuck off. I have a life. I'm *happy.* Also, *really,* you? While you're sort of a sock puppet given you work for them, I never figured that you'd do something like this."

Turning, I took off, trying to put as much space as possible between us.

"Buttons, wait," Matty called, running after me.

But I was *fast.* Matty must skip cardio often, because by the time I reached the caged golf carts, he was gone. Still, my heart pounded as I flung myself into Clark's arms.

"What's wrong?" Clark asked, wrapping his arms around me.

"The dads sent Matty after me." My body trembled. "I... I should leave, right? Go back to New York?"

"Gwen, breathe. Who's Matty?" Clark stroked my hair.

"One of my brothers." My heart pounded. "I knew I shouldn't have come. I'm so stupid."

"Can people even do that legally? Both track your ID and come after you? I mean, you're not missing, you're not a runaway, you're an adult," Clark said.

"That didn't stop them last time." Okay, that was out of context. In hindsight, they had a good reason to want me to stay in Vancouver.

At the same time, I hadn't wanted to drop my classes, leave Austin, New York, hockey, and move back into my old room, because they *thought it was best,* without regard to *my* wants and needs.

Unfortunately, I couldn't trust them to not do it again.

Clark looked around. "Last time?"

"When I crawled out the window. I... I should go back to New York, I..." I began to hyperventilate.

"Can they not go to New York? Would you be safer there?" Clark led me to a cart, rubbing my back. I noticed someone with a clipboard herding us into the carts.

I shook my head. "Not really."

After all, *he'd* found me in New York. Not that I had to worry about my stalker anymore, but I pushed that thought away.

"Let's go on the tour, see some animals, take a breath, and we'll go from there. You're an adult. They can't take you and make you go with them," he assured, as we got into a cart. "I'll keep you safe, so will everyone else. Stay close to me."

I leaned my head on his shoulder as someone closed the cage–it was so the animals didn't get too close. Usually people did this trail in their cars. "Okay."

"How many siblings do you have again?" Clark turned on the radio that would broadcast the guide.

"Seven. Four omega sisters, two of which are twins, and three alpha brothers. Matty's second oldest. I'm the youngest. Maricella's the oldest–she's nineteen years older than me." And had always resented me.

I wasn't sure why. When I was born, she'd been away at an omega academy, so it wasn't like she had to watch me. I wasn't given her room. She never got less due to me. If anything, she got more of the parents' attention–and was the reason I spent so much time with my nonna. Mom always said it wasn't me, but it still hurt.

Especially when she was no longer there to tell Maricella to *stop*.

"Isabella is the second youngest and is eight years older than me. All of my siblings were graduated and mated before Mom died. Well, except for my brother Joe." I kept my head on his shoulders, but I opened my eyes. "I was the oopsie beta that just wanted to play hockey."

The parents had been disappointed when I'd tested as a beta in middle school. Given Mom's family's disposition to have omega girls and alpha boys, it had been expected I'd be an omega like my sisters.

I'd been delighted to be a beta. But I'd naively thought it meant I could do what I wanted, which was attend school instead of being tutored and be able to focus on hockey instead of figure skating.

Sadly, they didn't agree, thinking it was a mistake. At fifteen, they'd still figured I'd be an omega–and at nineteen were surprised

I wasn't. Most omegas blossomed between eighteen and twenty-one, a little earlier or later not uncommon.

"I adore that oopsie beta that just wants to play hockey. She's one of my favorite people," Clark said. "You haven't talked to any of them in years?"

"It's better that way." I sighed and leaned into him. He pet my hair like he often did. Why was that such a turn on?

The guide began her narration over the radio as we drove the cart down the path with all the other caged carts, going all the way to the end of the trail. On the walk back, we ran through the treetop course with the bridges. Then we stopped off at the 'Wolf Den' where a keeper gave a talk about the wolves.

The one I'd been watching yesterday, and this morning, came over to the fence. He got close and sniffed me. I yearned to pet him, but the keeper warned us about putting our fingers through the fence.

If not friend, why friend-shaped?

The wolf whined. I squatted down. "Hi, Wolfie. I wish I could pet you. Do you want to come home with me? Just don't eat my cat."

"He likes you. Huh," the keeper told me. "He lost his mate and pups about a year ago and has disliked all women, to the point where we kept him away from the public for a while. Even now, he only really likes widows. Glad to know he's working through his grief."

It was a dagger in my heart. How did Wolfie know?

"Hey. It's hard losing someone, isn't it, Wolfie?" I asked, sitting there in the dirt.

Clark sat there with me, and I leaned against him, watching Wolfie, who laid down there with me, ignoring Clark.

Finally, we headed back to the lodge to meet Carlos and Dimitri at the bar. I kept looking around warily in case Matty came back.

"There you are." JP appeared in the lobby. "Peter's here. You need to meet him."

Clark looked at his phone and his brows furrowed. "Peter?"

"My friend from university, he's a goalie. He and Ladybug will be great friends." JP dragged me to the bar where a bunch of people were drinking.

Including a guy in a cowboy hat?

"Peter!" JP called. "This is Ladybug. You'll love her."

Cowboy hat spun around. A giant grin broke out on his bearded face. "Babybug. I'm so happy to see you."

"Cooter!" My heart exploded.

Cooter swung me around, like we'd been friends forever, instead of people who'd only ever talked on the phone and insta-chatted.

"Of course you know each other." JP laughed.

"He's besties with Bucket," Dean joined us. "Hey, Cooter, is Bucket your date? Or did you bring your wife?"

"It's Double-D-Cup! The wife didn't come, she's too busy wrestling bears," Cooter laughed. "Tenny may not have realized who's wedding we're at. He's up in the room, texting this one, because he's a big sap."

Awww. Cooter brought me Tenzin and didn't tell him. Adorable.

Mmmm. Would Tenzin sleep over in our gigantic bed?

"Oh, Cooter, this is Clark," I added, hauling both of them toward me. I took a picture of us, then sent it to Tenzin, who had texted me more than once.

Me

At the bar. Come down.

Tenzin

I'm going to kill Cooter.

Relief flowed through me. While I felt safe with Clark, I'd be even safer with both of them.

"Will someone tell me who Bucket is?" JP looked perplexed.

Dean laughed. "No, find out when you meet him like everyone else did."

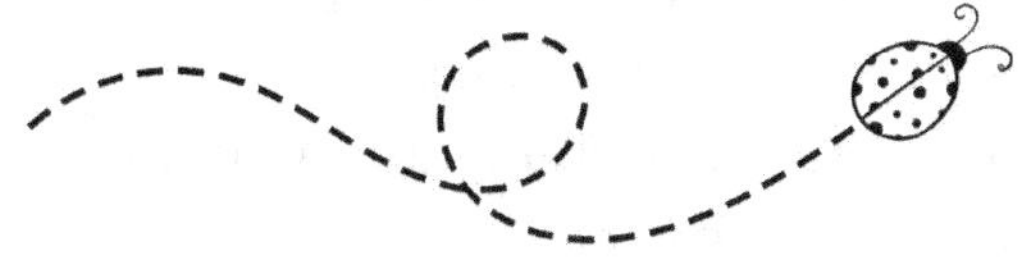

Chapter Forty-Three

TENZIN

At the bar. Come down.

I looked at the photo of her, Clark, and *Cooter*. Fuck.

I'm going to kill Cooter.

Served me right for not asking more questions about the wedding Cooter wanted me to be his plus one at.

It had been nice seeing my Sasquatch teammates, and I'd missed them. But I missed Gwen and Clark more.

The moment I discovered we were going to Quebec, I'd wanted to see if she was close, but my phone had died. Even though my phone had little charge, I shoved it into my pocket. I barreled down the stairs, heading straight to the bar.

Cooter stood with a bunch of people I didn't know—and some I did, like Dimitri, Clark, and *Gwen.*

Gwen waved me over. "Hey, Big Guy, welcome to the party."

"Hey, Firecracker." I gave Cooter a look. "Seriously?"

He couldn't have told me we were going to the *same* wedding as Gwen and Clark? All I knew was that it was some friend of his from university. Jonny.

"Bucket!" Dean waved. "Come join the party. Hey, I didn't know you were coming?"

"I didn't either." I gave Cooter another look.

Cooter smirked again. "Tenny, meet Jonny Boy. We went to university together. He's now a goalie for this obscure team called the New York Knights. Johnny Boy, this is Tenny. We played on the Sasquatches together."

Jonny Boy waved. "Jean-Paul, but most people call me JP. Only Peter calls me Jonny Boy."

I couldn't tell if Jean-Paul was calling him *Peter,* or if Cooter sounded that way with his accent. Peter wasn't Cooter's name before, it was Cooter.

"I'm Tenzin. It's nice to meet you. Congratulations on your wedding," I told him.

"This is Bucket," Dean told Jean-Paul. "Ladybug found him in the freezer section and now we have a new defender."

"Tens." Clark came over holding a beer. "I didn't know this was the wedding you were going to. I'm so glad you're here."

He looked *relieved.* What happened?

Cooter shrugged. "I thought it would be a fun surprise, since you're a Knight now. You could meet some of your teammates."

"Welcome to the Knights," Jean-Paul told me.

"You're the missing person in the goalie dance. JP, didn't you go to university here?" Gwen said to Cooter.

"So..." Cooter ran a hand through his hair, looking bashful. "You know how you think a school is one place, and it's really somewhere else, just has a similar name? That happened. I was so surprised with everyone speaking French. But, hey, we played good hockey, am I right?" He patted Jean-Paul on the shoulder.

Cooter, Jean-Paul, and Gwen started speaking in rapid French, with Dean joining in. My French wasn't that good, and Cooter had quite the accent.

"Is everything okay?" I asked Clark as I got a beer from the bar.

"Gwen's brother is here. I didn't see it, but she was upset." He frowned. "She thinks he's here to bring her back to Vancouver."

"He's here to what?" I frowned. No wonder she was upset.

"I'm confused. She's an adult and a beta. Her brother can't throw her over his shoulder and take her back to her dads' house." Clark frowned. "She also said the last time she was in Canada, she had to crawl out the window."

Huh. She had told me that she'd changed her name because of safety reasons.

"Oh, Babybug, I made you a present," Cooter said, in English, digging something out of his pocket.

That only cemented the fact that the fucker knew Gwen was going to be here and *didn't tell me.* Asshole. I should have suspected something, since he'd only invited me to be his plus one a few weeks ago.

He put the leather cord around her neck. "I made this to protect you. I have one, too." Cooter took his out from under his shirt.

I put my hand over my face. "Cooter."

She admired the piece of bone on the cord. "This is bone?"

While he meant well, I wasn't sure what she'd think of wearing a raccoon penis bone as jewelry. But this *was* Gwen, and it *was* a raccoon.

"Raccoon. Don't worry, it was humanely acquired," he replied.

"Thank you." She grinned. "This is so nice, and I could use this right now."

Clark looked at it, and his eyebrows rose. "Um, isn't that..."

"Yes." I sighed. While I loved Cooter like a brother, Cooter Cootering in public could be a bit much for me sometimes.

Jonas chuckled. "This is the most goalie thing ever."

Gwen blinked. "I think it's sweet."

"I still have the one you made me. Wear it for all the big games," Jean-Paul replied.

"Excuse me." A nicely dressed alpha in his late thirties appeared. He had wavy brown hair, olive skin, and hazel eyes.

Hazel eyes that reminded me of Gwen's.

"Gwen, can we talk, please?" he pleaded, turning to her.

"Is this your ex who hurt you?" Cooter blocked her with his body, eyes narrowing at the stranger.

"No." She shook her head, burnt sugar fear overpowering her mint scent.

"She's an adult and has a life and people who care about her." Clark joined Cooter, scowling. "You need to leave her alone. She's also great at hockey."

Carlos stood next to her. "Oh, fuck, your asshole dad is here."

"I think you should leave," I told him, taking a step toward the stranger, Gwen's fear tugging on my alpha instinct to protect her.

"I swear I'm only here for Flavie's cousins' wedding, nothing more. Look, I didn't know you were here. All I want to do is talk." The man looked at Carlos, horrified. "I'm *not* her dad."

"That's Matty, my brother." She pulled Clark to her.

"Your brother's *old*," Carlos chortled. "Old enough to be your *dad*."

"Thanks." Matty's voice went dry.

"Ladybug, you don't have to go with anyone or do anything you don't want." Jean-Paul joined me. Most of the Knights surround-ed her.

"I can call security," Jonas said.

"Is everything alright?" Dimitri joined us, looking fierce as usual.

"Gwen's super-old brother is here," Carlos replied.

Matty rubbed his forehead. "I'm not that old. Gwen, I just want to see how you are." He turned to Clark. "I know she's good at hockey. But it's terrifying to watch her."

"Why?" I held his gaze. When she was in the zone, it was poetic.

"Um, because giant alphas flinging pucks at her head is scary? The kids would love to see you. We're staying in chalet three." With that, he turned and left.

She looked like she was about to burst into tears. Clark squeezed her hand, then took off after him.

I'm not sure she even noticed. She was between Jean-Paul, Cooter, and Dean, with Dimitri and Carlos standing guard. They were all comforting her. I caught Dimitri's eye, then jerked my head in the direction Clark went, then followed them.

"I'm not here to hurt her," Matty said, standing in the hallway where Clark had cornered him. He was almost as tall as Clark and broad shouldered, but not nearly as big as most of our teammates.

There was something about him that would make most people think twice about messing with him.

No one messed with Gwen.

"So, your dads didn't track her ID and send you to bring her to Vancouver?" Clark demanded.

"No. Though I can see how Gwen thinks that. We're here for a mating party for my omega's cousin. Our pack came early, since the kids like the animals," he told us.

Clark's expression clouded. "Gwen deserves to be supported. Your family tried to stop her from playing hockey after your mom died."

"Gwen got *massively* injured playing hockey right when we found out our mom's cancer came back. While she made a full recovery, we weren't sure she would, and I swear she did out of spite.

After our mom died, the dads wanted her to stay in Vancouver. Not only because they were afraid she'd get hurt again, but because they'd lost their omega, and Gwen's the baby of the family. They went about it all wrong, which they often did when it came to her." He sighed.

"Oh." I nodded. "I could see that."

"In case you haven't noticed, my baby sister is possibly the most stubborn person on the planet. More stubborn than even the dads. They did a lot of trying to out-stubborn each other." Matty rubbed his head.

Clark looked at Matty's expensive watch. "Still, you abandoned her. She lived in a closet at the ice rink after she broke up with Austin. She sold her *Maria Barilla rookie card* to pay for her tuition last year."

"When did she live in a closet?" I turned to him, angry at the thought of Gwen being abandoned.

"After she broke up with her ex, but before she moved in with me. No one knew, otherwise we would have done something. As soon as I found out, I fixed it," Clark replied, then scowled at Matty.

"There's a lot that's not mine to tell," Matty replied, frowning.

"Last time she was in Canada, you all tried to keep her from going back to New York," Clark retorted, taking a menacing step toward him.

Clark's desire to defend and protect Gwen was hot.

"The *dads* did. Assholish, but well-meant. She's been through some shit, and they were worried about her," Matty told us.

"Worried?" Gwen stood there with tear stains on her face, arms wrapped around herself. "They demanded I drop out, leave New York, and stay in Vancouver, like I was a little kid."

"That was shitty. However, I understand why they thought it was a good idea, just not how they did it." Matty got closer to her.

She shrank and nestled into Clark's arms. I stood between Gwen and her brother to create a shield.

"I have no idea who you two are. Like I know *who* you are, and it's obvious that you two care about her, but *who are you?*" Matty asked.

"They're *mine*. I'm old enough to date. Most of my sisters were getting mated at my age." She made a face at her brother, while she stayed in Clark's arms.

"We are?" Clark beamed at her. "I'm so happy."

Hers? I'd take it. We belonged to her.

"Me, too." I gave her forehead a kiss. Forehead kisses make everything better.

"I'm not going back. I'm doing fine." Tears streamed down her face.

I gave him a look to let him know that we'd protect her wishes at all costs.

"I know. Last year at NYIT. Wow. Also, that final one with the six overtimes was insane," Matty assured, not moving closer to her.

Her head ducked. "I... I thought I saw you at the game."

"Lenny and I were there. Joe, Papa, and Babo, too. It was so hard to keep Babo from finding you afterward. We were trying to respect your request for independence," he told her. "I've caught a few of your games, which are still terrifying to watch. I feel like your leg is going to snap off any time you go into full butterfly."

Oh. There were *definitely* some complicated things going on here.

"I do my yoga, I see the physio, I'm okay," she assured. "Papa came? He hates me playing hockey." Her nose scrunched.

"The dads love you, which is why you always get your way, eventually. They just have to be assholes on principle first," he told her.

That, too, I could see. Especially if any of the dads were alphas. They'd want to protect their youngest, shield her, and get their way.

"I don't like that." Gwen scowled. "Now you'll tell the dads and they'll get me and…" She started to cry and Clark stroked her hair. "They sent me away. They don't get to keep me only when it's convenient," she sobbed.

Her fear, her tears, put me on edge and I growled at Matty.

"Buttons," Matty soothed, putting his hands up in surrender. "I don't have to tell *anyone* I saw you. Also, even though the dads are assholes, when you left last time, they *let you go*. They kept their distance and hoped that you'd come back when you were ready."

"I don't want to talk about it." She flinched.

"You never want to talk about it, which is a big part of the problem. Eventually, the lies you tell yourself are going to catch up to you." His voice gentled. "The dads are getting old, Buttons. I know how much not going to the grandparents' funeral hurt you. How will you feel if something happens to one of the dads, our siblings, or your nieces and nephews, and we can't tell you because you block us?"

"If I talk to any of you, they'll find me." Her chest shook. "It's bad enough I talk to Lenny sometimes."

"I'm glad you talk to Lenny." A pained look crossed his face. "While the dads are worried about you, they're not going to kidnap you and take you back to Vancouver."

She gave him a defiant look. "Why not? It's what happened last time."

"You were *hurt*, Buttons. You needed the hospital and when you were released, you needed to be cared for. I'm sorry they always fuck things up when it comes to you," her brother soothed.

My hands fisted. Who'd hurt her?

"I'm sorry we didn't protect you better. However, not dealing with it isn't helping you. I guess you haven't told them that story?

Sorry, not trying to boundary stomp. I'm genuinely worried."
Matty gave her an apologetic look.

"I try not to tell anyone that story. Ever." Salty sadness filled her scent as she burrowed into Clark's arms.

My heart broke for her and everything she'd been through. I'd give everything to make it all better. She deserved the world, and it seemed all she ever got was heartbreak.

Chapter Forty-Four

GWEN

My worst nightmare came true, as Matty brought up what happened in my second year in New York. What caused my nightmares. What I tried to forget.

"You don't have to tell us anything," Tenzin assured.

I should tell them. Especially before we got too serious, in case what I'd done was a deal breaker and they wanted to leave me. But at this moment, I wasn't ready.

"Hey, whatever it is, we'll still love you, Gweny. We love you so much," Clark said. "We all have unhappy things in our past and it doesn't define us."

Shit, I needed to hear that.

Also, Clark *loved* me? I wasn't ready to say it back, but it warmed me to my very core.

"That makes me so happy. You both mean so much to me." I sobbed again as memories of that gunfight assaulted me. What happened with Officer Jones hurt me even more than being kidnapped by Lucius.

"It's okay," Clark soothed, tucking me back into his arms. "Do you want to go back to the room?"

"I didn't want to upset you. I'm sorry. All I wanted was a chance to tell you some things–and the kids will want to see you," Matty told me.

"I..." It was an ugly sob.

"I know. You've been through so much." Matty held out his hand. "Let's get some drinks and catch up? Lenny told me about your breakup. Also, if you haven't figured it out, I'm the one he sells your shit to, so when you're ready, you can have everything back."

"You're shitting my dick. That knotwaffle. I don't need their money." I flinched. The betrayal cut deep. Though part of me was happy that I could get my Maria Barilla rookie card back.

"Who's Lenny?" Clark asked.

"Did your siblings ever have a friend that pretty much lived at your house? That's Lenny, Matty's bestie. He's a procurer of things and I fence shit through him," I replied.

"You make him sound nefarious," Matty chuckled. "He authenticates art for a living and comes to New York a lot. I never asked him to find you or buy your things. I *do* make my own money–that's the money you got. Working for the dads doesn't make me a sock puppet."

I made a face. "Yes, it does."

He shook his head. "No. But I understand you wanting to be completely independent. I was only trying to help."

"I know." My brother tried to help me. Usually I shut him down and I'd get mad at him for doing so.

I'd be angrier if he stopped offering and I think he understood that.

"So..." Matty asked.

Clark turned us, so his back was to Matty. "What he says about trying to fix things with your dads, since they're old, is valid. So is staying no-contact, because some hurts never heal. Getting an update on their health might help you gauge things though?"

"You're right. That's probably what he wanted to talk about." I nodded. *It's not all about you, Gwen.*

"Do you want us to stay, or go? I don't mind either way," Tenzin told me, getting close to us.

It felt selfish to ask them to stay. According to the wedding schedule, there was a fun *animals and cocktails* walk before the dinner tonight.

"I'll catch up? I'm sure you're both really confused and I promise I'll fill you in eventually, just perhaps not tonight." My belly twisted as I pulled them both in for a hug.

"Only if you want to," Tenzin assured me. "Text us if you need us."

I took a deep breath and wiped away my tears. "Matty, let's go have that talk."

It was time.

Matty took a bite of burger. "Mmmm. So good. With the dads having health problems, Flavie is after me to eat better."

"Are the dads okay?" I asked, as we sat at a picnic table by the lake. I had fries and a beer. If I was being honest with myself, one thought I'd had when I'd seen the dads last was that they looked *older.*

I might think they're assholes, but I'd be sad if something happened to them.

"Papa had a heart attack and had to make some lifestyle changes. It's making him reconsider his life," Matty replied. "He's been thinking about you all summer, debating coming to one of your games when the season starts, then asking you to dinner."

"Oh, is he okay? Papa? Not Babo?" I frowned. Papa was head alpha, and we clashed a lot over the years–mostly over things like hockey, academic performance, and activities. We'd had some good times, but he wasn't the cuddly dad. Or that dad that relented on things.

"Fortunately, he's okay. I told Lenny in case he talked to you. But I know you don't always want to know." He took another bite.

I usually didn't. Guilt shot through me. Still, it wasn't like I'd rush to the hospital to see him unless it was dire.

If it was, they'd get me. Wouldn't they?

Huh. Maybe I should unblock someone other than Lenny.

"Papa has always had a massive soft spot for you. That's why Uncle put you as a prize in his takeover plan, when he tried to overthrow the dads after Mom died." Matty took a drink.

I gave him a look. That was one of the times I didn't like to think about.

"They're all in their *seventies*, Buttons. Babo has to watch his blood sugar, Dad has to be careful about his cholesterol, Popi is becoming forgetful–and I know Grandpa Gary's dementia hit you *hard,* so I want you to know all these things. I'm not saying you need to move home–or even come home for a holiday–but dinner? It's clear they miss you." He took another bite.

"Maybe?" Shit. Popi was always there with a kiss for the boo-boos and a way to scare off the bed monsters. He was also the only one who didn't brush off how awful I felt after killing Lucius. Babo was the most supportive of me playing hockey, too.

Still, them not fighting for me when Lucius was after me when I was sixteen, cut deep. Parents should protect you. Even from stalkers with powerful parents.

Matty nodded. "Absolutely. But if you want to come home for the holidays, you can."

I gave him a skeptical look. "That sounds like a clusterfuck. Remember last time?"

After everything with Lucius and what happened at the lake house, I'd spent the holidays recuperating at the dads'. More than one sibling made it clear I wasn't welcome.

Another reason to crawl out the window.

I didn't fit in with my family anymore. If I ever really did.

"The dads have other houses. You have seven siblings, most of whom also have other houses. Pick a location. Pick a holiday. I'll be there." He leaned in. "Choose somewhere Maricella hates, so she won't show up? Please?"

I started laughing. "Maybe." Then it hit me. "If I go home, I could get pictures of Mom. My ex destroyed pretty much everything I owned. Including my one photo of her."

"I can send you pictures right now. Will you unblock me? Or give me an email or something?" He picked up his phone.

"Promise not to abuse it?" I frowned at him. He wasn't the one who overstepped. Still...

Really, I wanted some physical pictures. But I didn't have any digital ones, either. I'd hidden the hard copy in the lining of my suitcase, when I'd been sent into hiding–the one Austin wrecked. Sure, I could have gone online, but I'd worried about leaving a footprint.

"Pinky swear." He held out his pinky.

I linked it.

Matty grinned. "Oh, now you've done it. Constant stream of pictures of the kids for you."

I laughed. "I'm okay with pictures of the kids. I just don't want mean texts. Like Maricella telling me her kids wouldn't get into a good school, because I'm a murderer."

"What?" Matty took an angry bite of burger.

"Yeah, her and Dario," one of her mates, "and Chiara," one of the twins, "texted me all sorts of super nice things. And not only after everything at the lake house. They did it at the beginning too, when I was sent away to Rockland. Like even though *I was supposed to be in hiding,* I got so many nastygrams my host mom wanted to get the police involved."

I had to change my number multiple times.

A horrified look crossed Matty's face. "They were texting you mean things after you went into *hiding*? They weren't even supposed to know your number. You had someone at the law firm to contact in case of an emergency. Did you tell them?"

"I did. I was told to grow up, and that Maricella was right–it would have been better if I had died instead of the grandparents. Not what I'd expect for a law office." I took a long drink of beer. That had hurt my naïve little heart, that still expected adults to help and protect me.

I did tell my contact for the protection program, mostly to keep my host mom from going to the police. I'd changed my number again, and then the texts had stopped.

"I still have that response and all the nastygrams, both from when I was sixteen, and after... after the lake house." It was hard to talk about my kidnapping.

Some of my siblings blamed it all on me. *Sorry if me defending myself made your social life awkward.*

"Um, yes, can you forward those to me, please? I'll send you my email. Send me anything you have from the law office, too," he told me.

"Sure." I stuffed fries in my mouth. I'd do it later.

"It's not okay for them to say things like that to you." He sighed. "I'm sorry."

"You have a lot to be sorry about." My eyes teared. "It's one thing to send me to Nonna's instead of heading off the problem, given I *wanted* to go back after Mom died. We all know I was more at home there, more a part of their family than ours."

He flinched, because he knew it. It was why he and his pack tried so hard to include me in things.

"It was shitty abandoning me when Lucius didn't quit when I left Canada. Being ripped from my grandparents and sent to Rockland, changing names, not being able to talk to *anyone* in my old life, having to basically start over, was terrifying. I was *sixteen*." At the time, I'd obeyed and trusted the police.

Now that entire plan seemed completely batshit. It wasn't even official federal protection either. It was the local police who knew and loved my grandparents and did everything they could to keep me safe for her until I graduated high school.

"The whole thing was *entirely* for your safety," Matty told me. "You're right. It was a shitty idea, and we didn't like it. We also had no idea it would end like it did—even before the grandparents got the police involved. It was so delicate given who Lucius' parents are. We couldn't take care of things like we'd usually do."

"I know. I'm not worth the trouble." They would have done it for the others. The dads were powerful.

Just not as powerful as Lucius' family.

Still, they should have tried. I was a *child*.

"You know that's not true," he shot back.

"Yeah? If one of the others got kidnapped, would they have spent *weeks* with their captors?" I challenged. That had stung, finding out they'd known where I was for days before they came.

Matty flinched again. "We *came* for you. Yes, it took a bit, since we had to be cautious. We could have gone to jail—or worse. Look, things got complicated, you don't understand."

It was my turn to flinch. I'd been told that all my life. At the same time, I knew it was for the best that I never fully understood.

"If you'd come when you'd found me, Officer Jones wouldn't have died," I fired back. His death would haunt me forever. Lucius killed him, because he'd come to rescue *me*.

"I'm sorry." He dabbed his beard with a napkin. "Um, you *tell* people the dads are assholes?"

I shrugged. "Most university students have parents involved in their lives. I have to have a reason why no one ever comes to my games, or family weekend, or why I don't go home even for summer. *My dads are assholes* is a pretty succinct explanation."

"Fuck. I totally forgot that family involvement is still a thing in university." His look grew pensive. "We can come to stuff. This is your last year. Do you have graduating player things for hockey coming up?"

"I do. You'd play my dad?" I grinned. They lived in Vancouver, and it was a distance. But they also had privilege, which always made travel faster, easier, and more comfortable.

"If you want me to."

It was a kind offer, and it would be fun to show the kids around the campus. "Maybe? I'll think about it."

As we ate, we updated each other about our lives, and I got plenty of cute pictures of the kids. Giulia was *twelve* now. Davey was nine. After the kidnapping, while I was recovering at the dads', those two spent a ton of time watching movies and hockey games with me. Matty also had twins–and a little baby that I hadn't met.

"Isa misses you. She's in New York *a lot* for work. Please talk to her?" Matty pleaded.

My sister Isabella worked for a fashion house in Paris and was mated to a movie director and two actors. None of which the dads had approved of, though eventually they relented.

"I..." I squeezed my eyes shut.

The thing was, someone *had* told Lucius my whereabouts. Not only my location, but about my life. He could have hired a detective, but according to his taunts, someone *had* talked to him about me.

It hadn't been Lauren, the figure skater I'd run into in a club that knew my old name, either.

He sighed. "I need you to pick a therapist and handle your shit. I'll send you names and pay for it. If you're serious about going pro, you *need* to get your house in order."

"I'm seeing a therapist at the university clinic so I can handle my Austin issues." I focused on eating the rest of my fries. "You have a point. I have a public social media account now, and I sort of freak out every time I post. Therapy is hard. It's easier to pretend it all didn't happen."

While some of it had been helpful, I didn't like the direction my old therapist had wanted to go in. I didn't want to be anyone's science project, even if it could help others.

"I know. It *did* happen and affected you. It's great that you're seeing one at your university, but I think you should try again with someone who specifically handles things like this. Soon." He got out his phone and made himself a note.

I made a non-committal noise. It depended on which thing. I had several very separate issues to handle from my ordeal with Lucius at the lake house.

"Um, also, maybe love on Giulia a little? She tested as a beta and she's feeling insecure about it, because we don't have many beta family members for her to look up to. Well, Maricella said something, but that won't happen anymore."

My brother got that look on his face that reminded me that even my family members, who soothed my nightmares and made me milkshakes, were people to be reckoned with.

"That bitch. Ugh. Of course. I miss Giulia. Just don't do to her what the dads did to me after I tested as a beta?" I pleaded.

"Um, let you continue ice skating and dance lessons and have private tutors, while looking the other way when you ditched things for hockey practice?" Matty's brows furrowed.

I sucked in a breath. "They knew that?"

"Yes. Just like they knew you didn't really want to move to New York with Nonna in order to focus on skating, you wanted to play hockey with Mia. Ultimately, like always, they let you," he pointed out.

What?

"I... I don't know how to feel about that. Still, I wanted to go to school and play hockey, not continue fucking omega lessons." My eyes teared. "You alphas got to go to high school, why couldn't I? All the ballet in the world wouldn't activate that dormant gene."

Some betas had that little extra that had the potential to wake up and push them over into omega status. Something that an illegal street drug used by traffickers could exploit.

"I know. They were trying to continue to treat you equally. However, I can understand why it felt like that, since they didn't listen to what you wanted." He took a sip of beer.

They never listened to what I wanted. Which was the problem. And part of why I worried they'd find me and make me come home.

All my life they didn't listen. Why would they start now?

"Is it safe for me to have contact with people from before?" I asked, frowning as I toyed with my beer. "No one ever told me and there's some people I'd like to talk to."

I worried about danger. The grandparent's death wore on me. If I hadn't run to them, Lucius wouldn't have had them killed.

Matty's look softened. "Talk to whoever you want. Mia and her pack have been asking about you. I guess they saw your skating video?"

"Oh, they did? I miss them and keep hoping I'd run into them at a Knights game or something." Though she'd been coaching hockey in Italy with one of her other packmates for years.

Matty's phone lit up. He looked at it, then at me. "Incoming."

"Zia G." Giulia came running across the grass, sending a flock of birds flying.

"Giulia." I gave her a hug. She looked like Flavie, with her light-brown hair and blue eyes. Most kids with an omega parent favored them, which was why all eight of us looked a lot alike, while not all having the same biological dad.

I didn't even know who mine was.

"Zia G, are you courting the Yeti? I saw him hugging you." Davey joined her, looking perplexed. "He's so tall."

"Courting, no. Are we something? Maybe? He's *very* tall." I giggled.

Courting was when an alpha wooed an omega to show them they could be a suitable mate. It was like dating, but shorter, more intense, and fueled by the intent to bond with them.

"You know Double D is here. Grif Graf, too," I added. A couple years ago, he'd liked the Knights.

Davey's face lit up. "They are?"

"One of the goalies from the Knights is getting married. That's why there's all these hockey players here, why I'm here," I told him. Though I knew the cousin of Flavie's that was getting married. We'd been good friends when we were little. Maybe there were other people I knew here?

"Buttons." Flavie gave me a big hug, the baby on her chest. She, like most female omegas, was shorter than me. She was perfect, tiny, and dainty, with light-brown hair and blue eyes. They'd met in Vancouver at a mixer between her omega academy and his university.

"Where's everyone else?" I looked around.

"With the twins at the treetop walk, but you can see them if you'd like," Flavie assured.

Matty and Flavie mated first, then found a pack, so I knew her best. Just like I was closest to Giulia and Davey because they were older.

"Hi, what position in hockey is your favorite," I teased the sleeping baby, who was a big boy. "Defense?"

Flavie laughed. "Probably."

I got a bunch of pictures of Clark on the animals and cocktail walk. It looked like they'd be at the arctic foxes soon.

"Do you want me to show you how I stole an arctic fox last time I was here?" I asked the kids.

"I'm going to tell the Yeti to check your suitcase." Matty laughed.

Giulia looked at me, shocked. "You stole a fox? That's against the rules."

"I gave him back." I threw my stuff in the trash. It was nice to see them. I'd missed this. Them. "Let's go find my friends and I'll tell you about the time I rescued a baby tiger."

Chapter Forty-Five

CLARK

The outdoor pavilion sparkled with lights. People drank, chatted, and did karaoke. The lovely dinner, which was full of speeches from friends and family, with memories and pictures of the couple, was long over. Cooter's speech had been *spectacular*.

The Sasquatches' goalie was hysterical, and I could see how he was Tenzin's bestie. He was a good foil for the reserved defenseman. Even if I had trouble understanding his thick Appalachian accent.

I sat at a table with Tenzin, Dimitri, and Carlos. Cooter was currently on the karaoke stage, singing a country song about a woman who dumped her ex's truck in the lake.

Tenzin checked his phone and frowned. Gwen had showed up for a bit on the animal walk, introduced everyone to her niece and nephew, chugged a cocktail, had some ice cream, then left with them.

I guess she knew a lot of people here for the other wedding and went to say hello. Made sense. The people from that wedding seemed fancy and there was a lot of security.

Carlos, Dimitri, and some others took a turn singing, leaving Tenzin and me alone. I'd already been up there with Carlos. Carlos had disappeared during the animal walk and appeared right as food was being served, looking a bit rumpled.

"Hi." Gwen slipped into *my* lap, still in what she'd been wearing earlier, and not cute evening outfits like everyone else.

"Hi." My arms wrapped around her, trying to pour all my love into her, and she nuzzled my neck.

"Hey, Firecracker. Are you okay? Are you hungry? Dinner's past but there are snacks. Would you like a drink?" Tenzin asked, brows knitted.

"A beer?" she asked.

Tenzin squeezed her hand and went off to the bar.

"Did you have fun?" I asked. She leaned into me, eyes closing as I played with her hair.

"It was good to catch up. I miss Matty and his family. It was nice to see some of the others. I knew his mate's family pretty well." Her face stayed buried in my chest, so I held her tight.

Snuggling Gwen was my favorite job.

I'd give her more if she wanted. She might like some physical reassurance later. Or maybe she'd like to sleep nestled in my arms like last night. Eating her out on my motorcycle had been fun, maybe she'd let me taste her on the bed? Or take a shower with her?

Tenzin came back with a beer and a plate of food from the snack buffet. "Here you go."

"Thanks." She downed half the beer. "I'm so sorry I kept going with them."

"Gwen, it's fine," I replied.

"I feel bad. Here you are and I'm running off to see other people. I'd forgotten that I like some people and I've missed them." Her head ducked.

"If you *want* to see them, you should," Tenzin told her, as he put two fingers under her chin and pushed it up. "I, too, have a brother that I haven't talked to in a long time. If he and his mates and children showed up and wanted to see me, I'd absolutely drop everything." A wistful look crossed his face.

"You have a brother, Tens?" I asked, still holding Gwen on my lap.

"Yes. When our parents died, he was studying at a university. My younger sister and I were with our parents when they died. I was the only one to survive." The pain in his voice, his scent, was evident.

"Tens," I breathed, and squeezed his arm. Survivors' guilt was a bitch.

Gwen got up and sat on *his* lap. "I'm so sorry."

He wrapped his arms around her. "I went to live with Zaya in Nashville, because he was mad that I'd lived and no one else had, and convinced some of our relatives to send me to her. I've tried to reach out, but he's even returned the gifts I've sent his children."

Ow. "I'm so sorry you're treated like that."

"That is really shitty." She put her head on his chest. "You have us now."

"You do," I told him. Someone was mad because his sibling *survived?* How awful.

"Thank you. He'd always been my favorite, so it hurt for a long time. It is what it is." His expression grew pained as Carlos, Dimitri, and the others crooned in the background.

Gwen moved to get up, and he pulled her back down.

"Eat, Gwen." His voice grew growly.

"Clark, I didn't mean to dismiss what you said earlier. I hear you, and it means everything. Please forgive me if I don't say it back yet?" Her look turned pleading, as she shoved cheese in her mouth, like she hadn't eaten all day.

What did I say? Oh.

"I'm not going anywhere," I assured. She could take her time in saying *I love you* back.

As she ate her food and drank two beers, she showed us pictures of her ice skating and of her family and childhood. Her mother was beautiful, and her dads were all very imposing. My favorite was Gwen: tiny goalie.

"Hey, what does your family do? They have a company that some of your siblings work for?" I asked, trying to figure everything out a little more.

"They're in shipping. They have trucks and boats and planes. You see them all over Canada. They also partner with other companies in other countries. It's their money, not mine. I'm not poverty cosplaying, if that's what you're asking. I'll be super pissed at Austin if he was." She popped a little tiny sandwich in her mouth.

"I don't even know what that means," I told her.

"All I have is what's in my bank account. I'm happy to show you that balance." She grabbed a handful of nuts from the bowl on the table. "My parents didn't have an education fund or trust, or anything like that for me. I was told that much when I was younger. If any relatives left me anything, no one told me."

"If you didn't have an education fund, did they not expect you to go to university?" I frowned. While my education fund hadn't had much in it, I had one.

"Oh, they did. But you had to ask the dads and, of course, they'd only pay for it if they approved. Which was why my sister Isa attended an omega academy in Vancouver and not a fashion school in Paris, like she wanted to."

Oh. That seemed mean.

"My mom left me some jewelry when she passed, but it's at my dads', if it hasn't been pillaged by my siblings." She sighed. "If... if you want me to pay rent and stuff, I'll make it happen. I guess when I was living in a closet, I could have called Matty, but I'd rather live in a small, dusty space, than ask my family for help." Gwen lifted her head, eyes teary.

"The fact you'd rather live in a closet than take their help says everything," Tenzin told her.

"I don't need you to pay anything. That wasn't why I was asking." I shook my head.

"Yes. I'd rather be broke and happy than have all the money and be chained to a bed." Her eyes pleaded with me.

My heart broke, and I pulled her to me. "Gweny. I care so much for you."

Her head rested on my shoulder. "I care for you, too. Can we dance for a bit?"

"Um, sure." It wasn't really dancing music, but I'd give her whatever she wanted.

We stood, and she wrapped her arms around my neck, while JP and Celine sang a love song almost on key. Her hand snaked out and grabbed Tenzin's wrist, pulling him to her.

The three of us swayed to the music, her in the middle, as the day was clearly taking its toll on her. Eventually, her body relaxed into me. Her scent also changed to something less sad and more needy.

"Do you want to leave the party?" I asked, as someone sang something that made me hope all the kids had gone to bed. "Go back to the room. Maybe watch a movie or cuddle."

Have some naked, full body snuggles in that gigantic bed we have. Tenzin can join us if he wants. Even if he only wants to watch like he did when we were on the bubble wheel.

She nodded. "I'd love to go back to the room and, um, *snuggle* with the both of you, please? Maybe some full body snuggles with both of you at the same time, with me in the middle?"

"I'd be happy to, Gweny. Thank you for communicating your needs with us." I stroked her hair. "Just so you know, I've never done anything like what I think you're asking."

"I've never had two people at once. But I need you both. Possibly twice." She bit her lower lip, an anxious look on her face, though her eyes were lit with desire, her scent full of arousal.

"What I'm hearing is that my sweet little Firecracker needs us at the same time to make her feel better?" Tenzin's lips moved close to her ear.

I'd never done that. But I'd do that with her–and Tenzin. *Mmmm. Yeah. Not a hardship.*

"Please? You can decide between yourselves who gets what hole." That minty scent turned sour and her lower lip quivered. "Unless I'm asking too much, too soon?"

"Firecracker, I'm so glad you feel safe coming to us. It's been a big day for you. I'd love to make you feel better." Tenzin squeezed us to him.

She moaned softly in our arms. "Good. I *really* need you both tonight. Maybe more than once."

"My dick is yours, Gweny. We're happy to take care of you." It was rock hard, so I rubbed it against her, to let her know what she already possessed.

Gwen took both our hands. "Please, Alphas, take me to bed."

Those words went straight to my cock. I squeezed her hand. "As you wish."

Gwen held both our hands as we walked toward our villa, swinging them a little. Her face tipped up. "The stars are so pretty. Is the golden beetle out tonight?"

"It is." I put an arm around her and pointed it out. It made me think of the night Tenzin and I laid on the beach, looking at the stars.

Yeah, I was in love with that man. Just like I was in love with her.

I took Gwen's hand, then gave him a coy look as I outstretched my hand toward Tenzin.

He growled. "Don't you dare."

"Tag." I tapped his shoulder and started running, still holding Gwen's hand. She giggled and ran with me.

Tenzin let out a long, rumbling growl which echoed through the dark night. A wolf howled in the distance.

"Caught you." He picked up Gwen and threw her over his shoulder, and she squealed. His eyes focused on me.

I smirked. The moonlight made him look like a sculpture.

His nostrils flared. Holding my gaze pointedly, he gave a little grunt, then continued walking, Gwen still over his shoulder. Catching up to them, I ruffled her hair as we made our way across the grass to the villa.

I let us in—it was so quiet. Everyone else was still at the party.

"Oh, look at the wolves." Gwen, upside down, kicked a little and Tenzin put her down. She pressed her face to the glass window.

One of them watched her. The same one from earlier, maybe?

Tenzin came up behind her, pressing his body against her back, sandwiching her between him and the glass. I joined them, putting an arm around her, sliding it between her and Tenzin's bodies.

The wolf came up to us and gave Gwen a little yip, looked at Tenzin, growled, and went off. Animals could sense designations, too.

"Where's your room?" Tenzin picked her up again, and she yelped.

I flipped on the light, closed the door behind us, and turned on the fireplace, since it felt right.

Tenzin kicked off his shoes and flopped her onto the bed. "What are your expectations for tonight, Firecracker? I'd love to make you feel better by eating that pussy of yours. Also, I claim your ass first. Is there anything you don't like?"

Gwen stretched out onto the bed, toeing off her shoes, looking like a painting. "That sounds delightful. I don't want to be tied up or blindfolded, and I don't like mean words. The only expectations I have are that I want your knots and your cuddles. I'm happy you're willing–I'd understand if you're not."

"You want my knot, Gweny? You're a beta, will it hurt you?" I'd never knotted anyone before. But I'd give it to her. I'd give her anything and everything. After all, she already had my heart.

"Me? No. I might just be a beta, but I can take a knot real good in either hole. I... I've been fantasizing about both your knots at the same time. I've never done that. It should still feel as good for you." Her voice was breathy and part pleading. "Again, I'm sorry that this is such a jump, I..."

"There's no *just* about you, Gweny. You being a beta changes nothing, diminishes nothing. Please, communicate your needs to us. I will give you everything and anything. Also, I *really* don't like you talking bad about yourself." I took a step closer to the bed.

I didn't like her thinking her being a beta wasn't good enough for me. Us. Or that she shouldn't ask to have her needs met.

"Okay." She leaned into me.

My arms wrapped around her. "That's my good girl."

"We're happy to be here with you. We care about you so much and if you need to feel better we'll comfort you any way you'd like," Tenzin added.

The fact he said that made me feel good, given his previous hesitations about us. Though he had been the one to chase her in the fun house and have her fuck me on a ride. This felt different, and I was happy for the progress.

I brought her into my arms, then fell backwards on the bed with her. I pressed my lips to her temple. "Please don't talk bad about yourself. You have the best heart of anyone I know. It's part of why I love you so much."

"Okay." She nuzzled into me. "I adore your big heart, too."

Awww.

I kicked off my shoes, hearing them clunk on the floor, then I wrapped my legs around her. I attacked her lips, tangling my hands in her hair, trying to show her how much I cared about her.

A hungry growl filled the room and Tenzin stood there, shirtless, holding a washcloth.

"Come here, Firecracker, let me clean you up a bit." Tenzin sat on the corner of the bed.

Mmmm, shirtless Tens. I couldn't wait to see him naked.

Gwen crawled across the bed, and he stripped her, then gently ran the washcloth over her. I took off my shirt.

Tenzin kissed her forehead. "Think of a safe word. Something we wouldn't usually use in bed, just in case you need to slow down or stop. You never need to worry about using it. It is *always* okay. We can use it too, since this is new for everyone."

A safe word? I'd never heard of that. It seemed like a good idea though. I wasn't sure how both of us knotting her at the same time was going to work.

Gwen considered this for a moment as he finished washing her. "Raccoon."

Of course that was her chosen word.

"Perfect." Tenzin kissed the top of her head. "Don't be afraid to use it."

"Yes, Alpha." She gave him a coy little look.

"Good girl," he growled. "Now get on the bed and sit on my face."

Chapter Forty-Six

GWEN

I pulled off my shirt and bra, then tossed them aside, heart pounding, pussy throbbing. Tenzin took the washcloth back to the bathroom.

Clark looked me up and down as he took off his shirt and pants, leaving his boxer briefs on. "I like seeing you naked."

Same. Mmmm.

He lowered the lights, giving the room a soft glow.

When Tenzin returned, he lay down on the bed, like a beautiful, muscular pillow. He gave me a pointed look. "I was serious. Sit on my face, Gwen. I don't mean hover. If you suffocate me, then well, I'll go happily."

Those words made me gush.

I'd taken an enormous risk asking them to take me to bed. Something I'd debated. To have both at the same time was a lot.

But I needed them and hoped at the very least they'd snuggle me for a bit. If Tenzin returned to his room, Clark, at least, would knot me good if I asked.

Now here I was, about to act out my fantasies with these two guys, who'd quickly become my world, my obsession. Who held me, fed me snacks and beers, listened, and cared for me.

I'm a lucky, lucky girl.

"I'm waiting," Tenzin growled, opening his arms from his spot on the big hotel bed. "Come as much as you need to, okay?"

"Okay." Sit on his face? Sure, I had no problems trying something new.

Crawling over to him on the bed, I sat on his face. His tongue made contact with my clit and I gasped. My back arched as his mouth caressed me.

"That feels good, Tens." I moved my body with his motions as his hands clamped firmly against my thighs.

Clark got on the bed with me, straddling Tenzin's bare chest, facing me. As Tenzin continued to tease me with his tongue, Clark kissed me like he could heal everything in me that was broken.

Maybe they could. I hadn't only wanted them because I was horny and sad.

A gasp escaped my mouth as Clark played with my breasts as we kissed.

"Your boobs fit perfectly in my hands," Clark whispered. "I love all the cute little sounds you're making for us."

Another ripple of pleasure shot through my body. Yes. I needed physical contact. Human touch. Knots.

"Tens," I cried, as he hit the right spot, his hands now gripping my ass.

"That's it, Sweetness. Fall apart all over Tens' face," Clark whispered between kisses, as my hands ran up and down his muscular body.

Sweetness? That was the cutest nickname ever. This *was* Clark.

Clark's kisses peppered my jaw, then explored my neck. Tenzin continued to lick and suck me, driving me closer and closer to completion.

My body rocked over Tenzin's mouth and into Clark's, as if I could absorb both of them into me and make myself whole.

I wasn't going to last long. As if Clark knew, which he might, given my scent always changed a little before I came, his mouth stopped kissing my neck and clamped around my breast.

"Shit." My body bucked and pleasure crested through me. Tens and Clark held me in place, neither of them stopping as the orgasm shuddered through my body. I slumped into Clark's arms.

Tenzin pushed me down his body and brought my face to his. His face was slick with me, and I kissed my juices off his mouth.

"My turn." Clark dove between my legs, continuing what Tenzin had started.

Clark slid two fingers into me as he licked. Another orgasm shot through me. Oh, I liked being between both of them. *Would definitely recommend.*

Tenzin had my chin in his hand. "Eyes on me, Precious. Keep going, Clark. Make her fall apart."

Precious? Another amazing nickname, making me feel treasured. Wanted.

"She tastes so good," Clark murmured.

Tenzin stroked my face, his eyes holding mine. "Perfect. Come one more time, then we'll fuck you."

"Yes, yes please," I wiggled my ass a little. Clark seemed to enjoy eating pussy–and I'd happily offer mine.

Tenzin's kisses and teases were deliberate, focused. Clark ate me like his favorite dessert.

Clark's fingers worked faster. "Come again for me, so we can make love to you," he muttered into my pussy. "We're going to fit into you so perfectly. Everything bad today will go away and be replaced with all the pleasure we're giving our sweet, perfect girl."

I moaned. That. Dirty. Talk.

Fuuuuccck.

"We're going to knot you until you scream. Until you forget everything but us, know no knot, no pleasure, but ours," Tenzin growled, switching breasts.

Mmmm. *Talk dirty to me, Alphas.*

"Yes, yes, please," I begged. Clark *bit* my clit. Tenzin clamped down hard on my nipple with his mouth, fingers pinching the other. The orgasm crashed down on me hard and fast.

Tenzin's lips let go of my breast, and he caught me as I collapsed into his arms. Clark joined us, sandwiching me between their bodies. Three orgasms? This was exactly what I needed. I relaxed into them, feeling so safe, so loved.

Clark stroked my hair. "You're such a good girl."

Oooh, I liked being called a *good girl*.

"I can't wait to bury my knot in your pretty ass." Tenzin's face nuzzled my neck as he gave me some playful kisses that tickled, making me giggle.

"I love that giggle." Clark blew a raspberry on my chest, right under my boobs, so his face was partly buried in them. "I love these boobs."

"I love this ass." Tenzin squeezed mine.

"Since we're declaring love for body parts, I love these lips." I kissed Tenzin. "And these lips." I turned and kissed Clark.

Clark grabbed me and we made out again and I ground against his boxer briefs.

"Clark, please tell me you have condoms and lube," Tenzin said. "Precious, I'm not on birth control. Even if you are, I'd rather use condoms to be safe. I recently got tested, and I'm clean."

"Yeah, I don't need a dorm baby. Though I'm on birth control and I'm clean." I was glad I'd gotten tested the last time I'd gone to the campus clinic. I'd wanted to be cautious in case my ex had been cheating. Just like I had a birth control implant, because while I loved kids, it would be a long time before I was ready to have any.

"Yeah, me too. I got a birth control implant recently." Clark blushed. "I have lube and condoms. Um, I... I wanted to be ready in case you asked me for a super-good full-body cuddle. Especially since we were going to Canada and you're afraid." His look grew shy.

"That is so sweet. You're mine." I pounced on him, pinning him to the bed and kissing him. Awww. So fucking sweet.

"Yes, I surrender to Queen Ladybug." Clark grinned up at me.

Tenzin made an annoyed little growl. I looked over and he was naked. While I'd seen him shirtless, I took a moment to appreciate his very muscular body. Tree trunk thighs. Abs that you could cook pancakes on. Biceps on tattooed biceps. A cute little happy trail leading down to his monster cock.

Shitballs, that was one long, *thick* dick. His knot, that mass of muscles at the base that only alpha males had, was starting to inflate. It would get bigger with his arousal, and eventually he'd shove that whole thing in me, and it would *lock*–sticking inside me and holding us together, while he pumped me full of his hot cum, and he wouldn't be able to pull out until it deflated.

Which could be minutes, or it could be an hour.

Clark, too, had his eyes fixed on Tenzin's giant dick, scent flaring with desire. It made me happy that they seemed to be starting something, too.

"Do you two like what you see?" Tenzin's voice grew amused.

When I read romance novels, I always rolled my eyes at the heroines who were like, *It's so big. Will it even fit?* Like it's a dick, girl, it'll fit. But as I appraised that fine specimen of an extra gigantic cock, I now kind of understood where they were coming from. Because it was *huge*.

Oh, I'd fit that monster cock inside me or I'd die trying.

"Yep, dick me dead and bury me pregnant," I breathed. *Here lies Gwen, who took too much massive Yeti cock in her ass.*

"Same," Clark whispered in my ear.

Clark stood and went to his suitcase. Tenzin pulled the covers down, then sat onto the bed with me.

"Is this what you still want, Precious? If you're not ready, we can take you one at a time, or we could have you and not knot you." Tenzin's hand cupped my face gently, his thumb smoothing my temple.

"Please, Alphas, I want your knots. I need you both to dick me down so hard I see stars." The want for them to be inside of me grew.

Tenzin made another little growl. Clark joined me, holding a box of condoms and a tube of lube. Which I was grateful for. Unlike omegas, betas were not self-lubricating.

"Clark, strip and lie down on the bed," Tenzin directed.

"Yes, Alpha." Clark waggled his eyebrows, took off his boxers, and jumped on the bed, bouncing a few times, then flopped down onto the pillows, splaying himself out like a happy puppy.

Clark was slimmer and leaner than Tenzin, but just as muscular. There was no little happy trail, just an adorable little puff of curls and that beautiful, bejeweled dick.

That piercing *had* to be uncomfortable in a jock, though he probably took it out. While it wasn't quite a monster Yeti cock, his dick was still a sight to behold. His knot was bigger than Tenzin's.

Yep. I wanted to be fucked by two giant alpha cocks and made to come until I passed out.

"I can't wait to have that inside me." I looked at Tenzin, then back at Clark. "Better than a blow job from a dinosaur."

Tenzin's hand smacked my ass, filling the room with a crack. It didn't hurt. Instead, it made my clit throb.

"Precious, you're not supposed to say that anymore," he growled.

"Oops. I forgot." I batted my eyelashes.

Tenzin handed me a condom. "Put that on Clark. You're going to ride him."

I bounced onto the bed and opened the packet. My eyes met Clark's as I straddled him and slowly rolled the condom down his cock. At some point, I wanted to taste him.

Something splashed on my pussy and ass, then warmed a little, making me wiggle. "Oooh. Warm."

"I got the warming kind. I figured you'd like it better," Clark told me, smiling. He held out his hands. "Whenever you're ready, Sweetness.

I took his hands in mine, and slowly speared myself on his pierced, hard length, sighing as it stretched and filled me in all the right ways. "Oh, yes, that's it, Tesoruccio."

"Did you just give me an Italian nickname?" Clark moved his hips, hands still holding mine.

"Yes. You're my little treasure." Letting go of his hands, I placed mine on his shoulders as I slid up his length.

"Oh, I like that. And, you, Sweetness, are a sight to behold riding me like this. You fit me perfectly." His hands went to my hips.

"You look beautiful riding his cock. I'm going to get you ready, so you can take me, too." More warmth coated my ass as Tenzin started playing with my hole. "Breathe, Precious," he whispered, kissing my neck as he slid his finger in. The kisses trailed down the stars tattooed on the middle of my spine. "These are beautiful."

It was a delicate vine of tiny stars, forget-me-nots, hearts, and even a moon.

"Thanks. I designed a lot of it myself. Originally, I'd wanted it to travel down my entire spine, but I didn't have enough money. One day I'll get it finished," I told him.

As Tenzin played with my ass, I leaned forward to kiss Clark. His hands cupped my breasts now, as he teased and touched them. I slid up and down Clark's beautiful cock. Each time I stopped just shy of his knot.

"This feels so good." Pleasure built so fiercely inside me that I was afraid I'd come before Tenzin had me.

"Are you ready to take me, Precious?" Tenzin nibbled on my ear.

"Yes, please, Alpha. Give me Mostriciattolo," I sighed as his fingers slipped out of me.

"Please tell me that's Italian for monster cock," Clark whispered, giving me a slow, sweet kiss.

"*Little monster.* That's what his dick is called now. Please, Alpha, put it in me." I looked over as Tenzin rolled the condom over his cock.

"Oh, I will." He climbed back up on the bed and rubbed more lube on my ass. "What do you say if it's too much?"

"Raccoon." I stilled on Clark's dick. This was the moment.

"Come here." Clark pulled me close, running his hand through my hair, the other up and down my back, as he kissed me, sweet and slow.

The tip of Tenzin's dick broached my hole. He kissed my neck, my back, covering my body with his, running one hand over me, reassuring me, as the other guided him into me, past the ring of muscles and...

Tenzin bit down gently on the lobe of my ear. "Breathe."

I took a deep breath, and he pressed further into me, stretching me, first to the point of pain, but as I was about to cry out, pleasure burst through me, replacing it. It wasn't quite an orgasm, but it made me moan.

"That's it. Take him all, like a good girl, just like you took me. It'll feel so good," Clark whispered. "I can feel his big monster cock through you, and it feels terrific."

"Oh, it does," I sighed, as he kept filling me up. I felt so stuffed, so stretched, that I wasn't sure how much more I could take. But I wasn't ready to tap out. Nope, I wanted it all.

Yep, dick me dead, Big Guy.

"You feel incredible, Precious," Tenzin told me, as he pulled out and pushed in again, the sensation overriding me, as I tangled my hands in Clark's hair. "I'm so lucky."

I was done with being gentle and playful. "Pound me. Fuck me. Make me scream."

"As you wish, Sweetness." Clark held me tight, as Tenzin pounded my ass, moving his giant cock in and out so hard his balls slapped against it.

"Yes, yes, take me hard, Big Guy. I want it all. You, too, Tesoruccio." I kissed Clark and started to move, trying to match my motions with Tenzin. Pleasure overrode me as a moan escaped my lips.

Clark's hips pulsed. There was so much sensation, as wave after wave of pleasure washed over me, bringing me closer and closer to my release.

"Is that what you need, Sweetness?" Clark murmured. "I love seeing him in your ass."

"Yes, don't stop, I'm going to come." My eyes closed, because the pleasure was getting to be too much, but I didn't want it to stop. I was so full. Someone's hand rolled my nipple, as a mouth sucked on my neck.

"That's it, let go," Tenzin soothed, as he continued to thrust into me relentlessly. "We're right here. I want to see you shatter all over our cocks."

The release exploded out of me, hard and fast shudders ran through my body as I clamped hard on both their dicks.

"Knot me, Tesoruccio." I sat myself down on his cock so hard and fast, I saw stars as his giant knot stretched my pussy, seating itself fully, deep inside me. I came again, my body trembling, as I lay on his chest, my heart pounding.

Clark kissed me, arms wrapping around me. "You took my knot so good, it feels amazing being inside you."

Tenzin's hand caressed his face. "That was beautiful. Now, come again for me, so I can knot you."

Clark ground against me. With the knot inside, he couldn't move much, but what he was doing sent lightning sparks straight to my clit.

Tenzin grabbed my hair, turning my head, so he could capture my mouth.

"That's it. Come for me like a good girl," Tenzin growled.

Another orgasm shot through me, leaving me breathless as Tenzin pulled out and thrust inside me all the way to his knot.

"Alphas," I screamed, back arching, as that knot made its home in my ass, locking itself inside me. The gesture pulled against Clark's dick, which was still locked inside of me.

"Take everything you need," Clark growled, as he continued to grind against me, attacking my lips with his mouth, teasing my nipples with his fingers.

Tenzin's mouth fastened to my neck, sucking on the cords in a way that made me clench, as he ground his knot against my ass.

"That feels good. Both of you look so beautiful," Tenzin murmured.

"I love how I can feel your knot inside her," Clark told him, going past my shoulder to steal a kiss from Tenzin.

My body bucked at the sight of them kissing. They continued making out as the two of them sandwiched me between them, grinding and moving against me as I wretched and cried in pleasure.

"That's it." Tenzin clamped down at the juncture of my neck and shoulder–a popular place for alphas to claim their mates.

It wasn't hard enough to claim me, or even draw blood, but the gesture awakened every instinct in me, setting my body on fire.

Clark did the same on the other side.

I screamed their names as they wrung one more orgasm out of me. Now spent, I flopped onto Clark's perfect form. His arms wrapped around me, as he and Tenzin rolled us, so we were on our sides, since both of them were still firmly inside me.

Tenzin kissed my temple. "Are you okay? That was intense. But you took us so well."

"Shitballs, you two make me feel good," I muttered, still drunk on their scents and pheromones, as well as all the orgasms. *Would highly recommend.*

"Are you okay, Clark?" Tenzin asked, throwing a blanket over us.

"That was incredible." Clark kissed me again.

"I like being between you two." I snuggled deep between them, warm and safe amidst my two alphas. The gas fire flickered, making it feel so nice and cozy, and both of them held me, peppering my face with tiny kisses, stroking my hair, and telling me how good I'd been.

My eyes closed. I just needed a little nap. Then we could do it all again.

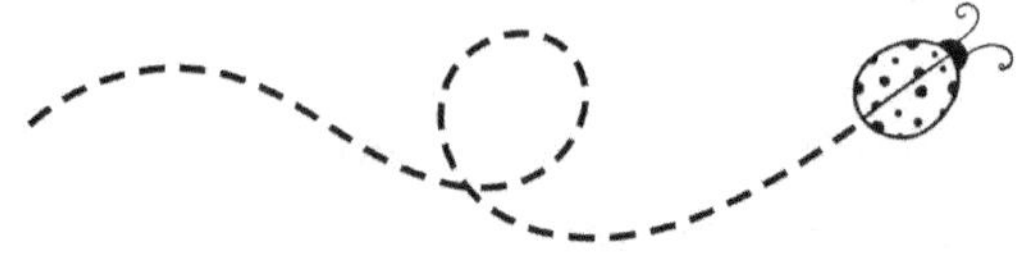

Chapter Forty-Seven

TENZIN

Both of them slept in the giant hotel bed, Clark's arm draped protectively over her. Sharing Gwen with him–twice–had been a pleasurable experience. She took a knot so incredibly well for a beta. Not to mention the way she took direction.

We'd gone hard that second time, so much that I'd ended up holding back, because I'd been afraid they might throw me into a rut. Betas didn't usually do that to alphas.

However, in just a few hours, my attraction to Gwen had gone from strong to magnetic.

Even if I still wasn't quite ready for a relationship, there was never any doubt I'd say *yes* to taking her to bed, when she'd asked us back at the dinner. She needed our care, our love, our knots–something I wouldn't deny her.

She was *mine*. They were *both* mine.

And I was theirs.

The large room was dark, with only the gas fire for light. I rolled out of bed, to use the bathroom.

"Tens, please don't run," Clark murmured in the darkness. "I know we pushed you tonight, but please don't leave us. We'll give you whatever you need."

"I'm just going to take a piss. I'll be back." When I came out of the bathroom, Clark slipped in, still looking a little upset.

An electric kettle sat on the counter next to a coffee pot, and I started some water for tea. I didn't like the tea offerings in the container next to the kettle. So, I tossed on the robe I'd discarded earlier after we'd all taken a shower together and ducked out to the kitchen.

All the lights were on in the empty living area. Snacks were strewn across the counter, like someone had come back hungry. Beer bottles covered the coffee table, looking out onto the wolf window. In the cupboard, I found some better tea and two mugs.

"Tens, Tens, where are you?" Clark's quiet voice was frantic.

"I'm right here," I whispered, hurrying back to the room and closing the door behind me.

Clark stood there, stark naked, a worried look on his face.

"Don't go." His eyes teared.

I set the mugs and tea down. "Hey, I only went to find some tea." I bundled him in my arms, not knowing what else to do. "What do you need?"

"I... I don't know." He put his head on my shoulder. Clark's scent was a little sour.

"Okay." I ran my hands through his hair, reassuring him that I was here. It wasn't simply spending the night with her that was extraordinary, being with him was something as well.

Seeing that beautiful body naked. Feeling his knot through her.

That pierced cock.

Mine.

The kettle went off, and I let go of him, then made us tea.

"Here." I handed him a mug, and we sat down on the couch. Taking a throw blanket, I threw it over us.

"Sorry, I didn't mean to freak out. I don't know why I did that?" he eventually mumbled.

"Alpha drop is a bitch and they don't talk about it enough in alpha classes," I offered. "It's also *completely* normal to feel like this. Gwen pushed you, too. First time knotting someone, first time being a threesome."

While his dirty talk was delightful, I got the idea that his past experiences were pretty straightforward.

"I guess I should go online and learn some things if that's how it's going to be. I know there are things she wants to try. Her ex wasn't adventurous." He glanced over at the bed. Gwen had spread out in the middle of the mattress like a starfish.

"I'll send you some reputable sources." I took another sip of tea. "You did a good job with her."

He'd also followed my directions so well. Mmmm, I did like good boys.

"Don't leave us. Everyone always leaves us." His eyes closed.

Us. I could see Gwen's massive abandonment issues, both from her ex and her family. But Clark? I knew nothing about his past romantic relationships.

"I might need more time, but I won't leave. Promise." Whatever this was, I wanted it. Even if it ended up with my heart being in pieces.

Again.

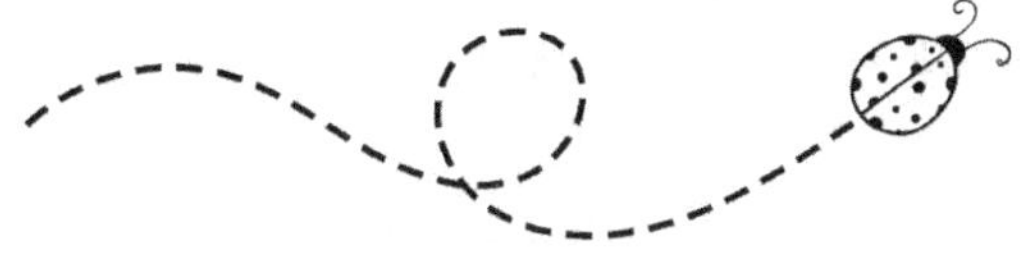

Chapter Forty-Eight

GWEN

"Good job, Ladybug." JP gave me a fist bump after dance practice. "See you tonight."

"Are you sure you're okay? Tenny's my friend, but I'm not afraid to kick his ass," Cooter asked me for the hundredth time this morning.

"I'm fine, Cooter. It's nothing that breakfast and a trip to the spa won't cure. Thanks for bringing clothes for him." I threw the bag over my shoulder.

Okay, I wasn't all right.

"Clothes? Like you're keeping a naked Bucket hostage in your room?" Dean laughed.

"Until I get my breakfast, yes." I shrugged. Clark and Tenzin were waiting for me with breakfast and snuggles, and I desperately

needed both. I'd been tempted to miss practice, but I knew someone would drag my ass there, so I came willingly.

"Are you giving me a ride back, Dean?" I'd driven over with him
in a golf cart, as their villa was next to ours.

Dean checked his phone. "Yes."

We got in the cart and I texted them.

Me

On the way back. Tens, if you want your clothes, my breakfast better be there.

Tens

Breakfast is waiting, M'lady.

Me

That's what I like to hear.

Clark

Your snuggles are waiting, too.

Me

Perfect

"Are you feeling better?" Dean asked as we drove across the
grass, the early morning air pleasant.

"I told you, I'm fine." I'd woken up upset and clumsy. It happened sometimes.

"Okay. You know you can trust me, right?" He frowned a little.
"Did they say or do something that set you off? Also, I hate to say
this, but your eating habits suck and good nutrition will make you
feel so much better. Fuck. Are you on legal shit? Illegal shit can
fuck with you. Grif used to see a doctor that helps hidden omegas.
I can give you her info."

"I'm not an omega. Will everyone stop?" I snapped. Last night had been amazing and I didn't like how I now felt shitty. I should still feel amazing... It wasn't guilt, either.

Dean flinched like I'd slapped him and regret filled me.

"I... I'm sorry. My dads wanted me to be an omega like my sisters. When Austin and I broke up, he'd said he always thought I'd be one." And *him*. Fucking Lucius. Tears streamed down my face.

The golf cart stopped and Dean pulled me to him. Omegas were usually pretty huggy people. He smelled like a cozy sweater, along with wisps of his mates' scent.

"It's okay, Ladybug. It's just that right now you seem to be stuck halfway between an omega drop and a spiral." He looked worried. "I don't know if bringing you back to your naked boys will make it better or hurt you more. I don't know how to fix this."

Ugh, I really was broken, wasn't I? Given I was with Austin when everything happened, I didn't notice much difference. But now...

The tears kept coming.

"If you're not an omega, maybe you should take a gamma test," he said softly. "And I mean this out of love. Something's wrong."

Gammas were essentially failed omegas. Something in their environment was dangerous enough that their body stopped a biological process, because it felt dangerous. It used to be things like war and famine. Now it was mostly asshole parents.

My dads were assholes. But not like that.

It didn't show up on the basic test, you had to do a special one.

"I had one a couple of years ago. Omega test, too. I come up as a beta on everything. I just need food and snuggles," I admitted. As much as I didn't want to have this conversation with Tenzin and Clark, they should know how damaged I was before we got deep.

"Okay." Dean drove me back to the cabin, worry resided in his scent.

Before I'd even gotten out of the golf cart, Tenzin stood there, in nothing but a pair of too-short drawstring shorts, that were Clark's.

"Precious." Tenzin scooped me up. He kissed my forehead. "I have breakfast–and Clark." He turned to Dean. "Thank you."

"If you need me, please call me." Worry gleamed in Dean's eyes.

Tenzin carried me into the villa. Valya was sitting at the table on her phone. She snickered a little as we walked by.

"Have fun," she called, as Tenzin and I went into the room and shut the door.

The overwhelming aroma of food and coffee made my stomach growl. A delicious spread sat on the low table by the couch, which had been moved, so we could look out the window at the wolves. The fire flickered in the background and the room smelled nice, like lavender.

Clark was there on the couch in boxers and a shirt, drinking a cup of coffee. "Ladybug, what's wrong?"

"I'm broken." I sobbed as Tenzin gently placed me on the couch.

"You're not broken, Precious. It's normal. I didn't take good enough care of you last night. That's all." Tenzin sat down next to me and wrapped a blanket around me.

I shook my head, hating that he thought any of this was on him. "It's not you. It's me. I didn't think it would be a problem, but it is. You should know. Um, I have to start at the beginning. Do we have anything stronger than coffee?"

Clark stood and came back with a bottle of champagne. "It came with breakfast. Who drinks champagne with breakfast?"

"You mix it with juice." I took the cup of coffee Tenzin poured for me and leaned into him.

"Okay. Do you want it with juice?" Clark picked up a glass.

"Sure." I didn't want to be hungover for the wedding later.

Clark brought me a mimosa that looked like it was mostly champagne and sat down next to me.

He opened one of the covered dishes. "We got this one for you. I got myself waffles. You can have them instead if you want."

They'd gotten me a meat with vegetables omelet and crispy potatoes. His was whipped cream with some waffle. Maybe. And a strawberry rose with a mint leaf for posterity, along with a side of fried ham and loaded hash browns. While I did like strawberry waffles I was feeling eggy.

"Thanks." I devoured my eggs. I should start talking, but I was hungry.

They let me, keeping my coffee full and feeding me bites of their meals. Tenzin had steak and eggs, along with potatoes and toast. The food was delicious and beautiful.

Finally, I downed the mimosa, then made myself another.

"You don't owe us anything," Tenzin stated, rubbing the back of my neck as I returned to the couch.

"I have to, if I want this to work. And after last night... I... I want this," I pleaded. Tears pricked my eyes. "But..." My head bowed. "I don't even know where to start. I broke my hip while playing hockey when I was fifteen. At the time, I was living with my grandparents in New York, so I could train with a specific figure skating coach, though it was a ruse to play hockey. The dads brought me home to Vancouver to recuperate, since my mom was dying of OOC and she wanted me there. My mom and I were close, even when I was living with my nonna."

I sniffed. Other than my nonna, she'd been my biggest advocate and supporter. OOC was a type of cancer that only affected Omegas.

"Her death devastated the dads, after all, she was their bonded omega. It was *rough*. My uncle, one of Dad's brothers, was trusted with helping them run their shipping company, so that they could spend time with Mom while she was dying–and later grieve for her.

He staged a takeover of the company. I don't know much about it, other than he conspired with some powerful people and offered them things to help. It failed. Badly. Uncle was ousted."

I took a sip of champagne. I was one of those things.

"After my mom died, I wanted to go back to my nonna's. I was making a very good recovery, and I liked my life in New York. The dads wanted me to stop playing hockey, so I wouldn't get injured again, and to stay with them in Vancouver. It was a huge fight. Nonna offered to fight for legal custody–and had a case given I'd spent years living with her already."

That had caused a rift with my siblings. Some agreed that I should be allowed to return to New York and live my life. The others told me that I was being mean to the dads and should suck it up and stay.

"There was this guy that I'd known for some time casually, mostly from social stuff my parents made me attend. While my mom was dying and I was recovering, we started messaging a lot. His situation had changed, and he'd been feeling lonely. We were just friends–if that." Thoughts of Lucius made me want to retch.

He went too far. Got away with too much. Some people blamed me. Apparently betas were only kind to alphas because they were flirting.

"Oh." Clark's voice was soft.

"His parents were some of the people helping my uncle with the failed takeover. I still don't know all the details, but my uncle had promised me for Lucius, as part of their payment for helping. The idea of me leaving Canada made Lucius angry. He *wanted* me even without the deal. His family's rich and powerful and it became easier to let Nonna and her pack get legal custody and have me leave Canada, than for the dads to put a stop to his nonsense." In some ways, Matty was right. One misstep and the dads could go to jail.

I still felt betrayed.

"They didn't get the police involved? They simply sent you away?" Clark made a face.

"His family is powerful. For a time, I was so happy with my grandparents, playing hockey and going to high school. But Lucius was a spoiled, wealthy, young alpha used to getting his way. Things got scary. Nonna and her pack got the local police involved, even though the dads said not to, and..." I winced. "And that led to my name being changed, and me being sent to Rockland alone at sixteen, emancipated, and hidden in junior hockey."

Which had taken some work. One simply didn't just get on a team like that, and I couldn't exactly bring my old name's records with me. But I wouldn't go anywhere if I had to give up playing hockey.

Still, starting over had cost me a lot. Not to mention the work I had to do to separate myself from her. That life.

The fear I'd lived with. The loneliness I'd felt at having to leave everyone and everything behind.

"I'm so sorry that happened to you," Tenzin added, rubbing my neck again.

"Shortly thereafter, my grandparents were in a car accident. I wasn't allowed to go to the funeral–which hurt, since they raised me more than my dads. The police could never prove Lucius caused Nonna's pack's death, but later Lucius told me he did it, to punish them for taking me away from him, because I belonged with him." I made a face. "Which would never happen. I wasn't some trophy. While sure he *said* he'd support my dreams, I had *zero* interest in him romantically."

His entitlement still rankled.

"Why was he after you? For the conquest?" Clark frowned, squeezing my hand.

I sat up and poured more champagne, not adding juice this time. "He was convinced we were scent matches and that my omega would wake up and we'd bond and be soulmates." I shuddered.

"Yeah, no. Not going to happen. I didn't like his scent that way. But he was insistent."

"Fuck." Clark put an arm around me. "Your family should have done more to protect you. You were a kid."

"They should have," I agreed. "I was scared. Sure, the police changed my name, and hid me. Helped me the best they could. Still, I was terrified. So I did other things, like I intentionally took pucks to the face, dyed my hair, changed my mannerisms and speech, tried to alter the way I played, stuff like that." Took illegal growth serum, so I wouldn't be so petite. Anything to make me different from *her*, so he wouldn't find me.

He'd found me anyway.

"Gwen." Pain coated Tenzin's voice as he cupped my face with his hand.

"Fast forward to my second year in New York. I'm living with Austin, playing hockey, working, and studying accounting at the community college. I hadn't talked to my family in years and I felt pretty abandoned by them. One night after hockey practice, someone attacked me and I woke up tied to a bed in my uncle's lake house." I shuddered at the memories.

My uncle had helped him, but he hadn't been the one to tell him where I was.

"He kidnapped you. After all those years?" Tenzin pulled both of us to him and I snuggled into the comfort of his body.

"Apparently, even with Lucius' family's political power, they were afraid his actions would reflect badly on them. So he wasn't allowed to do anything as long as they were in office. He was using this time to wait for me to grow up a little, and awaken as an omega. After all, I was only nineteen. Then someone told him where I was—and that I had a boyfriend. Which angered him so much he kidnapped me, *so we could be together like we belong*." The words tasted bitter in my mouth.

"Shit." Clark stroked my hair.

"He was frustrated I still wasn't an omega, so he…" I buried my face in Tenzin's chest. I didn't like this part, because he'd literally tried to strip me of my autonomy, of myself.

At least he hadn't succeeded.

Tenzin rubbed my back. "Did he hurt you?"

"Worse. He injected me with that street drug the traffickers use, mega-push, the one that can turn betas into omegas. He wanted to prove we were scent matches and was tired of waiting." I sobbed into his chest.

Not that I'd ever want to bond with an alpha like him. I was so glad he hadn't simply bonded my beta self and hoped it did the trick, since alphas *could* bond betas.

"Sweetness." Clark buried his face in my neck.

"It didn't make me omega. It made me sick. Probably a bad batch, given I have the genetic marker. That means I have the potential to push over to omega," I explained. Some betas had the potential to be other designations, and it never woke up.

"Oh, Precious. So you think you're broken, since the drug didn't work?" Tenzin's hands ran up and down my body.

My body shook. "Oh, no. The story gets so much worse–though he never bonded me, thank fuck. Given I went missing, Austin got the police involved, and they eventually tracked me to Canada. There, the local police wouldn't do anything about it, because of payoffs and other bullshit."

"What about your family?" Clark asked.

"Lenny discovered I was missing and told Matty. My family looked for me, trying not to involve the police or anger the other family, since Lucius' parents are the fucking prime ministers. Corrupt prime ministers, because they, you know, tried to help my uncle overthrow my dads while they were grieving their omega and owned a bunch of police." Okay, I could see why they needed to tread carefully, but still…

They took too long.

"Your family found you?" Tenzin snuggled me tighter between the two of them.

My heart hurt with the memory. "Enter the intrepid Officer Jones. He'd only been an officer for a year or two and felt like he *had* to find me, even though his superiors warned him away. They tried to dismiss it like I ditched my boyfriend in New York and ran off to Canada with another alpha. Officer Jones didn't believe it. He mostly worked off the clock, pulling in favors, trying to solve the case and find me."

Idealistic and sweet Officer Jones just wanted to make the world better. If he'd listened to his boss, he might not be dead.

But I might not have been found in time.

"The New York police had given the Vancouver police my picture and some of my clothes." I bit my lower lip. "Officer Jones apparently said it was my picture and scent that drove him to look for me in the first place."

Tenzin frowned. "He's an alpha?"

"Beta." I shook my head. "When he found me, his boss wouldn't give him officers to raid the lake house. He tried to rescue me himself with the help of his off-duty roommate, an ex-military friend, and his friend's retired scent dog. When Officer Jones found me tied up, I thought I was free and..."

My eyes squeezed shut as the memories bombarded me. "I was sick and weak. My leg was broken, because I kept trying to escape. I was terrified. Being made an omega against my will then force bonded to a delusional alpha was the thing my nightmares were made of.

Then Officer Jones came and..."

"You don't have to go on," Tenzin whispered, tenderly stroking my hair, trying to reassure me.

"Lucius came back before he could get me out." I looked away as the memories continued to assault me.

Clark squeezed my hand. I squeezed it back.

"There was a gun-fight. I got shot in the crossfire, but not badly. Lucius also gave me a bloody face for trying to run. Officer Jones shot the guard, but Lucius shot Officer Jones. Not wanting to be a captive any longer, I got Officer Jones' gun and shot Lucius," I sobbed.

"I murdered Lucius. The prime ministers' son. The man who'd been obsessed with me for years. I... I killed him."

In that moment, it seemed like the right thing to do. He could have shot me next or taken me somewhere else. There, he would have injected me with the new drugs and bit and bonded me before anyone even knew we'd moved. I'd have been his permanently. Sure, bonds could be reversed with drugs, but it was a difficult legal process.

While I hadn't expected shooting him to be cathartic, I hadn't anticipated feeling so guilty about it. Or to be made to feel bad about it.

Or have people think that I was a murderer.

"It's self-defense, not murder. He kidnapped you," Tenzin soothed.

"Only because I refused him and he felt he had no other choice. Officer Jones was still alive, though barely. I used his phone to call emergency and held him in my arms. While I did what I could, it wasn't enough and I watched the life drain out of his eyes, his face. It was *awful.* He died trying to save me," I cried. "He died because he considered me worth saving. My own family took their time, but a stranger literally defied orders for me."

For several moments I cried, hard, into Tenzin's bare chest as he and Clark murmured sweet things to me. That kind stranger who gave his life for me.

"You're worth saving," Clark whispered. A low rumble filled the room, making me vibrate, and filling me with comfort.

I nuzzled Clark, taking the reassurance his purr offered me, until I'd calmed down enough to finish the story.

Sometimes I wondered if I had any worth at all.

"The dog found me first. He and his owner had been taking care of the other guards. They'd also run into a group of people Lenny and Matty gathered to find me." The words barely came out through the tears. I rarely talked about Officer Jones. It hurt to do so. He'd had this wonderful life–and helping *me* took it away from him.

"He was gone." Clark's eyes filled with compassion.

"And with him, some of me," I admitted. This was the hardest part to talk about, especially since not everyone believed me.

Because I was a beta.

"When he touched me, I felt something. When his eyes met mine and he said, *I knew I'd find you. You're safe now,* there was a connection. When he died, it ripped something away. Broke me." It was hard to say, but true.

The wolf knew. In many ways, I was a widow.

"What happened to you is traumatic and awful, but you're not broken." Clark frowned as he snuggled me. "You need to stop saying that."

"It's called a dead-match. One of the many theories why scent matches are so rare is that not everyone's match manifests. There are plenty of betas with the potential to be alphas and omegas that stay betas. Like me. Basically, if I'd been an omega, and he'd been an alpha, we would have been soulmates. Him appearing there in the lake house took my breath away and not only because I thought I was free." The sobs came harder. "It was that latent connection that drove him to find me."

That hurt me so much more than killing Lucius.

"Dead-match. I... I've never heard of it," Clark replied, still holding me tight. "Makes sense. I'm so sorry you went through that."

Tenzin put my face in his hands. "Gwen, Precious. You're *not* the reason he died. It was Lucius. A good officer died in the line of duty, and that's devastating. It's not your fault. None of this is your fault."

My chest shook a little. "Sometimes it feels like it was. If I'd relented to Lucius when I was younger, none of this would have happened."

Some of my siblings told me that I should be flattered that he liked me and to accept him, since a beta like me would never find anyone better—and he was too good for me as it was.

"And be tied to an alpha you didn't love." Clark shook his head. "You deserve love, Gwen."

Did I?

"Dead-matches rarely bond, because we're betas. Marry, but not bond. There's also not a ton of research on it. But we did. They think it had to do with both of us bleeding and all the adrenaline." I turned away. No, I didn't deserve them. "We bonded, then he died."

Clark sucked in a breath. "The wolf who lost his mate who likes widows. He knew."

I nodded. "Animals often do."

Tenzin's hand went to his heart, anguish in his scent. "That must have been so traumatic, Precious. I've heard it's quite painful when your soulmate dies."

"It hurt. Physically. It felt like my heart was going to stop. They said I wouldn't let go of his body and I didn't talk much for quite some time. It took everyone a while to figure it out, since I had no way to describe all this. No one, not even me and Officer Jones, knew we were dead-matches. I had no idea what had happened to me, just that it felt like my soul had been ripped from my body."

I looked at them through tear-filled eyes. There had been so much pain and anguish. So many emotions.

Some I still didn't fully understand.

I was lucky I even knew this much. So much of this was con-sidered stories, not actual knowledge. One of the nurses noticed the way my scent changed and knew what it meant. She'd taken it upon herself to figure everything out.

"Now you know. The broken bond didn't really affect my relationship with my ex, so I didn't think it would affect my relationship with you. As you can see, it did. Also, how can you be sure I want to be with you because of you and not only because I'm trying to fill the cracks in my soul and you're there?" I got up from the couch, then threw myself on the bed and sobbed harder.

There, I'd said it.

"Um, I know you like me, Gweny." Clark crawled on the bed with me, straddled my back and started rubbing it. "This constellation, *hope*," he traced my spine tattoo, "is because you have hope. Hope for love, hope for peace, hope for healing. It's okay to grieve what you lost. It's also okay to let go and move on."

It was a fictional constellation from my favorite space books. But he was right.

"I try to have hope. But it's hard." It had been easy to go back to Austin, given he was familiar. He'd held on to me fast, helping me reenter the world.

"It can be." Clark sighed. "Gweny, you're not broken. Wounded, but not broken. People who lose their mates do love again, sometimes even mate again. I want to fill all those cracks up with cuddles and kisses until you feel whole."

"I accept." It hurt when your soulmate died. Sometimes you died, too.

There were times in those first weeks where I wished I had. Especially given no one understood. Originally, they'd thought maybe Lucius had managed to bond me. A posthumous bond test on him had been negative.

It wasn't negative for me. Or for Officer Jones.

None of this was in my medical record, because even though it was a government test, it *didn't count,* since we were both betas.

"Thank you for sharing such a painful story." Tenzin came onto the bed with us. He peppered my face with tiny kisses as Clark continued to knead my shoulders.

"Are you seeing someone for all this?" Clark asked.

"I was. It's hard. So I stopped, and told myself lies, so I didn't have to think too hard about it. But…" I sighed. "Matty wants me to go back to a specialist. He's right. My alternate narrative could cause harm. Like I've missed a lot of everyone's lives. Though my dads *are* assholes and I want nothing from them. They abandoned me, didn't find me fast enough, then after everything I'd been through, had the audacity to tell me that I should come back to Vancouver and leave behind the life I'd made for myself."

That was the rub. I'd fought tooth and nail to make my own life. I'd been so young, and I'd still needed my family, my parents, and they all abandoned me for 'my' safety when it felt like it was more to protect them, their life, and their business.

Then they told me I belonged with them and should move back like nothing happened.

Like fuck I would.

They also didn't like to be told *no,* which was why I feared that one day they'd just take me.

Like Lucius had.

Because those with the money made the rules.

"I'll support you," Clark asked. "Um, so how does your ex fit in with all this? He reported you missing?"

"Austin never knew much other than an obsessed alpha from my childhood kidnapped me and I was forced to kill him in order to escape. He didn't make me talk about it, though he knew there was more to it. I was kidnapped in November, so I did most of my recuperating at my dads' over break. When I had the fight with my dads and I crawled out the window in Vancouver, it was time for the new semester to start and they didn't want me to go back to New York. I missed my life—and Austin. While he'd offered to come out, he still had work and hockey and everything."

I also didn't want him to see that part of my life. It wasn't me.

"Not to mention Lucius didn't do this alone. He'd promised to help my uncle get back what he lost during his failed takeover. Uncle is now in jail, as are some others who helped. I had zero interest in staying in Vancouver." I sighed again. "I told my dads that if they had any money for me, to give it to Officer Jones' family. He was a good guy. I attended his memorial, met his family and dog, and talked to his friends and co-workers."

If I'd ever met him under other circumstances, we would have been friends.

Maybe even more.

"I hope they did that," Clark told me. "Um, what's the name you were born with? Will you tell me? Curious."

"Gabriella. It was great for ice skating, but I never truly felt like a Gabriella. I also detested being called *Gabby,* which Maricella, of course, only calls me. Some people called me Gabs. Mostly my family calls me Buttons."

"Because you're cute as a button?" Clark booped my nose, which made me giggle.

"Because my sister, Isa, decided to potty train me after watching a video online and used chocolate button candies as a reward and I became obsessed with them." I still loved them and would bribe people to bring them to me from Canada. They were pricey here in the gift shop, but maybe we could stop at a grocery store on our way to the train station.

"What do you need, Precious?" Tenzin asked.

"I still want to snuggle in a big pile like you promised." I needed it before my paid-for spa afternoon.

"In bed or on the couch?" he added.

I eyed the couch. It wasn't big and cozy like Clark's. "In bed."

Clark rolled me under the covers and the two of them fluffed pillows, got more blankets, and made everything nice and cozy before squashing me so tight between them they might just manage to squish my broken soul back together.

"Better?" Tenzin kissed my forehead.

"Much." For a moment I luxuriated in warmth and cuddles. "You two are actually okay with the fact that I grew up with another name, that I essentially lost a mate, and I killed someone?" It seemed too good to be true.

"We all have things in our past, and I'm sorry for everything that you have gone through. I'm here for you. You're a lovely person and I enjoy spending time with you. I look forward to where you lead us next," Tenzin told me.

Awww.

"The terrible things that have happened to us don't define us," Clark told me. "It's what we do following it that counts. After all, I killed someone once, too."

Chapter Forty-Nine

CLARK

As the words left my mouth, I winced. I might as well tell them the story. I didn't want to keep secrets from them. Also, maybe it would help Gwen a little. None of that was her fault, and I felt awful for her on so many levels.

Gwen looked up at me, her hazel eyes still a little teary, minty scent tinged with concern.

"Her name was Yelena. We were high school sweethearts. I was getting a lot of attention on the hockey front. I wanted to go to Natty for engineering–and hopefully play hockey for them. Because I was so confident, I did early decision, and was ecstatic when I was admitted," I told them. Natty, National Tech, was just as prestigious as NYIT and well known for engineering.

"You got into Natty early decision? Shit, you're smart," Gwen told me.

Considering I struggled sometimes with reading it had been a huge accomplishment for me.

"My parents were happy for me, even though we had no idea how we'd pay for it if I didn't get enough scholarships. Yelena and I had a huge fight. She didn't want me to go so far away. I might have gotten mad and accused her of being unsupportive. Not my finest moment, because she *was* supportive. She called me selfish, grabbed her stuff, and stormed out." I closed my eyes, trying to shut out the fight, the ugly things we'd both said to each other.

You're so selfish, Clark. It's always all about you. You and hockey.

Why is it okay for you to go to New York for fashion school, but I can't go to Natty?

I regretted that fight so much. It turned out that her grandma was sick, and she was planning on staying local for a while–and wanted me to as well. But she hadn't told me that. Also, she *had* gotten into fashion school. One day I'd start a scholarship there in her honor.

"Ma made me hot cocoa, hugged me, and helped me craft an apology text. But Yelena didn't reply. She didn't answer her phone, either. Then I got a call from her mom when she didn't come home." My chest shuddered at the memories of that cold winter night.

Gwen snuggled further into me, concern on her face. "She never made it?"

"No. She lived a farm over. She cut across the pond, which was frozen. But with ponds, they're frozen until they're not. The ice cracked, and she drowned. Never had a chance." I closed my eyes, trying to block out her blue body as we pulled her from the icy depths.

"Oh, Clark." Gwen pressed her face into my neck. "It was an accident. A horrible accident. My nonna had a pond. I know how they work."

"She was a great person, and it was a terrible thing that happened. For a very long time, I blamed myself. Others blamed me, too. After all, she wouldn't have cut across the pond if we hadn't fought." Okay, it was a logic leap. But to this day, some people thought that–like one of her moms.

"I'm so sorry that happened." Gwen touched her forehead to mine.

"There was nothing you could do." Tenzin squeezed my arm.

His touch blazed on my skin. Why did he have this effect on me?

"No, there wasn't. It took time and a whole lot of work to get over the guilt I felt. It was hard. I still feel it sometimes–like every time I see her family." I leaned into the both of them, grateful for our snuggly, warm cocoon. I kissed her forehead, hoping she understood.

"The moral of the story is that I need to see a therapist, got it." She rested her head on my shoulder.

"The moral of the story is that we can't keep blaming ourselves for things that aren't our fault. It's not healthy. Moving on isn't disrespectful. I eventually moved on. It took time, but I did. But... then he abandoned me when I got signed." Again, I winced as I remembered telling Tenzin last night that everyone left us.

"Who even does that?" Gwen asked.

"Not everyone wants the lifestyle the PHL offers. We're at the whims of our teams. It's not always comfortable." Tenzin smoothed the hair out of her face.

Gwen still looked skeptical. "I'm sorry he did that, Clark. I'll stay regardless of what team you're on, as long as you want me."

"Me, too." I looked at her, then at Tenzin. "I understand that things don't always work, but he literally ghosted me. It wasn't even open for discussion."

That hurt. He even came to my games and cheered me on. It would be one thing to talk about it and then decide to break up, but he wouldn't even give me that. He just ghosted me.

It had been terrifying, because his silence reminded me of when Yelena disappeared and we found her in the pond.

"Let's not do that, okay?" I added.

"Got it. But..." Gwen's look grew anxious. "Please don't abandon me for an omega, okay? You're alphas, and I'm..."

I gave her a look, daring her to say the words I told her not to.

"I'm me." She shrugged. "Taking two amazing alphas all for myself."

"That will never happen. If we want an omega at some point, we'll talk about it and if we *all* agree, you'll be at the center of the search—sitting on my lap as we go through the books at the matching center, and on my arm at mixers," Tenzin assured. "They'll know you're a very important part of this relationship."

I liked the picture he was painting of a life together. Maybe not adding an omega. I didn't think I needed one. Not all packs had an omega at their center.

Any omega would have to love and respect Gwen.

"That's not going to happen." I shook my head. "The way we get an omega is that one day, Gwen brings one home. Possibly not in a bucket."

Gwen chuckled. "A wagon. Or..." Her look went coy. "My own motorcycle?"

"I don't even like you riding on his. You need to learn to drive." Tenzin shook his head as one of our phones beeped.

I grinned at him. "You're just jealous that you haven't gotten to be my backpack."

"Oh, I'd love to see that," Gwen breathed.

Me, too. Not that mine was made for two alphas.

"Why do you even have a motorcycle? You're going to get hurt." He frowned, concern wafting off him as the phone beeped again.

Awww. Tenzin was worried?

"I used to help my grandpa and uncle fix theirs. I've been riding around on them for years. Always wanted one of my own." I bought it out of my second paycheck. The first mostly went to my parents. Though driving out here differed from farm country.

"I see." Tenzin picked up his phone off the nightstand. He frowned at it and sighed.

"I used to help my Gramps fix his antique cars. Is Cooter summoning you?" Gwen looked at Tenzin.

"Yes. Unfortunately, I need to go." He grimaced and rolled out of bed.

"I understand. I have things today, too," she told him.

Tenzin got dressed, as I continued to hold Gwen tight, since she showed no interest in moving.

"I hope you're feeling better. I'll see you later." He planted a kiss on her forehead.

I looked at him longingly, wishing I'd get a kiss, too, as I recalled him holding me last night, making me tea.

Tenzin reached out and ran his hand through my hair. "I appreciate you both sharing your stories."

He slipped out the door, closing it behind him.

"I should take a quick shower. It's nearly time to go to the spa. We're getting massages and facials and I don't even have to pay for it. Then we're going to do each other's hair and makeup," Gwen told me, still not moving.

"Do you want me to shower with you? Soap you up really good. Wash your hair." *Make love to you against the wall.* I ran my hand down her face, and she shuddered slightly. Hearing her story was devastating. Gwen was so young when it all happened. That asshole stole her childhood from her. She probably wanted some comfort.

Also, I had an alpha need to comfort her and reassure her.

She nodded. "Please?"

We got into the shower and I took extra care in soaping her up, my hands gliding across her breasts, her stomach.

A groan escaped her lips as I soaped her lower half, and her arousal filled the shower.

"Do you like shower sex?" I whispered in her ear, as I slipped a finger inside her trembling passage, the warm spray coming down on us.

"Very much," she murmured, snagging my lips, arms wrapping around me.

"Can I make love to you bare?" I pressed her up against the shower wall. I was pretty sure I knew the real reason she'd been so upset this morning. It had nothing to do with being broken *or* not being taken care of well enough last night.

She nodded and wrapped her hand around my hard dick, guiding me into her waiting warmth.

My lips crashed into her, as I fully entered her, taking her hands and holding them up against the wall. I kicked her legs out slightly, so I could get her at precisely the right angle.

"Clark," she gasped, as I hit that spot over and over, relishing in her expression as I pounded her into the shower wall.

I loved making her feel good.

"You feel amazing," I told her as I thrust in and out. "Do you want my knot? We don't have to."

Her eyes met mine. "Can you hold me under the shower spray until it deflates?"

"I'll happily do that." I continued to explore her mouth with mine as I let go of her arms. My hands traced her muscular body, bringing the both of us closer to our peaks.

"Come for me," I murmured, knowing I wouldn't last much longer. I loved being inside her.

Oh, making her come more, what a hardship.

I kissed her again as I played with her clit. Her body shook with pleasure. Pulling out, I thrust in, seating myself in her fully. Her pussy fluttered, accepting my knot and clenching my cock, causing my release to happen as I came inside her.

Gwen's body shuddered again, not quite a full orgasm but definitely in happiness. "Oh yes, that's what I need, Tesoruccio."

Bliss coated her face.

"It's all yours," I whispered, continuing to kiss her. Yes, that was exactly what she needed. I'd been right.

Alpha cum contained chemicals that helped the body produce all those happy hormones. When she wanted comfort from us last night, her body didn't only want knots, it wanted some alpha happy juice. But we were responsible and wrapped it up. She didn't suck our cocks, we didn't rub our cum into her skin.

She wasn't broken. Her body was having a hissy fit because it expected something and didn't get it.

Given we were both on birth control, I was glad I could give it to her now.

My arms wrapped around her tight as I held her so that she could get more of the warm spray and not be cold. She'd been with an alpha for a long time. There were reasons why alphas never used to date–just hookup or court with the intent to mate.

Being in an intense relationship with an alpha at a young age could have lasting effects. I'd gotten that lecture multiple times when Yelena and I got serious, especially since I awakened as an alpha at sixteen. Obviously, Austin wasn't as careful with her as he should have been.

I stroked her hair. "Do you feel better?"

"Much." She snuggled into me and I held her until my knot deflated enough to release her and we finished our shower.

Now that I knew, I'd be more mindful. Whatever happened last night, this morning, I wanted this. Forever.

I'd do everything I could to keep it.

Chapter Fifty

TENZIN

There were a lot of well-dressed people here in the main lodge, probably for the other event happening tonight. Well-dressed, fierce-looking people, speaking French. There was also a lot of plain clothes security. Perhaps someone famous was part of the other party?

It was amazing being with Clark and Gwen last night. My heart ached at everything they'd been through. If only I could've stayed with them.

But I'd see them later.

Maybe we could all spend the night together again? I wasn't quite ready to make a move on Clark, but I'd happily have a repeat of last night.

I frowned at my phone. In addition to being summoned by Cooter, Jacen had called several times this morning. The urge to call him back tugged at me. What if something was wrong with Morgan or the baby?

No. She wasn't my girlfriend. It wasn't my baby. They weren't my pack.

It was time to put Morgan and Jacen aside so that I could get in the right headspace and be what Clark and Gwen needed.

My phone buzzed again. *Jacen.* I ignored it and deleted his voice-mails. Should I block him? Yes, like I had Morgan. It was time.

I blocked him. As I walked through the lobby, I felt lighter than I had in some time.

"Did you fix whatever was wrong with Babybug? I'm not above beating your ass." Cooter looked up from his phone, as he sat in a chair by the window, when I entered our room.

"It's fine. She needed more cuddles." I'd have to make sure to really take care of her. Her feeling like she needed to tell us her past possibly had something to do with it.

After yesterday's run-in with her brother, I knew it was complex. I just hadn't expected it to be like that. *Shit.* The Prime Minister's son had stalked and kidnapped her. She took things into her own hands, then she held her soulmate as he died.

I could see how her parents might not have been able to go after them. Also, I could understand how it had hurt teenage Gwen's tender heart. You expected your family to protect you, and when they didn't, it ached.

Like when my brother turned his back on me after my parents and little sister died.

"You were with her all night?" Cooter smirked.

"And Clark." Might as well lay it all out. After all, this was Cooter.

"Clark? The puppy with glasses that's always with Babybug?" Cooter's eyebrows rose as he handed me a beer from the mini fridge.

"He's sweet, kind, sexy. The three of us fit comfortably, whether it's practicing hockey, watching TV together, or anything else." I took a drink.

"Good. You deserve to be happy. Also, Jacen's pack was pretentious as fuck. Sure, they were your friends, but they weren't your pack." Cooter opened his beer and sat next to me on the bed.

"True." Not sure that pretentious was quite the right word.

"It's time to cut Morgan and them out of your life, so they don't ruin whatever you might have with Babybug and Glasses," he told me.

I took a long drink of beer. "I blocked him. She's been blocked for a while."

The slightest bit of guilt tugged at me. I pushed it back. *Not my mates, not my problem.*

"Good." Cooter nodded.

"Last night was a lot." I took another drink. "Was I quite ready? No. Do I regret it? Fuck no." I took a deep breath, remembering how nicely she took us. The anguish as she told us her story–and he added his. Two beautiful, wounded souls.

"I know it might feel like a lot, but I think you're pretty fucking lucky. She's a keeper and not only because she plays with baby tigers," Cooter told me.

Cooter hadn't been very lucky in love. He hooked up a lot, and his couple of longer relationships had all been pretty disastrous. However, based on something he said when drunk, once on a fishing trip, I got the idea that it was a choice. That someone had broken his heart or gotten away, or something.

I nodded. "Yeah, I am."

This was special. I wanted to not rush things. I wanted to be ready for them. No. I didn't want to fuck this up.

"Thanks for bringing me with you. Even if I still think you were an asshole for not telling me where we were going," I added.

A wide grin spread over his face. "It's more fun this way." The grin faded. "Her brother's not a threat, right? No one's taking her back to Vancouver?"

"No. It's a heartbreaking and complicated story. But no one's forcing her back to her family. Given all the security here, I *am* curious about her brother's mate's family. If the security is even here for that," I told him.

Also, I needed to do more research on dead-mates so I could take better care of her. Losing a soulmate you never knew you could even have? Devastating.

Cooter snorted. "Security? You sheltered boy. But then the mafia in Quebec looks different."

I blinked. The mafia in Portland was mostly Chinese and Russian. Their reign spanned from below the Bay Area to almost British Columbia. "Mafia?"

"The mating party is made up of French-Canadian organized crime families. That's not wedding security. Those are the guests. The omega is a fucking assassin. Your girl's brother married into them. Which makes me wonder about him and *that* family. One doesn't simply marry into the mob." He took another drink of beer.

"There are mafias in Canada?" My brows furrowed in puzzlement. "They must be the most polite mafia ever. *Pardon me, but I'm going to shoot you now. So sorry.*" I chuckled.

Cooter looked unamused. "Mostly it's all silent, hidden under reputable businesses and polite society. Learned that real quick when I went to university here."

"Gwen's family is in shipping." And possibly quite wealthy.

"Shipping." He nodded. "Would that change anything?"

"No. Gwen wants nothing to do with her family." That could also explain a lot, like her not wanting their money so fiercely. And her needing to cut everyone out, even those she cared for, as well as her fear of them simply taking her.

It could also make some of her resentment toward her family make a lot more sense. If they were mafia, they couldn't simply go get her, guns blazing, if the *prime minister's son* had her–especially if the police were already bought. The repercussions could be so much greater.

Huh.

Cooter looked at his phone. "If you're done being a sap, we have shit to do. Tonight's the wedding. You can dance with Babybug. Just enjoy yourself–and them. Everything else can wait."

Chapter Fifty-One

CLARK

"This wedding is *amazing*. One day I'll have one as fun as this," Carlos said as he took a sip of beer at the reception. Music played in the background as people danced, drank, and had a good time.

"You want to get married?" I asked, grabbing a candy from the bowl on the table and unwrapping it.

Carlos seemed to be a serial dater, as was pretty common with kappas. It had to do with the thrill of the chase and them being adrenaline junkies. Also, if he was ever going to get married, he needed to stop hooking up with his ex, who he'd been texting again.

"One day, when I find the right person." Carlos waggled his fingers at one of Celine's friends as she walked by. "Not sure if I want an entire pack though."

"I'd like a pack." I glanced over at Gwen, who was talking to Verity and Valya. I'd always wanted a wedding—or at least a big mating party.

He snorted. "I think you're on your way to getting one."

My cheeks warmed. "I'd love that. Um, this is a really lovely wedding."

The wedding itself had been down by the lake, under a canopy of lace and flowers and had been sweet and a little silly with music choices, dancing down the aisles, and everyone throwing paper airplanes, as the happy couple retreated. It had been mostly in French, which added a fairytale component to it.

Even now, at the reception, the outdoor pavilion we were in felt like something from a movie, festooned with flowers, lights, and lanterns.

Did Gwen want a wedding? Probably. She'd look fantastic in a gold poofy dress—or whatever color she wanted to wear.

Gwen looked *stunning* tonight. The strapless blue gown accentuated her curves and did amazing things for her breasts. A slit showed off her muscular legs. Someone had done her hair and makeup and she sparkled.

"She's so pretty," Tenzin said softly.

"She is," I agreed.

The dinner had just finished, and the program would start shortly.

Gwen came over to us. "I've got to get changed, but I'll be back."

She left, and I noticed others leaving too—like Cooter and Dean.

Celine did a dance with her parents, which was beautiful. She and JP had danced together earlier when they'd entered, right before dinner was served.

That would be fun, too, to dance with Gwen like that. I wanted to keep her. We could make it work no matter where we went for hockey. Together, we'd work through our pasts.

We'd be so good together.

Hot damn, Tenzin looked sexy tonight, in a dark gray suit. But that man looked good in everything. And nothing.

It was hard not to think about last night every time I looked at him.

JP's sister, who'd been acting as the MC, got back on the microphone, calling Celine up to the center of the floor, where a chair had been set.

"We all know living with a goalie can be an experience," his sister laughed. "My brother and his goalie friends have prepared a special dance for you, as a welcome to your new life as a goalie wife."

The thumping bass of trendy club music filled the pavilion as JP burst onto the dance floor. He had changed into a jersey that said *Team Trembley* in the wedding's colors and black pants. Following him were his goalie friends.

Everyone cheered as they circled her, gave her flowers, then took position in front of her and started their dance. I wasn't sure exactly what I was expecting, probably inflatable costumes and silliness. This wasn't it.

Well, the song choice was borderline inappropriate for a family affair, featuring a warehouse remix medley of songs about ass shaking, being naughty, and getting freaky.

"Shit, that looks *difficult*," Carlos whistled, finishing his beer.

"Hard on the knees," I agreed. "I'm not sure how poor Coach Kirov can keep up."

The entire group did the splits, then scooped their bodies on the floor, and did some sort of thing with their legs and turned and got back up again. People whistled and cheered.

"Fuuuck," Tenzin muttered as Gwen did the splits again.

She had good rhythm and was one of the better dancers in the group.

Celine was grinning and laughing, occasionally with a hand over her mouth, eyes gleaming as she clearly enjoyed the sassy, sexy, and upbeat show.

They finished their high energy routine and landed in a multi-level pose, featuring Jean-Paul in the center, in full splits, who blew a kiss to his wife.

Everyone applauded. Then Celine and some of her friends did a dance for him. Another club song played and the two of them got up and danced with each other. Her dress was pale gold, puffy and sparkly, catching all the lights. The music changed and their attendants came up and joined them.

After that, the music changed again, and they invited everyone to dance and have fun.

Before I could get to Gwen, Tenzin was whisking her across the floor in some formal ballroom dancing stuff I only ever saw in the movies. Gwen's eyes gleamed, and she laughed. They looked cute together.

"Dance with us." Gwen bounced over to me.

I took her manicured hand and she pulled me up out of my seat. "I'd love to."

"Getting tired, Ladybug?" I stroked her hair as we put our empty glasses on the tray of a passing server.

"A little."

The music changed. She grabbed my wrist, pulling me and Tenzin to her, so she was in the center of us, reminding me of that day in my living room, when she'd kissed me and made my dreams come true.

Heat built between us as we swayed to the music. Her head was on his chest, her ass rubbing against my dick. Both of their scents took on tinges of arousal.

"Should we go back to the room?" I whispered in her ear. "You're in charge. Also, what happens in Canada stays in Canada. We can go right back to how things were before the wedding when we get back to New York. No pressure to be physical again until you're ready."

The last thing I wanted to do was push her. Though if she wanted to climb into my bed every night for snuggles, I wouldn't complain.

If he wanted to sleep over...

Gwen nodded, then looked at Tenzin. "I... I like that idea. We're still at the wedding, so will you both come back with me?"

"I'd like that if you'll both let me. Last night was amazing." Tenzin's gaze traveled from her to me, searing right into me.

It was? Good. I wanted this for as long as I got it. Forever would be ideal.

"I'd love to see you suck his cock while I have you. Would you like that?" I'd make sure she got plenty of cum inside her tonight.

"Yes, please," she sighed.

"That sounds amazing, Precious," he told her.

We gathered our things, said our goodbyes, and slipped out. Gwen held both our hands, as we walked back to the villa under an expanse of stars, much like last night. The mood was more playful. As we entered the dark villa, I picked her up and spun her around. We said goodnight to the wolves and I brought her into the room, leaping onto the bed with her. She giggled as I tickled her.

Tenzin closed the door as I started undressing her. Slowly, I took off her heels, unzipped her dress, then removed her beautiful matching strapless bra and panties. Tenzin watched us while he lit the fire, turned down the lights, and took off his shoes and jacket, heightening everything.

I nuzzled her side with my nose. "Can I have you bare tonight?"

"Oh, yes, please, Alpha," she sighed.

My dick stood up at attention through my pants, liking it when she called me *Alpha*.

"Sweetness, present for me." I gave her ass a pat as I stripped down to my boxers.

Giving Tenzin a coy look, her pink tongue licked her lower lip as she took up the position on her hands and knees, wiggling her ass at us. The light glowed over her olive skin, which glistened faintly with glitter.

Want and need shot through me, seeing her present for us like that.

"Beautiful." I stroked my hand down her back and across her ass. "I think I need more dessert."

I feasted on her pretty pussy as she watched Tenzin undress. My tongue teased her clit. The smell of her sweet arousal, as well as our desire, permeated the air.

"Tesoruccio, that feels so good," she whimpered.

"Do you want this, too?" Tenzin asked her, climbing up onto the bed with us. "Are you okay sucking me bare and swallowing me down?"

"Yes, please, Alpha, I want mostriciattolo," she begged, licking her lips again, like his dick was a delicious treat.

It was quite delicious-looking.

Gwen eagerly sucked his cock, all her happy noises going straight to mine, making it hard

"You're so wet for us. I love seeing how deep you take his cock. Now, I'll bury my dick in your warm, ready pussy. I'm going to make love to you, while you keep sucking him down so sweetly. Then, I'm going to knot you and fill you up," I murmured, planting kisses down her back.

I lubed her up, then met Tenzin's eyes, giving him a sly grin as I slipped inside her.

"I love the way you feel." My hands cupped her breasts as I pulled out, then thrust in her again, and adjusted my rhythm to meet her.

"Look at you, taking both of us. What a good girl," he praised. "I'm so close, Precious."

Her body trembled as I toyed with her clit with one hand and rolled her nipples with another. She was close, too. Seeing her swallow him down was beautiful.

Tenzin's eyes also kept meeting mine. Part of me hoped he was wondering what it would feel like for *me* to be on my knees, taking his cock in my mouth.

One day.

"I'm not going to last long, Sweetness," I muttered, my hips slamming against her taut ass hard and fast. "We can always do this again."

"I'm going to come," he told her, eyes closing. "That's it."

I felt her tremble under my hands. "Suck him down and come for me, then I'll knot you. You're my good girl. Good girls get dicked down hard by their alphas and get to come over and over."

Her body bucked. I pulled out, then thrust into her hard. My knot slipped inside her. She moaned with the stretch as it locked. I continued to thrust as much as my knot allowed, because she seemed to like it.

"Oh, you take my knot perfectly, Sweetness," I told her.

Tenzin pulled out of her mouth and ran a thumb down her face. "That was perfect."

"You taste amazing, Alpha," she murmured. Her body bucked again, and Gwen leaned her head back. "Clark," she cried, coming.

"You look so beautiful when you come," I murmured. So did he.

We slumped to the bed, still locked together. I rolled us onto our sides. Tenzin threw the blankets over us, then crawled in, so he was face-to-face with Gwen. My arms wrapped around her and Tenzin.

Gwen kissed him, then leaned back and kissed me. "That felt so good."

"It did," Tenzin agreed.

"I love seeing you take both of us," I told her. "We're so lucky to have you."

Gwen beamed and snuggled deeper between us.

Tenzin caught my gaze. I loved watching him with her. Would he take me like that?

Only time would tell.

But, oh, how I hoped that one day the answer to that would be, *yes.*

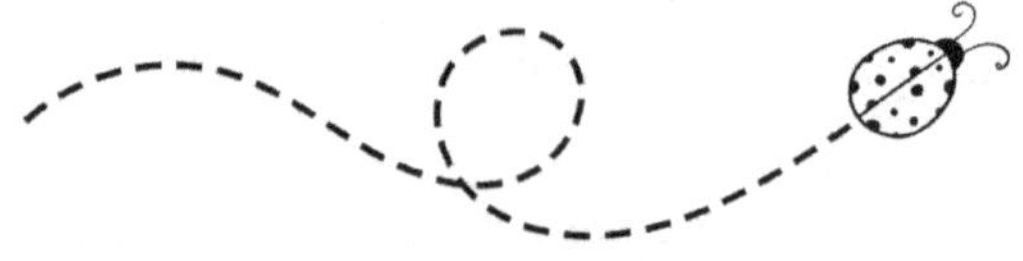

Chapter Fifty-Two

TENZIN

"While we had these two lovely nights together, what happens now?" Clark asked as Gwen used the bathroom. It was early, but Cooter and I had a flight to catch.

"I'd like to see where this goes. But I need to take it slow," I admitted. That I could do. A little at a time. I'd start with her, and then...

Clark nodded. "Understandable."

"Please take care of her while I'm gone? She gets touch starved easily. I'll do my best to text while we're on our fishing trip, but we'll be on a boat, so I don't know how reliable it will be," I told him. Cooter and I were going after swordfish. Something we'd wanted to do for some time.

While she seemed better, she'd need lots of snuggles and care.

"Of course. Always. Snuggling her is my superpower." His look softened. "I... I had a great time with both of you. I... I do like you, Tens, and I hope you understand that."

Oh, I did.

"That makes me happy. I had an amazing time with both of you. Please continue to be patient with me?" I pleaded, running my fingers through his hair.

"Me, too? I loved it. And I really appreciate that you went too fast because you wanted to take care of me. I see you." Gwen came out naked and put her arms around me.

I kissed the top of her head. "I want to be here for you."

"Me, too," Clark agreed.

"We'll support each other. I know I have a fuckton of shit to work through." She kissed me on the cheek.

"We're all in this together," Clark told us. "We'll go as slow as you need."

"Thank you." Relief flowed out of me.

"No, thank you for being there when I needed you, Big Guy." Gwen's arms tightened around me. "Take the time you need. Have fun fishing. See you when you get back."

Gathering my things, I kissed her, savoring it. Then I leaned in and kissed Clark, tentatively, gently. A promise that I liked him, too.

His hand cupped my face. "We're here."

"So am I." I put my hand over his.

I got my things and walked back to the lodge. Yes, I'd take this fishing trip to get my shit together. For them.

And for me.

Cooter was right. It was time to get over Morgan, Jacen, and them for good, so I could get on with my life.

I texted Cooter to order some food, so we could eat before we headed to the airport. We'd go back to his ranch first, since all our stuff was there.

My phone was filled with texts from *Imogen,* Jacen and Ilya's omega. We never really texted, so I hadn't thought to block her.

Imogen

Did you block them? You need to call Jacen. It's about Morgan. Please.

My finger hovered over delete.

Imogen

It's an emergency. Please call someone.

An emergency? Fine. I unblocked him and called.

"Tenzie?" Jacen's voice was sleepy. It would be even earlier there in Portland.

"Sorry for calling so early. She's okay?" I asked.

"Not really. It's been touch and go. Why didn't you call me back?" His voice was judgmental, frantic, and tired at the same time.

"I'm out of town, and honestly, I can't do this anymore. I'm sorry she's having a rough time. While I want nothing bad to happen to her, you're not my pack and it's not my baby. Also, I've found two amazing people and I don't want to fuck things up." My belly dipped.

What if...

"I don't want to fuck things up for you. That's not my intention. Sorry, I haven't slept. We've been through every test imaginable. Morgan will be on bedrest for the rest of her pregnancy. It's making her unhappy, because of her med school rotations and residency interviews, but they're willing to work with her. The babies are fine, too. For now. There's a chance she's not taking them to term," he told me.

"Them?" I sucked in a sharp breath.

"There are two. One was hiding, which was why we didn't get it on the scan. I'm not sure why we didn't pick up the other heartbeat, but it happens apparently," he told me.

"Twins. She's having twins." My heart sped. No. No. No. *Please don't say what I think you're going to say.*

"They'll keep a close eye on her. She and the babies are fine. Fraternal twins. A side effect of the enhancers she was taking," he told me. "They did tests on the babies to make sure they were okay. We know this changes nothing. We want you to be happy in New York and the last thing we want is for you to think we're manipulating you."

"Jacen, what are you saying?" But I knew. My grip on the phone tightened.

"You're going to be a father," he told me. "While our daughter is mine, our son is yours. I'll send you the tests, so you can have proof."

"I have a son." All the air whooshed out of me, like I'd been sent into space.

I was going to be a dad. The only problem was that I lived on the other side of the country and had no desire to move—or get back with Morgan.

What I wanted was Clark and Gwen. Did that make me a bad dad already?

"Tenzie, are you okay?" Jacen asked.

I squeezed my eyes shut. "Fuck."

"I know." His voice was soft. "Honestly, we don't need any financial support. This is about doing the right thing, not money. You can absolutely set up an education fund or something for him and have plenty of visits or even partial custody. We want you to have a relationship with him. We know how much you wanted to be a dad—and how amazing of a dad you'll be. If this is something you want, we're committed to making this amicable and we'll love him so much," Jacen told me. "And if you don't, we'll understand."

I sucked in a sharp breath. One of the babies was *mine?*

It was a trick wasn't it? But I didn't think it was.

Which meant I had a son.

"I... I have a son." Shit.

"You do. We're going to need your medical history," he added. "Also, if you have input on names, we'd love to hear them, especially if you want to name him after one of your dads or something. Morgan said you'd talked about it. But I'm getting ahead of myself."

"Yes, I... I can get that right to you. We had talked about naming him after one of my grandfathers. He was a doctor." My hands shook as I went into my medical record to give the doctor access.

I was going to be a dad?

"I like that. Thank you. I'll be in touch. We can make this work. If you want to be a dad, we want you to have that opportunity–and if you don't want to be a dad, we won't judge, promise." Jacen ended the call.

Test results showed up in my texts. I had a son. While I had no intention of making up with them and joining their pack, or trying to get traded to somewhere closer, this still changed *everything*.

I wanted to be a dad. But I wasn't sure I could do this without messing everything up. Including myself.

Fuck.

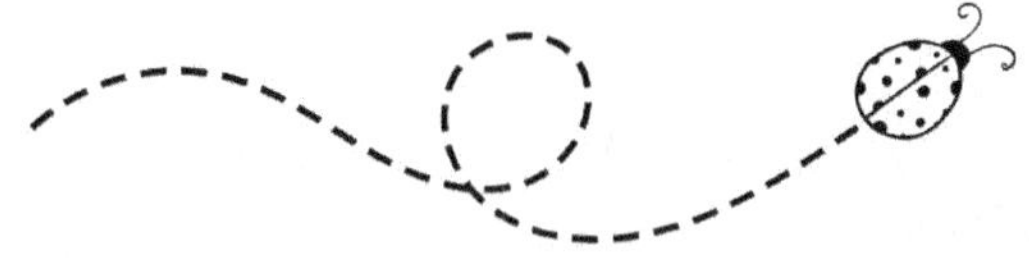

Chapter Fifty-Three

GWEN

The doorman opened the door of Clark's apartment building for me, greeting me with a smile and a *"Hi, Gwen,"* as usual. On the way to the elevator, I waved at the desk lady. I always felt so fancy. A door attendant *and* a desk person? So fancy. It differed greatly from my old building, which didn't even have a security door or a working elevator.

I took the elevator up to Clark's floor, my equipment bag and new backpack over my shoulder. I was still a little tired from all the festivities, but yesterday had been a holiday, so I'd gotten some rest. Today was the first day of my last year of university.

This year I had some interesting courses. I also had a *paid* internship, which I was doing at the rink. My hockey team was still riding the high of winning our division championship. This would be a fantastic semester.

"Clark, are you home?" I called as I entered the apartment and tossed my bag onto the kitchen counter, while I took out the protein bars and hydrogels I'd taken from practice, and put them in a bowl.

Then I removed some cushy socks, two headbands, ultra sporty deodorant, and mini packs of odor removing detergent, which were all from the care cupboard the athletics department kept for scholarship students. I plopped my equipment bag on the bench by the door, that was there for that purpose.

Clark sat at the kitchen table, working on his laptop. He looked up. "Hi, Gweny. How was your first day?"

My heart flipped at that grin.

"It was great. My class on detecting fraudulent reporting is going to be *amazing.*" I put my backpack on the counter and got out a baggie full of over-the-counter medicines, vitamin and energy shots, and first aid supplies from the campus clinic. Also, some star-shaped noodles, carrot and ranch packs, tiny containers of peanut butter, and little bags of celery, along with a baggie of chopped tomatoes and onions, that I'd taken from the salad bar in the dining hall.

Snowball napped on the top of her tree. I took out a feather cat-toy wand and shook it. Hearing the bells, she woke up, jumped off the cat tree, and bolted over to me.

"I think our team's going to be pretty good." I'd gotten a shit ton of side-eye. Windy had been flapping his mouth all summer talking about how I'd cheated on Austin, then dumped him when he didn't get signed. We all knew each other, and I'd have to deal with that at some point.

I dangled the toy for Snowball and she batted at it. "The treasure room had *cat toys*. I'd never even thought to look for stuff like that."

"Treasure room?" He pushed his glasses up, which had slid down his nose.

"It's what NYIT calls their needs pantry. We're the *Kings*." I grinned at Snowball as she jumped at the toy. "Feel free to take some carrots or celery. The little packs are great on the go. Maybe next time they'll have bottled smoothies or yogurts."

Still dangling the toy for Snowball, I put the veggies in the fridge, except for the baggie of tomatoes and onions, which I put in the freezer, then grabbed a beer.

"People can have pets in the dorms?" Clark held out his hand and I gave him the toy. Snowball bounded over to him.

"You can in family and pack housing." I sat down and opened my beer. "A lot of the stuff is donated. There were tons of school supplies today, too. But I used my points for snacks and a cat toy."

"That's great your school has that. My old college had one, too. The jam factory nearby always donated the jars with the messed up labels," he told me. "Don't feel like you have to use your points for meal stuff for us. Also, please order what you need on the grocery account, even extra things, like protein shakes and snacks. I want you to have enough food and I know you can't always get to campus to eat."

My hand went to my heart. "Thanks, that's so sweet. I need to make some pasta sauce this week. If I can't find the right fresh herbs in the greenhouse, behind the athlete's dining hall, I might buy some."

Sometimes I felt a little guilty that he paid for all the groceries, but I managed to feed myself a lot, so hopefully it balanced out. I tried to be a good shopper, but there were also foods I missed eating.

"Go for it. Pasta sauce? Sounds delicious."

"Can I use your slow-cooker?" I added. Yeah, it was cheating. So was freezing my tomatoes, since it took a bunch of trips to the dining hall to take enough, since I only took a little at a time, so it wouldn't be unfair. Every time I tried to grow my own in pots they died.

Clark blinked. "I have a slow-cooker?"

I nodded. "It's a little one, still new in the box. I think it was a *welcome to the team gift* from the MASOs last year, because there's some super cute hockey-themed potholders with it and recipes."

Some of which I wanted to try.

"Um, go for it. Hey, you got a package." He got up and brought me a large box.

"A package?" I frowned. "I didn't order anything."

"Do you want me to open it?" Clark offered.

I nodded. "Please."

Just in case it was weird.

Getting a knife, he sliced open the box and removed something roundish and purple.

A helmet? But I already had goalie masks.

Clark looked at the box and the paper in it and laughed. "Tens sent you a motorcycle helmet. I was going to take you to get one, but this one's cute."

"That was nice of him. I like it." I texted him a picture of me with it. It was all different shades of purple with *stars*.

Me

> **Thank you. It's so cute.**

Tenzin

> **You're quite welcome. I just want you to be safe.**

Awww. My heart melted.

"Hey. Do you want to go to that Thai place you like for dinner? If you're hungry, that is?" He pushed his glasses up, which had slid down his nose again. "Though, first, can we have a serious talk?"

Oh. My belly dipped. "I... I was thinking maybe I should pay the electric bill, since I'll be around more than you. Or the water bill, since I take so many bubble baths? I don't mind contributing to groceries. Also, I won't get my distribution until the end of the month if you need me to move out. Housing doesn't have any singles, but said they might in a few weeks."

"Don't move out." His look became stricken as he sat back down at the table. "I mean, unless you need to live on your own for a bit to be your best self. I'd support that. Don't move out because you think I want you to. Did we make it weird at the wedding? I like you living here."

My heart continued to thump as I joined him. "What? Never. You like me living here? I... I like living here."

"Okay, then I want you to stay. Um, you don't have to pay anything. I'm happy to cover everything." He looked adorably flustered. "That wasn't what I wanted to talk to you about. Um, do you want to be on my health insurance?"

"You want to add me to your health insurance?" That was *not* what I thought this conversation would be about, and I relaxed.

Clark nodded. "Yeah, this way, if you need additional visits to the physio or to see specialists, you can do that. It's really good–there's dental and mental health, too. Maybe they'll have whatever special therapists you need to see, and then you can be in control of it yourself, instead of your brother paying for it."

My jaw dropped at his reasoning. "That's so thoughtful."

I'd been fretting a little about it. I only had the free insurance everyone had–and campus healthcare. The types of people I specifically needed to see were either not available on campus or had long wait lists. But I didn't want Matty to pay for it.

I stood and gave Clark a kiss. "Can you? I mean, we're not mated, married, or pack."

Which were the usual sorts of things extra insurance plans required to cover someone.

He turned the laptop around. "One option is that I can add someone if we cohabitate, prepare and eat food together, and share household responsibilities. That's us."

"It is. Wow. I love that." It also sounded like the setup for a rom-com.

"I was trying to think of ways to help you," he added.

"Thank you so much." The school therapists were fine for some issues, but not for truly dealing with what had happened in the lake house. I wasn't an omega, so I couldn't get free care through the Omega Center, which was where most of those specific resources were.

I pulled my chair close and helped him fill out the forms.

"Okay, I got pet insurance for Snowball, too. Now, next item." He submitted it. "Want to be my person?"

"Be your person?" I blinked, having no idea what he was talking about.

"Yeah, so you can go to any Knight's game you want, not only the ones you're on duty for. I know how much you love watching hockey live, but rarely get to go. If you get to go for free and have a seat in the family section, it wouldn't matter if you came late from practice, or had to leave early to study. You can go to away games, too. Also, you'd have access to the family room, so you can get free food. Not that Carlos' mom's purse enchiladas aren't delicious." His look grew anxious.

I sucked in a breath. Again, not what I expected, and super cute. "I won't be taking anything away from anyone, will I?"

"Not at all. I can still get tickets for my family when they come. It gets difficult and expensive for them to travel all the way to New York. They're not on a direct ultra-bullet route. It's easier for them to catch some of my games that are closer to them," he told me.

His parents came a couple of times last year. I loved all of them. Especially his beta mom. Last year, he brought her to the fundraising gala for the Squires.

"I'm in your guest room." I frowned a little.

"My family usually stays in a hotel, since there's a lot of them," he replied. "Mostly it's the occasional friend or whatever. Now I don't have a guest room, because it's *your* room. Guests get the sofa."

What did I do to deserve this hunk of adorableness?

"Um, so... want to be my person?" His look went earnest.

"Of course. I can't wait. Thank you." I loved that he thought of me like that. Now I could always sit with the MASOs, which I wouldn't get to do outside of when I was on duty.

How much fun would it be to go to the opening game and just relax and enjoy it?

I bit my lower lip. "Does this mean I can wait for you after games in the family room, then ride to Tito's with you on the back of your motorcycle?"

"Absolutely. I love it when you ride behind me. And now you have your own helmet." His look became shy as he typed on his laptop.

"I do. Maybe one day we'll convince Tenzin to give it a try?" I did a little dance at the thought. I'd gotten pictures of him and Cooter at the beach.

"Mmmm, I'd love that, too." Clark licked his lips as we finished the form. "That cock..."

"Oh, yeah, when it's your turn, you're going to love how it feels." I stole a kiss, remembering seeing *them* kiss.

"I can't wait. Hey, did you get invited to the championship cup dinner? If not, want to be my plus one? It's going to be so fancy," he told me, pulling me onto his lap.

Right. The Knights winning the PHL finals meant they got a special party. This was where the championship cup was officially presented to them and the players got their rings.

"I'd love to. Thank you." I could wear the blue dress I wore to the wedding.

"Great. Do you want to get that Thai? We can take my motorcycle. We can send Tens pictures, so he can see that you're wearing the helmet."

It was getting late, but I didn't have any classwork. While I had to work on the schedules for Coach Kirov, that could wait. "I always have room for Thai food."

He beamed at me. "Good. Let's go for a ride."

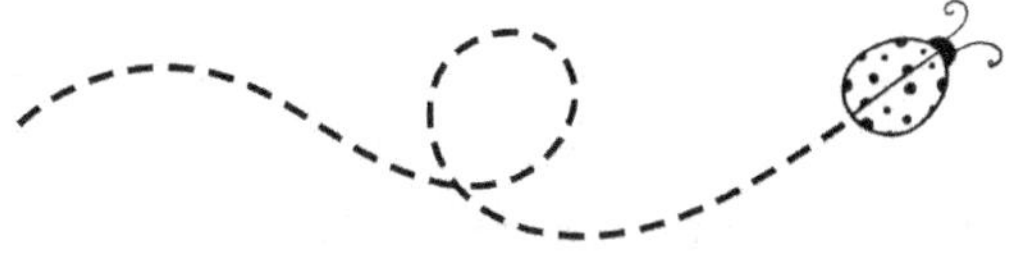

Chapter Fifty-Four

GWEN

"**I** don't like the teams I'm scheduled for, who wants to trade?" Arden made a face.

Of course she didn't like her games. I'd worked hard on those schedules, too.

Arden was an alpha and our new EBUG. She attended Barwyn, which was a fancy humanities-based university and nearly as old as NYIT. Every bit of her screamed money and privilege.

After two years of being the only female EBUG, I'd been excited for there to be another. But so far all she'd done was complain.

"I like mine," Tyler Yamato shrugged. Ty was an alpha and goalie for UNYC, and was friends with Austin *and* Windy. He was a good goalie—and knew it. The Boaters had drafted him, but he hadn't been signed yet.

Today was day one of our two-day EBUG training as we prepared for the Knights' pre-season to start, since we were there for those games, too.

We'd gone over rules and expectations. Marcel from HR took the time to teach us how to read a contract and go over ours. Sure, we worked for free, but this protected both us and the team.

The Knights needed to make sure we didn't dip part way through the season when we got busy. It was also nice to know they couldn't fire us because someone wanted to give their nephew the job.

Maryellen, who ran the community and educational programs, came in holding duffle bags. Technically, this was an educational program, not a prospect program.

"Here's a little token of appreciation from us." Maryellen gave us each a black and silver bag with Nat the Knight on it. We'd already gotten our EBUG shirts we had to wear sometimes.

"Ooh, Gwen, what did you pick for us?" Ty pulled out a heavy-duty black Knights' hoodie with silver embroidery and a big pocket on the front. "This is nice. Though I still like that jacket you have from your first year."

"Hoodies and PJ pants, are we twelve?" Arden pulled out the loose, black and silver plaid flannel Knights' PJ pants I'd also chosen. They said *New York Knights* along one leg and had the logo on the thigh of the other.

Tyler gave me a look. "Oh, those aren't for us. Thanks, Gwen. You know this will be Damien's new favorite to wear to class every fucking day. They're even his size, not mine, aren't they?"

"I aim to please. Damien's going to rock them." I grinned. His boyfriend was with the New York City Ballet. I could see Damien wearing *both* the pants and the sweatshirt over his gear to company class every morning.

I'd chosen things *I* liked. As head EBUG, *I* got to pick.

Okay, maybe the pants would fit his boyfriend.

"Did you hear, Damien got promoted to soloist." Tyler beamed. Those two were adorable together.

"He did? Amazing. I salute him." Standing, I grabbed my ankle and pulled my leg over my head.

Ty laughed and took a picture.

Coach Kirov sighed at our antics, her hair up in her usual bun braid. "Get down on the ice. I want to see how hard everyone's worked over the off-season."

"Why did you give me the home opener?" Ty said softly, as we got our stuff. "Don't you want it?"

"I'm going to the game, and I'm going to drink beer and have a great time," I replied. Yeah, I was going to seize that rare luxury.

EBUGs could get called in to play for *either* team. As much as I wanted to play in a pro game, something about the Gears always made my skin crawl.

"Thanks. I got to play in a prospect tournament with the Boaters, and there was this player for the Motor City Gears that bothered me. Like I'm sure I've played with him before," he told me.

"Oh? Maybe someone you played against as a kid?" I'd had that happen to me many times. We filed into the small upstairs locker room the EBUGs used.

"Maybe?" Tyler put on his shoulder pads. "I don't know what his name is. We didn't have names on our jerseys, just numbers, and his teammates called him *toilette.* They were assholes when I tried to talk to him. Sure, it's the Gears, but really? He also wore a gaiter with a skull face on it the entire fucking time, like he was in one of the dark romances Damien reads." He rolled his eyes. "I have no idea what he looks like, other than he has short blond hair and blue eyes. Oh, and is an alpha forward."

I'd played a lot of blond alpha forwards with blue eyes and attitudes over the years.

"Castle was telling me about him being a dick—and the skull gaiter." And not that good, apparently. "She was wondering if he was yet another Deloitte nepo baby. You know, *toilette, Deloitte.*"

I laced up my goalie skates. The skates from my university were all nice and broken in. I was trying to use those for practice and save the ones from Tenzin for games. This morning he'd sent me a picture of a big fish.

Tyler frowned as he put on his own skates. "But I don't know any Deloittes. I'll send you the couple of videos I took. Maybe you'll know? Like I think it's someone UNYC played regularly or something."

"Um, sure?" I replied, not sure how I could help.

"Also," his look grew pained as he put his pads on. "What happened with you and Austin? The entire team has been talking about how you cheated on him with Clark, then dumped Austin when he didn't get signed. And that you're the reason he hasn't talked to *anyone* all summer, not even Windy, disconnected his phone, and deleted his socials."

Here we go. I sighed.

His frown deepened. "I know Clark has a crush on you, but he doesn't seem the type that would move on another alpha's girl. I know how much you loved Austin. It was clear in all those lunches you made him for away games and how you pinned notes to his lucky socks."

"Look, I didn't cheat on him. I haven't heard from him since the night he didn't get signed. All I know is that his dad was making him come home, be part of his family's business, and mate an omega chosen for him. We had a big fight, because I knew nothing of this, and I hoped we could still make everything work, maybe convince his dad to give us more time." I rubbed my scar absently and tried to keep the irritation out of my voice. "Things got... heated. I dumped him and left the apartment. When I came back, he'd moved his stuff."

Ty blinked. "I thought his dad was dead?"

"Me, too." I sighed, still rubbing my scar. "I don't want to get into it. Our breakup had nothing to do with cheating, lying, or him not getting signed. I don't want him back."

"Okay." He frowned at my head.

"Get down to the ice," Coach Dodd called from the doorway. He was one of the assistant coaches who helped with us EBUGs. He didn't travel with the team, so he ran our practices when everyone else was away.

We put guards on our skates, took the elevator down, and made our way to the ice.

The three of us warmed up, and by then we had an audience. Constantine was in the stands. Dean was there, too, and gave me a silly grin, Jonas with him.

Excitement built inside me.

"Ready for us, Coach?" Grif Graf stood there with Nia, geared up and ready for practice.

"Yep. Some people think that the EBUGs need more time fielding pucks from the forwards." Coach Kirov gave me a look. It's something I'd brought up.

"Ladybug, you're first. Grif Graf is going to shoot pucks at you," Coach directed. "Don't go easy on her. Pretend she's Double D."

"Yes, Coach." Grif nodded.

I adjusted my mask and got ready. Grif Graf fired puck after puck at me. Like Coach instructed, he didn't hold back.

He also shot *hard,* which was why I'd asked Coach Kirov for this. The PHL forwards shot harder than collegiate ones. Grif Graf was the best forward in the PHL right now and one of the hardest hitters.

I leapt, slid, and full butterflied, as both Coach Kirov and Coach Dodd pointed out all my flaws, using me as a teaching tool. I didn't listen too hard, since I had to focus on the puck. Maybe someone recorded it.

Sweat dripped down my back. It was hard work and Dean would have an easier time stopping most of these, due to his size. Each time I let a puck in, Arden smirked or made a noise or comment.

However, this was *Grif Graf*. I didn't let *that* many pucks in. If I were getting tacos for every blocked shot, I'd be good for weeks.

"Okay, that's enough," Coach Kirov directed. "Good job, Ladybug. Someone has been working hard all summer. Thanks, Grif Graf. Ty, you're up with Nia."

I plopped down by my things and got my sticker-covered water bottle out of my bag. Shit, that was a good workout. Coach Dodd caught my eye and grinned. He was older, with white hair, and reminded me of my Gramps.

"Good job. I recorded everything for you, so you'd have Coach's notes," Dean told me. "Jonas is recording Ty. He needs to get serious if he wants the Boaters to sign him."

"Thanks. I'd like to do that more. I think you and Grif Graf are so good partially because you have each other to work off of," I told him honestly.

Dean thought for a moment. "Huh. Possibly. You need to work on control and holding back. You play every game, every practice, like you're playing for your life. Smarter, not harder. Your joints will thank you in a decade."

I gave him a skeptical look. "Dean, I'm a beta. I'm *always* playing for my life."

Ty let in more pucks than me, though he wasn't bad. Arden was next, facing off against Grif Graf. I had to admit, she was good–and smooth. She still let in more pucks than me.

Not that I was counting.

"Gwen, when did you get good?" Ty joined us, hair sweaty, a perplexed look on his face.

"Why do you UNYC asshats think I sucked my way to two national collegiate titles? Yeah, I know, beta sports parity laws and shit, but that's not why NYIT took me." I rolled my eyes.

While we were on good terms, and used to hang out a lot back when Austin would bring me to things, I always considered him more Austin's friend than mine.

Clark texted me and I texted him back, grinning.

Coach called me back up and repeated the exercise, only now Jonas was acting as defense, while Grif Graf shot pucks at me. Dimitri had arrived to help as well. We all took our turns. Finally, she dismissed us and reminded us we had more orientation tomorrow.

"All EBUGs, mandatory meeting in the dining room. It will be short. There are snacks," I told everyone. "Double D, I need you, too."

Dean gave me a mock salute, "Aye Aye, Captain Ladybug."

We took off our pads and skates, grabbed our gear, and headed upstairs.

"You seem to know Double D well." Arden gave me a look.

"This is my third year as an EBUG. You get to know some of them," I replied, as I swiped my badge to let us through the door. "Oh, Coach didn't mention this, but if you're uncomfortable in the press box, you can get permission to sit with the MASOs instead."

Arden's manicured eyebrows rose. "Why would I be uncomfortable?"

"Yeah, you probably won't have a problem with alphas pinching your ass and offering to *help* you with your career. I just wanted to throw it out there." In the dining room, I plunked my stuff down on a chair and got out the bag with the necessary things.

There was a nice little buffet of snacks for us, including sports drinks, fruit, sandwiches, and other tasty options.

"Before we snack, we have to take care of important goalie business." I took the bag and went over to the picture of Maria Barilla on the wall. I took a deep breath. Soon, I'd have to pass this on to someone else, like it had been passed on to me.

"This is Maria Barilla, New York Knight, Queen of the Goalies, and as the season begins, we always honor her with a sacrifice of noodles." I took the noodle necklace I'd made last year off the corner and wrapped it around my wrist. "She was an EBUG once, too, which is why it's our job," I explained.

There was no formal program back then. It was literally a *wait, the equipment manager's daughter is a goalie and is here and it's better than nothing* sort of situation.

It had been her big chance to prove to all the teams that had turned her down that she could do it. Especially when the Knights signed her.

"Her sauce is reported to be almost as good as my nonna's." I added a cheesy grin. Out of the bag came noodle necklaces I'd made out of the star noodles from the treasure room, embroidery floss, and glitter.

Everyone stayed silent and respectful. Ty and Dean knew the drill, but even Arden didn't make a snarky comment. You didn't mess with goalie superstition.

"As the new season starts, we give you this offering of noodles and ask you, Queen of the Goalies, to guide us and help us both in and out of the net." I hung the nicest and most sparkly of the necklaces on the corner of the picture. I think she'd like the star noodles and glitter.

"We ask to be steady, and fast, and patient." I put a noodle necklace around everyone's neck.

I took out the small container of pasta sauce and a single lasagna noodle I'd begged off the dining hall yesterday. "We ask to be as strong as you, to be good people, and good goalies." Because she was also a *nice* goalie–well except to designationist assholes.

Taking the lasagna noodle, I put some sauce on it and used it to paint some on Tyler's forehead. Then Dean's. "Help us bring the sauce to every game."

While Arden hesitated, she let me anoint her with sauce, using the lasagna noodle.

"The goalies are doing a goalie thing. Can you wait a moment before going in?" Grif Graf told someone, without a hint of teasing. Like even he understood the importance of this moment. I appreciated his respect.

I put down the noodle and sauce and got the bottle of Chianti out of the bag, which I'd already opened. "We ask this of you, our goalie queen. May we all have as many shutout games as you. In pasta we trust. Garlic toast."

Taking a swing of Chianti, I passed the bottle to Ty, who took a drink, then passed it on. It made its way around the circle.

"All Hail the Queen of the goalies," Dean said, bowing his head. He then looked over at me. "Thanks for including me."

"Can I wipe the sauce off my head now?" Arden asked.

Tyler touched the sauce on his face, then tasted it. "You made the sauce from scratch again, didn't you?"

"My nonna's recipe." I wiped the sauce off my head.

"It's so good," Ty told me. "If we get invited to any pre-season parties, will you bring some of your lasagna like you always do?"

"Yep." It was my go-to dish.

For a moment, we all stood there, looking at the picture, passing the bottle back and forth.

"Is it safe for non-goalies to enter?" Grif Graf called.

"Yes, thank you, Gumdrop." Dean wiped the sauce off his head, but not before tasting it and nodding.

Grif Graf, Jonas, Dimitri, and Nia came in. Their eyes flickered over the noodle necklaces and the bottle, but instead of saying anything, they headed for the snacks.

I downed a sports drink and gobbled a sandwich, then put another sandwich, drink, and some chips in my bag for later.

"Gwen, Ty, can I talk to you two?" Coach Kirov called from the doorway.

"Sure." I came out into the hallway, trying not to be nervous, Ty following me.

Coach gave us each a pretty envelope. Like the kind Celine had given me to invite me to her and JP's wedding, complete with a wax seal with the Knights logo on it.

"Here you go. Do either of you have Marcos' address? I wanted to send him one, too," Coach Kirov told us.

I opened up insta-chat. Marcos and I weren't super close, but we'd been EBUGs together for two years and followed each other on social media. "I don't, but I can get it. He's already in Argentina with his new team."

"Please." She nodded.

Ty examined it, but didn't break the seal. "What is this for? The gala isn't until February."

"We won the championship, which means we're having a championship cup dinner for last year's players and staff," she told us. "You three were there for us–especially with that whole double EBUG debacle in the finals. Gwen, you partially dressed out so many times. Not to mention ditching class to go to fucking Portland with us. Coach Dodd and I are proud of you. You, too, Ty."

Aww, they were?

Someone had decided that for the finals, *two* EBUGs needed to be provided for each game. It had been *insane,* even with the regular collegiate hockey season over. Like when the Sasquatches noped out of providing a second and made it *our* responsibility to bring one to Portland.

"Wow, we get to go, that is amazing," I breathed. Okay, I'd already agreed to be Clark's date, but the fact that I got my own meant everything.

Maybe I could bring Tenzin as my guest. That would be fun. He looked good in a suit and was a great dancer.

"Let us know if you can come," she told us, then left.

I sent Marcos an insta-chat. Too bad he probably wouldn't be able to get back for it.

Ty had opened the envelope. "Damien is going to shit himself. It's at the Harcourt. I'm going to see if he can snatch us tuxes from the costume room, because I only have suits."

"Harcourt? Fancy." I whistled.

Too bad I wasn't going home anytime soon. My mom had so many dresses for things like this. Sure, I was six inches taller, but there might be something that would work, given she liked really high heels. But my blue dress from JP's wedding would be fine. We returned to the dining room.

"Anyone want to grab a beer at Tito's? Double D's paying." Nia laughed.

"I've got to go to work," I replied, wishing I could go with them, as I put the invitation in my bag. Sure, I wasn't overworking myself, but I still was doing shifts at the rink.

"Windy said they fired you from Tito's." Ty frowned.

"I have other jobs, Ty. Bills don't pay themselves. Don't believe everything Windy tells you." Both Ty and Windy had allowances from their parents and lived in the dorms, and went home for summers where they did fancy summer training. They never had to sell their things to pay bills. Ty, being a graphic arts major, did some work for Carlos' brother-in-law's print shop. But that was beer money.

"Windy. Like hoodlum, Windy?" Jonas gave me a look.

"Yep. Anyhow, this has been fun. See you later." I grabbed my stuff and headed down the hall. I was working at the skate counter for warehouse skate tonight.

"Ladybug, wait up," Constantine called. "You look good out there. All that work this summer paid off."

"Thanks." I hadn't seen him or been by to feed Maddox all week. "Did you enjoy our orientation?"

"I did. Thanks for inviting me. Keep up the good work," he added. "You're still okay with a safe place to stay?"

"Yeah. I'm good. Thanks." It was nice that he checked in.

He nodded. "Good to hear. Um, you admire Maria Barilla, right? Someone told me that it was evident in your playing."

"I do."

He leaned in. "We're honoring her this year. Trying to decide if we take her number out of rotation or not."

"Wow, that is quite the honor," I replied. PHL goalies seldom wore the number 0 anymore, mostly wearing 1, 30, and 31. However, EBUGs were always 00. Sometimes female or beta goalies choose 0 as a token of respect. I did. So did Molly of the Belugas. before she came out as an omega, she'd hid as a beta.

"You're an accounting major and this is your last year, right? Do you need an internship?" he added.

"I'm going to be doing it with the rink accounting department." Not really forensic accounting, but my advisor was letting it count, which was nice. Not to mention, I got paid *and* class credit.

"I'll pay you more," he added.

I laughed. "You can't. Even a paid internship with you is against the NACA rules. It's why you give us EBUGs coupons for the food court and subway codes when we're on duty, instead of per diem. We don't even get paid if we play, we just get to keep the jersey."

"Oh." His look grew thoughtful. "Yet, you can work at the rink and do Squire camp? Curious since I didn't play collegiate athletics. I did theater."

"The rink is its own entity and is classified as an entertainment facility, not a professional sports team, so there's no issue with me working there. The foundation running the camp is also a separate entity and classified as a non-profit," I replied.

It was a little weird and complicated, but I always did my due diligence. I didn't want to lose my collegiate athlete standing, because I accidentally violated a rule.

"I see. Well–"

"Constantine, where are you? Do you know what those fuckers did–" Mr. Longfellow came down the hallway and stopped abrupt. The alpha GM was older and, as usual, wore a nice suit. He gave me a puzzled look, but his alpha scent was pure panic. "Excuse me, but I need Constantine."

Hopefully nothing was too wrong.

"Of course. Have a great day, Mr. Longfellow. You, too, Constantine." With a wave, I headed down to the rink staff locker room, stowed my things, and put my uniform on. Time to go to work.

Chapter Fifty-Five

CLARK

"This is delicious," Carlos said as he twirled more pasta around his fork. "Are you sure we're allowed to eat this?"

"Yes. She labeled the container for us specifically," I replied, as Carlos, Dimitri, and I ate pasta with Gwen's homemade sauce, along with the garlic bread and salad they'd brought.

We sat around my little dining table, which now had flowers in a vintage glass jar on it. I think the flowers may have come from the same place the fresh herbs in the fridge came from.

"Her sauce is so good. Sometimes she trades my mom containers of it for tamales." Carlos grabbed another piece of bread. "Did Gwen take everything from the dining hall again?"

"Yeah, she's been bringing home baggies of vegetables all week, then made it last night in the slow-cooker." I wasn't exactly sure why she needed homemade pasta sauce, a bottle of Chianti, and necklaces painstakingly made from noodles.

I also knew better than to press for details after she waved it off as *a goalie thing.*

"Why don't you just buy her ingredients?" Dimitri looked puzzled as he took a bite of salad.

"Gwen likes to contribute." I didn't have a problem with it. She didn't take too much at once and always used what she took.

She was so inventive, like Ma. I enjoyed her being around. Right now, it was a bit of a lull for me. Soon enough, training camp and pre-season would start and it would get busy.

Another reason for Gwen to stay here. Then I could see her at night and in the morning. Already she was busy with class, practice, and work at the rink. It had stopped my heart when she mentioned moving out, and I was overjoyed when she stayed. I didn't care about bills or any of that.

All I cared about was her.

Maybe I could talk her out of working as many shifts at the rink when she got her scholarship disbursement. I understood her not wanting to quit entirely, given she both enjoyed it and her privileges, but I wanted her to have time for what was important–like hockey and homework.

My phone buzzed. It wasn't Gwen who was working, but Tenzin. He'd sent a ridiculous picture of him and Cooter with a giant fish. I missed him. He'd be back soon.

Our phones lit up all at once, with Anders blowing up the group chat.

Anders

The multi-team trade fell through. Fucking shit. Motor City tanked it to sign another Deloitte, instead of taking me.

> **I've never even heard of this guy.**

> ***Bronson Deloitte.* Sounds like a tool.**

Nia

> **I'm sorry. We're not so bad.**

Anders

> **No, you're not. I've just been expecting the trade to go through.**

> **Fuuuuccccck.**

I felt bad for him, since he really wanted to go to Motor City. They *had* strung him along all summer. It was already *September.*

Me

> **That's awful. Call your agent. Maybe something else can be arranged?**

Grif

> **Another Deloitte nepo baby? Probably an asshole like the others.**

"What the fuck, man," Carlos said, trying to eat and read the group chat at the same time, getting sauce on his phone. He wiped it off with his thumb and licked it.

"This trade was doomed to fail once it got past four teams." Dimitri frowned. "In Russia, it would not have been legal to have such a trade."

It seemed large and awkward.

"Weren't we expecting a forward out of this?" I asked. The texts came flying through, mostly comforting Anders, teasing him about having to be a Knight again, offering advice, and lambasting the Deloittes.

Dimitri nodded. "From the Scorpions. Castle could do it. We'll be fine."

Dean

Wonder if this Bronson asshole's the one Castle was talking about.

Carlos looked up. "Sounds like an asshole."

I frowned. "He could be nice. We shouldn't assume all Deloittes are mean."

I didn't know him. At the same time, wouldn't the Gears have planned for another Deloitte? It wasn't like a fully-formed PHL-caliber forward would come out of nowhere. Huh.

"Not everyone's a good person, Clark," Dimitri replied.

We turned on the sports news, taking our food into the living room.

Grandpappy Deloitte, the owner of the Motor City Gears, was giving a press conference. "I'm so pleased that my grandson, Bronson Deloitte, has chosen to follow in his brothers' footsteps and join the Gears as our newest forward."

Next to him was his son, Coach Deloitte, and a blond guy with a bit of a beard in a very expensive suit. The guy kept moving his head in a way that made it hard to make out exactly what he looked like. He wore sunglasses. Inside.

"We're getting a fucking line of Deloittes." Carlos made a face. "We're playing them for the home opener, too."

"Ignore the trash talk. That's what I do." I finished my pasta. It was so good and I texted Gwen to let her know that, along with a picture of my empty plate.

"Welcome to the team, Son," Coach Deloitte said, giving Bronson a Gears hat.

Bronson put it on, posing with his grandpappy and dad. I still couldn't see his face.

"Thank you so much for this opportunity. I can't wait to join my brothers and cousins on the ice and uphold the long upstanding tradition of Deloitte excellence in hockey. I'm looking forward to being coached by my dear old dad." Bronson grinned at his dad, who gave him a light cuff on the arm, also smiling.

Something about this whole press-conference seemed forced.

"Why didn't we know about Bronson? Were you hiding him away?" one reporter asked.

Coach Deloitte shrugged. "Not everyone enjoys growing up in the spotlight. He's here now, where he belongs and ready to help lead our team to a championship. New York Knights, we're coming for you."

"The fuck they are," Carlos muttered, using his garlic bread to mop up the sauce on his plate.

"Mr. Deloitte, in signing your grandson, you've also shut down the multi-team trade. A lot of teams were counting on key players to fill their roster. Aren't you worried about the havoc it could wreck on the league this late in the off-season?" another asked.

Grandpappy Deloitte looked completely baffled. "Why would I be? I shouldn't have to take a trade I don't need. Training camp hasn't happened yet, and free agents can be signed until the end of the year. The teams have plenty of time to figure things out. Besides, it's good to shake things up."

"Shake things up my ass." Carlos sighed.

Dimitri was on his phone, consoling Anders. The group chat was still popping off, including memes and clips from the press conference.

It ended, and they focused on a shot of Bronson going over to a tiny, pretty woman, picking her up and spinning her around like she was the love of his life.

We cleaned up and did the dishes, and I got my skates, helmet, and keys. We were going to blackout skate tonight. "I'm sure the team will be fine. Let's go bother Gwen at work."

"Hey, Tony." I waved to the rink manager and Gwen's boss as we arrived. Blackout skate was going hard, as music thumped and people skated around with their glow necklaces.

"Hey, you missed all the excitement." Gwen's brow creased as she sold glow necklaces and handed out skates. She wore the light-up necklace I'd gotten her at the wedding. "Mr. Longfellow had a heart attack. The ambulances came and took him away."

"Oh no, I hope he's okay." I frowned. The Knights' general manager was really old and worked too hard.

Shit, was it the news of the trade tanking maybe?

"Me, too," she told me.

We kept Gwen company while she rented skates, then went on the ice for a while. Gwen eventually got to join us, which was always a good time.

She cleaned up and took my arm, her backpack, and a small bag over her shoulder. "Let's go. My hockey stuff can stay here. We have more EBUG camp tomorrow."

I handed her the purple helmet Tenzin had gotten her. "Care for a ride?"

"Always." She did a giddy dance as she put it on.

I loved that little dance. She looked so cute. We rode back to our place.

"Hey, I got my own invitation to the cup dinner." She pulled out a black envelope from her backpack when we were back inside our place.

"Wow, I'm so glad you got one." It made sense, considering everyone got to come from the trainers and equipment managers, to the front and back office staff. Technically, the EBUGs were staff. Unpaid staff, but staff.

She bit her lower lip. "Maybe Tenzin will be my date? Or do you want to ask him?"

"Go for it." I sighed. I missed him.

She removed the invitation from the envelope and took a picture.

"Are you going to wear the dress you wore to the gala last season? You looked like Aquatica." It was blue and fluffy with sparkles. She'd even dyed her hair to match.

She giggled. "I borrowed that dress. Maybe I'll wear the blue dress I wore to the wedding. I could dye my hair blue again."

"You looked *nice* in that dress." I nodded, remembering how it made her look like an old-fashioned movie-star. "Do you want me to make some popcorn? My mom sent me some today."

"Sounds great. I'm going to hop in the shower." She gave me a kiss and left the room.

I made us popcorn and settled onto the couch while she took a shower. Sports news was still full of the trade falling through.

Gwen padded out in some flannel Knights PJ pants and a shirt that said *EBUGs do it when no one else can*. She flopped onto the couch, then stole the popcorn bowl off my lap.

"Tenzin says he'll go with us." She beamed.

Her in a pretty dress, Tenzin in a tux, a fancy dinner, and a championship ring? Sign me up.

Highlights of the Gears press conference and them signing that baby Deloitte came on, this time with commentary. They showed highlights of him skating at the prospect tournament, and lamented the lack of knowing anything about his collegiate hockey career, if he even had one. Then they engaged in lots of speculation about why no one had ever heard of him.

The whole time Gwen watched the TV intently or on her phone, frowning.

"Is everything okay?" I waved the feather wand for Snowball, who had the zoomies.

"Castle and Ty mentioned him. There's something familiar about the way he plays. It reminds me of Austin. Maybe they played together." She went back to her phone.

"True." I waggled the wand again. Snowball could jump high for a kitten.

Gwen frowned at her phone. "There are zero good pictures of him online. He's either wearing the gaiter, or sunglasses, or has his head tilted, so you can't see it."

"Maybe you played with him... before?" My voice grew tentative. "Do you ever run into people who know your old name?"

"Sometimes. You're right, I probably played with him or against him at some point." She nodded. "Just because he reminds me of Austin, doesn't mean he is. That would be wild, right? Family business, my ass."

Austin? She thought Bronson Deloitte could be *Austin?* Huh.

"Can I give Matty this address? He wants to mail me my hockey cards," she added, changing the subject.

"You're texting Matty? Is that good?" I asked her, not knowing if I was supposed to like her brother or not. "You can give out this address if you're comfortable. If not, I have a post box we can send it to."

She shrugged. "He's one of the better ones. I'm sure they know where I live. I think I want Matty to send me a picture of my mom. Maybe a few other things."

"We can get some frames and put your hockey cards on the wall with my comics." I pointed to some of my most precious comics, which were framed and in the living room. They were here, so my siblings and cousins didn't borrow them.

Gwen beamed. "I love it. I can put my mom's picture in my room. Oooh, I have a print of Dumas' *Almost Perfect* that Lenny got me for my birthday one year. Maybe Matty will send me that and I can put that in my room, too."

"That's a great idea." I put my arm around her as the news continued to talk about Bronson Deloitte and all the players upset by the trade being canceled.

The Knights would be fine without whoever we were supposed to get. Anders was on the trade because he *wanted* to be, and it would be easy to find another forward.

"Um, I'm well aware I'm doing to you what Austin did to me. I... I'm hiding my real name, what my family does, and not using their money and letting others buy things for me." Gwen sniffed a little. "I... I'm happy to tell you whatever you want."

"I understand *why*. That's the difference." I wiped the tears from her eyes.

Gwen planted a kiss on my nose.

"While there aren't many videos or things online about me any-more, here's me figure skating. This wasn't long before my hockey accident." She showed me the video.

There she was, dark hair full of sparkles, her outfit filmy and white with gold and silver. She looked innocent and full of unbri-dled joy. This was before her mom died, before her injury, before she left home and changed her name, before that asshole obsessive alpha stole her joy.

Gabriella Capaldi, Vancouver, Canada, Beta, the caption said.

"Thank you. Though it doesn't matter." I gave her a kiss on the forehead and smoothed the worry from her brow.

"Movie? I want to take my mind off this," she offered.

We watched a movie, and then she headed to bed. I showered and sat in bed with my phone. I felt guilty as I looked her up. Like she said, there were very little—some stats for ice skating and hockey, a few videos, mostly from official accounts. I guessed someone had hidden the kidnapping and trial from the media.

Her offhand comment about Austin being Bronson bugged me. I looked him up and couldn't find any good pictures, either. I texted Dimitri and Carlos.

Me

Do you think this Bronson asshat is Austin?

Carlos

Not sure Austin's a Deloitte.

Dimitri

Do you want me to find out?

I will.

I considered this for a moment.

Me

Not yet.

I'd just turned out the light when I heard sobbing from her room. Rolling out of bed, I stood in the doorway of her room, the door open, since Snowball liked to go back and forth between our beds.

"Gwen?" I called into the room only lit by her fairy lights.

She sat up. "Only a nightmare. I'm okay."

The stench of fear and sadness in her room said otherwise. *Only my ass.* I walked over to her bed and picked her up.

"Clark." She kicked her feet a little, but her protest wasn't strong.

I took her back to my bed and tucked her in. "Sleep with me. It'll be okay."

"Okay." She rolled into my arms, head on my chest, not fighting me.

"That's my girl." I planted a kiss on the top of her head and tightened my arms around her. "What do you need?"

Her lips met mine, the kisses hungry. Her breath hitched in her chest as her minty scent grew sweet with arousal.

"Does my Sweetness need to come? Or does she need to be fucked?" My voice became growly. I'd be happy to make her feel better any way she wanted. She was my world. I was her moon, ready to orbit around her and be subjected to her every whim.

"Fuck me, Alpha." Gwen struggled to take off her clothes.

"Gladly." I stripped bare, tossing her clothes on the floor. Holding her to me, I savored how right her naked, muscular body felt in my arms.

This. My hand ran up her back. This was *everything*.

My fingers trailed down her back, tracing her tattoo, then cupped her ass. She squealed as I squeezed it. So perfect. That hand curled around her body to caress her dripping pussy.

"Please," she gasped.

As I continued to toy with her wet folds, my cock hardened, yearning to plunge into her silky depths. Her breath came out in little pants.

"I need you inside me, Tesoruccio," she gasped.

"Always." Rolling on top of her, I slid inside her. Her eyes went half-lidded as her sweet aroused scent wrapped around me.

Kissing her, I pumped in and out of her, gently, tenderly. This was a love letter to her body, not a race. With each thrust, I tried to fill all those little cracks in her soul, so she'd feel whole again.

She was already whole to me.

"You feel so good, Sweetness," I told her, as I kissed her jaw, her throat.

"Yes, right there," she gasped as my pierced cock hit just the right spot. Her hands ran up and down my back.

"There?" I teased, nibbling on her neck as I hit it again.

And again.

One day maybe I'd sink my teeth into her, marking her for everyone to see.

"Clark," she cried, gasping as an orgasm wracked her body, making her tremble as her scent changed slightly, like it always did.

I took a deep breath, trying to stave off my release as her pussy squeezed me delightfully.

"I need your knot," she moaned. "Please, you feel so good."

How could I deny that?

"Always. I love being inside you. I'm going to knot you and fill you full of my cum and hold you so tight no nightmares can get through," I assured her, capturing her lips with mine, as I thrust all the way inside her, my knot pushing past her entrance and locking.

My cum flooded her, and I kissed her again, trying to tell her with my tongue how much I loved being inside of her. It was perfect.

She was perfect for me.

"Do you feel better, Sweetness?" Locked in her, I rolled us to our sides and held her to me, reassuring her with my touch, as I kissed the top of her head.

"So much better. I love being in your arms," she sighed.

"They're all yours," I assured, playing with her hair.

Her eyes closed, and her breathing slowed. By the time my knot deflated enough to slip out, she was fast asleep.

Good.

Closing my eyes, I got comfortable keeping her close. Snowball padded in and curled up with us.

I hoped Bronson wasn't Austin. Even though I was curious as to his explanation, no reason in the world took away the fact that he hurt Gwen.

If Bronson *was* Austin, I was going to spend most of our home opener in the penalty box.

Oh, but I wouldn't regret it one bit.

Chapter Fifty-Six

GWEN

I finished up my filing, at the accounting office, at the rink, waved to the accountant, clocked out, and headed upstairs. Yeah, I needed to thank Valya's friend for choosing such nice outfits for me at the boutique, and for creating those lists of what went together.

Back then, I hadn't realized I wouldn't be wearing my rink uniform when I worked in the back office.

Clark and some others were in the small rink doing drills, but I needed to get my cardio in. With my schedule, and because I lived off-campus, getting to my university team cardio and strength training workouts got hard. Coach Hirata was fine with me doing them here as long as they got done.

The main weight room had a group of rookies doing an organizeverid workout, and another group was doing drills with cones in the other workout room. Rookie camp was in progress, with a scrimmage against the Jersey rookies tomorrow, and a rookie tournament on Saturday. That would help determine who got to come to training camp on Tuesday.

Us EBUGs had gotten to help a little with rookie camp, which was always fun. In fact, Coach expected me down on the ice soon.

Rusty and a couple of Maimers were in the dance room with the choreographer, working stuff out for this season's dances before *their* season began.

I let myself into the small workout room, which was empty and quiet. This was the *no alphas* workout room—and mostly for Dean's comfort. No de-scenter or cleaner in the world could make the big workout room smell like anything but sweaty alpha.

Putting on some music, I got to work, setting an alarm, so I knew when to go down to the ice. While it was fun working out with people, sometimes it was nice to have quiet. I sort of missed those late-night solo workouts on the ice, back when I was staying in the closet.

I didn't miss the closet.

"Oh, it's just you. Hey, Ladybug." One of the trainers stood in the doorway, peeking to see who was inside.

"Yep, it's me. Not a rookie being hazed." I was almost done and down to my stretches. Currently, I was on the mats, legs in the splits, chest to the floor. Sometimes alpha rookies were told this was the rookie workout room as a joke.

I popped up and grabbed my phone, then opened the app Coach Hirata had me tracking my cardio, strength training, and conditioning on. "Can you sign off for me?"

"Sure." He took my phone and signed off.

Coach Hirata didn't care who signed. Various Maimers had done so for me many times, as had Dean, Carlos, and Dimitri.

"Thanks." I took my phone back, finished, then checked my email and texts.

Tenzin had sent me a picture of him and Cooter at Cooter's ranch. He came back tomorrow. I sent him a picture of me sitting on a stability ball. Clark texted that he was meeting with the conditioning coach.

The apartment building had messaged that I'd gotten a package from Matty. Nice. That must be my hockey cards. Mercy also wanted to know if I wanted to come over tonight. Hmm. Clark had a sponsor thing, and Mercy and I hadn't hung out in a while.

Another notification made me pause.

And... oh? So soon? I did a little happy wiggle, still sitting on the ball. I hadn't expected my scholarship disbursement to hit my bank account today. It was way more than I thought it was going to be, too.

Amazing. The first thing I wanted to do was buy a meal or coffee for the meal walls at the places that still did it. Just like when I got a big tip.

The alarm on my phone went off. First, time to help out with the rookies.

"A pastrami sandwich with fries and extra pickles and a cookie, to go please," I told Zia, as I ordered at the Italian deli. I hadn't been here in a while. "Oh, I'd like a meatball sandwich with extra cheese, fries, and a cookie too. I... I can pay. I got my scholarship money today," I told her as she rang me up.

Earlier today I'd gone to some of the places where I used their meal boards and bought things for it to pay forward the kindness people had shown me. It felt good to do that.

Since the deli simply fed me for free, I wanted to buy things.

She looked me over. "Good for you. You sure? Who's that for?"

"I am. School year's going well. It's for, well, I guess he's my boyfriend and don't worry, he's much better than the last one." I eyed the total, which was only for Clark's meal. But I paid. They didn't have a tip jar, or I'd stuff it.

"Good. He should be good to you. If not, let me know. Study hard," she told me as she handed me my food, but not before she tucked extra cookies in there.

Order in hand, I took the subway back to the apartment. I got my package at the desk, then went upstairs, hoping Clark hadn't left yet for the sponsor thing with the hair gel people.

"Hey, Gweny." Clark wore a navy suit, with a light-blue shirt, and a striped blue tie, feet bare. His hair was neat and slicked back.

"Hi, Clark, I got you a meatball sandwich. I know you have a thing tonight, but I can put it in the fridge." I put the food and package on the counter, and my backpack and duffle on the bench, then kicked off my shoes.

Clark swooped in and kissed me on the cheek. He found it and took a huge bite. Bliss coated his face. "So good. Where's it from?"

"A deli not that far from the zoo. I got my disbursement today." I'd scarfed my fries and the cookies down on the subway, even though they'd fed us after practice. "If there's any bills you need me to pay, let me know."

Clark grinned, sauce on his face. "That's how I felt after I got my first PHL paycheck. I think we're good. You probably have things to buy before the fancy dinner, like getting your dress altered or new eyeshadow. Though Snowball says she deserves a treat."

Snowball was on the counter, trying to eat Clark's fries.

"Do you need a widdle treat?" I picked her up and gave her a kiss.

She yowled as if to say, *yes please,* then jumped down to sniff my shoes.

"How was class?" He took another bite.

"Fraud class was great. After class, I studied and had coffee in the campus center with some classmates." All the campus center places took either meal swipes or dining dollars. "Then we had practice, which ended early."

Using a knife, I opened the big box from my brother. At the top was a small box, with all of my hockey cards I'd fenced.

"Oooh, is that your Maria Barilla card?" Clark leaned into me, making me *very* aware of his hay and sunshine scent.

Since the night I'd ended up in his bed after the nightmare, we'd been going to bed together a lot. He always let me take the lead. If I needed to snuggle, we snuggled. If I needed knots, I got knots.

If I needed to be eaten out on the seat of his motorcycle, we did that.

Mmmm, I could get used to this.

"Yeah." I ran my finger down the case the card was in. I was so happy to have it back. I'd like to think she wouldn't be too mad that I sold it, considering it was for my education.

I showed him the others, including the signed Mario D'Angelo card my brother Luca had given me. Mario had played for Venice and the Italian national team and had been Luca's favorite player. It was the nicest thing he'd ever done for me.

Clark took some photos out of an envelope. "Is that your mom?"

There was a picture of my mom holding me as a baby, the dads with her. "Yep."

Clark smiled. "She's beautiful and looks a lot like you."

Tears pricked my eyes. "I miss her."

"I'm sure you do." He hugged me to him.

There were a couple of other pictures, including a family photo from Isa's wedding of all of us, one of me and mom at a skating competition, and one of Matty and me at his mating party, at the wildlife park in Quebec.

"I love seeing these pictures." Clark shoved the last of the fries in his mouth and looked at his phone. "Ugh. I have to go. What are you doing tonight? Study? Party? Work?"

"There's a party. I should study. I think I'll go to Mercy's and make cookies and play video games. We haven't done that in ages." I carefully put the photos back in the envelope.

Clark put his shoes on, then grabbed his keys and helmet. He kissed me long and deep. "Have fun. See you later."

I waved as he disappeared out the door. Mmmm, I liked me some goodbye kisses.

Mercy

Are you coming? Kaiko's here.

Me

On my way.

There were a few other things in the box—including the jewelry I'd sold Lenny, minus the things from Austin. At the bottom was a paper sack with pink fabric. The dress. The pink looked lighter than I remembered—not that my memory was perfect by any means. I texted Matty.

Me

Thanks for all the stuff.

Matty

I'm glad to give you your things back. I sent pictures and found the dress. It was always my favorite of hers.

Was it? Okay.

However, my painting wasn't in the box. Maybe it didn't fit, and he'd mail it separately.

I grabbed the bag and my backpack, put the envelope of pictures in it, and took off for Mercy's. The building Verity and her pack lived in was close by–and fancy. They owned a two-story penthouse with a patio.

I texted her from downstairs and the elevator buzzed; the doors opening. The elevator went right into their living room like a TV show. As the doors opened, I saw Dean, Jonas, and Grif were watching TV together, drinking beer and eating something that smelled good. Their place was huge with the kitchen and dining room opening up onto a stellar view of the city.

"Hi, Ladybug. Mercy and Kaiko are upstairs," Jonas told me. "What's the plan tonight? You know, I'm still finding beads from all those bracelets you made for her birthday party."

"I think we're baking cookies." I looked around. "Is Team Mom home?" I could ask Verity if I needed some dress help.

"She and AJ are on a date." Dean's voice grew sing-song.

"Nice. I get to go on one tomorrow with Tens." I did a little happy dance. He'd texted me earlier. We were going dancing.

"So you are dating both of them?" Dean asked, leaning into Jonas as he gave me a teasing look.

"Yeah." My cheeks warmed. I'd signed the papers in HR, so other than reassuring Coach K that I wasn't being pressured into it, everything was fine.

With a wave I headed upstairs, where Mercy's room and the living room we hung out in was.

Mercy and Kaiko sat in the living area, which had beanbags and cozy couches with pillows, along with a TV and her gaming systems.

"Gwenifer." Kaiko stood and gave me a big hug. She was several inches taller than me, with light golden skin, killer legs peeking out of short shorts, and hair up in two little puffs. Pink streaked her black hair. She was nineteen and had joined the Maimers last year with Mercy.

"You're back!" I put the bag and my backpack down, then hugged her. She'd gone back home to her parents for the off-season.

Kaiko was an alpha and played swing. That meant that mostly she played crusher like Mercy, trying to stop the other team's bullet from scoring, but she could be tagged in as the Maimers' bullet. You had to be versatile and fast.

She picked up a box. "I got you a present. I didn't know these were your favorite, or I'd have my parents put them in their care packages."

In her hands was a giant package of little bags of chocolate buttons, like the kind you'd get from a vending machine. "Shit, this is for me? Did you rob the business warehouse store?"

"My parents have a membership," she told me.

I did a happy dance and opened it, pouring a bag into my mouth and offering bags to them. "Thank you so much. What do I owe you?"

This would keep me in buttons for a while. So many chocolate buttons!

Kaiko waved me off. "Don't worry about it. How did I not know you were Canadian? Aren't you from upstate?"

"Thank you. Um, that's where I lived with my grandparents."

"Are you from Kaiko's part, Jonas' part, or somewhere in the middle? Pretty sure you're not from Quebec." Mercy took a handful of spicy cheese puffs from a bowl on the table. Jonas was from Toronto.

Kaiko opened her mini-fridge and held up a can of soda.

"I grew up close to you, Kaiko." I caught the can she threw. "There was this dance shop I loved to go to because they had much better stuff than the one by us. Or so my tiny self thought."

Kaiko grinned. "Is it the one between the bookstore and that little tea shop with the purple chairs? We usually go to one on the other side of town, but sometimes we went to birthday parties there."

"They have the best mini swan cream puffs." Usually my mom and sisters would have tea, while Babo went with me to the shop and got me what I needed. Sometimes I talked him into a trip to the bookstore. I took a sip of soda and plopped down on one of the couches.

Mercy took another handful of cheese puffs. "I feel like baking chocolate chip cookies."

"Sounds good. Should we make food first?" Kaiko held up her backpack. "I brought back those ramen noodle packs you like."

"Oooh, and rice sprinkles?" I grinned. Tenzin had like ten different types of rice sprinkles.

"Of course. Hot sauce, too." Kaiko started pulling food out of her bag.

Tenzin had given me a new appreciation for hot sauce.

"Oh, I got my package from Matty, so I brought the dress for the dinner," I added.

Mercy's eyes fell on the rumpled white paper sack. "Who are you going with, Clark?"

"Yep, we're bringing Tenzin, too." The idea of dressing up and dancing with Tenzin made excitement shoot through me.

"Fun. I'm going with Verity and the guys, since dressing up and eating free fancy food sounds fun," she told me.

"My brother mailed pictures of me and of my mom." I took the envelope out of my bag and handed it to her. "Since you wanted to see me in a skating costume. Anyhow, my mom always had such pretty dresses. I'm surprised one of my sisters didn't take it. They took a lot of them after she died."

Like to the point I'd hidden two of them in the attic, so they wouldn't take them. Both dresses would be too short for me now, which was why I'd asked for this one. It made a dress-puddle on her while she wore heels, so it should work okay for me.

"Awww, you're so fucking cute." Mercy showed Kaiko the picture of me at the skating competition.

"This one's pink, bare shoulders, ties in the back with a bow, and pools onto the ground. She looked like a princess in it. I'm going to need some alterations. Her post-eight kids rack is bigger than mine." I opened the sack.

The dress had been stuffed in the bag and not even folded. A little mustiness wafted off it. I tore open the bag and pale pink fabric with pink flowers flowed out. Huh? I removed the dress, careful of all the food and drinks.

"It's so wrinkled. Did he just stuff it in a sack?" Mercy laughed. "I have brothers that would totally do that."

I shook it out, not that it did anything for the creases. The dress was beautiful, off the shoulder with a V-neck. Delicate pink and green flowers decorated a shimmery overlay on top of pale pink fabric. The skirt was full and had a bit of a train with a corset back.

It was beautiful. Too beautiful for the likes of me.

And very much not the dress I thought he was sending.

"Ooh, look at that," Kaiko cooed. "That lace-up back."

"You're going to need one of those poofy slips," Mercy told me. "If Verity's are too long, maybe Valya has one? No, that might be too short."

I held the dress up. "This isn't the dress I asked for. It's so beautiful."

Kaiko took the dress from me and laid it out over one of the beanbags. "It's not the dress? It does tick off all the boxes."

"True. I think I might wear it anyway, if it fits. It won't be too fancy, will it?" It was fluffy, not sleek.

"Is there such a thing? You're going to look like a fucking princess. I can't wait to see the expressions on your boys' faces," Mercy chuckled. "They are your boys, right? Valya says you were hooking up with them at the wedding, but Dean says you're dating."

"Yes." My cheeks burned.

"Clark is one hot tater tot. You should absolutely fuck him and keep him. I've only seen pictures of the other one, but hoo boy, he's a sexy man." Kaiko threw a cheese puff in the air and caught it in her mouth.

"He's taller than *Grif.*" Mercy grabbed a handful. "If they treat you right, go for it."

"They do. I don't know what we are? Like it's serious and exclusive, I think. Tens and I are coming off breakups. Though I'm ready and Clark..." I exhaled as I remembered last night...

"The man bought you books and bubble tea. I'm pretty sure he thinks you're dating," Mercy laughed.

Kaiko nodded. "There's nothing wrong with dating again. If anyone says anything, they can fuck off."

"True. I mean, they're already mine." I looked at my phone and Matty had texted me more.

Matty

> **Flavie thought you wanted some hot pink one. But I knew when you said *looked like a princess*, it was this one. Chiara has that one, anyway.**

> **Send me a pic from the hockey dance.**

Me

> **I will**

> **Thanks again, it's so pretty.**

"Oh. A sister I don't like has the other." This was much prettier. It was surprising no one had taken it.

"There's a little damage to the fabric, mostly fraying at the seams, and there's a big rip, but it's fixable in the hands of the right person," Kaiko told me. "Let's go into Mercy's room. You can try it on and we'll see what we can do. Mercy, bring me straight pins."

Mercy's room was done in earth tones, and on the wall was a nature photo she'd taken, that had been blown up on a giant canvas and hand-tinted by Dean.

Stripping out of the sweats I'd put on after practice, I stepped into the delicate dress. Kaiko had already undone the back.

We pulled it up, the soft fabric cascading over me. It was tight in the shoulders.

"That's pretty. Look." Kaiko finished lacing the back.

I looked in the mirror, on her closet door and sucked in a breath. My hands smoothed the full skirt. "Wow."

The girl who looked back at me was unfamiliar. Shit, she looked good.

"The sleeves are cutting off the circulation to my arms." I tugged at them, the tightness taking away from the rest of the dress. A rip rang through the room and I looked at the fabric in my hand, horrified. "Oh, fuck."

"Hey, it's okay. We were going to have to alter that, anyway. Clearly your mom had chesticles, but she must have skipped arm day," Kaiko soothed. "There's enough boning to make it strapless. That's beyond what I can do—if we're allowed to alter it?"

"We're going to have to if I'm going to wear that, and I want to." I bit my lower lip. "My sisters alter my mom's dresses, so it's fine."

I didn't stalk my sister Isa's socials, but I'd seen her on the red carpet in more than one of my mom's old dresses and she'd absolutely have to alter them.

"Here, let's try." Kaiko undid the lacing, helped me take my arms out, then redid it, tucking them in. She frowned and pinned a few things. "It'll take someone cleverer than me, though. I just know the basics from years of helping out with my sibling's dance shit."

"I do feel like a princess. Is it too short? I can see my toes." I looked down and wiggled them.

"You'll have to wear flats." Kaiko got on the ground with the safety pins.

"Verity probably has a good tailor? Like the one who did all the beads on that dress she wore to the gala last year." I swished the skirt.

"That person's out of town. We'll figure it out–you *have* to wear that dress," Mercy told me.

"I'll text my cousin, she lives here and fixes costumes for the opera and ballet. Can I send her pics?" Kaiko asked. "She'll charge you a fair price and she does nice work–especially on old and fragile dresses. One of the museums had her fix the dress on one of their sculptures."

"Sure. That sounds good." I'm sure Verity paid premium prices, and while I appreciated quality and the time it took, my money only went so far.

Kaiko took a bunch of pictures, then took some tape and put it on all the frayed parts.

Mercy picked up the bag. "Hey there's something in here." She took out a little bag. "There's a note, *I can't find the necklace mom wore. But this is close.* Oooh, pretty."

She held up a triple-strand pearl necklace and some earrings that I recognized. They'd belonged to some aunty or nonna or something.

"Here, let's put on the necklace." Mercy helped me with it. "Oh, yeah. We can do our hair and makeup together. I'm going with Verity and the guys. Valya's going with Dimitri. We'll make it a party."

"I like that idea. Maybe we can get pedicures, too." I couldn't help but stare at myself in the mirror. I'd need shoes, possibly a haircut by then, but yeah...

Mercy took a bag out of her closet. "Gwen, do you want to try on some of the shit I outgrew and take what fits."

"Sure. You have cute shit. Thanks." I swished again, not ready to take the dress off. Never had I worn something so beautiful.

Kaiko looked up from her phone. "My cousin thinks she can do it. At least we have a couple of weeks. I'll bring it to her tomorrow?"

"Perfect. Thank you."

Oh, I couldn't wait for Clark and Tenzin to see me in this dress.

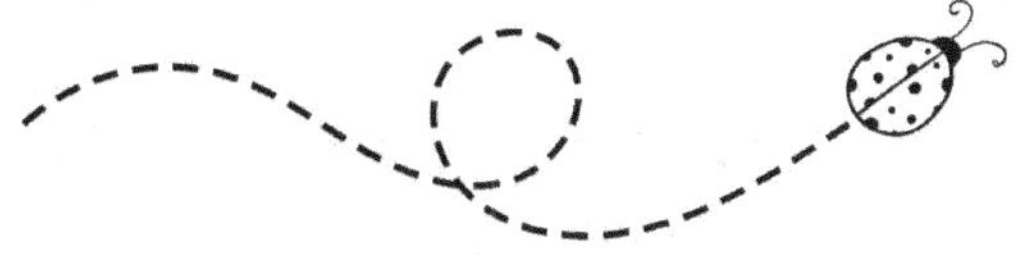

Chapter Fifty-Seven

GWEN

Humpy skated across the ice with the puck, then smacked it right at me as I crouched in the net. Nothing like a Friday afternoon practice to get out the aggression of the week.

I stopped the shot with ease, then tossed the puck at him. "Come *on*, is that as hard as you can go?"

"That's what she said." Bonnie laughed. Half the forwards were taking turns whacking pucks at me, while the other half were down at the other end with our other goalie and our assistant coach. Coach Hirata worked with defense in the center.

NYIT had their *own* ice rink, which was used for hockey, skate smash, figure skating, speed skating, and the ice cheer squad. They also had community skate time and fun nights, not unlike warehouse skate at the training center.

"Suck my dick, Di Rossi," Humpy said, taking another go at the net.

While I wasn't much of a trash talker during games, busting my teammates' balls during practice was one of my favorite pastimes.

This time he hit harder, but nothing compared to Grif Graf. It also didn't make it in the net.

"Kiss your boyfriend with that mouth?" I teased. His boyfriend was one of the hockey cheerleaders.

"Just my girlfriend." Humpy smacked another one at me. His girlfriend was team captain.

I caught it again. "Maze, your boyfriend is hitting on me," I mock-tattled.

"I know. It was my idea. My turn. I bet I can sink it in the net." Maze grinned. "I can be a better alpha than him." Her eyebrows waggled as she half-sang the words, which were from a popular song.

"Show me." I made a *come at me* gesture at our team captain.

Maze skated right toward me with the puck. Fierce and powerful, she had barreled into more than one goalie last season. The Bay Sharks had drafted her and she was the best forward on our team. As expected, she smacked it right into the net.

I ate ice trying to catch it.

Mine.

"Now that is how it's done," I praised, getting up off the ice. "Do it again, but *harder.*"

"That's what she said," Bonnie giggled.

"You wish." Maze laughed at Bonnie.

"Mmmm, so do I." Humpy tried to pinch his girlfriend's ass, and she hit him with her stick.

Coach looked over at us and narrowed her eyes. Yep, the hockey team for one of the oldest and most prestigious universities in the country was super mature.

"I spent the summer practicing with some of the Knights. They hit *hard*. Catching Grif Graf's shots is like wrangling a freight train. Also, Carlos' shots punch fast," I told them.

Maze took a few more shots. Most of which I caught, but she brought on the force.

"So much better," I told her.

"My turn," Bonnie said, coming at me with the puck. "So, um, you're dating Carlos Rodriguez? It was fun when he, Clark, and Dimitri came out with us."

I laughed as I caught it. "Um, *no*. He's still hung up on his ex and I'm not his type." Which was svelte and full of trouble.

Like the kind that ended up with me doing him a solid by keeping a snake in my shower for a week.

"Harder, Bonnie. I barely felt it," I yelled.

"Oof." Maze laughed as Humpy said, "That's what she said."

"Eat a bag of dicks," Bonnie laughed, trying again.

This one got in. "No thanks, I'm full."

"Why is there a Yeti in the stands?" one of the first year's asked as he moved to take his turn.

"We're going dancing tonight." I shrugged, catching it with ease. "That was weak. Do it again."

I was so excited about our date. He'd come back to town today. I'd missed him a lot.

"It's not Carlos and Clark, it's Clark and the Yeti," Bonnie's voice went sing-song.

"Go dive in a dumpster of dicks, Bonnie," I told her, as the first year came at me, glower on his face. Baby alpha didn't like being told what to do by a beta.

"That sounds amazing. I'm severely lacking in genitalia to drown in." Bonnie's look turned wistful. She was a pretty beta, but a lot of guys were put off by how smart she was.

"Why would the Yeti date you?" the firstie grunted as he took another turn.

"Shut the fuck up, Firstie. You're as messy as a badger in a dumpster of waffles. That's all for you today," Maze snapped as I caught it.

The forwards finished coming at me, then Coach gathered us all up for a cooldown and announcements.

"Strength training, conditioning, and cardio is *mandatory*," Coach lectured, giving us a hard look. "I know you have busy schedules, but that's why we have a variety of times, days, and options. Only exception is people who are taking part in other training programs with permission and get sign-offs."

Which would be me.

"Go on, now," she told us, the skate smash team was waiting for the ice.

I skated over to Tenzin, grinning so hard my face hurt. "Hey, Big Guy."

"Hey, Firecracker. The *mouths* you all have." He smiled and handed me a bag.

"I know. The university's founders would be proud. See you in a few." I took the bag of clothes I'd asked Clark for. Today was a longer practice day, and it was easier to simply shower, change, and leave from here, than go back, given I could put my things in Tenzin's truck.

I skated off and headed for the locker rooms. There I showered, changed into the dress and boots, and fixed my makeup.

"What are you dressed as? Weren't you going dancing?" Maze eyed my outfit as she got dressed in sweats.

Most of them were headed to a party later. Normally, I'd want to go, but I'd rather go out with Tenzin. I'd missed him so much my heart hurt.

"We're going country dancing." I twirled. This wasn't the sundress I'd asked Clark to get, but the blue denim dress was cute with these boots.

"Have so much fun," Bonnie told me. "I'm jealous."

Tenzin was waiting for me outside the locker rooms. He took my backpack and equipment bag from me, then slung them over his shoulder. "Ready to go?"

He looked stunning in a button-down, tight jeans, and his boots. Our hats were probably in his truck.

I took his arm, relishing in the feeling. "I can't wait."

"Do you want to watch an episode of our show? I finished my classwork," I asked as we walked down the hall of the building. Tomorrow was Saturday, so it didn't really matter. I didn't even have to work.

Normally, that would freak me out. After getting my scholarship disbursement, I'd done the math and realized that since I got paid for my internship, and I was still giving goalie lessons, I could just work rink shifts when I wanted to.

After all, thanks to Clark's generosity, my expenses were minimal. My savings weren't anything fancy, but if I didn't work all the time, I'd be okay.

A crazy feeling, but given the season was starting, it was a good thing, so I could focus on what was truly important.

And have time for things like this. We'd gone out to a restaurant on our list, then went dancing at our favorite place. It had been fun hearing all about his adventures with Cooter, and to spend time with the two of us.

Something felt off, but he'd flown in today and was probably tired.

"Not tonight, Firecracker." He shook his head.

"Oh. Tired?" I deflated.

His look grew pained and my heart stopped. Oh shit. Something was wrong.

"I need a little more time, Firecracker. I also have some things to do early tomorrow." He squeezed my shoulder. It had started to rain, so he'd wrapped his sweater around me

"Oh, okay. I'm absolutely fine with that. Watching our show wasn't a euphemism. I just wanted to spend more time with you." If he made a move, I'd take it. Tonight I was a horny little beta. If he didn't, I'd happily sit and watch TV with him. I'd missed that simple act.

We stopped in front of my door and he set down my bags.

"I know." He cupped my cheek with his hand.

"Okay. I... I missed you." I tried to gulp down the lump in my throat. "Oh. So no yoga and a visit to see Marty tomorrow then?"

"I'm sorry. Want to practice on Sunday?" he offered.

"Sounds good. Text me." I deflated. He probably had a shit-ton to do before training camp began.

"I will. I had a lovely time. Oh, I missed this. Good night, Gwen." Tenzin's enormous arms enveloped me in a hug.

"Good night." I bit my lower lip as I opened the door with my code and held it with my foot. "Thanks for a great time."

I took my things, then slipped inside and dropped my stuff onto the bench. My eyes teared as the door closed behind me.

"You're home early." Clark sat on the couch, playing a video game with his headset.

I kicked off my boots and dove onto the couch, burying my face in his side.

"I think I've just been friend-zoned." That hug felt like goodbye, and sadness welled up inside me. I should have known better. He'd gone finishing with Cooter and realized he couldn't be with someone like me.

"Hey, Gwen's home. I'll see you tomorrow," he said as he ended the game and took off his headset. "Sweetness, what's wrong?"

"He needs more time." I cried. "Tenzin didn't even want to watch TV. He walked me to my door, hugged me, and said goodnight. He even turned down yoga. That's like even worse than friend-zoning."

We were over and he didn't know how to tell me.

Clark stroked my hair. "I'm sure it's not like that, Sweetness. I'll go to yoga with you. Or we can go out to breakfast, then visit Marty."

"It's me, right? How could I have been so dumb?" I sobbed. "He doesn't know if he wants to be with a broken beta like me. A murderer with secrets."

"Hey, hey." Clark tipped my head up. "No talking bad about yourself. You're not broken. We have *no* reason to believe this has anything to do with you. He had a pretty traumatic breakup and everyone deals with stuff differently."

"You're right. It's just..." My chest shuddered. "I... I got really vulnerable with you both, revealed my deepest secrets, pushed you, and now..."

He held me tight, nuzzling my neck. "I'm sure that's not it."

"Okay." I gulped again, grateful for Clark's calming presence. "You're right."

"I'm right here." Clark held me close, and I inhaled his hay and sunshine scent.

"Who were you playing video games with? Your siblings or Carlos?" I asked, trying to calm that part of me that felt abandoned.

Clark was right, it wasn't me. He simply had a lot to do.

"Anders. He's still disappointed about the trade falling through, and the options his agent has for him aren't what he wants. The Knights wanted to keep him, which is a smart move." His lips brushed against my neck, as his hand rose up my thigh. "Is this okay? I don't want to push."

"I... I like it." I melted into him.

Clark's fingers grazed my pussy, and I clenched. My heart pounded as one of his fingers slipped inside me.

I sighed. "That feels good."

His lips grazed my collarbone. I gasped as a second finger slipped inside. The rhythm they created was maddening, and I yearned for another finger to join them.

My hand slipped under his shirt and roamed his broad and muscular chest.

"You're so wet and ready for me. You know, if you ever want me to join you in the bathtub, I'll touch you real good," he growled, as he scooped me up like I was a princess.

He knew what I got up to in the bathtub? That was alpha noses for you.

"What do you want, Sweetness?" he asked as he carried me into his room. "Do you want me to fuck you? Touch you? Take you in the shower and wash your hair? Just want to sleep? Do you want me to keep you company while you finish any assignments? Hey, wasn't there a party? We can go. It's still early in party time."

I gushed. While I adored him putting my needs first, him putting my *wants* first, like he was doing now, was sexy as fuck.

"Is this an alpha thing? I smell like him, so you need to fuck me and cover me with your scent?" I looked up into his beautiful eyes and cupped his face.

He laughed. "I don't care if you smell like him–I like how he smells. I don't even mind if you wear his clothes, just not to bed with me. Feel free to stuff it under your pillow, like that shirt of mine you stole."

My cheeks burned. "I... I sleep better that way. Always have. Your blanket that you gave me after my stuff was destroyed, brought me so much comfort in those early days of the breakup."

It still lived on my bed. It was little things like that, things I'd done even before everything with Officer Jones, that possibly led my ex to think I might eventually awaken as an omega.

Clark held me in his arms, swaying gently, as we stood in the middle of his room. His built-in shelf housed his special-edition Defender League collectibles, some posed in a scene with the pocket square I'd gotten him for Christmas, as the backdrop. He bought a figure every time he scored a goal.

There were also hockey cards, comic books, graphic novels, photos, bobble heads, action figures and other things. A small lamp illuminated the room and there was a graphic novel by the nightstand.

His bed was also *very* comfortable. I adored his Defender League sheets. His comforter was plain blue. Captain Everything blue.

"Please, steal my blankets. I want to fuck you because you smell like you need to be stuffed full of my cum." He brought me over to the bed and slowly took off my clothes.

"Yes, Alpha." I looked up at him. Clark was right. It wasn't us. If we truly cared about Tenzin, we'd be patient and give him the time and space he needed.

Clark pulled me onto the bed with him. "How do you want me, Sweetness? Hard and fast? Soft and slow?"

He slid off his grey sweats–which had *nothing* underneath and got into bed with me.

"This." I climbed on top of him and kissed him softly, staring into his eyes, as if by doing so, I'd learn everything about him I needed to know.

"Oh, yes, please. Ride me, Cowgirl," he teased, thrusting his hips.

Grabbing his hands in mine, I ground against his inflated knot. I sighed in pleasure as I moved up and down on his thick, hard shaft.

"Tesoruccio," I gasped, angling my body, so that pierced cock got exactly where I wanted.

"That's it, take what you want, Sweetness. What you need, what you want, that's all I need and want." He grinned up at me.

Those sweet words did as much for me as his dirty talk.

I leaned forward, my pleasure rising. "I want your knot," I told him.

He captured my breast in his mouth, nipping it.

"Clark," I cried, slamming down all the way onto his knot as an orgasm shook my body.

His hips took over as he *kept moving,* locked inside me as he filled me with his cum.

"That feels good," I gasped, as his tongue lapped at my nipple.

Another orgasm shook me and I collapsed on top of him, spent. His body stilled. Clark's arms wrapped around me. He kissed me deeply, a sense of content flowing through me.

"You're amazing–and you can ride me anytime." He kissed me again, body wrapped around me, partially on top of me, squishing my nicely filled soul back into my body.

"You're not so bad yourself," I murmured, snuggling against his muscular chest.

This time, when I fell asleep, I had no nightmares.

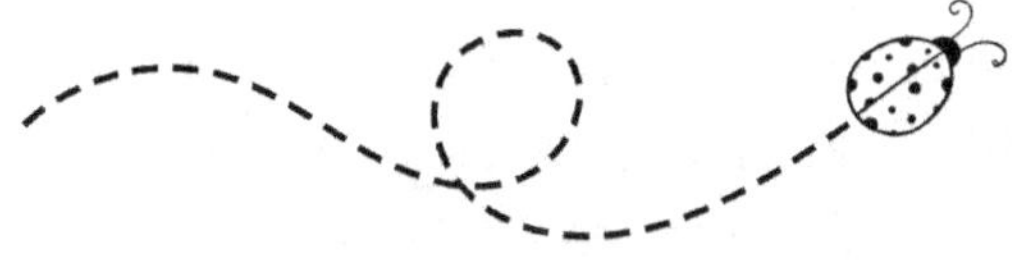

Chapter Fifty-Eight

TENZIN

"Are you coming to Carlos' mom's for dinner?" Gwen asked me, as we worked out in the weight room in the training center.

I shook my head as I lifted free weights. "I have to meet with a potential new sponsor tonight. They're in town for the golf tournament tomorrow. I'll see you there, right?"

The pre-season golf tournament was a fundraiser for the Knights' youth programs.

Gwen's eyebrows rose as she used one of the leg machines. "Me, at the golf tournament? I can't play golf. Also, I have class, work, and practice."

"Oh. I was hoping you'd be able to drive around in the golf cart with me. Clark, you'll be there, right?" I looked at him.

Clark shook his head from his spot on the bike. "I don't know how to golf."

My heart sank. "Oh. I signed up for it because I thought you two would be there. Well, that and the team wants to finally formally announce they signed me. Will you go to the party after at least?"

"I have practice." Gwen sighed. "You can come over after?"

"Training camp starts the next day. I need to finish getting ready." I was so behind, too. Being unprepared wasn't a good look when starting a new team.

"Oh. Well, routines are important." She nodded as she finished her set.

The defeat on her face broke my heart. I hated missing yoga and a visit to Marty yesterday, but it was when my lawyer could meet–and it was only the first of many meetings.

I was redoing my will, and starting a trust and education fund for Squiggles, which was what Morgan was calling our son. Bean was her and Jacen's daughter, and Pickles was Imogen and Ilya's baby. We were also working out some preliminary parenting agreements.

All that was just the work I had to do on the legal end. The work I needed to do on myself before I became a parent was much more painful.

It was still difficult to wrap my head around the fact that I had a son on the way.

How did I even balance having the life I wanted with making sure my son got what he needed? I wasn't sure where I fit. Where I wanted to fit. There was so much, and I was terrified of messing it up.

Instead of taking the fishing trip to get my shit together, the news I'd be a dad sent me into a tailspin. I'd spent most of the trip drunk and depressed. So much that I had to tell Cooter what was going on.

Though there had been some *excellent* fishing, and we'd had a good time despite everything.

Right now, Cooter was the *only* person who knew, well, besides my lawyer and therapist. I wasn't ready to tell anyone else. Telling people made it real. I hadn't even told Zaya. When I did tell people, Gwen and Clark should be among the first.

I looked over at Gwen as she dabbed her forehead with a towel. A forehead that still had a scar.

What would those two think of me being a dad? It changed things. I wasn't getting back with Morgan, but I had other responsibilities now, including wanting to spend time with my son during the off-season.

So much about all this confused and overwhelmed me. Why? Why did it have to be me when something good was starting to happen with them?

"Everything okay, Tens?" Gwen's scent turned concerned as she went over to another machine.

"I have a lot going on, Firecracker." I finished my set, not ready to burden them.

"Okay. We're here if you need us." She started on the leg press.

"I know. I'm so very grateful," I assured her.

"Yeah, I've got to get myself sorted for training camp, too. Have to show Coach I'm not just a wonder rookie, that I can be an asset," Clark added.

I hated telling them that I needed more time. Really, I'd much rather be with them, than meeting with a lawyer and therapist. But I had to figure out my feelings before he was born. I didn't want him to suffer because I had a complicated relationship with his mother.

Which meant this had to be my focus right now, even if I didn't want to. Not that I was completely neglecting them. I'd been researching how to best take care of Gwen. There wasn't much information on dead-matches. Hopefully, someone would get back to me.

My timer went off. "I have to get ready for my meeting. I'll see you later? Oh, I found little lunchbox-sized packets of the cookies you like when I was at the market, Gwen. You might want them for your backpack."

Gwen's face brightened. "Thanks, Tens. I hope you get this new sponsor."

"Me, too." I grabbed my stuff and headed down to the parking garage.

These sponsors would want me, right? It felt weird to be negotiating things like this, without much help from my agent–she was still on maternity leave. They were a big athletic shoe company. It could be a great thing. Making sure I was financially stable, that I had money for the future, was more important than ever.

Not only for my son. But the life I'd build with them.

As soon as I got my shit together.

Chapter Fifty-Nine

CLARK

Sweat dripped down my back, as Coach Atkins called us in. I skated over to him with the rest of our group. The next group, ready to take our place on the ice, joined us. Training camp had been grueling, with the coaches working us to the brink over the past three days.

This wasn't to get us in shape. We were expected to come ready. This was about showing the coaches what we could do for the team this year. I wasn't sure how people who went on vacations right before camp, like JP and Tenzin, did it.

During the upcoming pre-season games, the coaches would pay close attention not only to how well we played, but how well we played with each other, and whittle it down to this year's roster—not everyone here at training camp would be on the team.

Realistically, there were only a couple of open spots and several rookies, free agents, and Bantams fighting for them. For most of us, the Knights had the right to trade our asses at any time if they found someone better. So we had to keep that edge.

Mr. Longfellow's heart attack had been bad, so Constantine was acting GM, and he'd been watching us, mostly with a blonde woman I'd seen around before, and a couple other suits, one of which might be the owners. The assistant GM before our previous one had come out of retirement to help out, too.

Castle skated over to me. Last year we'd gone to developmental and rookie camp together, played the tournaments together, and had even gone to training camp together. I'd stayed. She'd gone down to the Bantams, but she'd played some games with us last year. I grinned back. She had everything to prove and was giving it her all.

"As we come to the end of training camp, it's time to name this year's team captains. The skates Elias and Winston Royce left to fill are huge," Coach Atkins announced. "This year's captains are Nia Watkins and Jonas Seong."

Everyone applauded, but it was a surprise to none of us. Especially since the other obvious choices, Pauley and Nakey, didn't want it.

Nia gave a rousing speech about how we were going to win the championship again.

My group left for off-ice training, conditioning—and snacks. Tenzin and his group took our places on the ice.

"Clark." Gwen stood there, in a pleated skirt, knee socks, slip on tennies, and *my fucking sweater,* which hung close to the hem of her skirt.

I had told her she could wear my clothes. I just didn't expect her to look so delicious in public while wearing them.

"Gwen. Off to class?" It was Thursday. She had her fraud class today.

"Yeah. Don't tell the Maimers but I just hid one hundred tiny ducks in their locker room. Anyway, I need to head to campus early today for a study group for data systems." She gave the rink a wistful look. "Coach Kirov says we can join you tomorrow. Oh, for one of the scrimmages this weekend, they're putting me and Ty in as goalies. Something about testing defense. Have you gotten your pre-season game assignments yet? I hope you play the one I'm on duty for."

"I think we're getting them after lunch," I told her as everyone disappeared into the Knights' locker room, to change out of our gear and skates before heading upstairs. "You look great in my sweater."

If only I had time to take it off her. I ran my hands up under her skirt, cupping her ass.

"Yeah?" She looked around, leaned in and gave me a kiss. "Hey did you ever get a necklace or ring, or anything, when they gave you goodies the other day?"

I blinked, frowning. "Um, I don't think so. The bag. The training camp hoodie I gave you. There were a few other things. You can rummage through it and see what else is in there. A necklace would be fun."

"Right? Earrings, too. Maybe I should see if the MASOs are ordering cute stuff. See you tonight." She kissed me again.

I entered the locker room in time to hear one of the free agents ask about the *'hottie in the knee socks'*.

"That's Clark's girl," Anders joked as he changed, blond hair up in his usual man-bun. "Touch her and he'll pulverize you in Go-goKart."

"Hey, don't sit on Lucky," Dean yelled at one of the Bantams as they went to sit down.

Everyone started laughing. The Bantam looked baffled.

Nia looked at me. "Good for Ladybug. Aren't goalies supposed to date hot people?"

The entire room erupted in guffaws, because clips of the commercial I'd done for Bare Armor had gone viral for my 'hotness.' I threw my towel at her.

Every day, Gwen and I grew closer. Tenzin had been so busy. Sure, he had stuff going on. At the same time, we seemed to be further back from where we'd been before the wedding. I had no idea what to do.

We went to conditioning and off-ice training, then the whole team gathered to eat in the dining room.

"Scrimmage rosters are posted for Saturday," Coach Atkins told us. "Two EBUGs will be the goalies for scrimmage game B. You'll meet all of them tomorrow and you'll be seeing them around all season. The roster for the first two pre-season games is also posted."

"I call Gwen," Jonas laughed. "Nia, you can have Ty."

"Eat my dick, Jonas, I get Ladybug." Nia threw a wadded napkin at him.

Coach gave them a look. "You two don't even know which EBUGs are playing. You're also both on scrimmage game A."

He talked a little about the EBUG program, then launched into the *'do not harass the EBUGs and it's a bad idea to date them'* speech.

A couple of people smirked at me.

After I ate, I checked the roster. They assigned Tenzin and me to the same team for our first away game against Boston. The coaches would be mixing things up and figuring out the roster and the lines.

After we finished for the day, a bunch of us headed to Tito's. I saw Tenzin going to his truck as I got on my bike.

"Hey, are you going to Tito's?" I asked. "I miss hanging out with you."

He shook his head. "Unfortunately, I have to take care of some things."

"I get it. Hey, we're going to Dimitri's tonight. Come join us? Gwen would love to see you," I added. She missed him a lot.

Those little packs of cookies he'd given her had made her day.

"I can't. But I'll be at the barbeque at Nia's tomorrow, and the pool party at Coach Atkins' on Saturday." His look grew anxious. "I don't know what to bring. We never brought stuff to Sasquatch parties, it was always fully catered."

"I'm bringing artichoke dip. Gwen's making lasagna. You know, if you text her, she'll have ideas." Bringing things–and seeing what everyone else brought–was half the fun.

"I'll do that. Thanks." He got in his car and drove off. I stood there, frowning.

"Clark, hey." Atticus, Nia's omega, came over to me. He was a slim, well-dressed omega that was about Gwen's height, and in his late twenties. Their pack had twin toddlers and he worked in marketing.

"Hey, Atty." I saw Nia talking to Pauley and Nakey. Pauley was a forward like Nia and had blond, beachy hair. He was mated to Nakey, who had dark hair and played defense.

"You added Gwen as your person, right? I'm head MASO this year, so I have the list," Atty added.

"I figured it would be nice for her to have access to the family room and be able to come to games. Oh, and get snacks." Because she was always hungry.

"I heard she's living with you?" Atty smirked.

"She couldn't get housing and I had an extra room. Are you ordering things? I think she wants some cute jewelry." I thought back to what she'd said earlier.

"There will be some in the goodie bags for opening night. Now, did you just want family room access for her, or did you want her to be part of the actual MASO group? For example, AJ has family room access, but isn't part of the MASO group. But Verity and I have both."

"They made me meals last year." And gave me the slow-cooker. Gwen had made some delicious queso dip in it the other day.

"Yes. We do things for the team and have some social activities, also a group chat. Did you want her to be part of that? It's fine if you don't. Everyone in the MASO group contributes at the beginning of the year and it covers some of the things we order and do," he offered.

"Yeah, she'd like that. Send me a request and I'll pay it. Thanks for including her, that's so sweet," I told him.

"Great, we adore her. I'll put her down. Thanks." He waved and got in the car with Nia.

I went to Tito's and joined Carlos, Anders, Dimitri, and Mitchy at a table. Next to us was a table of Bantams and free agents.

"Who do you think is staying?" Mitchy asked, eyeing them.

"Castle," I said with a nod.

Mitchy had also been working his ass off. At some point, Sarah would come back from maternity leave. So someone would get traded or moved down to the Bantams, since she'd get her spot back.

Maybe it would be Mitchy, maybe someone else. But it wouldn't be until much later in the season, or even next–she hadn't even had the baby yet.

Anders looked around. "Where's Bucket?"

"He had things to do," I replied with a shrug.

"What's more important than the team? He's the new guy. Bucket should be here getting to know everyone like Vickers." Mitchy nodded toward the table where Vickers, our other new defender, had a french fry basket on his head as he talked to Pauley and Nakey.

My phone buzzed with the payment request for Gwen to join the MASO group. I paid it immediately. It would be fun for her. She was already friends with a bunch of them.

"Bucket's been weird since he got back from fishing. Did he and Cooter have a fight?" Carlos teased as he took a drink of beer.

"He's busy. Moving across the country and changing teams is no joke." I wasn't sure. After all, Vickers had done the same.

"I get that. I just sort of miss him," Carlos said as he texted someone.

Maybe Tens and I could talk about him making more time for Gwen. She was having nightmares nearly every night, and while I loved snuggling her, I think she needed him.

Well, that and I missed him, too.

Chapter Sixty

CLARK

We boarded the team jet to Boston, in our suits for our first pre-season game. Nia was captaining this group. Jonas had the other, which had played the Royals yesterday at home. Nerves were high, given all the things these games determined. It wasn't just who stayed and who went, but who made up the lines.

I liked my line from last year and sort of hoped they kept mine the same. I could see them putting Grif with Nia and Pauley, though. Carlos and Grif were magic together.

"Do you want to sit together?" I asked Tenzin as he took a window seat.

He gave me a startled look, and my heart sank. We hadn't even driven together. I'd asked about it and been brushed off, because he had something going on. He'd been at the barbeque and pool party. We hadn't talked privately, but he'd hung out with us and spent a little time with Gwen.

Still...

I shook my head. "It's okay. I don't want to disturb your routine."

A lot of players had very specific routines, like Grif Graf, who had to sat in the third row, left side. Or Carlos who always wore those little pink under eye mask things my sisters liked.

"I... I like to read on my way to games. We can sit together." He gestured to the empty seat next to him. "My hesitation was that Gwen packed me a lunch, and I didn't want to share. Then I remembered she probably packed you one, too."

"She did." I told her she didn't have to. Our team jet had food, but she'd wanted to. It was nice that she made him one, too. For some reason him not wanting to share something she made with me stung.

I'm sure he didn't mean it that way.

Right?

"Oooh, what did you get? Verity made me *fried chicken* and chocolate cookies." Dean grinned at us from the seat in front of us. He was sitting next to Jonas.

"Verity has a nutritionist-approved recipe for chocolate cookies?" I perked. "What kind of chocolate cookies? The kind Mercy and Gwen made at their sleepover? Those were good." Part of pre-season had been meeting with the nutritionist, who'd stressed that eating right played a huge role in performance.

While I'd tried to take care with what I ate, during the off-season I'd gotten lax. Also, Gwen kept making queso dip in the slow-cooker to have as a late-night study snack.

"Those were good. No, she made the crackly kind that's covered in powdered sugar. It's her big sister's recipe," Dean laughed. "Yeah, this snack is about as nutritionist approved as Gwen's lasagna. That shit is tasty. I must have had three helpings on Saturday."

Since Gwen had to make two, we'd gone shopping for the ingredients. She'd been excited to buy a special type of cheese. Also, she got ridiculously happy about olive oil.

Anything for that smile.

It seemed like I had to coax it out of her more lately.

She was taking Tenzin's distance hard. She also was now going to therapy with someone who had experience with broken bonds, which might be contributing to her mood.

Tenzin being sweet with her at the pool party had helped. When he hadn't come over to watch a movie with her, it made her sad again.

"It was very cheesy." Tenzin nodded, stowing his bag. "I like the sauce."

"Usually lasagna is cheesy." Jonas laughed, and then gave the attendant his and Dean's drink orders.

I ordered a lime soda and Tenzin got green tea.

"You don't like cheese," I breathed, getting it. Though I'd seen him try it at her urging.

"Not particularly. A little is fine. Gwen's lasagna is eighty percent cheese." He had a book to read again.

True. Especially when she didn't put meat in it.

"More on national parks?" I eyed the book in his hand. "Like traveling?"

For a second, his look grew bashful. "Like all the murders and disappearances that happen. It's fascinating."

Gwen texted.

Gwen

Want to come to my pre-season game against UNYC? You don't play that night.

I turned to Tenzin. "We should go to her game against UNYC. I feel bad that we can't make her away game in Toronto."

"I... I'll see. Apologies, there's so much for me to take care of before the season starts." His look went wistful.

Dean turned around again. "Are you talking about the NYIT vs UNYC pre-season game? Given both Gwen and Ty are playing, it might be fun for a giant group of us to go. Oh, silly little tip. While you don't have to pack Gwen a lunch for away games, I know she'd love a treat with a note on it snuck into her bag. Their meal service is usually a plastic bucket of prepackaged snacks."

"That's a great idea," I replied and texted her.

Me

Yes!

Gwen

Thanks. Good luck!

Tenzin was deep into his book.

"Hey, did we do something wrong?" I said softly.

Tenzin shook his head. "Not at all. I appreciate your patience. I apologize for being so busy. The pool party was so much fun. Please continue to take care of her while I get my shit together."

"Okay." I got out my game buddy so I could play Go-goKart.

He was quiet for the rest of the flight, but he ate the snacks Gwen packed and texted her thanks.

On the flight back from Boston after the game, he sat with Shawn Vickers, the new defender.

"Is everything okay?" Dean asked through the seats. "Did you have a fight?"

"I... I don't know what's happening." I frowned, because he was having a *conversation* with him.

Vickers was bald, with light golden-brown skin. He was around Dimitri's age and had moved into our building with his wife and baby. Castle and Anders had moved into our building, too. Though Anders had lived there last season, too.

The flight was brief and I took my bike back, and when I got home, I found Gwen on the couch, playing video games against my sisters. The remnants of a taco dinner sat on the table.

She gestured to the fridge. Aww. I warmed it up.

"You won." Gwen beamed, finishing her game.

"Barely." I joined her and ate my tacos. "I got two assists."

She leaned her head on my shoulder. "Yay. You'll smash this season."

I hoped so. When this season was over, I wanted them to re-sign me. I liked being a Knight.

"I tried talking to Tens. You're right, I think we've been friend-zoned while he deals with stuff." I sighed. While I understood, it still stung a little. We were more than willing to be with him, support him while he went through everything.

Her eyes closed and salty sadness mixed with her mint. "Is he still even going to go to the cup party with us?"

"I'm sure he will, I'll ask him." I hugged her.

"What do we do?" Her eyes were misty.

"Continue to give him space, wait for him to heal. You still have me." I kissed her forehead.

"I'm so glad."

I gave her another kiss. "You have me always."

And I wouldn't want it any other way.

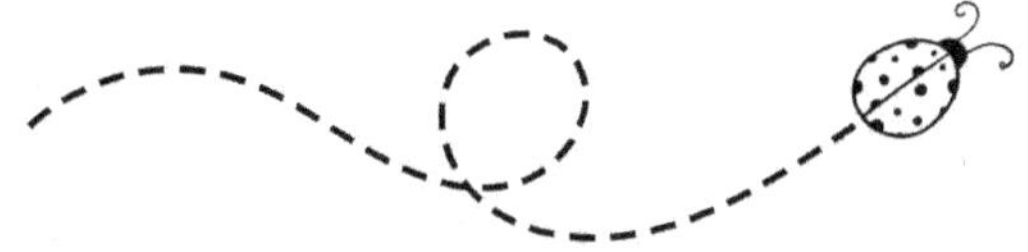

Chapter Sixty-One

GWEN

Doobie, one of the UNYC forwards, received a pass from Windy, and flew across the ice with the puck, headed straight toward me with all the force of a rhino, like he'd been doing the entire game.

Bonnie, Humpy, and Maze chased after him, trying to steal away the puck.

The packed rink went wild. The NYIT versus UNYC game was always a draw. Alfie, one of our defenders, chased Doobie around the net. Doobie passed the puck back to Windy. Maze took it from him, but she didn't get far. Doobie tripped her and Windy stole it, coming right for me. Windy took the shot.

But I didn't move that way, I moved the other way. I wasn't about to be fooled by Windy's fake shot.

Austin had taught him that.

I'd taught Austin.

Cheers erupted as I caught it. No goals for assholes. Not today. Not ever.

"You fucking cheating bitch," Windy spat, looking like he was about to punch me.

"Don't touch the fucking goalie." Alfie got in front of me and growled at him.

"Whatever." He skated off as his coach called for line changes.

I patted the goalpost. *Good post.*

UNYC had been playing rough and dirty. Knoblick had already been carted off for stitches.

Alfie shook his head. "Next time, just whack him with your stick."

"Are you going to sit in the box for me?" It was tempting. Goalies couldn't sit in the penalty box, so a player had to sit their penalty if they received one.

"Absolutely," Alfie replied, then skated off as he was called in. Actually, any of the defenders would.

He and Schmitty were replaced with Boondock and Freight Train. Those two were a team, like they'd been a defensive pair since they were twelve and no one felt like they needed to separate them–including NYIT who'd recruited them both. They hoped to go pro together.

"Go, Ladybug," Clark shouted, holding up a *giant* sign. While I knew Clark was coming, I hadn't expected most of the Knights and a good number of the Maimers to show up. It was sweet.

Dean even had a sign with my name on one side and Ty's on the others. Mercy's was covered in glitter.

We were in the third period and tied 2-2. I was revved and ready to go, mostly because I drank my usual concoction of energy drink, hydrogel, and vitamin water before the game. I sang as I danced around, waiting for the action to come back to me.

Oooh, Tenzin was here? He'd said he'd be late. I waved.

Giggles shot the puck at Ty, who shot it back, and it bounced off her helmet and into the net before Ty could blink. She looked absolutely baffled as everyone cheered.

"You scored," I shouted at her.

Giggles did a little dance as her song played, and she waved to her parents in the stands. Aww, they got to see her very first collegiate goal. Someone was going to get their helmet stolen.

I did a little dance in the net, since one of our firsties just scored on Ty with *her face*. I wasn't letting Ty live that down.

Now I owed Giggles one personal lasagna.

If Dean could bribe me with tacos, I could bribe the forwards with my homemade lasagna. We had to win this game. No question.

The line changed again. As Giggles returned to the bench, Windy body checked her hard, sending her sprawling to the ground. He did the, *"oops, I didn't see the bitty beta, I'm such a big alpha,"* bit.

The ref bought it. Ugh. How *dare* the refs buy that fuckery.

A few guys painted burgundy and gold–and nothing else–jumped onto the ice from the area the cheerleaders entered from and ran across it as most of the arena chanted, *"streak the ref, streak the ref."*

Streaking the ref when they disagreed with a call was a tradition. The naked guys were rounded up, but not before putting a show on the ice that rivaled our mascot and cheerleaders. Many people in the crowd were amused, but some were confused.

Wait until Maze scored three goals in one game and someone released the chickens.

The medic came over to Giggles. Shit. I patted the goal post again. *Please let her be okay.*

Windy came down the ice. I skated to the side of the net in anticipation. Boondock stole the puck and skated behind the net,

Windy chasing him, not caring if he ran right into me. I clocked him with a shoulder to the head and he went flying.

"Oopsie, this little beta didn't see the giant alpha," I sniggered, then patted the goalpost.

Windy peeled himself up off the ice as Doobie headed after Boondock, who had the puck.

"You fucking bitch." Before Windy could lunge himself at me, I smacked him again with my stick.

Boondock passed to Humpy, who passed to Maze. She slapped the puck toward Ty as a fight broke out, but Ty caught it. The ref blew the whistle. Both Windy and I got a penalty.

"I'll take it." Boondock sat in the penalty box, and someone threw an inflatable shark onto the ice. He grabbed the shark, did a dance, and put it in the box with him.

Windy tried to punch me and Freight Train slammed him against the boards.

"Don't touch the fucking goalie," she shouted.

A fight erupted and more penalties were awarded before we got started again. People dumped popcorn on Windy, which was a UNYC thing. Personally, I considered it a waste of good popcorn.

The clock ticked down, and the gameplay focused on UNYC's end, as Maze tried to score a third goal. I danced around to keep my energy up. Mercy and some Maimers saw me dancing and started dancing with me.

Wait, was that...

I shook my head. No. It couldn't be. Even if it was my ex, I wasn't going to let it phase me. I'd been working hard with my therapist to move forward, so I could be confident in my choice to be with Clark and Tenzin–and be comfortable with myself.

Yeah, I had this.

Tenzin waved and flashed a heart with his hands. I made one back.

"Miss me?" Boondock asked when he got out of the box and came back onto the ice, Alfie going back to the bench. He'd tried to take the shark onto the ice with him and the ref wouldn't let him. Now it was being tossed around the crowd.

"Aways." I got ready as Doobie took the puck. Windy was still in the box.

There wasn't much time left. Bonnie stole the puck and headed toward the net. She took the shot, but Ty deflected it, setting Maze up for a corner rebound shot. The crowd counted down. The puck slid in right before the buzzer.

"RELEASE THE CHICKENS," the announcer yelled, as it came up blinking on the screens and the silly chicken dance song played.

Three live chickens, one for each goal, waddled onto the ice. They wore little booties, so they didn't hurt their feet, and had little sweaters to keep warm, all made by the admin for the biology department.

Much better than throwing bones on the ice like at PHL games.

"We won." I did a happy dance and thanked the goalposts as our mascot chased the chickens around the rink. Their names were Puck, Stick, and Jock. They were the pets of the biology department.

Sure, this was an exhibition, but it was nice to win. I felt a tiny bit bad for Ty. But I didn't feel bad for Windy, who was still being an ass about my breakup with Austin.

I took off my goalie mask—which was my good one that Carlos got repainted for me. It was burgundy with gold accents and had our mascot on it, chasing three chickens. It also had a *crown* painted on it.

The mask went well with my new burgundy goalie pads, which I'd painstakingly altered to fit me perfectly. One leg said *NYIT,* the other had our mascot on it—a king with long flowing locks. For hockey stuff, the mascot held a hockey stick instead of a sword.

Like always, I wore 0 on my jersey.

Clark was right there waiting for me off the ice.

"You did so good." Clark *picked me up* and raised me a little like he was going for a lift, then spun me.

"You're wearing my jersey." My eyes teared as I realized what he was wearing. A burgundy and gold NYIT Kings' jersey with *my* name and number was on his back. *Oh, my heart.*

"Of course I am." He beamed.

"Where did you even get one?" They didn't sell them with our names and numbers.

"Oh, Carlos did it for me over at his brother-in-law's print shop. I'm so glad you like it." His eyes sparkled as he set me down.

I leaned up and kissed him. Where was Tens?

"Di Rossi, are you coming?" Coach called.

My cheeks burned. "I'm happy you came. Wait for me outside?"

"Always." He gave me a squeeze.

In the locker room, the coaches gave us notes and let us know everyone injured would be okay. *Thank the goal.*

"Di Rossi, let's not make goalie penalties the theme of this season," Coach Hirata added.

"Yes, Coach." I removed my gear in a specific order, just like I put it on.

"Please thank the Knights and Maimers for coming out. It was fun to have them," she replied. "The Knights are hosting an after-party for both teams at Tito's."

Awww, how nice.

"Hey, my mom's sending the slip so you can wear it for the Knights' party," Bonnie told me as we hopped on the bikes to cool down.

"That's nice of her." Since I knew Bonnie's petticoat fit from wearing it with her dress to the gala last year, I'd asked to borrow it again to wear under the pink dress.

We showered, changed and when I got out of the locker room, there was a massive crowd outside, as people asked the Knights and Maimers for pictures and autographs.

"Gwenifer," Mercy hug-tackled me. "That was insane. I love the thing with the chickens."

"Me too." Clark joined us. He kissed me again, hard, his hay and sunshine scent wrapping around me. A couple of the Knights whooped.

Scratching my nose with my middle finger, I leaned into him.

"Where's Tens?" I looked up at him. "I saw him in the stands."

Clark's brows furrowed. "He had to leave."

"Oh." My heart dropped.

"I know, Sweetness. But he saw a lot of it." Clark pulled me to him and kissed my head.

"I loved how you clocked that guy, then hit him with your stick," Dean laughed, coming over to us and giving me a hug. "Great job. That was Hoodlum, right?"

"Yep." I rolled my eyes. "Knotwaffle."

Ty joined us, looking baleful. "That was some game, Gwen." He looked at Dean. "Thanks for coming. I need notes."

Dean clapped him on the shoulder. "We'll go over some things. There's nothing you can really do about the face goal."

An older man came over to me. He looked slightly grumpy. "Di Rossi?"

"Yes, thank you so much for coming, Mr. Thomas." Excitement and trepidation roiled in my belly. This was Dean's agent. I'd invited several agents, since I knew this would be a great game.

"You play too hard," Stu Thomas told me. "I'll send the contract. *Read* it, maybe have someone else read it, too. If you're interested, send it back. If not, let me know promptly. Good game." Stu turned on his heels and left, but not before looking at Dean. "If she can learn to play smarter, not harder, she's going to come for your record."

Dean grinned. "Good."

"Did that just happen?" I whispered as Stu left. My heart sped. Did I now have an agent?

"Yeah, I think you got an agent." Clark took my hands and started dancing with me.

I looked at Dean. "I should say *yes*, right?"

"Yes." Dean nodded.

Ty blinked. "I can't believe that just happened."

Dean chuckled. "Ty, if you're going to make it in the PHL, you *have* to get your head out of your ass. You have an agent. Why shouldn't she?"

Clark took my bag. "Come on, Gweny, let's go to Tito's."

"Let's go." We had a lot to celebrate. If only Tenzin were here, too.

"There's nothing wrong with that dress, right?" I showed Verity a picture of me in the blue dress at JP's wedding that I'd put on social media. Isa found me and messaged me about the importance of not being a fashion disaster in public.

Which confused me, since Valya had chosen the dress at the fancy boutique. I'd also had help with my hair and makeup.

"It's a beautiful dress, and you look amazing in it," Verity assured me as she took a sip of a fruity drink after we sat at a table at Tito's. "I don't know what her problem is."

"Me neither." Because Isa wasn't one of my mean sisters. If she was telling me something was wrong with my dress, she meant it sincerely.

I just didn't know what it was. But then I'd never been good at fashion.

Oh well.

"She can suck it. She better not have anything bad to say about the pink dress," Mercy told me.

"I hope the dress is done being altered in time." While I'd gone for a fitting, the delicate fabric was being finicky.

"You can never go wrong in a pink Dubois." Verity looked around. "No Bucket tonight?"

I sighed as I peered through the crowded bar. Tito's was lively and everyone was having a great time. "Maybe he'll come soon."

Tenzin had texted me and told me he was proud of me and sorry he hadn't made the whole thing. He often texted me, took a moment to talk when he saw me. Still, things weren't how they'd been before the wedding.

I couldn't help but think that it was all my fault.

Mercy joined us and Verity set off to find Grif.

"Hey, Gwenifer, is this you?" Mercy pulled up a video of a figure skating routine on her phone.

"Oh. That's Midwest Gabby. People mixed us up *a lot*, even though she was a little older." I wasn't a *Gabby*. Most skaters called me *Little Gabs* instead, which I'd liked.

She'd also stopped skating not that long after I moved to Rockland. I found out later her home had exploded in a drug raid.

"Oh." Mercy nodded. "Okay. Not you. I, um..." Her look turned anxious. "I have a friend that's good at... stuff. We started to look for you, but she said we should stop. So we did. This video randomly came up in my feed the other day and I was curious. Are you safe? She, um..."

I froze. "She knows my record is...."

Shit.

"It's all good. She fixes records to make people safe. Do you need help? I can get you help," Mercy asked, expression serious as she leaned in, voice quiet, scent concerned.

"The person I was hiding from is gone." I looked away. "I was told I could contact people again. But I have little in common with that part of my life anymore. I like the life I made for myself. I feel more like a Gwen, anyway."

"Don't worry, I'll keep your secrets," Mercy told me. "You have no family on your record. If you ever want an adopted alpha sister, for safety, my friend can add me really well."

Awww. "That's sweet. I'll let you know, thanks."

That was something to think about. I'd already added Tenzin and Clark as my emergency contacts. Having an alpha sibling on record could be useful.

"Here you go." Clark came over to me and handed me a beer, giving me a little kiss on the cheek.

"Thanks." I kissed him back.

Windy stormed over to me, clearly drunk. "Where's Austin? What did you do to him?"

Again? Ugh. "I'm sorry your bestie ghosted you, but don't get mad at me for it, Windy. Please, leave me alone."

"He wouldn't have just ghosted me. I'm his best friend. You did something to him," he shouted, pushing me.

I fell to the floor of the bar; the air whooshing out of me, as my beer spilled all over me, the glass bottle shattering.

"Leave her alone," Clark growled, helping me up. "Are you okay?"

I sighed, my burgundy NYIT Hockey hoodie soaked. "I'm fine."

"What's your problem, assfuck? You don't touch the fucking goalie," Mercy snarled at Windy, alpha anger wafting off her.

Jonas strode over, scowling, arms over his chest. "Hoodlum, you need to leave."

"How could you cheat on Austin with *him?*" Windy sneered at me as he gave Clark a snide glance.

"Not cheating on Austin. Stop being a dumbfuck. We broke up months ago. Which I've been trying to tell you." I tried to shake tiny pieces of glass off me.

Mercy handed me a bunch of napkins off the table.

"You murdered him like the other one, didn't you?" Windy's voice was loud, and people turned and stared.

"That's enough, Windy," Jonas snapped. "Gwen didn't murder anyone."

"Yes, she did. She ran off with her other boyfriend to Canada a couple of years ago. Then she murdered him. Austin was so worried when you went missing. He believed your bullshit story and took you back. But I know better," he shouted, lunging at me.

"Don't you dare touch me again, Windy," I shouted, willing him to stop as I stepped to the side.

The air sizzled, and he stopped mid-lunge. His face contorted. I shouldn't be able to do that. There were a lot of things I shouldn't be able to do. Some I had better control of than others.

"What the fuck?" someone whispered.

My cheeks burned. Those who've lost their scent matches being able to access alpha traits were documented. It was meant to help omegas protect themselves after they lost their alphas. I got omega shit, too, sometimes.

Clark pulled me closer. "Touch her again and you're going to regret it, Windy."

"I remember that. We helped Austin put up flyers. He was worried sick, and no one was taking him seriously." Ty stood there as Jonas pinned Windy's arms.

"Thank you for that." My voice was soft. "I didn't run away with some guy and Austin knew that. I didn't hurt Austin. He went home."

"I don't believe you. He would have told me. You killed him like the other one," Windy yelled as he fought against Jonas.

"Fucking shit, Windy," I snapped, tired of his bullshit. "Do I need to brick you down with shit dicks? I was kidnapped, and I shot my abductor in self-defense after he killed the officer trying to rescue me. It's not the same and none of your fucking business. Yes, Austin knew, and I guess he told you. I did *nothing* to Austin. He left *me* to go home after he didn't get signed by the Aces. Go eat a bag of dicks, you knotwaffle." I rubbed the scar on my forehead.

I made a face, not liking that Austin told Windy things I'd told him in confidence. But then the kidnapping had been hard on both of us and we'd done couples therapy for a while to help us through it.

"Fucking shit," Mercy muttered. "If I wasn't afraid of being banned I'd punch him."

Security came over. "Is there a problem?"

"He had too much to drink." Jonas thrust Windy at him.

A server I didn't know came over to clean up the mess.

"You're a fucking bitch. A beta bitch he wasted all that time on, because he figured you'd be an omega, and his ticket to a good team. You sucked on the ice after you came back, too. You'll never be anything," Windy yelled. The bouncers dragged him out of the bar.

"I'm so sorry about the mess," I told the server, making a note to tip her as much as I could.

"I can't find any of this online," Ty muttered.

"Please, leave it alone, Ty," I pleaded, as Clark held me tight.

Lucius' family had kept it all out of the media. As had mine. You could find a couple of small things about Austin Blake looking for his missing beta girlfriend. And a bit about my uncle being charged, for keeping his niece in his lake house against her will.

"But–"

"It's none of your fucking business," Clark snapped. "She's allowed to break up with knotheads, she's allowed to date again, she's allowed to defend herself, and she doesn't owe you anything because she used to date your teammate. If you want to be helpful, why don't you have your team lay off."

"Hoodlum and Ty's team is giving her shit?" Jonas' voice grew sharp.

"Yeah," Clark replied. "Gwen even gave them the police report, and they still think she cheated and buried Austin at the zoo."

"Ty, fix that," Jonas snapped. "Hey, are you okay, Ladybug?"

"I'm okay. Just wet. I didn't hurt Austin," I sobbed. "I don't know how anyone could think that."

Clark rubbed my back. "I'm so sorry he dragged all that up. It's okay."

"Okay." I closed my eyes and leaned against him. I couldn't believe I revealed all that with everyone there.

Though Windy had fucking started it.

"Do you want to go home?" he asked.

"Can we stay a little longer?" I still hoped Tenzin would come.

His arms tightened around me. "Anything you want, Gweny. Anything you want."

What I wanted was Tens.

Chapter Sixty-Two

TENZIN

"Thank you for taking the time to meet with me. I appreciate it." I shook hands with the expert I'd just had dinner with.

"My pleasure," the alpha replied, gathering his things. "I'm happy to help."

I left the restaurant, feeling bad that I'd arrived late to Gwen's game and had to leave early. Trying to track down this expert had been difficult, and he was only in New York for a short time.

While betas suffered when bonds with their alphas broke, no one seemed to care. Most of the research and services focused on omegas, since their bonds were two-way. There was a difference between breaking a bond and breaking a bond with your scent match when they *died*–though both were painful.

And dead-matches? Most people thought it was a fairytale. And two betas dead-matches *bonding?* Impossible.

Which was why I'd been so grateful he'd made time for me. He was one of the few researchers in the world studying dead-matches and the only one willing to talk to me without offering Gwen up as a subject. Dinner had been quite educational.

Also, heart-wrenching.

Gwen

Come to Tito's? I won the game!

Yes, I'd stop by for a few moments. I missed Gwen and Clark so much. Thank goodness they were being patient with me. Between therapy and being depressed, I wasn't fun to be around–or wanting to be around people much.

Knights and university students crowded Tito's. I looked around for Gwen among the sea of bodies.

"Bucket, there you are." Carlos waved me down, and I joined him, Dimitri, Vickers, and Anders. It looked like Gwen was sitting with Mercy. I didn't see Clark.

"Hey." I felt like I was settling in with my new team. Our season started in a couple of days.

"I think when we hit Glitter City I should rent out the champagne room at the Luscious again," Carlos looked at me and Vickers. "You're not a real Knight until you have a lap dance."

Vickers grinned. "Count me in. We just have to send my wife a video."

He'd been a great resource, given he had an infant. I felt bad confiding in someone I barely knew, when I hadn't told Clark and Gwen. But I needed someone other than Cooter to talk to about this. The only babies he knew about were horse babies.

I shook my head. "I'll pass."

Not interested in strip clubs, lap dances, or Carlos' hazing. Especially if it ended up with getting my dick pierced. While Clark's cock looked lovely with hardware, I had zero interest, unless Gwen explicitly asked me.

"Oh, so you take me to the piercing place and they get a lap dance?" Clark came over to us, frowning.

"You got a lap dance, too. Please, take them to get pierced or tattooed. We'll go with you," Carlos replied.

Clark shook his head. "I don't feel the need to haze someone just because I was. What do you like to do in Glitter City, Tens? I've always wanted to go to the Defender League Experience."

Glitter City was an oasis in the high desert of decadence, gambling, and shows—and not my choice for vacation spots. There was supposed to be some lovely hiking though.

I pondered this for a moment. "I'd love to see the Gugette, but it's always closed by the time we get to the hotel after the game and never open before we leave."

The Gugette was a satellite museum of the Guges Art Museum in France. It was in the L'Elegancia Hotel. I'd been to the main one in Paris, and it was wonderful.

"Museum?" Carlos snorted.

"Museums are nice," Dimitri replied with a shrug.

"I'm going to get a beer," I told them, leaving the table to go to the bar.

Clark followed me. "Hey, Gwen's having a tough night. Make sure she knows you're here?"

"Of course. What happened? Didn't they win?" I frowned as I ordered a beer from the bartender.

"Windy pushed her." Clark told me what had happened.

"I'm so sorry I wasn't there." Guilt flickered through me. At the same time, if I hadn't made time to meet up with him, I wouldn't have had the chance for months.

I had an alpha need to be able to take care of her as much as I needed to be able to properly take care of my son. Whoops, I was supposed to pick up those baby-care books I had on hold at the library.

"Tens." Gwen's face brightened, like the sun coming out from behind the clouds, as she walked over to us. "You came."

"Apologies for having to leave the game early. You looked great out there," I praised. She smelled of beer and sadness, and I wanted to hug her. Something about her seemed like she didn't want to be hugged right now.

"I... I think I have an agent. Thank you so much for all your help." She told me about Stu Thomas coming to her game. Venture was a top-tier agency.

"I'm so proud of you. Congratulations." I was so happy for her. He had a great reputation.

The three of us sat down at a table and Gwen told me about everything that was going on.

"What about you? Is everything okay?" The pleading notes in her voice tugged at my very soul.

"I'm fine. There's so much going on with the season starting and a bunch of other things," I assured, disliking her worrying about me. "Cooter says *hi*. So does my sister."

Who still didn't know I was going to be a dad.

"Okay. Want to talk about it?" She bit her lower lip as she absently rubbed the scar on her forehead.

"Not yet. I appreciate your patience," I told her.

Clark seemed a little broody as he sat with his arm around her. At least they had each other.

"Do I wear a tux to the dinner? I'm excited to go with you." I couldn't find my tux anywhere, so I'd need to get another. Maybe it was at Cooter's. At least I'd gotten that shoe sponsor and we'd be doing a photo shoot. It was incredible they'd wanted me, considering we didn't wear shoes when we played.

It was partially to promote their larger-size line, and I did have enormous feet, even for an alpha.

Gwen brightened. "You're still going?"

"Of course I am. I wouldn't miss it for anything." It was nice of them to invite me. Sure, it was a party essentially celebrating my loss, since the Knights had beaten the Sasquatches in the finals to win the championship, but it would be nice to be with them.

Clark nodded. "It's a tux thing. Gwen's got a fancy dress."

Ooh, I couldn't wait to see her in it.

"Can we go dancing soon?" she asked. "I miss doing things with you."

"Me, too. Soon. I'm sorry I've been so busy." I felt bad about it. Once the season began, I'd have even less time than I had now.

"It's okay." Gwen looked so sad. "Can you come over and watch a movie?"

"I can't tonight. I'm sorry." There were lawyer things I still needed to do. Also, I had a meeting with Yeti Soap Co. in the morning, since they wanted to do some holiday stuff.

"Okay." Her shoulders slumped. "I'm happy you're here."

"Me, too." Soon I could be more for her, like she needed.

I just had to finish getting my shit together first. Like my son, they deserved the best me–and right now I wasn't it.

Chapter Sixty-Three

GWEN

"Are you okay? Big test or something?" Tony asked as I clocked out this morning after completing my accounting work for the day.

Or something. But I wasn't going to tell Tony. I hadn't been planning on telling Clark what today was either.

Matty *had* told my siblings. That was part of the problem. He was supposed to be on my side.

"I have a headache. Though I have a test this afternoon." Which I wasn't worried about.

Concern flashed over his face. "Okay. Are you working too many hours?"

"No, it's fine." I was happy with the time I did here weekday mornings and the couple of shifts I picked up at the snack bar and skate counter.

Another text came through my phone as I was changing, so I could join in a Knights practice. Isa? Fuck. It was one thing for her to message me on social media, it was another thing to *text* me. On a number I didn't give her.

"Are you shitting my dick?" I muttered as I rubbed my forehead. I was going to murder my brother.

There was also the fact that I hadn't meant to fall down a certain path last night, but I'd been watching the Gears play the Boaters and...

My fingers itched to text Lenny and find out for sure.

I got on the ice. A few players gave me curious looks, since it was a team practice. Tomorrow was their home opener. Since JP had something this morning, it was me and Dean today.

"Ladybug, are you lost?" Mitchy joked. He was a cocky shit and knew a lot of the same people I did–like Windy and Austin.

"Suck my dick," I snarled, not in the mood.

His eyebrows waggled. "Yeah?"

Clark skated over and growled at him, putting an arm around me. "Fuck off, Mitchy."

He looked offended. "What does Clark have that I don't?"

"I'm sure Carlos could help you with that," Anders smirked.

If I wasn't so pissed, I'd laugh.

"Don't be a dick, Mitchface." Castle turned to me. "Come on, Ladybug, show those assholes some girl power."

While practice was a good place to work off my aggression, by the time I slunk into the small conference room with my coffee and second breakfast, my bad mood had returned. The Maimers were in pre-season and had decided to prank us by changing all the drinks in the drink machine to water, which hadn't helped.

The notification I'd gotten while I'd been practicing had also contributed.

Me

> **How dare you give my information to the dads?**

Matty

> **I only gave your info to Flavie, the kids, Isa, and Joe.**

> **The dads know where you are; they were respecting your boundaries.**

Me

> **Why are they disrespecting me now?**

Today of all days, too! Matty had been pressuring me to have dinner with the dads, but we weren't playing any west coast universities for a bit, and they didn't have any desire to come out here.

Figured. I wasn't worth the flight. Just like I wasn't worth starting a war with the government for.

Wow, I was a bitter bitch today.

Matty

> **Sending you a birthday present is not disrespectful.**

Gwen's birthday was in February. But Gabriella? Her birthday might be today.

Me

> **It's not my birthday.**

> **If you want to be helpful, send me my painting.**

For some reason, he wouldn't send me my Dumas print. I didn't understand why.

Much of my anger came from the fact that everyone couldn't waltz back into my life like nothing happened. It was an insult.

I let Matty know that.

"Wow, good thing I'm not whoever you're texting," Dean said softly, coming in with two drinks and a bunch of stuff. "Here. I think you might need this today."

He handed me one mug, which was herbal tea, along with a chocolate bar, a packet of pain relievers, and one of those little heat packs you put in your gloves while skiing.

It took me a moment. Dean looked at me expectantly.

"Thank you. Verity has you trained well." Beta and alpha female menstrual cycles were pretty similar. I could totally see how someone might think I was in a bad mood because it was shark week.

"That and Grif has nine sisters. Stu said you're all signed and good to go, congrats," he added, taking a seat and sipping his matcha latte.

"Yep. Thanks to you. I don't think I'd have landed an agent like him without your help." I appreciated his assistance. Never did I think I'd get an agent like that.

Dean shook his head. "It was all you. I only reminded him that good things can come in small packages."

"For that I'm grateful." I opened the packet and took the pain reliever for my headache. I guessed the heat pack was for cramps. Good idea. I put that in my backpack for another day.

JP came in and fist-bumped me. "Heard you did great today. Here."

He handed me a package of chocolate buttons. My heart exploded. Celine must be in town for a few days, since her airline had these in their kids treat packs.

"Thank you." I ripped the package open and dumped a bunch in my mouth. Sure, I was still working through the box from Kaiko, but more were always welcome.

Coach Kirov and Coach Dodd came in, Arden and Ty following. The coaches played a few clips, and we went over some things from when the Knights played the Aces in pre-season. Then we moved on to clips of the Gears, so the goalies would know what to expect. Ty watched with rapt attention–as he should since he was on EBUG duty.

"Watch number 16; he plays dirty," Coach Kirov told us. "He's new."

"Their entire line plays dirty," JP replied. Nepo baby Deloitte was number sixteen, joining his brothers 17 and 18.

Ty frowned. "Where do we know him from? It bugs me so bad." He gave me a pleading look. "Gwen, ideas?"

I froze as Coach played another clip. My focus wasn't on the play. It was on number 16's feet. More specifically, the maroon skates with gray stitching–which he hadn't been wearing in anything I'd seen so far.

Anger boiled inside me as I texted Lenny and Matty. Fuck that fucking knotwaffle with a pineapple.

Me

I want to know who Austin is. Today.

Lenny

Already know. I'll send it over.

Matty

What do you want us to do about him?

I knew what I'd like them to do. Even if it was wrong to want it.

"Gwen, care to share what's so important you're texting instead of watching?" Coach Kirov snapped.

"Nothing. Sorry, Coach." My hand shook. Lenny knew who he was? He'd probably done it back in August, and held onto it until I was ready, because that's how he was.

In all honesty, I wouldn't be surprised if there was a lot that Lenny and Matty were doing for me that I didn't even know about.

I *was* over his sorry ass. Now I was angry. Livid if my suspicions were correct.

Yeah, it was a good thing I wasn't on duty tomorrow. If I actually took the ice and got in the net, I'd whack him in the kneecaps with my stick and get suspended.

Coach Kirov strode over and snatched my phone from me. "You can have this back after practice. I'm disappointed in you."

Ugh. Could today get any worse?

"Coach, is Gwen here?" Silas stood there, holding a giant bouquet and two boxes. The beta was one of the equipment managers. He was in his forties and the one that worked the most with us EBUGs.

How dare they send gifts to my *work?*

"I didn't know it was your birthday. Happy Birthday." Silas put the flowers and boxes in front of me. One box was from a high-end boutique, the other from a fancy bakery.

"Who's Sof?" JP snatched the card from the flowers.

"Isn't your birthday in February?" Dean asked.

Tears brimmed in my eyes as the fragrance of omega lilies and roses filled the room. These weren't my favorite flowers. They were my mom's.

"How dare they?" I blinked back tears, not wanting to cry in front of the team.

I wanted to pick up the bakery box and chuck it across the room. That would be wasting food though and I couldn't bring myself to do that.

Instead, I stared at the stupid flowers, wishing they'd incinerate.

"Can we eat these?" Ty asked, taking the card off the bakery box. "Who's Joe?"

"My brother. Sof is my sister. They think it's my birthday. It's not." I gulped down the tears, trying to grow a pair.

I opened the giant box from the Fairytale Bakery, which held fruit tarts with sugar crowns, beautifully decorated brownies, and my favorite–tiny cream puffs shaped like swans. At least Joe sent me something I liked.

Ty took a brownie. "My mom stomps on my boundaries, too. Sucks ass. But we can't let good food go to waste."

"True. I... I'm going to put these outside." The smell of the flowers made my stomach churn. It was too much like her funeral.

I put them on the table outside the conference room and took a deep breath, trying to get it together.

When I returned, Coach Kirov reached for a pastry. "I'm sorry you're having a shitty day, Ladybug. We need to get back to work. Thank you for sharing your treats."

"Sorry. I don't mean to be unprofessional." My head ducked, and I bit my lower lip to keep it from quivering. Shit. Shit. Shit.

Dean pushed the box toward me. I took a swan and bit the head off.

We went back to the films, analyzing the forwards of the Gears and going over strategy. My fingers itched for my phone so I could read Lenny's email. By the time we were done, we'd demolished most of the box. I took brownies for Clark and Tens.

"Can I take Jonas a tart? They're his favorite," Dean asked.

"Take them all," I told everyone.

"If you're not going to, can I open it?" Arden picked up the brown and gold box from Faun off the floor. "I'm so curious."

"Isn't that where they sell the purses that cost as much as cars?" Ty asked.

"Yes." JP nodded sagely. It was one of Celine's favorite purse brands.

Dean shrugged. "I like their wallets."

"So does my dad," Arden replied. "The card say *"For Buttons. Please stop being a fashion disaster. Love Isa."* She shot me a sympathetic look as she undid the ribbons. "I have a sibling like that."

I still had no idea what Isa meant. Because even to class, I was mostly wearing all the cute stuff Valya got me.

"Shit." Arden took the small, dark purple bag out of the tissue paper. "If you don't want it, you can sell this easy peasy. Haven't seen one like this."

"Why do I need a fancy purse?" I eyed the leather purse. It was pretty, but...

JP grinned. "You need a fancy purse to keep up with the MA-SOs."

I took the tissue paper pillow out of the box and threw it at him. Most of the MASOs carried really expensive bags.

"Oh. It's a mini *Gwen*." Arden handed me the booklet. "That must be why she chose it."

Dean laughed. "It's a bucket bag. They make a Gwen purse that's a bucket bag."

"It is funny." I picked up the purse and admired it. The detailing was exquisite, down to the gold hardware and the drawstring. It wasn't a large bag, but looked like it could hold a good amount.

The others left and Coach Kirov handed me back my phone. "Gwen, keep your head in the game."

"Sorry, Coach." My head bowed. "I didn't know they were sending things. I didn't know they even knew where I worked."

"You were distracted before the treats came. When you're here, all that matters is the game. Not the fight you had with someone, or the test you bombed, or everything you need to do. Everything gets left at the door," she told me.

I knew this and gulped as I gathered my things. "Yes, Coach."

Coach Dodd was outside, admiring the flowers. "We can find a place to keep them until you can take them home. You've got class soon, right?"

"They were my mom's favorite," I said softly. "I... I can't stand the smell. It's too much. Sof was trying to be nice, but I..." Staring at them made me want to cry. "Would your mate like them?"

"She'd love them. Are you sure?" he asked. His omega had beat the same cancer my mom had, and we talked about it sometimes. I'd met her, and she was really sweet.

"Please. I want them to make someone happy." Things in hand, I headed off to find Clark. I walked through the door of the large workout room.

Clark put down his weights and came over to me. Tenzin didn't seem to be there. Pity.

"What's wrong?" Clark wrapped his arms around me.

"My sister thinks I'm a fashion disaster and sent me a purse. My dads and siblings have no boundaries." I buried my head in his chest, trying to hold the box and him.

We went outside the weight room and for a moment I just let him hold me.

"You heard from your dads?" Clark said.

"Worse, they sent me presents. Three of my siblings sent presents *here*. They think they can buy my love back," I sobbed. "Where have they been for six years? Where were they when I didn't have enough food? Where were they when I was living in a closet? Not that I want their money, but where were they?"

Where were they when I was being chased by a spoiled alpha?

I looked up at him through tear-stained eyes. "The shitty thing is two of those three presents were thoughtful. I didn't ask them to–and it's not my birthday."

Clark frowned. "Your birthday's in February."

I gulped. "Gwen Di Rossi's birthday is in February."

"Oh, *her* birthday is today. And your family decided this would be a good day to contact you after six years? That's a lot. What do you need?" Clark rubbed my back.

"This. That's what happens when I let them in an inch." I sniffed. "I'm afraid of what the dads sent to the apartment. Oh, and *fuck.*"

I'd forgotten about the email.

"Um, I asked Lenny to find Austin. I have suspicions." I opened my email on my phone.

Clark sucked in a breath. "You're ready for that? That's a big step and I'm proud of you. I'm right here."

There it was. Fuck.

Soundlessly, I handed the phone to Clark.

"That asshole. Go work for his family? They own a fucking hockey team, not a bean farm." Clark gave me back my phone. "Are you okay?"

"Not really. But I needed to know before the game, so I can face it better." Anger bubbled up inside me.

Clark wiped the tears off my face. "I'll throw him into the boards for you."

"You will?" That made the violent, petty part of me very happy.

"So hard. Maybe more than once." He grinned, looking blood-thirsty.

Nia came out of the weight room and picked up the box, which had fallen during our hug fest. "Please tell me you didn't take Atty's message about appropriate attire for the game too seriously? That wasn't for you."

For some reason, I'd been added to the MASO chat—and muted it. While they were a friendly bunch, I didn't have time for that.

"Faun makes a bucket bag called the Gwen. My sister thinks she's hilarious." I rolled my eyes. I took it out of the box to show her. It was very cute though, and she'd remembered that I like purple now, not pink.

It also made me a little sad—I missed Tenzin so much.

"That is funny. Also cute." Nia left, and I sent Isa a picture of me, the purse and Clark.

Me

I'm not a fashion disaster.

I was wearing *designer* leggings with my *puck off* crop-top.

Isa

You are and I love you.

Your boy is cute.

"Isa thinks you're cute," I told him, giving him a brownie. "It wasn't my idea to change my birthday."

Clark rubbed my shoulders. "It makes sense to do that. If you need to ditch class or practice for your mental health, do it."

"I'll be okay. I'm just not sure if I'm being a whiny ungrateful bitch or not." My eyes closed as Clark got the back of my neck.

My head still hurt.

"You're not," he assured.

"Is Tens around still? I got a brownie for him, too." I'd like to see him, too.

"I don't know. Do you want to text him?" Clark asked me.

I shook my head. "It's fine. He's so busy, and I don't want to bother him with my silly problems."

"Your problems aren't silly. But yeah, he's so busy and preoccupied. He's been sort of sad. Maybe he misses his old team? Or he's having complicated feelings about playing for the team he lost to?" His brow furrowed.

"Maybe?" The alarm on my phone rang. "Ugh, I have to go. I have a test."

Clark leaned in and gave me a kiss. "See you later? You don't have to come if you don't want to."

"I'll pop in for family skate, though I don't have much time between class and practice." Since tomorrow was the home opener, the Knights had a family skate today. I loved family skate, because it was a chance to see the players' and coaches' families.

Would Tens be there? It was optional. Should I text him about that?

No. I didn't want to come across as too clingy. He clearly still needed space, and it was only right to give it to him.

Hopefully, he'd come.

"Good luck on your test—do you need me to take you?" he offered.

"It's fine. Tonight we'll open my dad's presents together?" I was a little worried.

He hugged me tight. "Of course."

"Thanks."

I would deal with it all later, because it was time to take a test.

"Anyone home?" I called when I walked into the apartment. I wasn't sure if Clark was back yet. Something smelled *good* though.

Snowball gazed at me from her cat tree, but didn't move.

"What. The. Fuck." I put my stuff down and stared at the *giant* box on the coffee table.

"I got your packages from the desk." Clark stood in the kitchen, stirring something.

"Are you making dinner?" My heart burst with happiness. It made up for Tenzin not showing up at family skate. I should have asked him if he was coming before getting my hopes up.

Clark beamed at me from the kitchen. "I am. You got a delivery on the counter. It's been hard not to open it."

On the counter was a box from a very fancy local cupcake bakery. I opened the card. *Happy Birthday, Zia G, love Giulia, Davey, the twins, and Baby G.*

Awww. Matty said he gave the kids my address.

I opened the box. Inside were a dozen *beautiful* hockey-themed cupcakes. They had little sticks, pucks, and helmets on them. One of which had a little sign that said *happy birthday.* Picking it up, I sent Giulia a selfie of me and the cupcake along with my thanks.

"Those are so cute. They'll make a great dessert. Well, if I can have one." Clark came up beside me and kissed my neck. He wore a hockey-themed apron. *Adorable.*

"Eat as many as you want." I leaned over and kissed him. "Do I have time to open them now? Do I even want to?"

"We can open them now. One's from Matty." He covered the pots and turned down the heat.

Grabbing some scissors, I went over to the table and grabbed the small box that said it was from Matty. Inside, packed in a bunch of paper shreds, was a delicate necklace. *This was Mom's,* the note said.

It was a cornicello, a horn meant to ward off evil. I'd gotten one once. I didn't know Mom had one, and it was much daintier than I ever saw her wear. It also looked old. There was also a gift card to the bookstore. Nice.

I texted him thanks as Snowball chased the paper shreds around. Taking a picture, I sent that, too.

Sighing, I stared at the box from my dads and opened it. *Happy Birthday, Buttons. Here's to another winning season,* the card said. All four of them had signed it.

What? Tossing out some paper, which Snowball attacked, I pulled out a box.

Inside was a sparkly goalie mask done in all different shades of pink. Little hot pink ladybugs with rhinestone ladybug trails decorated it.

"Wow," I breathed. "They've never gotten me hockey gear before. It was Mom or Nonna or someone. Pink isn't my color anymore, but it's pretty." I used to wear pink all the time, not only since it once had been my favorite, but for my mom.

"They know we call you *Ladybug*," he said as he traced the ladybugs with his finger.

I found the next box, which was from a very fancy ice skate brand that only did custom skates. Inside were hot pink, quilted goalie skates, complete with fur trim and rhinestones.

"Fourteen-year-old me is squealing. I didn't know Cordelle made goalie skates. Sometimes I'd get their figure skates to match my different competition outfits." I held them up.

"They're adorable," Clark agreed as he inspected them. "And very well made."

"What else is inside?" I pulled out another box. "Viper?" They were one of Bowman's boutique brands and a lot of their work was custom. I withdrew the hot pink, sparkly goalie catching glove and blocker that matched the skates and mask perfectly.

My eyes teared. Why couldn't they have done shit like this when I was a teenager?

Clark wrapped me in a hug. "Clearly, they're trying. Even if they don't know your favorite color is purple. It'll look striking on the ice."

"I'd be a big sparkly target for the other team," I laughed. I wasn't sure if and when I'd wear all this. I wore my team colors for NYIT games.

"There is more." Clark tossed another piece of packing paper out.

Snowball crouched as if hunting, peering at the paper. She pounced, attacking it, and batting it around.

I took a video. "You're such a good hunter, Snowball. You get that paper."

"Gweny. Look." Clark pulled out something large and hot pink, wrapped in plastic. They were sparkly and had the Viper logo, which was a snake wrapped around a hockey stick, on it.

"Matching goalie pads?" Tears streamed my eyes as I opened the plastic. "From Viper? Shit."

Wow. Goalie pads on top of all this? They looked like they'd fit me, too. I'd make my own alterations. Oh, they had rhinestones on them, too.

My chest shook, and I sobbed. Color aside, this was an expensive, thoughtful, useful gift. I tried everything on.

"You look cute. You should wear this," Clark told me.

Maybe I would. Or at least parts of it? It would be nice to have quality backups. Obviously, if they ever watched me play, I'd wear it. I wasn't sure how good the goalie skates were.

I took a picture of the gear and texted Matty.

Me

Please tell them thank you for me.

They should be thanked, but texting them meant they might text me back. I wasn't ready for that.

Matty

Happy you like it. Everything fits?

Me

Yes. Everything is cute. Very pink, but cute.

A timer buzzed.

"Dinner's ready." Clark picked up the paper and put it in the box.

I finished cleaning up as he took something out of the oven, with the hockey potholders that had been with the slow-cooker.

Snowball climbed into the box. I sent the videos and pictures to Matty.

Me

Snowball likes the paper and boxes.

"I'll set the table." I placed our dishes and silverware on the table as Clark finished getting everything ready.

Clark brought over a steaming hot meatloaf. A fucking meatloaf. My mouth watered. I don't think I'd had meatloaf since high school.

He added a bowl of mashed potatoes, some gravy, and green beans.

Yeah, I was keeping him.

"Sorry, I forgot to buy rolls," he said as we sat down and we served ourselves.

"More room for cupcakes." I took a bite, savoring the savory, meaty goodness. "Amazing. Ma's recipe?"

"Yes. I figured after having an emotional day, with your family stomping all over your boundaries, you'd like some comfort food." He took a bite of mashed potatoes and gravy.

That man.

"Thank you." Oooh, did the green beans have *bacon* in them?

We finished our dinner, and since he cooked, I did the dishes.

"You can have a cupcake. I'll have one in a moment," I told him as I loaded the dishwasher.

Clark hopped up on the counter next to the box. He got one and took a bite.

His eyes closed and the look on his face made me want to do something to cause him that much bliss.

Throwing a detergent pod in, I started the dishwasher.

"Are they that good?" I teased as I stood in front of him as he sat on the counter.

A bit of white frosting was on his lip. Leaning in, I licked it off. It was good frosting, not too sweet.

"Mmmm, more, please." Clark pulled me to him. He kissed me long and deep. Then he took another bite, getting frosting *all* over his face.

"So messy." I kissed the frosting off his face. Grabbing one, I took a bite. Oh, these were good. I looked at him in time to see that look on his face again.

Hmmm.

I unzipped his pants.

"Sweetness, what are you doing?" Clark gave me a smoldering look as his scent grew sweet with arousal.

"I want you to look at me the way you look at the cupcake." I took his cock out and felt it harden in my hand. Taking my cupcake, I smeared some of the frosting on his dick. "Whoops. I'm going to have to clean that up."

Getting down on my knees on the kitchen tile, I swirled my tongue around the frosting on his cock.

"Gwen." He sucked in a breath and made a cute face.

Not the face I wanted. Why I was jealous of a cupcake, I didn't know. But it had been one hell of a day.

I traced the tip and shaft with my tongue, trying to get all the frosting. Every once in a while, I glanced up at him.

Nope. Not quite.

"That feels so good, Gweny," he sighed, tangling one hand in my hair. Not in a controlling way, more as if grounding him.

The tip of my tongue teased his piercing, taunting the little balls and my hand reached up for some larger ones, caressing their undersides softly. Before my eyes, I watched his knot inflate.

"What a good alpha you are for me," I murmured, running a finger over his knot.

"I'll always be good," Clark gasped as I took him into my mouth. "Fuuuck."

Oh, there was that look. Satisfied I could please him as much as a cupcake, I bobbed up and down his hard length, sucking and teasing it.

"I'm going to come. There's a towel on the counter if you don't want to swallow," he gasped.

No. I planned on sucking all his cum down. Maybe he'd even call me a *good girl.* Why did I like it so much when he said that?

The salty cum, which tasted a little of his hay and sunshine, shot down into my throat and I swallowed, his hand entangling in mine. For a moment I laid my head on his thigh.

"Wow, you sucked down my cum so well, like the good girl you are," he murmured as he stroked my hair.

Getting up off the floor, I leaned into his arms.

"Here, you didn't finish your cupcake." Clark held me to him and fed me bites of it.

That made it a lot better.

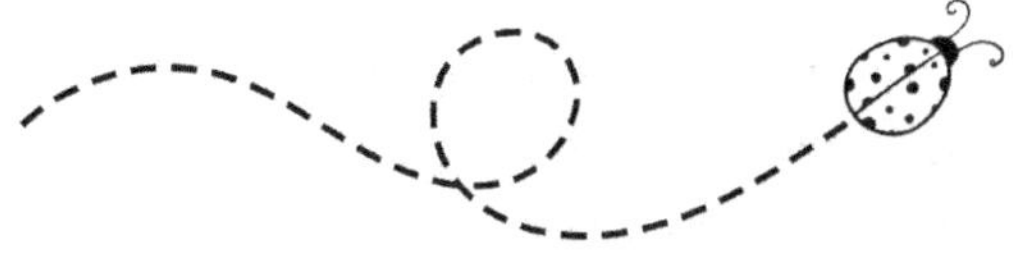

Chapter Sixty-Four

CLARK

The alarm beeped, and I rolled over to shut it off, then popped up out of bed. Snowball gave me the stink eye, watching me from the other pillow.

"Sorry, I have to get to the game," I told her as I went out into the kitchen and made a protein smoothie, then shook myself awake from my pre-game nap with my usual stretches. Today was our home opener.

Coach Atkins had gotten us pumped and ready this morning at our team meeting and morning skate, finalizing the roster. While Anders, JP, and a few others had gone out for sushi, I'd taken a nap, so I could be in top form for tonight.

Fuck. Austin Blake was Bronson Deloitte. We were playing that jerkface and his whole asshole family tonight. Number 16 would pay for what he did to Gwen.

Finishing my smoothie, I made sure Snowball had lots of food and water. I got out a new toy for her from the bag of *widdle treats* Gwen had gotten and put in the cupboard, then hopped in the shower. After, I put in my contacts, making sure I had my glasses for later. Then I dressed in a pinstripe suit and the cute tie Gwen had given me this morning.

Grabbing a cupcake from the box on the counter, I took a bite, letting the chocolaty goodness explode over my tongue. Cupcakes were just muffins with frosting. It also made me remember the blowjob she'd given me in the kitchen last night.

Fuuuuck.

I might have had her good last night. Okay, I was making love to her every night to help keep the nightmares away.

As I left our apartment, I glanced at Tenzin's door. Given Gwen wanted to ride on the back of my motorcycle after the game, it wasn't like we'd carpool. Our social media guy had texted me to let him know when I was on my way. He wanted to get a shot of me pulling into the garage on my motorcycle for our channel. So I texted him and Gwen.

When I pulled into the garage, he was ready and waiting and got a nice shot of me pulling into a space, and taking off my helmet.

"That was great," he told me.

I grabbed my helmet–and Gwen's.

Fans were already gathered at the arena as I headed to the player's area. I got waves and cheers as I made my way to the players' area and one of the social media interns was there, catching everything for our channel.

"It's your first home game of the season. How do you feel?" she asked me, holding up her phone.

I smiled, imagining slamming Austin into the boards. "We're going to crush this."

As always, I was one of the last to leave the ice during pre-game warm-ups in the arena, given I liked to take my time. Like I'd taken my time doing my off-ice warm-ups, wrapping my stick after our pre-game meeting, and eating dinner with the team.

On game day I didn't want to rush, I might miss something.

Since this was the home opener, Castle, being a rookie, had been forced out without her helmet, to do her rookie lap at warmup. It was tradition, even though we'd made her do it last season when she'd been brought up when someone was out with an injury. I'd done it, and one day Gwen would do it, too.

The Gears had made Bronson and another player do it, as well. They were warming up on the other side of the ice, several of them skating around and being showoffs.

While some players were serious and locked-in during warmups, Dean and Grif were being goofy with each other, smacking each other on the ass with their sticks. My heart squeezed a little. I wanted Tenzin to chase me around the rink after I'd play-smacked his ass with my stick.

Carlos was trying to put pucks down people's pants. Silas stacked pucks carefully—which Carlos would knock over on his way off the ice. He always had to be last going in.

I grabbed a puck, because sometimes the kids asked for them. Gwen wasn't here yet. She had practice tonight and would rush over from campus. I took a quick survey of the signs and saw a kid with candy bars taped to hers, asking to trade candy for a puck. While she didn't have chocolate buttons, she had Gwen's other favorite.

Skating over, I held up the puck. Her eyes lit up and I chose a candy bar. She tossed it over the glass and I caught it. I threw her the puck. "Thanks."

As I skated off, a body in a grey and maroon jersey slammed into me. He knocked me to the ground. For a moment all I saw were skates. Custom maroon skates with gray stitching. I sucked in a breath.

No. It couldn't be. He'd been wearing black skates in the videos I'd watched.

Did he actually have the balls? I peeled myself off the ice, and standing there was number 16, helmet on.

He did. Anger swirled inside me. How dare he?

"How do you like my sloppy seconds, Wonder Boy?" he sneered, ramming me with his body, trying to knock me down again. "But then, she always did want your dick."

"You abusive asshole." I stood firm, then pushed him back. I was a little bigger. "Do you know what you put her through?"

"You know nothing, you hick," he snapped, shoving me.

"Try me, Toilette." I pushed him again. Hard.

One of his brothers pulled him away as Jonas did the same to me.

"You'll pay for what you did to her, you monster," I growled.

Jonas was pushing me toward the tunnel. "Off the ice, Clark."

We stumbled into the locker room. Most of the players had stripped down a bit. Music was playing, getting everyone pumped for our home opener.

I wasn't pumped. I was *fuming.* How dare he?

"Here, you dropped this." Carlos handed me the candy bar.

Coach Atkins stormed over to me. "What was that? Fighting during warm-ups? I know this is the Gears, but really? I don't care what he said to you."

Something in me snapped. "He's wearing the skates. That dick-head had the *audacity* to wear the skates he put her in the fucking hospital with, the ones she worked overtime to buy him. He also called her *sloppy seconds*. How dare he? That fucking asshole."

"You said he'd pay." Jonas looked confused. "That's their new nepo baby, right? Toilette or something? Who'd he put in the hospital?"

"Gwen. He's Gwen's ex. The one that disappeared before the police could go after him for hurting her. The one that broke up with her when he didn't get a PHL contract on his own, so he had to leave and go work for his dad. Well, that dad is fucking Coach Deloitte, and the reason no one's ever heard of Bronson Deloitte is that for years he went by Austin Blake," I spat, so angry I could barely talk. "She sacrificed so much for him. Fucking knotwaffle. What sort of psycho wears the skates he put her in the hospital with?"

"Knotwaffle?" Coach blinked.

"That's a Gwen word," Jonas replied. "Yeah, that's a dick move."

Dimitri's head popped up from the book he'd been reading. "Are you saying her ex *is* Bronson Deloitte?"

"Yeah. She found out yesterday. As in, she has proof." I felt like I needed to add that.

"You were right." Carlos punched his locker, his scent going spicy with anger. "Shit."

"That's why Ty kept saying that Bronson Deloitte's style looked familiar. They played together for years," Dean added.

Nia scowled, shaking her head. "Asshole."

"Yesterday? Well, that explains a lot," Coach Kirov said softly. "I still don't understand the birthday thing."

"What do you mean, Ladybug's ex *put her in the hospital?*" Pauley looked startled. "I thought they just broke up."

"She was bleeding in my arms. Carlos and Dimitri were at the hospital with us." Suddenly, I was back to that awful night. I was in the shower and missed her call. When she hadn't answered, I'd rushed to the rink, only to find her lying on the ice, bloody.

The day I died a little. Until her love revived me.

Nakey frowned. The forward had a sister her age. "Wait, that guy she was going to marry, *hurt* her with the skates she bought for him? I remember her picking up all those extra shifts at Tito's to get the skates."

"Dude, what? Austin's not a Deloitte. He's not an asshole like that," Mitchy replied with a roll of his eyes.

"Shut up, Mitchy." Castle threw a towel at him.

Dimitri gave everyone the short version.

"Breathe," Tenzin said softly, standing close to me.

I took a deep breath, getting wisps of him along with a whole lot of locker room. "I'm going to fuck him up."

"The scar on her head. He did that." JP stood. He didn't look good.

"She's not on duty tonight, is she?" Jonas asked me.

"Ty's on duty. She's coming to the game. If she was on duty, she'd be a fucking professional though." I poured one of my hydrogels in my mouth and put the candy bar away.

Jonas nodded. "And whack him with her stick like she did Windy."

"Ooh, I'm going to be sick again." JP ran off to the bathroom.

"I told you not to eat that," Anders called after him. He looked at me. "I'm going to beat Austin's ass. No one messes with ours."

"Do what you all need to do. Don't get badly injured. I don't want to see *any* multi-game suspensions. We need to *win*, understood?" Coach Atkins barked.

"Yes, Coach. That's a rousing speech." A woman wearing a vintage black and silver Knights Jersey with a 0 on it, a man whose vintage jersey said 7, and a person wearing slacks with a nice turtleneck sweater, came into the locker room.

While no one was naked this close to the game, a few people looked startled. Okay, Nakey was nearly naked. But he enjoyed being naked, which was why he was called *Nakey*.

The woman laughed. "Believe me, between playing and coaching, I've seen it all. My current team is a bunch of nudies. Also, my father was the equipment manager for this team back in the day."

Gray streaked her black, wavy hair. The others were the same age. The man in the jersey also had dark wavy hair and a similar olive complexion, the other had near white hair.

"Mia. Gio. Vail. Welcome." Coach Atkins grinned. "Mia, if I'd known all it took was inviting you to drop the puck, to get you to one of my games, I would've done so long ago."

Usually someone famous or a former player came and did a ceremonial puck drop for the first home game of the season for each team.

Mia chuckled. "I'm so sorry we didn't pick a closer team to coach."

"This is Maria Barilla-Russo, former Knights goalie and Giovanni Russo, former Knights defenseman. Both of them coach for the Venice team in Italy. This is their mate, Vail Russo," Coach Atkins told everyone. "Maria and Gio will be honored later this season. We go way back."

Maria Barilla? As in Gwen's favorite player?

Dean stood there, mouth gaping.

JP rejoined us from the bathroom and sucked in a breath, staring. "Merde."

One of the guys with her chuckled. "You have a fan club."

"Thank you," JP finally said, looking star-struck. "Thank you for everything you've done for hockey."

"Absolutely," Dean added, expression full of awe. "If you hadn't laid the groundwork, omegas never would have had a chance in the PHL."

"It's always nice to meet fellow goalies." Maria smiled and looked up at them. "My, what big boys you are. Goalies are giants now."

A couple of defenders were talking to Gio.

"Thank you for defending me after I was outed," Dean added in earnest. "You telling them I had a place on the ice meant everything. Same when you defended my mate."

"What happened to you was shitty. You're a great player. All I did was remind them of that. Same with Grif," she assured him.

"Are you staying for the game? You're my girlfriend's favorite. Your card is on our wall, right between my two most important comics. She'd love to meet you. She's a goalie for her university," I blurted. We'd gotten frames for some of her cards.

"Does Gwen know you're calling her your girlfriend?" Anders smacked me on the ass.

Nia laughed. "He signed her up for a MASO pass, so I hope so."

"Gwen's one of our EBUGs." Constantine joined them. "Solid goalie who's going places. I'm pretty sure she made the noodle necklace hanging from your picture at the training center."

Vail chuckled, arm around Mia. "I love how you've become the patron saint of EBUGs. Do they sacrifice a lasagna like the ones in Boston? Oh, there are the ones who make boats of spaghetti, set them on fire, and float them down the river."

"It involves homemade sauce and wine, I think?" I blinked. "Um, I don't get to know goalie secrets."

"It does," Dean replied. "Sauce, wine, and noodle necklaces."

"You're Vail Russo, the skating coach," Tenzin breathed, standing next to me.

"Yes." Vail nodded.

Where did I know that name?

Tenzin turned to me. "Gwen's figure skating coach. The one she trained with, so she could play hockey with his mates, the retired PHL players."

I sucked in a breath. Oh! "The ones that lived next to her non-na."

Oh shit. That was before she was Gwen. Did they even know her new name? She might not have had contact with them in years. That must have hurt so much.

"That makes so much sense, why she plays the way she does," Dean breathed.

Maria put her hand to her heart. "I haven't seen her in a while, but she holds a very special place in our family."

Okay, they knew. Whew.

"I'm sure you know all the good stories." I wanted to hear about tiny Gwen and all the animals she found. Did she bring them to the rink?

"You have no idea." Maria laughed. "She's why we have four cats and a turtle."

"Double D, JP, you two will be doing the ceremonial puck drop, as will the Gears' goalies." Coach eyed JP. "If you're well enough?"

JP nodded. "I'll try." He gave Maria a look. "Not contagious. Just tried some sushi I shouldn't have."

I checked my phone and took a swig of vitamin water. Gwen had texted that practice went long, and she was running late. Hopefully, she wouldn't miss puck drop. She'd want to see this.

Dean had everyone kiss his stuffed rabbit. Grif had won it for him before a game back when they were in high school. It had become lucky. Everyone kissed the rabbit. Not just because he was the goalie, but because his superstition allowed for it to be *washed*.

Unlike Pauley's socks, which were only washed when we lost, to wash away the bad luck. Grif was getting people to pet Lucky. I didn't really understand the whole imaginary cat thing, but it made people happy, so why not?

"When did Gwen find out who Austin was?" Tenzin growled, cornering me. His jersey was still off, so were his pads, and he wasn't wearing any sort of undershirt.

"Yesterday." I tightened my skates, trying not to look at all that bare Yeti chest on display, and his tattoos. *How did they taste?*

He frowned. "She didn't tell me."

"Why would she?" All my frustration exploded out of me. "She's so afraid of bothering you, that she couldn't bring herself to text you yesterday, when she was having a massively shitty day. You didn't even come to family skate. I get it, you're busy, but all she wanted was to hold your hand and skate around. Gwen was so sad that even the Maimers dressed in inflatable costumes didn't cheer her up. She misses you. I miss you," I yelled at him, well aware people were listening in as all my frustration poured out.

Tenzin recoiled like he'd been slapped. "I've been right here the whole time. I text you both every day. Yes, I haven't been able to take her on dates, but things have been hectic. I'm right there across the hall."

"Are you really that dense? You might as well be across the ocean for how emotionally unavailable you've been. We're trying to be respectful of your need for space, but it's hurting her." Hurting us. Glaring, I checked the tape on my stick.

Hurt wafted off Tenzin. He still stood there half-naked. Unmoving.

"She thinks it's her," I hissed, voice low. "That given everything she shared with you, you're taking so long because you're deciding if you want to be with someone like her."

"What? No." His look grew horrified. "That's not it at all. There's a lot to put in order with the season starting. Partially why it's taking so long is that I've been tracking down experts, so that I could care for her properly. I want to be with both of you. She thinks that? No wonder she's withdrawn so much. I figured it was the stress of class, work, and practice. Fuck."

The look on his face tore at me. But he *had* hurt her. She'd been near tears when he hadn't shown up at family skate yesterday.

"Experts?" I frowned. All Gwen needed was love, cuddles, and understanding.

Okay, and tacos.

"Yes. There's some big family things happening that I need to wrap my head around pretty quickly, which has taken priority. I'm so sorry you both feel this way. It was never my intention. She didn't text me about her bad day, because she didn't want to bother me?" He rubbed his forehead, scent anxious. "I... I didn't go to family skate since I thought she had class, so I was meeting with my therapist."

"Oh. Still, you need to talk to us and communicate. We thought it would be like it was before the wedding, and instead it's been so much less. We miss you. Is it that hard to come over and watch a fucking movie?" I pushed, still feeling anger.

Not at him, more at Austin, but he was right there.

Tenzin flinched. "I didn't realize that I wasn't doing a good job of communicating. Because I made a point of talking to both of you."

"You made her sad. Do you even still plan on going to the dinner with us? Gwen's spent weeks getting her dress altered and finding shoes, and is all excited to go with us." My arms crossed over my chest.

His look went bewildered. "Of course I am. I even got a new tux, since I can't find mine."

"Bucket, put some clothes on," Coach shouted. "Lover's spat can wait."

"Sorry, Coach." Tenzin turned back to me. "We'll talk after the game. I never meant to hurt anyone." He threw on his pads and jersey, and it looked like he took a moment to send a text.

Just because he never meant to hurt us didn't negate the fact that he *had*. I understood that family things may have derailed everything, but couldn't he have talked to us?

Taking a deep breath, I touched the tiny Captain Everything plushie keychain I kept in my bag.

"Hey, pet Lucky, you'll feel better." Grif offered me a handful of air.

I pretended to pet the non-existent cat. "Thanks."

Yeah, that didn't help. But I wasn't going to tell him that.

"It's game time," Coach yelled. "Let's kick some Gear ass."

Now that... that would help.

"Ladybug's watching. Let's show her we give a shit," Nia added.

"Keep your head in the game," Jonas told me as we left the locker room. "If that's her ex, I'm sure he and his brothers are going to come for us. Work it out with Bucket later."

"Thanks." I nodded. Them come for us? No, I was going to come for *them*.

"We'll get them good and make Mariquita proud," Carlos told me as he slung an arm around my shoulder.

"He's 16?" Tenzin said as we entered the tunnel, that would take us to the arena.

I nodded. "She's here, so feel free to harass Austin and show her you care."

"Okay. I can't believe he wore the skates. Ugh. I'm sure it was on purpose. I'll slam him good for her. Maybe twice. Possibly break his nose." Tenzin punched one gloved hand with another.

The venom in his voice made me smile. He did care about her.

That was a hockey *I Love You* if there ever was one.

I think I'd send her one, too.

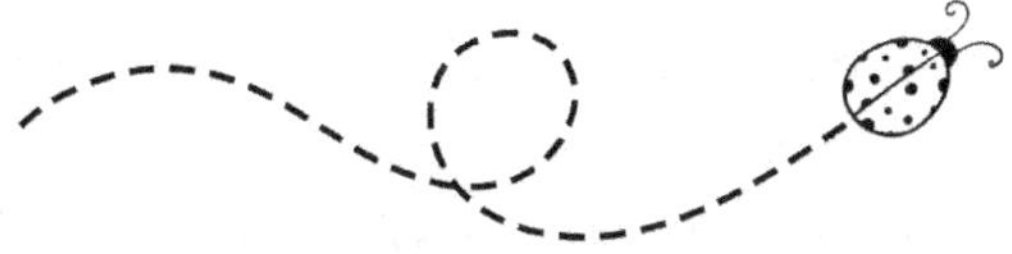

Chapter Sixty-Five

GWEN

"Again," Coach Hirata yelled, as the entire team did sprints, or 'buggies' as my team called them, across the ice.

Practice should have ended by now and the skate smash team was pissed at us, as they did skate drills on the other end of the rink.

"Fuck." A firstie ran over to the bucket the assistant coach had put out and puked in it.

My stomach threatened to rebel and my feet hurt. Fucking firsties. Coach had warned us that skipping out on cardio, conditioning, and strength training would merit punishment.

"Back in line," Coach yelled. "Keep going."

Taking a deep breath, I went again. This wasn't the day to wear my new skates–though they were more comfortable than I'd expected.

Also, better than I'd expected. They handled almost as well as the ones Tenzin got me.

I'd spent last night making some alterations and breaking everything in. This morning, I'd used the sharpener at work, and gotten the skate blades the way I liked them.

Here I thought it would be *hilarious* to wear it all to practice tonight and try everything out.

There was no clock, and I didn't wear a watch, so I didn't know how close we were to the Knights' puck-drop. I'd definitely missed watching warm-ups. Possibly dinner in the family room too.

Coach was fully aware that the Knights' home opener was tonight and that most of the team planned on heading to Marabou Mike's to watch it.

Finally, she let us go.

"Dinner's cold, but that's what you get," she snapped. "Now get out of here. Next time you better listen to me or it'll be worse."

"Worse?" Giggles looked like she was about to puke.

"Yeah, it can get worse." Bonnie gulped as we headed to the locker room.

Shit, I stunk. I should wash my hair, but there wasn't time. However, I did soap myself down twice in the shower. Shoving my practice clothes in a grocery sack, I tied it, so it didn't make everything else smell. Then I threw on my Knights' EBUG PJ pants and hoodie, and slipped my feet into the cloud-soft slides I'd stolen from Clark.

At least I had no blisters.

"Are you going to eat or go straight to the bar?" Bonnie still looked green.

"I have a ticket to the game." There was a super cute outfit waiting for me on my bed, along with my bucket bag.

I grabbed a couple of recovery drinks and some hydrogels on my way out, my bag full of my new hockey gear and my backpack over my shoulder. As I jogged to the subway stop, I checked the time. Shit.

The Maimers were doing a promo before the game to promote their season and I wanted to see it. This morning Constantine had told me who was doing the opening game ceremonial puck drop and sworn me to secrecy.

Yeah, I didn't want to miss that.

Did I go home and change, risk missing everything or head directly to the game as-is? The problem was that I had all my stuff with me and it would burn time to take it back to the locker room.

I'd go straight there and deal with that when I got to the arena, glad I always kept all my credentials with me. On the subway, I focused on not puking and getting the recovery drink down.

I entered through the back of the arena, like I did when I was an EBUG, flashing my EBUG pass. Usually, I stored my things in the equipment office, which was attached to the locker room.

This close to the game, I didn't want to bother anyone. Were there public lockers? It was almost time; I didn't even have time to go to the family room and get food.

Oh! The family room.

I kept running, since it was close to the locker rooms. There were cubbies for the MASOs to store diaper bags, strollers, and coats. I'd drop everything there.

At the door, I flashed my shiny new family room pass and stumbled inside. A bunch of the MASOs were still there, finishing dinner and drinking wine. A couple of little kids played hockey with mini sticks.

"Um, I think you're in the wrong room?" A MASO said, a baby in her arms. I'd seen her around. I think she was Vickers' wife.

"I have a pass?" My voice was a squeak. Maybe I should have worn what I'd worn to class, not that jeans, a cute sweater, and ballet flats, compared to most of their outfits.

Everyone was dressed perfectly, even the ones wearing black and silver Knight's jerseys with their players' names and numbers on them.

"Hi, Ladybug. Running late?" Atty laughed, looking dapper, as always, in slacks and a blazer, shoes expensive and shiny.

"Coach held us for punishment drills. Puck hasn't dropped yet, has it?" I looked for the cubbies. There they were.

"Not yet. The Maimers are about to go up," Atty told me. His dark curly hair was impeccably done, his blazer and slacks perfect. He was a little shorter than me.

The cubbies were too small, so I half tossed it on top. I'd keep my backpack with me.

"That is quite the fashion statement," Patrice smirked, sipping her wine, manicured nails tapping on the glass. "You're not on duty, right? If you are, you're cutting it close."

She was Pauley and Nakey's omega and that mom who could make a ratty T-shirt look glamorous. Tonight she wore a silver and black dress which showed off her mating bites. She was helping Atty with MASO stuff since Verity was too busy with her PhD program and work.

"Nope. Ty's on duty. So I can drink. Why did I never know about these shoes? Clark isn't getting these back." I wasn't feeling as nauseous now. Grabbing a water I chugged it, then I grabbed a beer from the small bar and chugged that.

"They're so big, make him get you your own pair," she laughed.

Eh. Between having older brothers and well, my alpha ex, and now my alpha boyfriend, I was used to wearing too-big stuff for funsies.

I put two bottles of fancy vitamin water and a lime soda in my bag, along with some snacks. They never had purple, my favorite color of water.

"Everyone, this is Gwen, otherwise known as Ladybug," Atty replied. "She's a student at NYIT and one of our EBUGs. Wonder Boy is her intrepid sidekick."

"Oh, the one in that underwear commercial where he's running across a roof? Nice. I think he lives in my building." The MASO with the baby grinned.

"That's the one," I nodded. The plates were all ceramic, so I grabbed a plastic beer cup and filled it with chicken pasta. There wasn't much left. Still, it was nice to have access, something I hadn't had previously.

Some of the MASOs would grab me snacks when I was on duty.

"Gwen, you can get more food after puck drop. Your pass works the entire game and they will put out more stuff at intermission," Atty told me.

I filled another with salad and covered both with napkins, grabbed two rolls and a fork, and put them in the cup holders on my backpack.

"Oh, yeah, I could, couldn't I?" I got my beer refilled and looked at the TV, which was broadcasting the ongoings from the arena. "Gotta go."

"We'll see you up there." Patrice waved. "Jackson, you need to eat your food."

Jackson, her son, was much more interested in playing with Atty's twins. Little Tori napped in her stroller.

"Wait." Atty ran over to me with a little gift bag. "Here."

He took a black and silver Knights cap with Clark's fifty-five on it and put it over my gross hair, then shoved the bag at me, which I slid around my wrist.

"Your goody bag. Um, only Clark put you down, so it's only his number." Atty winked. "Maybe it will make Bucket jealous. See you up there. We'll be there soon."

"Um, thanks." I darted to the elevator, trying not to spill my beer and crush my food.

Make Tenzin jealous? Ha! He'd barely noticed me all week. He hadn't even come to family skate yesterday.

I made it to the family section and found my seat right as the Maimers came on and performed one of the dance battle routines. Oh, I was right by Verity and AJ. They were already seated.

Putting my beer in the cupholder, I waved to those I knew. The coaches' packs and kids were all here. Cait gave me an enthusiastic wave and as did Coach Kirov's kids. Coach Dodd was there with his wife too. Often he watched from the press box–he didn't coach on the bench.

I got my cups of food and stuffed my face as I watched. Now that I was no longer nauseous, I was *starving.*

Mercy had taught me this Maimers routine and Tens was going to film it, so I could put it up with all the other dances. Well, he would if he ever found time for me. We'd already rescheduled twice.

Yeah, I knew hockey players had hectic schedules, but it felt personal.

The Maimers were good, but then they had an *amazing* skating coach. Also, their DJ was the best and had made another fire arrangement for them.

Everyone cheered as the Maimers finished their dance, and the announcer talked about their upcoming season. Nat the Knight came on and shot some shirts at the crowd to get them riled up.

"Oh good, you're here." Verity waved at me. "Rough practice?"

"Buggies until the firsties puked." I made a face.

"Shit, I'm sorry." AJ grimaced. He wore Grif Graf's jersey. Verity wore a custom one with Grif, Dean, and Jonas' numbers on it.

"Hey, Clark got in a shoving match with someone from the Gears during warmups. Jonas had to tear him away. Do you know what that's about?" Verity asked, leaning over the back of her seat.

Taking my beer, I gulped half of it. "Number 16?"

"Yes," AJ said.

I drained the rest of the beer. "That's my ex. I have a feeling Clark is going to be spending some time in the sin bin tonight. I just hope he doesn't get hurt."

"Oh. I didn't realize your ex got signed. Are you okay with being here? I'll cover for you if you want to leave," Verity told me.

Aww, how sweet.

Tonight I wasn't feeling sweet though.

"I want to see him smashed against the boards," I snarled as I got out a vitamin water.

The intros started. First came the Gears. I booed every single Deloitte. Seven of them if you counted the coaches.

I also remembered I had a goody bag, and I looked at all the cute stuff with Clark's number on it.

"Verity, why did I get a party favor?" I held up the earrings with 55 on them. There was also a bracelet with *Edwards 55* and a little hockey stick.

"Clark had you added to the MASO group and paid your fee," Verity replied. "We missed you at the welcome tea party. I tried to tell them you had class, but it's what worked for most everyone."

"Oh. Nice. Everything is super cute." Immediately, I put the bracelet on and put the earrings in my ears.

"Yeah, though my earrings are really dangly with three numbers." She laughed and showed me.

"Oh, is that why I'm in the group chat?" I hadn't known that. I hoped the fee wasn't expensive. It covered things like baby, wedding, and mating showers the MASOs threw, and gifts–like the bracelet Janessa got when Elias and Winston retired, with little charms on it, like their numbers and a hockey stick.

And goodie bags, apparently.

"Yes. You'll get invited to *all* the stuff now," she added.

They did lots of fun things, like sip and paint nights, and going to the spa. The MASOs helped each other out–making meals when someone was sick, getting injured players to appointments, and babysitting for each other. Being with a hockey player could get hard. They also did things to help out the rookies and players that didn't have significant others.

The Knights came onto the ice and had their intro, which was full of smoke, lasers, and Nat the Knight, pretending to ride a horse. I cheered hard for everyone as their names were called and they skated out, wishing I had more food–and beer. They announced the lineup and played the national anthem.

"We welcome retired New York Knights, Maria Barilla-Russo and Giovanni Russo to do tonight's ceremonial puck drop," the announcer said, as both teams lined up out of respect.

They said a few things about Mia and Gio and their accomplishments. I wanted to visit them before they returned to Italy, but things had been so busy.

The goalies from both teams came to the center. Usually they had a carpet for those dropping the puck to walk out on, but Maria and Gio skated, wearing their old jerseys. Shoving my now empty beer cups of food under my seat, I stood and cheered, grinning, as my phone started vibrating.

Ty

You think she'll sit in the press box?

Me

If she does, text me.

I could use one of her hugs. There was also a text from Tenzin.

Tenzin

Hey Firecracker, I'm so happy you're in the crowd tonight. I'll look for you. I'll get you a beer at Tito's after the game?

Me

Yes, please. Good luck tonight.

Awww. That was a much more meaningful text than I'd gotten in weeks, and it warmed me that he took a moment before the game to text me.

Mia and Gio dropped the puck. JP, who looked a little unsteady, gave her the puck, which she got to keep. She and Gio left the ice and everyone was cheering.

The opening offensive line was Nia, Pauly, and Anders. That had made Anders a lot happier about staying with the Knights. Though Anders was also an excellent player.

Jonas and Tenzin were on defense. Tenzin looked for me as he skated out. I waved at him, and he waved back.

However, the Deloitte brothers were all in their opening line. Austin wore the skates I bought him.

"The balls on that knotwaffle," I muttered as I rubbed my scar. No wonder Clark got into a fight with him during warmups.

It looked like choice words were said as the puck dropped and things immediately got rough with Anders slamming into 16, as Nia stole the puck and went for the goal, being chased by 17, one of Austin's brothers.

Nia faked a pass to Pauly and got it in the goal between the goalie's legs. The crowd went wild. Anders tripped 16 as the line changed.

The Deloitte brothers weren't called in. The Gears kept their players on the ice a little longer than the Knights. Clark, Grif, and Carlos came out. I braced for it.

3... 2... 1

Grif stole the puck and Clark slammed Austin into the boards, hard. A fight broke out, with players from both teams coming to fight.

The ref and linesman broke it up. Clark and Grif got sent to the penalty box, as did the Deloitte brothers and the Deloitte defenseman.

Clark tapped on the glass in front of the family section as he was escorted to the box and blew me a kiss. I blew one back.

"Aww, he beat him up for you. That's so sweet." AJ grinned at me.

"It really is," I replied as Clark flashed me a heart from the box.

First period was an absolute bloodbath, the refs continually blowing their whistles. As soon as Austin returned to the ice, Tenzin slammed him into the boards. Austin fell to the ground. Nia tripped Austin as he got back up.

The thing was, it wasn't only Clark going after Austin. Or even Tenzin, because I could see Clark telling him.

It was *everyone.*

I sucked in a breath. "They *all* know Austin is Bronson Deloitte."

Not that I minded. If anything, the fact that the entire team was defending me like that was sweet.

AJ nodded. "I'm sure after the warmup fight, Coach asked Clark what he was thinking. Clark, being an honest guy, told them everything."

My phone buzzed.

Constantine

Can you come up to the press box at inter-mission?

Me

The period ended, and I stood. So far, the Gears hadn't scored on us.

"Getting some more beer?" Verity asked.

"I've been summoned to the press box. Get me one if you go down?" Making sure I had my phone and credentials, I left my backpack on my seat and headed over to the press box.

"Hey. You look comfortable," Ty snorted, looking at my PJ pants and hoodie. While he wasn't wearing a suit, he was dressed nicely, per the program rules.

"I came straight from practice. It ran long because firsties are asshats, so I didn't have time to get cute," I replied. Oh well.

Good thing Isa didn't follow hockey, so she couldn't call me a fashion disaster if I ended up online, from one of the fashion reporters that liked to show the player's suits and the MASO's purses. My hair sort of deserved it. At least I had a hat.

"My boyfriend stole both my PJ pants and my hoodie." Ty rolled his eyes.

"I'm sure he looks amazing in them." I grinned.

Ty frowned and looked at me. "It *is* him, right? He always wanted those skates. That's why he plays so familiar?"

"Yeah. It's him." I rubbed the scar on my forehead.

"Huh. It's so weird." His nose scrunched.

"I know. But I don't care. I don't want an explanation. I don't want justice. I've moved on and I'm good," I told him. If Austin was missing a few teeth or had a black eye after the game, I wouldn't be sad.

The door opened and Constantine walked in with a bunch of people.

Ty started happy-dancing. "She's here."

I hung back a little as Constantine introduced Mia, Gio, Vail, Hazel, and Jules to everyone. Hazel and Jules were teachers.

"It's an honor," Ty said. "You're Gwen's favorite." He pushed me forward.

"Hi, Mia, looking good out there." I grinned. "You, too, Gio."

"Buttons." Mia gave me a big hug. "You're so *tall* now."

Yep. I'd only been four-foot-nine when I was fifteen and the doctors didn't think I'd be much over five feet. When I'd had the opportunity to use *normally illegal, unless you had a really good reason,* growth hormones to make myself taller, to change my profile back when I was being hidden, I took the chance.

There was no way I'd make it in the PHL as a five-foot goalie. Now I was the same height as her.

"Long time, no see." Gio hugged me so hard my feet lifted off the floor. He was almost as tall as Grif Graf.

"Maria Barilla is your aunt?" Ty gave me a look. "That answers so many questions."

I laughed. People had thought that before. "I wish. When I was little, my grandparents lived next door to them. She's the reason I'm a goalie and not a figure skater." I looked over at my old skate coach. "Hi, Vail."

"Hi, Buttons." They gave me a side hug. "Next time you're going to put up skating videos, please warn me," he teased.

Right, the Russo pack hadn't known this name, leading Mia to ask my family about me and message me on social media.

"Sorry." I grinned back and went to greet the others, while people talked to Gio and Mia.

"Buttons, I made you cookies, hoping you'd be on duty. Happy Birthday." Hazel, the tiny Russo omega, gave me a hug. She smelled like chocolate and hazelnuts.

"Thank you." I took the container she handed me from her bag. "But, um, my birthday is in February. It's okay. My family decided to start talking to me yesterday and sent me all sorts of nonsense *to my work.*"

"Oh." She looked startled. "I didn't even think of that. I'm sorry."

"It's fine. I will take all the food. Especially your cookies." I hugged the container tight.

Vail looked concerned. "*Start* talking to you? They haven't talked to you since..."

"Pretty much. It's safe now, which is why I answered Mia when she messaged me. I wasn't ignoring you. It's just that I wanted you to be safe." I gulped.

"Understood. Gwen Di Rossi?" Jules grinned. "Really?"

Gwendolyn Ross was the badass main character in my favorite sci-fantasy series I'd loved as a teenager, *Gwendolyn Ross, Intrepid Space Explorer*. The ones Clark had got me at a bookshop by his house to replace what Austin wrecked. The same author wrote the new space romantasy series he'd bought me on our bookstore date.

"I needed to be brave. I wish I had a space whale." That's what happened when you let a teenager pick their own name.

I had zero regrets.

"Her new series is good," I added. I wasn't sure if I'd rather have a space dragon or a space whale. Both maybe?

We talked a little longer and Mia gave me a big hug. "Gio and I have to go back to Italy, but we'll return in a few months. Also, visit the barn *anytime.*"

The barn was Vail's training center on their property. When they bought the old farm next to Nonna's, they'd converted the giant dairy barn into an ice rink and opened a training center.

Ty looked jealous after they left. "You got cookies? And you know her?"

"Knew. Haven't seen them since my grandparents died," I replied softly, opening the container and letting him have one. "I'm going to go back down."

I stowed the cookies in my backpack, not interested in sharing more. Second period kicked off with Grif getting the puck and a fast and furious race for the goal. At one point Tenzin *and* Clark were in the box, both flashing me hearts with their hands.

The Gears' goalie, a Deloitte cousin, got cut by a skate and had to go for stitches, though she'd stopped the puck.

"Shit," I muttered as another goalie took her place, drinking the beer Verity got me. I should stop after this one if I planned on drinking at Tito's later.

Whoops, I still needed to do some reading for class. Fortunately, I'd mastered the ability to study and watch hockey simultaneously.

Ty sent a picture to the EBUG group chat of him sitting in the equipment office half dressed in case he was needed, which was protocol. Yeah, I was so glad that he was on duty. That would be *beyond* awkward.

A few moments later, Clark, fresh out of the naughty box, had the puck. Austin chased him, so he passed it to Grif, the other two Deloittes barreling after him, as the two defensemen covered the goal. There was a giant collision as Grif scored a goal, bringing it to 2-0, Dean's goaltending game strong.

Another fight ensued–Grif, Clark, Austin, and a couple others going in the box, *again.* The announcer made a snarky comment about Clark getting another penalty. While Grif spent plenty of time there, Clark didn't.

The game didn't restart as the linesman was talking to the goalie, who was on the ground. My belly tightened as he was carried off the ice.

Ty

> **Don't hate me if I go in?**

Me

> **Play the shit out of this game.**

I was happy for him. Ty might only play for a few moments, while the goalie got checked out. He could play the entire game.

The ice crew came on and swept the ice, their patterns always so fun to watch.

Finally, the announcer finally spoke. "The Gears' goalie has been injured and taken for care. Since Deloitte is also out, you know what this means..." An alarm sounded through the area. "Did someone call for an EBUG?"

The EBUG song blasted and lights flashed. It was the song *Calling for a Hero,* which had been changed to *Calling for an EBUG.*

The crowd cheered. Everyone loved an EBUG.

"Let's welcome Tyler Yamato, tonight's emergency backup goalie. He's making his PHL debut, filling in as goalie for the Motor City Gears. This is his second year taking part in the New York Knights' goalie development program, and is a starting goalie for UNYC, where he's in his last year and studying graphic arts. The Great Lakes Boaters have also drafted him. Get out there and show us what you can do," the announcer continued. Ty's picture, which had been taken during orientation, flashed up on the screen.

Ty skated out in a grey Gears' jersey, UNYC pads, and a mask in Knights' colors. I stood and cheered. He might be covering for the Gears, but still was one of *mine.*

"If *our* EBUG is covering the Gears, what happens if we need one?" Verity asked as play restarted.

"There's *never* been a game with two EBUGs in play. Present, but not playing. An EBUG in play is rare enough. Theoretically, since I'm here, they might ask me. Coach Kirov and Coach Dodd are also allowed to step in." I took a big gulp of beer. "There's usually at least one goalie on the ice crew."

Coach K

Are you drunk? I'd understand if you were.

Me

Not drunk

Tired. A little thirsty. My feet hurt. But I was a university athlete. Two and a half beers was nothing.

If we needed you, could you go in?

Understand if it's no. I can see if Arden can stand by.

It was procedure.

Put me in, Coach

Dean hadn't let in any goals, and if something happened–which I hoped didn't–we had JP.

Still, I stopped drinking beer, switched to water, and took some painkillers. Fatigue pressed down on me and I wished I'd taken an energy drink.

Things were getting rough again. Number 17 had the puck and barreled across the ice, knocking LeeAnn down. Vickers got in his way. Number 17 passed to 16, who took the shot. I sucked in a breath. Austin had yet to make his first regular season PHL goal, and I didn't want it to be during this game.

Dean caught it and I cheered. Austin said something to Dean, and Vickers smacked him, another fight starting.

The line changed. Grif stole the puck from number 18 and raced across the ice as the Gears chased him *around* the Gears' goal, where Ty valiantly watched for the puck, ready.

Defense came from the other side. Grif looked like he was passing it to Carlos, but instead hit it to Clark, who shot it into the goal.

Clark's body stiffened as his goal music played and I could imagine how guilty he felt scoring on Ty. He might even say *sorry*.

But the Knights *couldn't* go easy on Ty–and Ty knew it.

Spinning in my direction, Clark turned and made a heart with his hands. Oh, the cameras caught that. I made a heart right back. 3-0 and a goal for Clark. What an opening game.

Celine looked upset and held up her phone to let people know she was taking a call. It was probably work calling her out early.

A moment later, a steward in a Knights' polo came over to me with a coffee.

"Thanks." I took the coffee, frowning. It was nice, but why?

My phone buzzed right as Dean tripped one of the Gears, who tried to take him down with him.

Coach K

JP has food poisoning and is being taken to emergency. I need you down here.

Now.

Me

Yes, Coach

AJ's head whipped around and I stood. "What's wrong?"

Oh fuck. But I was a professional, and this was my job. Sometimes you had to work with asshats. It was a part of life and I'd have to suck it up.

The chance of me playing was slim-to-none, anyway, so I pushed those butterflies away.

"JP's sick. I have to go down in case Dean gets hurt. Which I hope he doesn't." I winced as Tenzin got slammed into the boards, then shoved the offending player hard.

I'd lost count of all the firsts, hits, and penalties. It was only the end of the second period.

AJ gave me a hard alpha stare. "You've got this. If you go in, show that fuckhead that *you're* the one who belongs in the PHL, not him."

"Absolutely." This would end like every other time—with me eating snacks in the equipment office. Part of me wanted to whack Austin with my stick. I wasn't going in though. There'd never been a two-EBUG game, and we weren't going to start tonight.

And I was okay with that.

Chapter Sixty-Six

GWEN

"In case you need to tape your stick." Silas came into the family room, where I'd set up, and handed me some hot pink tape. Smirking.

"Thanks." I had momentarily forgotten that I didn't have the gear I usually brought to Knights' games. I didn't even have my ratty practice stuff.

No. I had my brand new hot pink gear. Because I thought today was a good day to be a smartass. I also didn't have a stick, since my dads hadn't bought me one, so for practice today I used the one I always did and kept there.

At least my pink gear passed Silas' inspection. It was good stuff and while I wasn't as comfortable in it as my usuals, at least everything had been broken in a bit. He'd been nice enough to find new base layers and socks for me, so I didn't have to wear my nasty shit.

Ty had forgotten his *mask* today. So I didn't feel so bad about not having a stick. The one Silas had for me was nice. It *wasn't* pink. Hence the tape, I was sure.

I sat in the family room, partially dressed, doing my usual warm-ups. It was now intermission, and I didn't want to disturb anyone and the snacks were better.

As I talked to some of the MASOs, I taped my stick up with the pink tape and watched the mascot entertain the crowd on the TV, in the corner. I might as well be pink and sparkly if I went out. Then again, the likelihood, even with JP in emergency, was slim.

At least JP would be okay.

Coach Kirov came in. "Get fully dressed. Coach Atkins wants you on the bench. You *are* up for this?"

I gulped. Coach wanted me on the *bench?* What? I'd never gotten to sit on the bench before.

"Put me in, Coach." This was my job. I could sit on a bench and wave at kids. I'd stuff some snacks into my pads.

"Good. Oh, you're going to need this." With a grin, Coach K tossed a bundle of black and silver fabric at me and left.

"I get to put one on?" I sucked in a breath,

AJ saw the bundle and put a hand to his heart. "Baby's first jersey?"

I nodded and unfolded it, hands shaking. It was still warm from someone ironing the letters. My eyes teared. While I'd partially dressed out before, I never got to the point where I'd get to put the jersey on, let alone *sitting on the bench*.

Given I was an EBUG, it had 00. On the back was *Di Rossi*. My name.

My name was on a fucking Knights' jersey.

I got to *keep* it.

Shit. My *name.* Usually it just said *EBUG*.

I finished getting dressed, keeping to my usual dressing order. It was almost the end of intermission, so I had to be fast. I sent some quick texts. One to my team's group chat, one to Lenny, one to my host mom, and one to Matty, all saying, *"Going to warm the Knights' bench. Can you spot the Ladybug?"*

Best Host Mom

I'm so excited for you.

I made an insta-chat and sent it to Cooter. "Going in. Got your necklace to bring me luck."

Several MASOs admired my pads and skates. Verity found a hot pink headband in her purse to help keep the hair out of my eyes fashionably.

The NYIT group chat was already popping off, because most of us knew Ty. It was filled with good luck wishes and that warmed me.

Lenny

Win and you get a pastrami sandwich.

Me

Bring me my painting?

Why won't Matty mail it to me?

I got my water bottle out of my bag and frowned. "Hold on. Fucking shit."

No. No. No. No.

Usually, I had the right colored things in my bag when I was on duty. All I had was the correct color of hydrogel. I hadn't been planning on going in tonight.

"Fuck, fuck, fuck." I didn't have what I needed.

Atty gave me a look. "Ladybug, there are kids here."

"They don't have the right colors. I know I won't go in, but I'm going on the bench and I have to be prepared and they don't have the right colors." I looked at AJ, my eyes tearing. There was no time.

AJ was at my side. "Hey. It's okay. What colors do you need?"

"I need a pink energy drink and a purple vitamin water. It doesn't matter if the water is caffeinated or not. Brand and flavor don't matter either, only the color." I frantically pulled bottles out as if that would make it appear.

While I found a pink energy drink, there was no purple vitamin water, not that there'd been any earlier.

Why was there never any purple?

"Ladybug, are you ready?" Silas called from the doorway.

"Give us a second," AJ called back.

My hand shook. "What do I do?"

It wasn't right. Nothing was right. If I went in, I'd fail, because it wasn't right.

"Hey, we have choices," AJ soothed. "We could do a purple energy drink and a pink vitamin water? Or we can do the pink energy drink in your hand and make purple from a pink and blue vitamin water."

"I have a bottle of purple sports drink in my diaper bag," Vicker's wife offered.

"Oh." My freakout paused. "Sports drink works. Thanks." I'd only switched to vitamin water since that's what NYIT had.

AJ nodded. "Anything else?"

I shook my head as I drained the water out of my bottle into my mouth. Taking the can and the offered bottle, I added half the can, then the packet of gel, then most of the bottle.

"I want to make potions," Jackson whined, tugging at Patrice's arm, as I capped my water bottle and gave it a shake.

"Ladybug's going to play in the game, so she gets to make a potion. It's like how daddy always has a banana sandwich as his after-nap snack before a game," Patrice explained.

Jackson beamed. "Ladybug gets to play?"

"Well, I get to sit with the players." I sucked half the drink down and sighed as my anxiety faded and all was right with the world again.

Jackson and the twins gave me good luck hugs. Which melted my heart.

"Thanks, AJ." I bit my lower lip. At least he'd understood my freakout. Hopefully, the other MASOs would, as well. They were the ones ordering bananas, washing–or not washing–the socks, and making sure everything was folded right.

I threw away the empty pack, but didn't know what to do with the open can and bottle.

"Don't worry about it," AJ told me, following my glance. "Anytime. I get it. Mine was a very specific type of pickles. Grif went to five stores once to find them for me."

I laughed. "Clark keeps pickles in his locker for between periods. One of his moms makes them and sends jars to him."

"At least pickles won't lead to heart failure." Atty read the can, grimacing.

At least I didn't mix my energy drink with *coffee* like Ty did.

"Ladybug, they're waiting." Silas came back in, grabbed my stuff, and left.

"You've got this." AJ squeezed my shoulder.

"We'll cheer for you," Verity added, as I grabbed my stick and mask, balancing it with my water bottle. The other MASOs echoed it.

I grabbed a few snacks, stuffed them in my pads, and ran out of the family room, following Silas.

"Thank you. My name is on it," I said softly.

"You're littler than the others, and won't fit in the one we have on hand. Always planned on making you your own. You've earned it. Also, Mia's here." He smirked. "Her dad trained me–and I remember you when you were tiny. You were her neighbor, right?"

"I was." Wow, he remembered me? Silas had never mentioned that.

Music blared when we entered the locker room. Everyone turned to look at me as I stood there in a Knights' jersey, hot pink pads, catching glove, blocker, and skates, with a pink mask and a pink-taped stick in my hands.

"Ladybug's going to warm the bench," Coach Atkins told everyone.

"Nice pads, Mariquita." Carlos laughed and smacked me on the ass.

I struck a pose, nearly dropping my stick. "I'm a pretty, pretty princess."

"Yep, almost as pretty as Vickers," Nia laughed.

Vickers strut around, then slapped her on the ass. Nia hit him with her towel.

"I love the skates," Nakey told me. He looked at Pauley. "Do you think we should get Patrice skates like that? Maybe in baby blue? She'd love the fur."

Pauley laughed. "Sure, if you think it will get her on the ice."

Patrice was that MASO who'd rather set up the snack table and have a gossip during family skate than actually skate. They'd carried her out more than once.

Then I realized what reporter was hanging out with them.

"Gwen!" Annalise from *SportsBeat* grinned. Her camera operator was with her.

"Look, I'm fully dressed." I did a little turn. She'd only ever seen me half-dressed, hanging out in the equipment office, in case they needed me.

Carlos started laughing. "Right, the goalie-in-waiting article. You know, I never did figure out where you got the fun snacks."

"I'll never tell." I grinned. Silas made me promise. Because the players would eat them all.

"You look incredible. I love the pink." She directed the camera operator to get some footage of me and Carlos. Clark, Dimitri, and some of the others crowded around us and it became us clowning around and being silly.

"Focus, we've got to go back out soon," Coach said as Dean picked me up and threw me over his shoulder, making me squeal and crushing my chips.

Coach Atkins gave last-minute instructions to the forwards. I downed the rest of my drink. Time to get my head in the game.

"Do you need a pickle?" Clark offered me the jar.

"I..." The weight of what was happening hit me.

Clark put down the jar and held out his arms. I took the smelly hug.

"I've got you. So does the Captain." He took out his tiny Captain Everything plushy and booped me on the nose with it.

Dean joined us, *huge* in all his gear. "You've got this, Ladybug. If you go in, you get a taco for every shot you stop. If we win, they become taco dinners. It's okay if you let pucks in, just try to let in less pucks than Ty."

"Let in less than Ty. I can do that." I shook a little as I put my mask on. While I'd prefer to let in zero pucks, I could definitely do that. Also, I could be bribed with tacos.

"Goalie hug." Dean slammed me to him.

I was pretty sure the camera operator got that, but everyone loved goalie hugs.

Tenzin came over to me as everyone filed out and pulled me to him. "You have this. I believe in you."

"You do?" My heart warmed as I snuggled into his smelly jersey.

He nodded. "Every single day. You mean everything to me."

"Same." That hug meant everything. I missed his hugs.

Whoops, I hadn't changed out my nose ring for my sporty one. I even had it in my bag. I'd swapped it after practice. It was too late now. It would be fine.

But I had Cooter's necklace, like always, on under my clothes.

Coach Atkins looked at my gear and skates and blinked. "Did NYIT change their colors?"

"My dads think this is my favorite color. Silas signed off on everything," I mumbled as we entered the tunnel. "I have this, Coach."

I hoped.

"I know you do," Coach Atkins told me.

We went out and the players skated around. Dean got in the net and carved up the ice just how he liked as music thumped in the background. I tried to get in the zone and sat down on the bench. Inside, I was a mess, excited and nervous all at the same time. But again, just because I was on the bench didn't mean I'd go in. A little kid peered at me and I waved.

And ignored the fact that the Gears were *right there next to us.*

Clark sat next to me and squeezed my hand. "You've got this. If you smack Austin with your stick, I'll take your penalty."

"Awww." I leaned my head on his shoulder.

Carlos sat down next to me on my other side. The smell of nasty farts filled the bench. Grif made a face.

"Ugh, Lucky." Carlos rolled his eyes. "Grif, stop feeding your cat cheese."

The Deloitte brothers took off toward our goal, determined to score, Nia and Anders chasing them. Number 17 swooped in and hit the puck hard at the goal.

The puck went high and hit Dean right in the mask, knocking him on the ground, sending the puck flying right back onto the ice.

That was hard.

Jonas immediately went to Dean, as Nia started punching number 17 and another fight broke out. You didn't touch the goalie.

My attention focused on Dean as the linemen came over to him, heart roaring in my ears. This was what I hated about my job–I only got to play if my friends got hurt or sick. Nausea rolled in my belly.

Clark squeezed my hand. "You're Gwen Fucking Di Rossi and you were made for this. What better revenge is there than not letting those Deloittes score? Think how therapeutic this will be. Put him behind you for good."

I swallowed hard. He was right. I wouldn't let the douche brothers score.

This would be good for me. I'd take all that anger, fear, frustration and hurt and channel it into my playing.

If I happened to have a chance to hit, trip, or punch Austin?

Well, that would be frosting on the cupcake.

Make them regret. Yep, I'd make Austin regret ever pursuing me.

Jonas and a linesman helped Dean off the ice. Hopefully, he was okay.

"Dean Donovon's being brought in to get checked out. That was a hard one," the announcer said. "Given that right before intermission, Jean-Paul Trembley was taken to the emergency room, the Knights are now without a goalie."

The fake alarm sounded. "This means we're having a historic game with *two* EBUGs. Did someone call for an EBUG?"

The EBUG music played.

Coach Kirov was right there. She grinned at me. "Ladybug, show them how it's done."

"Yes, Coach." I stood and took the snacks out of my pads, throwing them over the glass at the kids who'd been waving at me.

"You have this, Mariquita," Carlos told me.

"Break his kneecaps," Pauley added.

Coach Atkins winced. "Please don't. Don't get suspended. Try to win."

"You can do this. You get drinks at Tito's when we win," Carlos promised, slapping my shoulder.

Drinks *and* tacos? Nice.

I had this. I tumbled over the boards as the crowd went wild.

This is it. What I'd been waiting for, for the twenty years I'd spent in this sport. I was taking the ice at a PHL game. A *Knights'* game.

Mia was even here to see it.

"Making her PHL debut is EBUG Gwen 'Ladybug' Di Rossi," the announcer called out, as animated ladybugs filled the screens. "This is Di Rossi's third year in the Knights goalie development program, where she's head EBUG. She's in her last year at NYIT, where she's a forensic accounting major and starting goalie. Di Rossi has led *two different* collegiate teams to national titles. Welcome, Ladybug."

My picture flashed up on the screen.

I held up my stick and waved as I skated over to the goal. The crowd cheered, and I saw the MASOs waving at me. Jackson and the twins jumped up and down, along with some other kids, including Coach K's. The Maimers, who'd stayed to watch the game, started dancing. Somewhere out there were Mia and Gio. I'd show them I remembered everything they'd taught me.

Yeah, I'd make everyone who ever coached me proud tonight, even those who had no idea who I was now. Especially everyone who took a chance on the tiny beta girl who wanted nothing more than to be a goalie.

I'd play for every beta girl who wanted the same.

Dimitri and Nakey were there waiting for me at the goal.

"We have you, Bozh'ya Korovka," Dimitri told me. "They're rough, but we know you're not a delicate little flower."

"I am so a delicate fucking flower." My belly tightened as I skated back and forth a bit, marking up the ice just the way I liked it. "A carnivorous one."

The play began, and as expected, Austin came right for me, with those fucking skates. Even though we hadn't played together in years, I knew all his tricks–we'd still practice together.

Not to mention I'd studied him as I'd tried to figure out who he was. He'd been having a little trouble since his favorite shot *wasn't* PHL legal. I'd warned him, but he always knew better than me.

Austin took the shot and came in hard and fast, and I smacked it right back onto the ice, sending everyone scrambling for the puck.

Everyone except Austin.

"I'm not going easy on you," he snarled as the ice crew came out to sweep the ice.

All I could do was laugh. He'd *never* gone easy on me. That wasn't the relationship we had. We went all out on each other to help make each other good.

"Eat a bag of dicks, Toilette. You and your knotwaffle brothers are messier than a badger in a dumpster of waffles. You certainly aren't scoring on me today," I sneered back.

"Get out of here," Dimitri told him, and Austin skated off. He turned to me. "I'll buy you a present if you don't let him score."

"Keeping him from scoring is my present," I replied, giving the goal post a pat. *Good post.*

No, today was not the day Bronson fucking Deloitte would score his first regular season PHL goal. No goals for assholes. Not today. Not ever.

Play re-started and I monitored the puck as the action stayed down on the Gears' end, though I knew Austin and his brothers were going to come at me with everything they had.

The best revenge is to thrive.

Watch me fucking thrive.

Number 17 had the puck and headed for me, number 18 on his heels. They tended to tag-team and give each other the assist.

Nerves coursed through me. I was playing in a PHL game. Against my asshole ex.

Fuckity, fuck, fuck.

Think tacos.

Taking a deep breath, I pushed it away. Yes, because for every puck I stopped, I got a taco. Not one puck was getting in. All those tacos belonged to me. It was time to bring the sauce.

I'm Gwen Fucking Di Rossi and I was made for this.

Chapter Sixty-Seven

TENZIN

The puck struck Dean's mask, shooting back onto the ice, and he slumped to the ground. My belly clenched. This had been a rough game. At least we were in the last period. My ribs smarted. Clark had a black eye. Griff's face was cut.

Jonas and the linesmen helped Dean off the ice. Dean was out. Which meant...

The screens flashed and music played as they announced Gwen. Everyone cheered for her and pride filled me. Here was my little Firecracker, playing in a Knights' game.

Like she'd always dreamed of.

She looked as beautiful in that Knights' jersey as she had in the blue dress at the wedding. More. If anything, the pink pads and mask suited her.

Anger flashed through me as I was called in for a line change. The possessive alpha wanted to be there to protect her from Austin.

While the hockey player part of me knew that Gwen could handle herself, the alpha part worried about her getting injured. I was absolutely certain that her ex wasn't going to go easy on her–nor were his brothers.

"I've got her," Dimitri murmured as he took my place.

I knew he did. Dimitri cared for her like a sister. Clark was out there, too. Still, I itched to protect her, and I huffed in annoyance as I took my seat.

Coach Atkins gave me a look. "You'll get your chance."

My hands fisted in my gloves and my belly tightened, as Austin immediately jetted across the ice. *Get it, get it.* She deflected the shot with ease. He said something to her and skated off.

"Asshole," I fumed. How dare he?

A few seconds later, number 17 was back at her and she caught it.

"Get back in there." Coach sent me in with Vickers, since Jonas was still with Dean, given they were mates.

I skated out and went right into play, protecting the net and chasing those assholes around. When the ref blew his whistle and play halted I skated over to her.

"Hey, Firecracker, looking good," I told her.

"Hi, Big Guy. Hey, Vickers." She waved.

"We've got you," Vickers told her.

Play restarted and eventually we were called back out, but we were back in soon enough. As the minutes on the clock ticked down, it was evident that the Gears' forwards had orders to score. Number 17 came at her fast and hard. Back on the ice, I swatted the puck away from him toward Nia.

"Not today, fucknugget," I muttered.

Nia took it in their end, scoring another goal, bringing us 4-0.

I chased her ex around the goal, Vickers coming around the other side. Gwen was ready at the side of the goal, tripping him ever-so-subtly as he skated by, sending him sprawling.

The ref blew the whistle, but no penalty was called.

"Whoops. I didn't see you." Gwen's voice dripped with innocence as she patted the goalpost.

I was called back off. Nakey and Dimitri went in. Her ex came at her again, and I could tell what he was doing. Back when I first met her, she was struggling a little glove-side, and we'd worked on that.

Something he didn't know.

With the grace of a dancer and speed of an ultra-bullet, she deflected it. Her ex caught it on the rebound, and she sent it right back. There was no doubt he was pissed as he went right for her again, smacking it hard.

She dove, catching it, and everyone cheered. He got pissed and Dimitri threw him down. He got up and moved toward her. She poked him with her stick as Clark shoved him.

"Look at her go." Jonas sat down with me. "She could be as good as Dean in a few years. Better even. I love it when she gets feisty."

She was sparkling tonight.

"Is Dean okay?" I asked.

Jonas nodded. "He should be–and Verity's with him, so he sent me out here to help protect Ladybug."

"How do you do it? Sit on the bench, while Dean and Grif are in, without you out there to protect them?" I wanted to climb over the boards and stand in front of her, rules be damned. Also, Dean and Grif were both *omegas*.

"Time, patience, and trusting in them. I've also played with them since we were together at BosTec. Gwen knows what she's doing, knows the risk. It's part of supporting them. But yeah, it is hard, especially when they get hurt," he admitted. "You three had a fight? I've been curious. It's clear she and Clark are a couple, but you all seemed on well enough terms."

"I don't know. Whatever it is, I'll fix it. I don't want her to hurt." The fact that she thought this was her fault, that I didn't want to be with her because of what she endured, broke my heart.

This was on me. I thought I was communicating, that everything was fine.

It wasn't.

Yes, I'd fix it before it was too late. Before it ended like everything with me and Morgan. I'd thought I'd been doing fine there, too.

The ice crew came back out. The coaches went over a couple things and we went back out.

"Is Dean okay?" Gwen asked as Jonas and I took the ice.

"He'll be okay. How many tacos are you up to?" Jonas asked.

"Nine." She grinned. Then she frowned. "Ty gets tacos too, right? It's only fair."

Jonas nodded. "Absolutely. I'll make sure."

Tacos? Didn't goalies who didn't let in any goals not pay for drinks after the game?

"Dean's buying her a taco for every puck she stops," Jonas explained.

Ah, it was a Double D thing. He had a soft spot for the EBUGs. Bribing the university students with food to play well made absolute sense. My collegiate coach had bought us noodles after winning many times.

The ice crew left and the game resumed. Number 16 came back with a vengeance, determined to score on her. He stopped fast, spraying her with snow.

She caught the puck and snarled, "mine." Gwen poked him with her stick again. Not enough to be a penalty, but she was definitely issuing a warning. "That wasn't nice, Deloitte."

"Hockey's not nice, *Di Rossi*," he sneered. "What little girl did you steal your gear from?"

"Leave her alone," I growled, shoving him as he got closer to her than I'd like.

"It's a game, you giant moron." He shoved me back. "My literal job is to score. It's not personal. We don't go easy on the EBUGs. You're not going easy on ours."

I wanted to punch him, but her being in the net changed things. If I was sitting out a penalty, I couldn't protect her.

"It's okay, Big Guy," she whispered as he skated off, Jonas going after him. "That's how he is on the ice, a massive trash-talking, alphahole who likes to fight. I'm not afraid of him. But I'm glad you're here with me."

"Me, too," I told her, going back into the fray.

Jonas and I were called back in. It was clear the Gears were *desperate* to score and that the forwards were unhappy that an EBUG in pink gear was keeping all the goals out.

It was also clear that someone told them her weaknesses, as they kept going glove-side and shooting *hard*. Good thing we'd worked together over the off-season.

Finally, Coach had Jonas and I rejoin the game. Gwen took a puck to the chest and went down, but not before keeping the puck out.

"What's up your gooch, Deloitte?" Gwen swore at number 16 as she got up, the ref blowing his whistle.

"Not you," Austin laughed.

How dare he? I shoved him. "Stay away from her."

"You want a piece of me, Yeti? You fucking her, too? If anything, it makes me feel good that she needs *two* alphas to replace me." He took off his gloves and helmet.

My gloves and helmet hit the ice. He had a skull gaiter covering his face, but it didn't stop my fist from making contact with his nose.

"She deserves better than you," I retorted.

"While she tries her best, she'll never deserve better than me. Clark maybe, given he's practically trailer trash. He's been after her for so long. It's pathetic." He swung for me and I dodged.

"They're not *trash*," I growled, tackling him to the ice and pounding his face. While I'd slammed him a few times, I'd been wanting to do this the entire game.

How dare he insult them? The Deloittes might be rich, but they had trashy values. They gave factory owners a bad name, with the way they tried to exploit their workers.

The ref blew the whistle again as Jonas pulled me off him, and I got sent to the penalty box for fighting.

Shit. I couldn't protect her from here. However, there was less than a minute left. She'd be okay. I made a heart with my hands, when she looked at me, and she made one back.

It was the longest fifty-seven seconds of my life as I sat there in the box, watching the game, helpless.

At least her asshole ex was in the box, too. And he was bleeding.

Grif went in for his third goal of the night, and Ty stopped it, surprise evident.

Number 17 took the puck and barreled down toward Gwen as the seconds ticked down on the screen above. They wouldn't win, but honor was on the line. Clark stole it and went back for the Gears' goal.

Standing, I cheered for him, wanting him to get another goal. Number 18 stole it back and swept it across the ice. They kept going back and forth as the seconds ticked down.

Number 18 got close, but instead of going in for the shot, he feinted and passed it to Number 17, who was on the backside. He took the shot and Gwen dove for it. I held my breath as she stopped the goal.

"She caught it. Yet another amazing save from Di Rossi as she steals the goal from Deloitte. Nothing gets past her. Is it the pink gear?" the announcer said.

The buzzer sounded. "Dare I say it? It's a *shutout* for the Knights as they win against the Gears. What a game!"

The crowd roared as I tumbled out of the box, desperate to get to Gwen. She patted the goal posts.

The announcer continued to talk about how historic the game was and the last shutout with an EBUG was when Maria Barilla herself made her debut with the Knights. Huh, I hadn't known that.

The team rushed over and tapped their helmets to hers. Clark picked her up and spun her around on the ice and they laughed and danced. My heart squeezed. Yes, we'd have a good talk. I missed them so much.

Maybe I didn't need space. Perhaps I needed *them*.

I joined them and swept her up. "I'm so incredibly proud of you."

A shutout. Sure, she only played one period, but she still kept *every* puck out.

"Thanks. All the tacos belong to me," she laughed, her minty scent pungent and laced with sweat, anxiousness, and happiness.

"You got a goal. That is amazing," I told Clark.

He ducked his head. "I don't know if it really counts. Maybe I won't buy a figure."

"It totally counts, and you were going to buy an Aquatica one. I'd say scoring a goal in the home opener was better than a blowjob from a dinosaur." Gwen smirked at me.

I growled a little. "Don't be bratty."

"What are you going to do about it?" While her tone was teasing, that was pure challenge.

The ice crew came out and dumped plushies on the ice.

"Goalie hugs." Dean came onto the ice and stole her from us before I could answer, hugging her tight. While her skates and gear added a lot of bulk, and he wasn't wearing his pads, she still looked so small in comparison.

"Should you be out here?" Worry coated her scent.

"I'll be okay. They're just being cautious. I wouldn't miss this for anything." He put an arm around her.

Clark stood next to me, eyes on her. "She's the most beautiful girl in the world."

She was.

Tonight, I needed to let her know that.

Chapter Sixty-Eight

GWEN

We did it! We'd won the home opener against the Gears. The arena erupted with cheers as my teammates tapped my mask with their helmets, chests bumped me, and they hugged me and swung me around.

We'd gotten a shutout. I'd kept Austin from scoring. Also, I'd gotten *sixteen* tacos. That was a whole lot of stopped pucks for one period. They'd been vicious, coming at me with an intense ferocity I'd never experienced before.

I looked over at the Gears. They were hugging Ty and slapping him on the shoulder. Good. He'd played a great game and they *should* be nice to him.

Though I hoped their coach ripped them a new one in the locker room for not getting a single goal.

No goals for assholes. I'm sure they were having *all* the regret right now.

Yeah, that game would be thriving, right?

I went over to Castle, since this was her first official game with the Knights.

"We did it," she squealed. "You did amazing out there."

"You're not so bad yourself." It would only be a matter of time before she became an integral part of the team. She hustled even more than I did.

"Since we have *two* EBUGs making their debut, we get a double stuffie smash. Don't forget to stay for the shutout shootout," the announcer said.

Excitement zinged through me. I got to do the stuffie smash *and* a shutout shootout? That really was better than a blowjob from a dinosaur.

"Will our EBUGs please come to the center for the ceremonial stuffie smash? Congrats on a great game and welcome to the PHL family," the announcer said. "We can't wait to see you again."

After an EBUG played, they got to hit stuffies at the fans.

I came to the center as did Ty. "Ty, that was a great game."

"Thanks, you were fucking insane," he said. "Shutout. Fucking shit."

Analise came over to us, carefully walking on the ice, camera operator in tow. She must have pulled some strings to be able to do that. I'd been fully prepared for her to be in the tunnel or locker room waiting for us.

"Here I am with our favorite Knights Goalies-in-Waiting who finally got to live out their hockey dreams and play in a history-making double-EBUG match that ended in a shutout. How do you feel?" Analise held out the microphone.

"I'm still amazed I got to play in a game," Ty told her. "It was incredible to be out there and the Gears were great."

I'm sure Austin had taken his gaiter off in the locker room and I was so curious about how that convo went. But I wasn't about to ask.

"I'm glad Dean and JP are going to be okay," I told her. "After all those games of almost getting to play, having the chance to get on the ice with the Knights was *amazing*."

"A shutout, Ladybug. Good for you. First EBUG shutout for the Knights since Maria Barilla herself. Who's here," Analise told me.

"I'm proud to be part of the Knights legacy of goalie and EBUG excellence." I hoped she and Gio were proud of me–and I wished that Nonna and Mom were here. I sniffed a little.

Analise looked at the camera. "There you have it. Our Goalies-in-Waiting are waiting no more, as Knights EBUGs, Tyler Yamato and Gwen 'Ladybug' Di Rossi, played in this historic game."

The camera went down.

"We're going to get some shots of the smash and the shootout. Great job, you two. Gwen, I hope some of the teams watching you take note. Also, the pink looks *fantastic* on camera." She waved, and they went over toward the plushies.

The crowd chanted *stuffie smash, stuffie smash*. I danced in excitement as the EBUG music played. We skated around the rink, hitting stuffies over the glass at the fans, laughing. Nat the Knight came out on the ice and helped us.

As Ty whacked the last stuffie into the stands, the ice crew was already leading tiny kids carefully onto the ice. I wasn't sure where they got the kids for the shootout, but they were all wearing little skates and helmets, a few held up by parents or older siblings.

So stinking cute.

Another tradition for when the goalie got a shutout at a home game.

Dean joined me, grinning. The kids excitedly got in line and someone explained the rules. Basically, each kid got a turn in the net. Dean and I gently hit swag and stuffies at them. They got to keep whatever they caught.

Well, that and Nat kept *sneaking* them stuff, which was *hilarious*. Nat 'stole' my stick, and I chased him around the rink. I knew the mascot. He ran the Knights' power skating practices. He was also the Maimers' skating coach, who did all their choreography. It was good fun.

"Come on, Firecracker." Tenzin held out a hand when I finished.

It had been so long since he'd shown me little courtesies like that, and I loved it. Clark took my other hand.

We posed for some pictures and then the three of us skated off the rink.

When I entered the locker room, it erupted in cheers. Red and black streamers were *everywhere*, along with silly signs like *Maimers Rule.* One had been scratched out and said *Gwennifer is Amazeballs.*

The Maimers had struck again. They'd defaced the locker room like this last year, too, when they'd done a promo before our game. Like last year, there was also a little cart with cake pops on it from Verity.

"Well done, Ladybug." Coach Kirov patted me on the shoulder, beaming like a proud parent. "Especially under the circumstances."

"Good game, Ladybug. The press is going to want to talk to you," Coach Atkins added.

"Yes, Coach." I laughed as I ate a cake pop shaped like a hockey puck. I'd just played in a PHL game. I couldn't get over it.

The coaches went over a few things.

"That was a great game," Dean told me when the coaches finished. "I'm so fucking proud."

"You are? That means a lot. And I get tacos." I did a dance. "Now I get to do a press conference in either my hoodie and PJ pants that I wore to the game, or the jeans and sweater I wore to class. Which one says *I'm not a fashion disaster?*"

Though they were designer jeans and a cute sweater.

Dean held up a dry-cleaning bag. "I have you. Verity was going to ask you if you wanted it anyway, which was why it was in the back of our SUV."

"Oh, that was nice." I loved the stuff Mercy had given me. I chugged some water, hit the ice bath and showers, and changed into what was in the bag. Which turned out to be one of Mercy's sparkly pantsuits she sometimes wore for Maimers games.

Dean and Carlos helped alter it, giving it a quick hem with sock tape and a few tucks with safety pins. Carlos knew how to do this from all his years of being on TV.

My hair was wild, so I squished some product in it, then swiped on lipstick and powder. That was as good as it was going to get.

Oooh, I looked good in this suit.

"Come on, they're waiting." Kylee, who was in charge of PR for the Knights, dragged me off, collecting Ty along the way. She was a no-nonsense beta, who in her heels was shorter than me, but had a presence that made her feel larger.

The Knights' logo was in the background of the press area and there were lots of people and cameras.

"Gwen." Ty hugged me, still hopped up on adrenaline. "We played a game."

"We smashed it." I grinned; well aware people were taking our pictures. Goalie hugs were the best.

"You certainly did," one reporter said. "Tyler, you were on duty. Did you think you'd end up playing for the opposing team?"

"We always know it's a possibility, but you never think this is going to be the day you play at all. Still, it's a dream come true. It was *amazing* being out there," he replied. "The Gears are great."

"I've been practicing with the Knights for over two years. They're my friends. I don't like seeing them get hurt and I'm so glad everyone's going to be okay. But yes, it's a dream come true." I grinned. "I've wanted to be goalie for the Knights for a *long* time."

"Ty, do you think the Boaters were watching?" someone asked.

"If they were, I hope they remember I was up against Grif Graf," he laughed.

"Can we talk about the pink gear, Gwen? It seems like an unusual choice," a reporter asked curiously. "Honestly, if pink gear means shutouts, then maybe everyone should wear it." He chuckled. "Does it have to do with them calling you, *Ladybug?*"

"JP gave me the nickname when I first started. Because I'm a lady EBUG," I snorted.

Everyone laughed. Yep, hockey players and their nicknames.

"As for the pink gear..." I had an answer. A partially true one. "My mom died of OOC when I was a teenager. She–and my Nonna–were my biggest fans and I miss both of them every day." My eyes teared. "I wish both of them were here to see this. I wear pink for my mom, and all the other moms and dads out there with OOC, and for all the kids who will never get to see their parents in the crowd at another game." I wiped my eyes with my hand.

Maybe I should start wearing pink again, at least sometimes.

"Shit, Gweny," Ty whispered. "Um, hi moms and dads. See, it was absolutely worth years and years of being hockey parents." He waved at the cameras.

"Were you two nervous? How do you combat nerves when you're out there?" someone asked us.

"Keep calm and think of tacos," I blurted.

"Tacos?" the reporter blinked.

I turned to Ty. "Double D says we get a taco for every puck we stopped."

Ty lit up. "We do? I could use some tacos right now. I'm starving."

"We're students, bribe us with food," I laughed as a few reporters nodded and muttered about recalling those days.

"Are you single, Ty?" someone asked.

"I'm very taken," Ty laughed. "Hi, Damien, I love you."

"Gwen, who are you wearing? It's quite flashy for hockey. You look like you stole it from a skate smasher's closet," a fashionably dressed reporter smirked, probably from the style beat.

Well, that was spiteful. Also correct.

I looked down. "I did. Have No Mercy's closet in fact. It was this or the hoodie I wore to the game, since I came straight from my university hockey practice. I never expected to play tonight, so I wasn't fully prepared. I was just here to watch their home opener. So, who wears it better? Me or Mercy? Wait, I don't want to know." I laughed and did a little spin.

They asked Ty a bunch of questions, but then he was the alpha male who'd been drafted.

"I love the Knights, but I'm a Wolves fan, hometown pride and all," he replied, "and the Boaters, of course. Gwen's the hardcore Knights fan."

"My nonna and her neighbors brought me to my first Knights' game when I was three. I got to go down to the glass and see warm-ups and sit on my neighbor's shoulders and Callahan gave me a puck. That was when I was told goalies were the best." I grinned. "I might have a Maria Barilla card on my wall, too."

The reporters got back on topic, talking about some of the plays.

"I think it's time to let them go. After all, it's a school night," Kylee finally laughed, and escorted us away.

"You were two." Maria stood there with Gio, pride on her face. "You were two when you sat on Gio's shoulders and Callahan gave you a puck, then grabbed you and flew you around the ice like an airplane."

I sucked in a breath. "I forgot that part. Wait, I did the shutout shootout once, didn't I?"

She thought for a moment. "At least once. You caught a fuzzy blanket that lived in your treehouse for years."

"I did, and the mascot gave me a toy." What had happened to my treehouse and everything in it after Nonna died? Was it in the boxes with everything from my room there?

"Good job, Buttons. Someone brought the sauce tonight." Gio pulled me in for a hug.

I looked at him and Mia. "I learned from the best."

"They'd both be so proud of you." Mia's eyes were teary. She was such good friends with Nonna. "*I* am proud of you."

I hugged her tightly. "I needed to hear that."

Reporters were taking pictures.

Mia let go of me and hugged Ty to her. "I'm so proud of you, too. It's not easy going in there mid-game."

"Thanks." Ty's eyes grew a little misty.

"Come to Tito's, Mia?" I wanted to talk a little.

"I'll see if anyone's up for it. We miss you." Mia gave me another hug and Kylee led us back toward the locker rooms.

"She brought you to hockey games?" Ty gave me a look.

"I spent a lot of time at my nonna's as a kid."

"Oh." His look grew pensive. "Where *did* the pink gear come from? It looks brand new."

"Birthday present from my dads." I sighed.

He blinked. "I knew your family were assholes, but it takes a special kind of shitty to get birthdays wrong. At least it's from Viper."

"They're all waiting for you two in the family room," Kylee told us.

"Great." Ty went off, but she held me back.

"Gwen, I want to circle back to the Bronson thing. Maybe tomorrow?" Her voice was soft. "The players were, um, talkative, during intermissions, and I have concerns. I made them shut up before Analise came in. Still, send me everything you might have, like police reports? Copy your agent." She winced. "The Deloittes can get nasty with their exes. I want to be prepared."

"Sure. I'll do that and stop by tomorrow morning after work." It made sense that she'd want to be ready if anything hit the press. Of course they were chatty; hockey players were fucking gossips.

I walked into the family room, and many of the players and some MASOs and family members were there. They all cheered for us.

"Gwenifer, you look amazing. I knew it would fit you. That sister who doesn't like your outfits can suck it. We should send her a picture," Mercy told me.

"We should." I got my phone from Clark, which had a million messages. I took a picture of her, me, and Verity, and captioned it *I'm not a fashion disaster* and sent it to Isa.

Nia made a speech and gave us our jerseys back, now signed. Ty having a Gears' jersey signed by the Knights was hysterical. Then again, the Gears had signed his Knights' mask.

One of Atty's twins was asleep, but I was hug-attacked by Jackson, the other twin, and Coach K's kids. Their excitement in seeing me play was *everything*.

"Let's go to Tito's. Goalies who get shutouts drink for free, and since Doc says I can't drink tonight, Gwen gets *all* the beer," Dean laughed.

I'd take all the free beer. Tony would understand if I was a little hungover tomorrow. Whoops, I hadn't let him know I was playing. I'd text him the picture Verity took of me in my gear later.

Clark handed me my motorcycle helmet. His glasses were back on, and they went well with that striped suit. "Ready to ride?"

"What do I do with my stuff?" I blinked. Perhaps I could ask Silas to put my gear with the team's to be taken back to the training center and pick it up from here?

"You can put it in my truck. It's not like I live far." Tenzin gave me a fond look that reminded me of better times.

"Thank you. I'd like that." I walked with the two of them down to the parking garage and put my stuff in Tenzin's truck.

Tenzin gave me an enormous hug, and I relished in it. I'd missed his hugs.

"I'm proud of you, Firecracker. I'll see you both at Tito's. Drive safe," he told us, smoothing my face with his hand.

"I will." Clark squeezed me to him. "After all, I have someone important on board."

Chapter Sixty-Nine

GWEN

Tito's was electric as I sat at a table, trying to check texts. I'd had a nice visit with Mia and now she was talking to Dean and some others.

Isabella

You are so a fashion disaster. I can't believe you wore that to a press conference. Also, you were voted the game's worst-dressed MASO. Do you need me to send you things? By the way, your hair is *wavy*.

She added a link to a post, ranking the outfits of the MASOs for the games played tonight. There was a picture of me in my jammie pants, hoodie, hat, and backpack. The caption was "*Not sure what player she belongs to, but she looks like she just got out of eight am calculus.*"

I rolled my eyes. All the stuff I needed to do my hair was expensive. Mercy and Verity sat down and Verity handed me a beer. I showed her the article.

Verity took a sip of her fruity drink. "That's funny. Look, they low-ranked every MASO who wore a jersey. Both Atty and I are near the bottom. *Don't know who she belongs to?* You're literally wearing Clark's number in the photo."

Whatever, anyone who ranked Verity and Atty near the bottom weren't to be trusted.

Mercy rolled her eyes. "I'll fix this."

She got out her phone and commented, "*She just got out of hockey practice. In case you didn't notice, she changed into a pink mask and a Knights' jersey later.*"

"Thanks," I laughed. Hopefully, my sister wouldn't think I looked like a fashion disaster in our mom's old dress. Kaiko picked it up today, and it was at Mercy's. The alterations were more than I expected, but from the pictures it looked like she'd done an amazing job, especially with making it strapless.

"Why *is* your sister hating on your clothes? That's a nice suit. I was sad when it got too short. Verity picked it out," Mercy added.

"I know. I don't get it. I love it. Thank you."

"Isa's a fashion snob who works for Vecci and thinks being badly dressed is worse than death. But she means well. The suit is nice, but not super couture or whatever her standard is." Lenny took the stool next to me and handed me a box. "One pastrami sandwich, as promised. With extra pickles."

"Lenny, what are you doing in New York?" I wasn't expecting a sandwich *tonight*. Was the deli even open at this hour? He wore a dark suit, but stood out among all the other guys in suits.

One of these guys is not like the other.

"Authenticating paintings for an auction house." He turned to Verity and Mercy. He gave Verity an appreciative look. "I'm Lenny."

"Verity," Verity replied, looking wary. "This is my sister Mercy. Gwen, your sister works for *Vecci?*"

"Yeah, I think she designed that dress you wore in that last show. I don't keep in close touch with my family, because they think boundaries are only for countries." I grabbed a crunchy pickle spear and took a bite. Mmmm.

Verity snorted. "I get that."

"I was watching the game with some clients in their box when you texted me. I'd been trying to figure out how to get down there and bother you. Is that Mia?" Lenny's eyes fell on her as she talked to Dean, Gio's arm around her.

"Yep." I took a bite of my sandwich, which had the perfect ratio of pastrami to mustard. Lenny knew Mia and Gio from tagging along to stuff at Nonna's over the years.

"Matty wants you to call him. Like now," Lenny replied.

"Who are you?" Carlos stood there, frowning. "This is not Popi. Other Popi?"

"Popi's bestie, so pretty much. Popito?" I laughed. "Most of the Knights think Matty is my dad."

Carlos snorted. "*No.* You need to work on your Spanish if you're going to Mexico City next year."

I nearly spit out my sandwich, and I took a big gulp of beer to wash it down. "Who says I'm going to Mexico City? I never reached five-foot-ten."

Not that I was against it. I'd take *any* PHL team. Clark would fully support me. Like I'd support him if he went somewhere else. It was part of the job. Hopefully someone was watching me tonight and liked what they saw.

"Oh, the Tigres are still watching you, Mariquita. And that pink gear? You're *perfect.* Besides, my cousin plays for them," Carlos replied. "He tells me things. See, Lucky agrees. He's proud of you, too."

True. They were besties. I *had* gotten a text from an old teammate of mine who now played defense for Mexico City, and she'd seen me on TV tonight.

Not that I understood why pink gear made me more attractive to them as a player. But I'd take it.

I pretended to pet Lucky. "That means a lot, Lucky."

Mercy turned and waved at someone. "Oh, there's Kaiko." She left the table, Carlos going with her, pretending to take Lucky with him.

"Nice to meet you." Verity got her pink crutch and her fruity drink. "I'm going to find Grif."

"Lenny, this sandwich is so good." I took another bite. Yep, just what I needed.

"Um, who or what is Lucky?" Lenny's eyebrows rose.

"Grif Graf's imaginary cat." I shrugged and ate a fry.

Dimitri eyed Lenny from across the room where he was with Carlos, Valya, and a bunch of other people. Kaiko and Mercy joined them.

"Why can't I have my painting?" I popped another fry in my mouth.

Lenny took another fry and gave me a look. "Why do you think?"

My heart sank. Not everything Lenny did was legal.

"It's *real*," Lenny replied softly. "But not stolen. Okay, maybe it was. The owners were shitty, and you deserved it more. However, your dads had a fit, since everything has to be above board with you. So they bought it."

"Above board?" I finished my pickle.

"Don't be coy, Buttons. I know you know what's what. However, if you want to continue to Gwen to the Gweniest, I'd be careful what questions you ask," he told me.

My belly twisted. I knew what people said about the dads. I'd seen things over the years. But no, I didn't want to know.

Wow, Lenny had *stolen* a painting for me. How sweet. And the dads had bought it to make it legitimate. For *me.*

Huh.

Wait. The painting on my wall was *real?* Wow.

"I... I like my life." I ate my other pickle, pondering this. "While I miss them, I text Matty a few times and suddenly I'm getting birthday presents at work when it's not my birthday from people I hadn't heard from in years."

"They miss you. They *are* capable of respecting your boundaries, but you have to make them want to." Lenny took a fry.

I grimaced. "I don't have that kind of patience."

"Who are *you?*" Clark came over to the table.

"Lenny." He eyed him. "Take good fucking care of her. I held her the day she was fucking born."

"Oh. Lenny, your brother's friend who bought your cards." Clark nodded.

"Yep. The one and only. He's in town for work. Saw me play, brought me a sandwich." I pushed the box toward him and he took a pickle.

"Finish up and call Matty. He's waiting," Lenny added.

I crammed food in my face, while Clark pumped Lenny for embarrassing stories about me. Then I held up my phone. "It's too loud right here. I'm going to go back by the bathrooms."

Which was where I'd sneak calls when I worked here.

Clark frowned. "Should I come with you?"

"I'm fine." I found that quiet place behind a ficus tree, where if you stood just right, the cameras didn't see you—so you couldn't get in trouble, as long as you kept it short and weren't missed.

I called Matty, and it immediately switched to a video call. With a sigh, I fished earbuds out of my pocket. I'd already video chatted with half my university team. And talked to my host mom, who couldn't stop squealing.

"Buttons." Matty beamed at me on the screen. "I'm so fucking proud."

"You are?" My eyes narrowed at the bookcases behind him. "You're at the dads?"

"Yes, I was here when you texted. We watched you together and now they want to buy the Belugas." He grinned.

My hand went to my face. "Please don't."

"But that would be fun. You played in a game!" Babo's weathered face appeared on screen and my heart sank. Not because I didn't want to talk to him, but due to how much he'd aged in three years.

"I did. Um, next time you come see me play, please ask me if I want to go to dinner. Coach might not let me, but I won't be mad." Now I felt awful, because they'd come to see me play and hadn't approached me, in an attempt to honor my wishes for space.

He beamed; blue eyes sparkling. "I'd love that. Looks like you're not near us until after the new year. You wore our present in the game. I'm so glad you liked it."

"I love everything. Thank you." I couldn't help but smile at his excitement.

The phone got passed around as my other dads talked to me about the game and I couldn't help but fill with delight. I'd been waiting for them to get excited about hockey with me for *years*.

But all of them seemed so old. Especially when Popi mentioned if I got good grades, he'd consider getting me a malamute puppy. Which was what I'd wanted when I was a teenager.

Papa took the phone. "Buttons. You looked *great* out there."

"Thanks. I... I'm happy in New York. I'm finishing up at NYIT. Doing an internship. Hoping to get signed when I graduate." I always wanted his approval most of all.

"I'm proud of you for getting into such a good university, and for doing so well on your own." He looked the least old of everyone, even though they were all pretty similar in age. But I could see it in his hazel eyes, hear it in his voice.

He was proud of me? I'd take it.

His look grew sad. "I didn't know you still wore pink for your mom when you played."

Oh. They'd heard that.

"It's been a while. I grew out of my pink stuff. Thank you for the new gear, I appreciate it. But my birthday is in February." There. A boundary.

I waited for him to smash it.

"Okay."

Okay? No, amused, *is that so?*

"I know you keep a disciplined schedule, which I appreciate, but you *are* invited to any and all holidays. Even if you can only stay a day. Mateo will help you with transportation if you need it," Papa added.

No please. No pleading. But he was head alpha and a powerful man, who ran a big transportation company. This was as close as it got—because it wasn't an edict. However, an offer to get my ass to Vancouver was thoughtful.

"Thank you. I'll check. With hockey we don't get much time off, even during winter break, since we still have games." I wanted to say *yes*. Who knew how many holidays they had left?

But my family was like a riptide. One misstep and I'd be pulled under. I had to be cautious.

"Good." He nodded. "The purple hair is nice."

Matty took the phone from him and slipped into the other room.

"That was uncalled for." I pouted, feeling so many things after a dad ambush.

"I needed you to see them. Please consider visiting."

"I like my life." And my bubble of ignorance.

"I know. It suits you. You can do your own thing and still see us. Promise. I'll get your ticket if you want me to. Good night, Buttons." He ended the call.

For a moment I sat there feeling everything all at once. Despite everything, I still loved my family. Even if the things people said about them were true. I didn't want to be a part of that any more than I wanted conditions on love or money.

However, they'd seen me play. They told me they were *proud.* I needed that.

"Babe?" The voice came from the other side of the plant.

My body tensed, and I took out my earbuds. A hoodie-covered head poked over the plant, and turned, so I couldn't see his face.

Even without that familiar fabric softener scent wafting toward me, I'd know it was him. I scowled. "Don't *babe* me, Austin."

Of course he'd show up. He knew this was where the Knights went after games from years of bartending here. He must have snuck in, otherwise someone would have texted me that they'd seen him. I texted Clark.

Me

Austin's here. Still by the plant. Find me in five minutes.

"A shutout. Shit. What a debut game." He leaned against the wall. "The NYIT game was good, too. You play like I remember. Back when you were good, back before you changed."

Still sitting, I put my head on my knees, I also hit record on my phone and shoved it in my jacket pocket. Just in case. The accountant in me liked backup.

So he *had* been at the NYIT game. Huh. But he might have been in New York for sponsor things or something.

"It's too bad that I couldn't be the one to bring it out of you. It hurt me so fucking much that I couldn't fix you after you got kidnapped. And that you didn't trust me enough with what happened." His shoulders slumped.

"You fixed me more than you know," I said softly, belly churning. "I wouldn't have made it without you. Mostly because you *didn't* make me talk about it. I don't even trust myself with it most of the time. But you're not here to talk about that, are you?"

"No," he admitted.

"I don't want an apology, explanation, or your money. You're unredeemable in my mind and will never get another chance. What you did to me was shitty on so many levels," I spat. "However, *please* let Windy know I didn't murder you. His accusations are going to cause him trouble if he doesn't stop."

"Windy thinks what?" Disbelief rang through his voice.

"Did you even ever love me? I loved you with my very soul, Austin Blake. It breaks me up that I gave you everything and to you I was just your bang maid." My voice shook.

I should leave. However, we were in a public place. Clark would come in a few minutes. Maybe I wanted a few answers...

"I loved you so much. It was like my heart got ripped from my chest when I knew it was over. I don't want this life. I wanted a life with you and losing that chance hurt. Seeing you on the ice in a Knights' jersey was a knife in the heart." His dryer sheet scent grew salty as he continued to keep his back to me.

"Then why didn't you fight for us? Five years, Austin." I sniffed. "You simply gave up. Gave me up. Gave *us* up. For what?"

"You don't understand what families like mine are like. I blew my one chance at escape. I can't fight this." Frustration leaked into his voice.

"Can't or won't?" I snapped. I understood more than he'd ever know. Also, never underestimate the power of a good spreadsheet.

"*Can't.* See, you don't get it. I couldn't take you with me, no matter how much I wanted to, and I'm so sorry." His voice grew soft, and he turned toward me, the hood hiding his face.

"So, instead of having an adult conversation, you put me in the fucking hospital? Are you shitting my dick right now?" Next he was going to tell me he wore the skates tonight to let me know he still cared.

"I... I put you in the hospital?"

"What do you think throwing a skate at my head did?" I moved my bangs, so he could see my scar.

He sucked in a breath. "I... I didn't know. I didn't mean to go that far."

"*That far*? You *meant* to hurt me? Of course, you didn't know; you fled the state and changed your name." Who was this alpha?

"No argument in all the world would make them change their minds. We had our chance, and we failed," he told me.

My eyebrows rose. "Given who they are, do you think they'd actually let you play for another team?"

Those conditions felt like he'd been set up to fail. They were probably friends with the other team and made a deal or something shady like that.

"They wouldn't do that." He shook his head. "We failed, and I had to keep my word. I also couldn't risk you following me into this life. There's no place for you here. I know your boundaries. I was only going to hurt you enough for you to leave and never look back."

His hand went to his face. "But then when you were calling Clark and leaving, I got so angry and I couldn't help myself. The skates were right there, and then you ran, and well, the alpha in me got–"

"That is such a load of bullshit." My hands fisted as I ached to punch him. I wasn't to blame for him hurting me.

"I was trying to protect you," he blurted, turning to face me, face still in shadow, though I could see the bruises from the game.

"Protect me by hurting me?" I scowled at him. How dumb could he get?

"Yes. You're a good person and I wanted to protect you from this life I now have to lead. You have no idea about the world I live in. You try so hard, but they'd eat you alive. You'd never fit, and you'd be so fucking unhappy. Or you'd lose everything I love about you trying to. This life wrecked my mom, and that's the last thing I'd ever want to do to you." His voice broke.

Oh. I knew he loved his mom. It still didn't excuse what he did.

"Did your mom even die? Or is she an asshole like your dad?" I snapped.

"She did die." His voice broke. "She was a beta like you. My dad knew the family would be bad for her. But he ignored it, even when it was too late. I'll never forgive him for it." Anger wafted off him. "Or my grandfather. There's no escaping them."

"I was good enough for you when you needed me to help you pay tuition, even though your family owns a car company. Then you graduate and suddenly I'm not? Not to mention the family business is a *hockey team*. That's not you having to give up your dreams. I wasn't going to ask your family for a job. I know how to not be embarrassing in public. Also, we'd talked about an omega." Would it have hurt him to have a conversation with me?

His laugh grew derisive. "No. You'll *never* be good enough for them. There's no place for you in my world. *None*. It'll end like my mom. Or worse. Ris, my omega, will hate you. You're *not* her people. Just like my dad's omega hated my mom. In another life..." He sighed.

Things pulled together. Again, it might be an explanation, but it was no excuse.

"Save your bullshit." Unfortunately, plenty of betas got dumped by their alphas once they'd outlived their usefulness.

I'd just never thought it would be me.

He flinched, and the hood fell back. His hair was neat and short, and his natural blond, which he hadn't been in years. I saw the full impact of the bruises he'd gotten during the game. Wow, they'd gotten him good. His nose looked broken. He also had a beard.

"I... I'd hoped everything would work out. But I had to be prepared. See, you don't get it," he snapped.

"You didn't talk to me. Was wrecking all my stuff necessary? I didn't take you for petty–you know how little I have. That was the only photo I had of my mom. Also, canceling the payments you'd already made for my tuition was downright shitty. We have a fucking contract. You left me in a tough spot," I admitted. I might as well let it all out.

His blue eyes widened. "Fuck. I forgot about the contract. I was trying to protect you. Erase the trail. I'll pay you back. I wasn't trying to use you; I just needed to figure out how to do it without anyone knowing."

Um, sure.

"I don't need your money." My arms crossed over my chest.

"My family doesn't know about you. I mean, they know I was with someone, but they were never interested enough to care. That's why I deleted all my social media and reversed the charges. I didn't want them to find you, or know you meant something to me. They can ruin your life, your career–and the Deloitte family loves to ruin people."

What Kylee said to me made sense. Shit, I needed to email her.

"I have no idea who you are." That hurt. While I'd hid a lot of my life from him, I never hid who I was.

Not to mention I'd been there with the asshole family of the entitled alpha that sought to destroy everything I loved.

"It was my brothers who trashed your stuff. I hid your hockey box so they wouldn't ruin your rings." His voice turned pleading like that excuse fixed everything.

While I appreciated that, I would've rather him protect the photo of my mom. Or maybe tell his brothers to *stop.*

"You can't tell people I'm your ex. I don't even know how you figured it out." He sounded hurt. Austin always liked to think he was the smart one.

"I know what you look like playing hockey." I rolled my eyes.

"Oh. Well, you shouldn't have told Clark–or Ty." A hint of anger rippled through his scent.

"Ty figured it out from your *playing*. You wore the skates I bought you and you pushed Clark while calling me *sloppy seconds*. Did you not think he'd figure it out? Your disguise is shitty." My voice went incredulous. Clark had told me what happened when they fought at warm-ups.

"Oh. Um, my anger got the best of me. Again. My family can't know. Your PHL career will be over. They can shadow-ban you, get you kicked out of school, make it impossible to get a job," he told me.

"Your anger got the best of you? Well, maybe you need anger management classes–or alpha suppressants." All the worry about my career and not a single worry about what it might do to him, given he was an alpha Deloitte, and I was just a beta.

"Yeah, like my family would be okay with that. I can't believe you're with Clark. You cheated on me with him, didn't you?" He stroked his stupid beard.

The old accusation made my eyes roll. "No. I didn't. But you cheated on me with Ris."

"She's an omega. It's not cheating. I've known her forever. We weren't promised until a couple of years ago." There was no remorse in his voice.

Not cheating because she was an omega? What sort of bullshit was that?

"You were with me for five years." I arched an eyebrow at him. "I don't believe that they don't know about me. How do you know they won't come after me, regardless?"

"I changed my nicknames that I called you with each new hair color, made it sound like you were different girls, and played it off like it wasn't serious."

My head snapped over to him. "You couldn't have told me any of this?"

I caught two unfamiliar scents and my body went on alert. Shit. This was not Clark coming to get me.

"I was trying to protect you," he growled.

"Protect her from what?" Derick Deloitte, the eldest of the Deloitte brothers, sneered. He was taller and thinner than the other two, but still muscular. He was number 18, winger for the Gears. "This doesn't sound like a blow job, does it, brother?" His short hair was the same shade of blond, but his eyes were brown.

"No, it doesn't." Tripp Deloitte was a little shorter and a lot stockier. His dirty-blond hair was long and hung in his blue eyes. Number 17 and co-captain with Derick.

Derick peered at me. "One of your bang maids is after you now that you're famous and mad you lied?"

"That's not what this is. She's no one," he blew off, sneering at me.

That didn't hurt the way it should. I *was* nothing to Bronson Deloitte. If anything, I was disappointed in myself for thinking Austin loved me.

I stood and tried to get back to Clark. The two brothers blocked me.

"Let me pass," I demanded

"Oh, I don't think so." Derick pinned me against the wall.

"Get your hands off me, Derick Deloitte, you don't have permission to touch me," I screamed, kneeing him in the balls, and ducking under him, needing to get past the plant, so that the cameras caught this.

I darted past Derick while Austin stood there like a lump. Tripp grabbed me.

"Tripp Deloitte don't touch me, you neither Bronson Deloitte," I shrieked as Derick grabbed me from behind, slammed me up against the wall and slapped a hand over my mouth, as I struggled and kicked, trying to scoot a little further against the wall, so I was firmly in view of the cameras.

While I might be hesitant to ruin Austin, I had no such qualms about Derick and Tripp.

"Don't move." Tripp slapped me hard across the face, both him and Derick making sure to stand where I couldn't kick.

My cheek burned as I struggled, and he slapped me again.

"You don't get a piece of him, you little beta whore," Tripp growled. "Don't forget that you signed a non-disclosure agreement."

No, I didn't. But I could see Austin getting backed into a corner and lying. Or even forging my signature.

My teeth clamped down on his hand and Derick yelped, letting go of my mouth as I screamed.

"Let go of my girl." Tenzin punched him in the face.

Clark came running, Jonas and Dimitri with him.

My girl? Tenzin still thought of me that way? Those words warmed me.

"Gwen. I'm right here." Clark came over to me, shielding me with his body.

"Don't touch the fucking goalie." Jonas punched Derick in the face.

Dimitri cornered Austin with his gigantic frame. "You should be ashamed of yourself, *Austin.*"

"There's no fighting in here." Ernie, my old boss, stormed over with the bouncers.

Derick slugged Jonas. "You're mistaken. We're the victims. Don't you know who we are? This little beta whore here–"

"Gwen's a lot of things. A whore isn't one of them," Ernie replied. "Austin, you have some nerve showing up here, then attacking someone, after what you did. Gwen, get some ice from the bar. You alphas need to take this outside. You Deloittes are banned, you too, Austin. Knights, this is a warning. No fighting in the bar. I'm only giving it to you, because you treat everyone nice."

"I'm the goalie that kept you from scoring, you dipshits," I spat. Ugh.

Wait, what did he do?

"Come on." Clark shielded me and we got some ice from the bartender.

"Where's Lenny? We need to get the footage before the Deloittes have it erased." I took my phone out of my pocket and stopped the recording, immediately sending a copy to the place I kept such things. I looked around the bar.

"On it." Mercy was right there, texting. "Those assfucks."

I took some selfies and added them to my vault, then sent everything to Kylee and Stu that she'd asked for.

Carlos brought me a beer. "You okay?"

"Austin is a fucking knotwaffle." I downed it, my mind still reeling from everything. He hurt me to protect me?

Matty

I'll take care of him.

How did he know? But Lenny might be out back, beating the shit out of the Deloitte brothers.

Me

The Deloittes could ruin me and wreck my career in the PHL.

"I'm right here." Clark wrapped his arms around me.

My body shuddered. "I'd finished talking to my dads. Austin wanted to talk. It cemented that he's a knotwaffle, since he claimed he hit me to protect me from his family, since I'm not good enough for them. Then his brothers came and..."

"You're safe." He held me tight.

"Thank you. Do you want some ice for that black eye you got during the game?" I offered.

"It's fine." Clark held me tighter.

Tenzin came back. There was a bruise on his cheek that wasn't there before, and he looked a little smug. "I'm right here. I won't leave you, promise."

"You won't?" I left Clark's arms and buried my face in Tenzin's chest.

"No. I'm so sorry if at any point it felt like I did." Tenzin's arms wrapped around me. "I truly appreciate your patience and I apologize if I seem distant. Things have been hectic and no, I'm not questioning whether I want to be with you and Clark. I promise. If anything, I've been trying to make myself worthy of you."

"Are you?" I peeked up at him. Everything he said soothed my ragged soul, and I desperately wanted it to be the truth. "I've missed you. It feels like you're not even my friend anymore."

"I'm so sorry, Precious," he murmured. "I didn't intend to hurt you. You both mean so much to me."

The look on Clark's face said it all–he was hurt by Tenzin too.

"It's not me? I mean, I'd understand if it was, but I'd want you to tell me instead of stringing me along or shutting me out." I buried my face in his chest again. He smelled so good.

"It's not you. I just needed to get my shit together. I still don't have it together, honestly. But I miss you."

The rawness of it hurt my heart.

"I don't have my shit together either, but that doesn't mean I don't want to be with both of you," I told them, reaching for Clark's hand.

"I want to be with *both* of you." Clark's voice was raw, honest. "Stay with us."

"I will. After this we can go home and talk this all out," Tenzin offered.

"I'd like that," Clark said softly. "This only works if we communicate. Which differs from talking."

Tenzin looked abashed, and I got the feeling something may have happened between them to instigate this.

"I want back what we had. I want to hold hands and watch movies and go dancing. I know we're all so much busier now, but you know what I mean, right?" Eyes tearing, I gazed up at Tenzin.

"I do. And I want it too." He pulled Clark to us.

Ernie came over to me. "You okay?"

"I am. But what did Austin do? I'm guessing it wasn't just ditching his shifts, because you let me in here," I replied.

"I regret firing you. I was mad at him and thought you were helping him steal booze and short tips." His look went abashed. "Found out who was helping him and it wasn't you. Which was why I asked you back."

Asking me to fill in was asking me back? Okey dokey.

"He was stealing?" It was weird that I didn't know that, but then I'd missed so fucking much.

"Glad you're okay." My old boss awkwardly nodded and went back to work.

For a long time I let the two of them hold me tight in the bar. Mia and her pack said goodbye and left. Some others went home as well. Lenny was nowhere to be seen. Oh well.

"I got it, and sent it to you," Mercy told me, returning. "My friend is super good at shit like that."

"Thank you," I told her. I found it and put it with everything else.

"Are you ready to go home?" Clark asked. "You have work *and* class tomorrow."

"I do." I looked at Tenzin and he nodded. Whoops, I never did my reading for class. I'd have to squeeze it in tomorrow.

We said our goodbyes. Tenzin looked at Clark and me as we got onto the bike.

"Be careful?" Tenzin asked. "I'll knock on your door with your things and we'll talk."

"See you there." I waved. I put on my helmet, wrapped my arms around Clark, and we set off. "Talking to him is good, right?" I said through the com system. I liked that we could talk to each other.

"It is. I don't think he realized he was hurting us," he said as we made our way through the streets of New York. "I'm curious about what has been keeping him so busy. He mentioned something about family stuff. I hope his sister is okay."

"Oh, me, too." I liked her. "Something's going on and I'm glad he's ready to talk about it. I want to be there for him."

If he wanted to do more than talk I'd be okay with it.

"Are you okay? I can't believe Austin's brothers did that. What did Austin say to you?"

I gave him a short version. "No apology. No proper explanation. Just that he hurt me to protect me."

"That is unbelievable. I'm just glad you're okay," he told me.

Me, too. With three alphas that could have gotten out of hand, quickly.

"I... I hope we can set things right with Tens," I sighed.

"If he doesn't spend the night with us, don't be sad. I've got you."

"Yeah?" My core warmed. I was usually horny after a game, and tonight was no exception.

"Yeah. Grif told me that, um, this is a Knights thing. Apparently goalies who get shutouts get oral from their partners. Not that I need a reason to go down on you. But..." Clark's head ducked.

I sucked in a breath. "Oooh, I'll take that."

Out of nowhere, a car flew at us.

"Fucking shit, what is this guy doing?" Clark swore. He swerved as I held on tight.

A crashing sound ricocheted thought the air and everything went black.

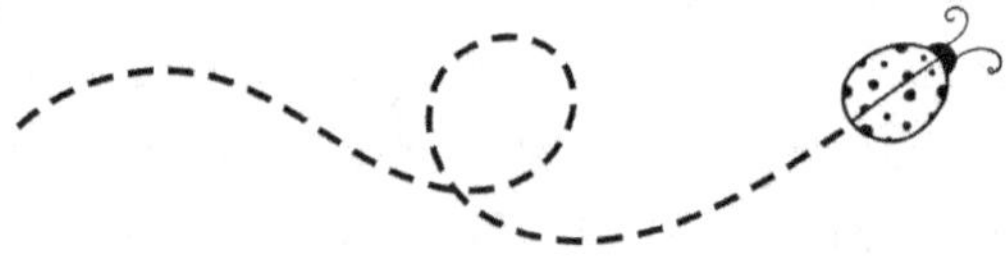

Chapter Seventy

TENZIN

I knocked on their door, holding her bag and backpack, but there was no answer. Oh. I must have beaten them home. Knowing Clark, he took her out to ice cream or something as a reward for a good game. He seemed like he'd grown up in the sort of house where all games got treats, not only the winning ones.

My sister was like that, always finding me a treat after a game, regardless of the outcome. Usually we'd stop at the grocers on the way home and I'd pick out some chips.

Sending Clark and Gwen a quick text, I showered and put on something more comfortable. I frowned at my phone. Still no text from either–and no answer when I knocked on their door again.

A quick scroll through the team group chat told me nothing. I called both of them, but it went to voicemail. Worry roiled in my belly. I didn't have access to either of their locations, so I couldn't tell if they were getting takeout or if something happened.

Of course. Nothing bad happened; they got food and weren't answering, because they were on their way back. I tried to push bad thoughts out of my mind and went to make some tea, to give myself something to do.

I sipped the tea and turned on the news. Sports news was full of Ty and Gwen's debut. The couple of clips they showed of her interview after the game were charming. Gwen had captured everyone's hearts, especially with the answer about the pink gear.

Where *had* the pink gear come from? It looked brand new. Someone had said her *birthday* was yesterday, which wasn't true. Her birthday was right after Cooter's.

Once again, I frowned at my phone. Still no text. I tried their door and called them both again.

Nothing.

Dread spread through me. This didn't feel right.

My phone rang, and I jumped. I didn't know the number, but it was a local area code, so I answered it. "Hello?"

"Is this Tenzin Brooks?" the female voice said.

My stomach sank. "Yes."

"You're listed as an emergency contact for Gwen Di Rossi," she said. "I'm calling from the emergency room of Manhattan General Hospital to inform you that she has been in a motorcycle accident."

... to be continued in Loving Ladybug, Part Two

Glossary of Select Terms

<u>**Designations**</u>

Alpha: Larger, faster, and with better senses, they make up about a quarter of the population. Their barks and pheromones can influence people. Male alphas have knots, female alphas have locks. Their scent has a distinctive note that marks them as alpha. Female alphas can carry children.

Beta: They make up over half of the population and are your average ordinary people. Like the other designations, they can have kids, join or form packs, and an alpha can mate with them.

Gamma: Essentially, Gammas are 'failed' omegas. While sometimes a genetic switch is thrown, halting development, most of the time it's environmental. Something is so dangerous in their environment that the body declares it unsafe to become an omega and halts a genetic process. Gammas can have many omega traits, but it varies from person to person. Gammas rarely respond to barks, pheromones, or danger the way omegas do. Common causes of gammas are war, famine, extreme poverty, and asshole parents.

Delta: They have a lot of alpha characteristics–especially in regard to size, speed, and senses. They make excellent soldiers and security, especially because they are bark-proof. They're rarer than the 'big three' designations (alpha/beta/omega.)

Kappa: The life of the party, they're usually adrenaline junkies with poor decision-making skills. They're an extremely rare designation.

Tau: Not a designation but a medical term referring to someone who lost their bonded scent match, also known *soulbroke* and *shadow*.

Omega: Omegas are usually smaller than the other designations and tend to be nurturers and caregivers. They're the most physically compatible with alphas, so they're often sought after as mates, even though they make up less than ten percent of the population. They can and do partner with other designations. Omegas have the same rights as everyone else. Omega males are *very* good at making kids. Omegas have an extra element to their scent that marks them as such. They also produce slick and perfume when aroused.

Sports

Boner: When one hockey player scores three goals in a single PHL game. Fans toss bones onto the ice in celebration.

EBUG: Emergency Backup Goalie. Amateur goalies who play during a hockey game if both of a team's goalies can no longer play. The home team is responsible for providing an EBUG who can then step in for either team. A lot of PHL EBUGs are goalies for their collegiate teams and are part of goalie development programs offered by many PHL teams.

Fútbol: Soccer/football. A sport popular worldwide, especially among betas.

IATS: The International Association of Team Sports is the world-wide governing body overseeing team sports such as fútbol, ice hockey, and rugby.

ICIS: International Coalition of Ice Sports is the worldwide governing body for sports such as figure skating, speed skating, skate smash, and curling.

MASO: Mates and Significant Others. A term that encompasses the mates, packmates, spouses, girlfriend, boyfriends, partners, and significant others of professional athletes in team sports.

PHL: The Professional Hockey League. It governs four conferences and eight divisions, totaling thirty-two ice hockey teams spanning four countries.

PSSL: The Professional Skate Smash League. It governs four conferences and eight divisions, totaling thirty-two skate smash teams spanning four countries.

Skate Smash: A contact ice sport where five players from each team skate around the ice trying to gain points. Ten two-minute successions comprised each period, with a thirty-second rest between each succession. They also have dance battles where they perform synchronized routines as a team.

<u>Other Terms</u>

Alpha-Blockers: A type of medication that dulls alpha senses and instincts. It's most commonly prescribed to violent alphas, young alphas who aren't in full control, and criminals. There's a huge stigma on them, so many who should take them don't.

Dead-Match: Two people who would have been scent matches had they not stayed beta.

Defender League: A popular superhero franchise with movies and comics.

Fried Lace: Funnel cake.

Game Buddy: A personal video game device that can also be hooked up to your TV.

Go-goKart: A popular car racing video game, often played on a Game Buddy.

Hydrogel: Electrolyte gel in a squeezy pouch.

Insta-Chat: Communication app where people send short video/photo messages to each other.

Location Finder: A location sharing app.

Mega-push: Drug that can 'push' a beta with specific genetic markers over to an omega. It is mostly used for trafficking.

Musify: A social music streaming app where users can both listen to music and create and share their own playlists.

Scent-Match: Soulmate. That perfect match between two people–usually an alpha and omega. They usually know it by smell. Scent-matches are rare and plenty of people have happy and long relationships without being scent-matches. Sometimes scent-matches dream of each other, but that's mostly in books and movies. A scent match can be 'lopsided' when it's not al-pha/omega.

Shadow (soulbroke): Someone who has lost their bonded scent match.

Spiral: Dangerous drop in omega hormones which can result in unconsciousness, irrational behavior, and/or hospitalization. Often a trauma response.

Ultra-bullet: Super-fast train that can turn an hours-long drive into moments.

The New York Knights

Forwards

Nia Watkins #23 (co-captain)
Pauley Diaz #14
Anders Larsson #37
Griffin 'Grif Graf' McGraff #26
Clark 'Wonder Boy' Edwards #55
Carlos Rodriguez #17
LeeAnn Tinsley #15
Vaino Virtanen #12
Shawna Castle #52
Jasper Michaels #73
Mitchy Vance #63

Ela Patel #36

<u>Defense</u>

Jonas Seong #42 (co-captain)
Tenzin Brooks #4
Dimitri Belikov #7
Roberto 'Nakey' Diaz #82
Miko Virtanen #13
Shawn Vickers #11
Mathieu Decker #88
Kimo Nakamura #3

<u>Goalies</u>

Dean 'Double D' Donovan #1
Jean-Paul 'JP' Trembley #31

<u>EBUGs</u>

Gwen 'Ladybug' Di Rossi
Tyler Yamato
Arden Kingsley

<u>Management, Coaches, & Staff</u>

Steve Atkins, Head Coach
Cal Daughtry, Owner
Louis Daughtry, Owner
Ben Dodd, Assistant Coach
Svetlana Kirov, Goalie Coach
Beauregard 'Bunty' Longfellow, General Manager
Lars Janssen, Assistant Coach
Constantine Alexander, Assistant General Manager
Devon Bishop, Operations
Kylee St. John, PR
Marcel Dupree, HR
Maryellen Bailey, Education & Community Programs
Silas Cooper, Equipment Manager

The New York Institute of Technology Kings

Forwards

Maze (captain)
Humpy
Bonnie
Giggles
Knoblick
Firstie

Defense

Alfie
Schmitty
Boondock
Freight Train

Goalies

Gwen
Jacky

<u>Staff</u>

Coach Hirata
Assistant Coach Moreno

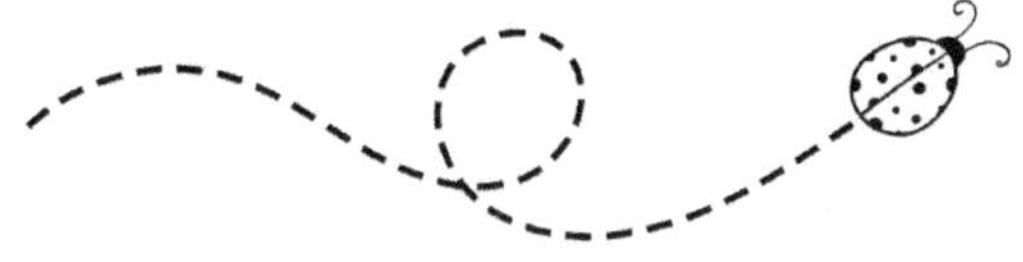

The Capaldi Family

The Parents

Tomasso Capaldi (Papa; head alpha, head of Vector Transportation)
Lorenzo Capaldi (Dad)
Vincente Capaldi (Popi)
Arturo Capaldi (Babo)
Ilaria Capaldi (Mom; deceased)

<u>The Kids</u>

Maricella
Mateo (Matty)–Corporate Lawyer
Sofia (Sof)
Chiara
Luca–Lawyer
Giuseppe (Joe)–Accountant/Podcaster
Isabella (Isa)–Fashion Designer
Gwen (Buttons/Gabriella/Little Gabs)–Student/Goalie

Loving Ladybug

Part Two

My ex doesn't know when to quit.

It's not enough that he has a hockey contract and an omega. No, he and his family have decided to go after me because I had the poor judgment to date him.

At least I've got Clark and Tenzin–and things are heating up between all three of us. Yeah, I might just keep those two forever. Also, the New York Knights are my family and have my back.

My past is about to catch up to me, but my ex is the one who should be wary. There's a good reason why I don't talk to my family much.

I've decided that despite my past, despite being just a beta, I deserve good things–friends, a hockey career, and two cute alphas included. And I'm not going to let anyone stop me.

Loving Ladybug, Part Two, is a why choose omegaverse friends to lovers hockey romance and is the second half of a *duet*. See what happens next with Gwen, Clark, and Tenzin in the conclusion of this m/m/f romance.

About Jane Handler

A hopeless romantic, Jane Handler grew up reading romance and often got them taken away by her teachers for reading during class. Now she writes why choose, omegaverse, and hockey romance, including the HockeyVerse series. When not writing she can be found drinking tea, reading, eating sushi, or binge watching TV with her family.

Keep up with Jane on Instagram, Tiktok, and her Facebook reader group.Follow her on Book Bub and Amazon to keep up with new releases.